"Child has long been one of the best contemporary thriller writers."
—*The Daily Beast*

"That this Reacher is so effortlessly larger than life is evidence of how intense the overall series has become."
—JANET MASLIN, *The New York Times*

"No one kicks butt as entertainingly as Reacher."
—*Kirkus Reviews*

PERSONAL

"Jack Reacher is today's James Bond, a thriller hero we can't get enough of."
—#1 *New York Times* bestselling author KEN FOLLETT

"Fans won't be disappointed by this suspense-filled, riveting thriller. Those who haven't experienced this irresistible series should definitely start at the beginning and catch up to this book."
—*Library Journal* (starred review)

"Reacher's just one of fiction's great mysterious strangers."
—*Maxim*

THE AFFAIR

"The novel fans have been waiting for."
—*USA Today*

"As usual, plenty of eggs get broken in spectacular style on the way to making a Reacher omelet. Child's mastery of high-octane plotting remains remarkable, as does his ability to inject what, in other hands, might have been cartoon characters with all the sinews that power human beings."
—*Booklist* (starred review)

"He is the best in the business and this only solidifies that truth."
—*RT Book Reviews*

"Exciting and suspenseful, with deceit and cover-ups, violence, and sex, this is another great entry in Child's compelling series. Reacher's many fans can only hope there will be many more. Highly recommended for anyone who likes intelligent, well-written, tense thrillers."
—*Library Journal* (starred review)

WORTH DYING FOR

61 HOURS

"Child's writing is superb. Not only is this thriller believable, but the descriptions of the blizzard will make readers want to hug their furnaces. Fast paced and exciting, this is highly recommended for thriller fans."
— *Library Journal* (starred review)

"Child keeps his foot hard on the throttle. . . . As always, Child delivers enough juicy details about the landscape, the characters, and Reacher's idiosyncrasies to give the story texture and lower our pulse rates, if only momentarily. . . . This is Child in top form, but isn't he always?"
— *Booklist* (starred review)

"Jack Reacher is much more like the heir to the Op and Marlowe than Spenser ever was. . . . Reacher is as appealingly misanthropic as ever."
— *Esquire*

GONE TOMORROW

"Hold on tight. This is No. 13 in Lee Child's action-packed series starring ex–military cop/pit bull Jack Reacher, and it may be the best. . . . This novel will give you whiplash as you rabidly turn pages, packed with layers of intrigue, murder, deceit and mystery."
— *USA Today*

BAD LUCK AND TROUBLE

"Electrifying . . . A top-tier Reacher book."
—JANET MASLIN, *The New York Times*

"As always, the action is intense, the pace unrelenting, and the violence unforgiving. Child remains the reigning master at combining breakneck yet brilliantly constructed plotting with characters who continually surprise us with their depth."
—*Booklist* (starred review)

"Perhaps there are action-lit writers more recognizable than Child, but the bet is that none of them will turn in a tighter-plotted, richer-peopled, faster-paced page-turner this year."
—*Kirkus Reviews* (starred review)

THE HARD WAY

"The best thriller writer of the moment."
—*The New York Times*

"Jack Reacher, the tough-minded hero of a series of best-selling noir thrillers, has all the elements that have made this genre so popular among men for decades. He travels the country dispensing his own form of justice, often violently and without remorse. . . . Reacher is doing something surprising: winning the hearts of many women readers."
—*The Wall Street Journal*

ONE SHOT

By Lee Child

LEE CHILD

Dell 🏛 New York

Personal

A JACK REACHER NOVEL

2015 Dell Mass Market Edition

Copyright © 2014 by Lee Child
"Not a Drill" copyright © 2014 by Lee Child
Excerpt from *Make Me* by Lee Child copyright © 2015 by Lee Child

Published in the United States by Dell, an imprint of Random House, a division of Penguin Random House LLC, New York.

DELL and the HOUSE colophon are registered trademarks of Penguin Random House LLC.

Originally published in hardcover in the United States by Delacorte Press, an imprint of Random House, a division of Penguin Random House LLC, in 2014.

This book contains an excerpt from the forthcoming book *Make Me* by Lee Child. This excerpt has been set for this edition only and may not reflect the final content of the forthcoming edition.

ISBN 978-0-8041-7875-4
eBook ISBN 978-0-8041-7876-1

Cover design: Carlos Beltrán

Printed in the United States of America

www.bantamdell.com

2 4 6 8 9 7 5 3 1

Dell mass market edition: May 2015

For Andrew Grant and Tasha Alexander,
my brother and sister-in-law:
great writers and great people

Personal

Chapter 1

Eight days ago my life was an up and down affair. Some of it good. Some of it not so good. Most of it uneventful. Long slow periods of nothing much, with occasional bursts of something. Like the army itself. Which is how they found me. You can leave the army, but the army doesn't leave you. Not always. Not completely.

They started looking two days after some guy took a shot at the president of France. I saw it in the paper. A long-range attempt with a rifle. In Paris. Nothing to do with me. I was six thousand miles away, in California, with a girl I met on a bus. She wanted to be an actor. I didn't. So after forty-eight hours in LA she went one way and I went the other. Back on the bus, first to San Francisco for a couple of days, and then to Portland, Oregon, for three more, and then onward to Seattle. Which took me close to Fort Lewis, where two women in uniform got out of the bus. They left an

Army Times behind, one day old, right there on the seat across the aisle.

The *Army Times* is a strange old paper. It started up before World War Two and is still going strong, every week, full of yesterday's news and sundry how-to articles, like the headline staring up at me right then: *New Rules! Changes for Badges and Insignia! Plus Four More Uniform Changes on the Way!* Legend has it the news is yesterday's because it's copied second-hand from old AP summaries, but if you read the words sideways you sometimes hear a real sardonic tone between the lines. The editorials are occasionally brave. The obituaries are occasionally interesting.

Which was my sole reason for picking up the paper. Sometimes people die and you're happy about it. Or not. Either way you need to know. But I never found out. Because on the way to the obituaries I found the personal ads. Which as always were mostly veterans looking for other veterans. Dozens of ads, all the same.

Including one with my name in it.

Right there, center of the page, a boxed column inch, five words printed bold: *Jack Reacher call Rick Shoemaker.*

Which had to be Tom O'Day's work. Which later on made me feel a little lame. Not that O'Day wasn't a smart guy. He had to be. He had survived a long time. A very long time. He had been around forever. Twenty years ago he already looked a hundred. A tall, thin, gaunt, cadaverous man, who moved like he might collapse at any moment, like a broken stepladder. He was no one's idea of an army general. More like a professor. Or an anthropologist. Certainly his thinking had been sound. *Reacher stays under the radar, which means buses and trains and waiting rooms and diners, which, coincidentally or not, are the natural economic habitat for enlisted men and women, who buy the* Army Times *ahead of any other publication in the PX, and who can be relied upon to spread the paper around, like birds spread seeds from berries.*

And he could rely on me to pick up the paper. Somewhere. Sooner or later. Eventually. Because I needed to know. You can leave the army, but the army doesn't leave you. Not completely. As a means of communication, as a way of making contact, from what he knew, and from what he could guess, then maybe he would think ten or twelve consecutive weeks of personal ads might generate a small but realistic chance of success.

But it worked the first time out. One day after the paper was printed. Which is why I felt lame later on.

I was predictable.

Rick Shoemaker was Tom O'Day's boy. Probably his second in command by now. Easy enough to ignore. But I owed Shoemaker a favor. Which O'Day knew about, obviously. Which was why he put Shoemaker's name in his ad.

And which was why I would have to answer it.

Predictable.

Seattle was dry when I got out of the bus. And warm. And wired, in the sense that coffee was being consumed in prodigious quantities, which made it my kind of town, and in the sense that wifi hotspots and handheld devices were everywhere, which didn't, and which made old-fashioned street-corner pay phones hard to find. But there was one down by the fish market, so I stood in the salt breeze and the smell of the sea, and I dialed a toll-free number at the Pentagon. Not a number you'll find in the phone book. A number learned by heart long ago. A special line, for emergencies only. You don't always have a quarter in your pocket.

The operator answered and I asked for Shoemaker and I got transferred, maybe elsewhere in the building, or the country, or the world, and after a bunch of clicks and hisses and some long minutes of dead air Shoemaker came on the line and said, "Yes?"

"This is Jack Reacher," I said.

"Where are you?"

"Don't you have all kinds of automatic machines to tell you that?"

"Yes," he said. "You're in Seattle, on a pay phone down by the fish market. But we prefer it when people volunteer the information themselves. We find that makes the subsequent conversation go better. Because they're already cooperating. They're invested."

"In what?"

"In the conversation."

"Are we having a conversation?"

"Not really. What do you see directly ahead?"

I looked.

"A street," I said.

"Left?"

"Places to buy fish."

"Right?"

"A coffee shop across the light."

"Name?"

I told him.

He said, "Go in there and wait."

"For what?"

"For about thirty minutes," he said, and hung up.

No one really knows why coffee is such a big deal in Seattle. It's a port, so maybe it made sense to roast it close to where it was landed, and then to sell it close to where it was roasted, which created a market, which brought other operators in, the same way the auto makers all ended up in Detroit. Or maybe the water is right. Or the elevation, or the temperature, or the humidity. But whatever, the result is a coffee shop on every block, and a four-figure annual tab for a serious enthusiast. The shop across the light from the pay phone was representative. It had maroon paint and exposed brick and scarred wood, and a chalkboard menu about ninety percent full of things that don't really belong in coffee, like dairy products of various types and temperatures, and weird nut-based flavorings, and many other assorted pollutants. I got a plain house blend, black, no sugar, in the middle-sized go-cup, not the enormous *grande* bucket some folks like, and a slab of lemon pound cake to go with it, and I sat alone on a hard wooden chair at a table for two.

The cake lasted five minutes and the coffee another five, and eighteen minutes after that Shoemaker's guy showed up. Which made him Navy, because twenty-eight minutes was pretty fast, and the Navy is right there in Seattle. And his car was dark blue. It was a low-spec domestic sedan, not very desirable, but polished to a high shine. The guy himself was nearer forty than twenty, and hard as a nail. He was in civilian clothes. A blue blazer over a blue polo shirt, and khaki chino pants. The blazer was worn thin and the shirt and the pants had been washed a thousand times. A Senior Chief Petty Officer, probably. Special Forces, almost certainly, a SEAL, no doubt part of some shadowy joint operation watched over by Tom O'Day.

He stepped into the coffee shop with a blank-eyed all-in-one scan of the room, like he had a fifth of a second to identify friend or foe before he started shooting. Obviously his briefing must have been basic and verbal, straight out of some old personnel file, but he had me at *six-five two-fifty*. Everyone else in the shop was Asian, mostly women and very petite. The guy walked straight toward me and said, "Major Reacher?"

I said, "Not anymore."

He said, "Mr. Reacher, then?"

I said, "Yes."

"Sir, General Shoemaker requests that you come with me."

I said, "Where to?"

"Not far."

"How many stars?"

"Sir, I don't follow."

"Does General Shoemaker have?"

"One, sir. Brigadier General Richard Shoemaker, sir."

"When?"

"When what, sir?"

"Did he get his promotion?"

"Two years ago."

"Do you find that as extraordinary as I do?"

The guy paused a beat and said, "Sir, I have no opinion."

"And how is General O'Day?"

The guy paused another beat and said, "Sir, I know of no one named O'Day."

The blue car was a Chevrolet Impala with police hubs and cloth seats. The polish was the freshest thing on it. The guy in the blazer drove me through the downtown streets and got on I-5 heading south. The same way the bus had come in. We drove back past Boeing Field once again, and past the Sea-Tac airport once again, and onward toward Tacoma. The guy in the blazer didn't talk. Neither did I. We both sat there mute, as if we were in a no-talking competition and serious about winning. I watched out the window. All green, hills and sea and trees alike.

We passed Tacoma, and slowed ahead of where the women in uniform had gotten out of the bus, leaving their *Army Times* behind. We took the same exit. The signs showed nothing ahead except three very small towns and one very large military base. Chances were therefore good we were heading for Fort Lewis. But it turned out we weren't. Or we were, technically, but we wouldn't have been back in the day. We were heading for what used to be McChord Air Force Base, and was now the aluminum half of Joint Base Lewis-McChord. Reforms. Politicians will do anything to save a buck.

I was expecting a little back and forth at the gate, because the gate belonged jointly to the army and the Air Force, and the car and the driver were both Navy, and I was absolutely nobody. Only the Marine Corps and the United Nations were missing. But such was the power of O'Day we barely had to slow the car. We swept in, and hooked a left, and hooked a right, and were waved through a second gate, and then the car was right out there on the tarmac, dwarfed by huge C-17 transport planes, like a mouse in a forest. We drove under a giant gray wing and headed out over open blacktop straight for a small white airplane standing alone. A corporate thing. A business jet. A Lear, or a Gulfstream, or whatever rich people buy these days. The paint winked in the sun. There was no writing on it, apart from a tail number. No name, no logo. Just white paint. Its engines were turning slowly, and its stairs were down.

The guy in the blazer drove a well-judged part-circle and came to a stop with my door about a yard from the bottom of the airplane steps. Which I took as a hint. I climbed out and stood a moment in the sun. Spring had sprung and the weather was pleasant. Beside me the car drove away. A steward appeared above me, in the little oval mouth of the cabin. He was wearing a uniform. He said, "Sir, please step up."

The stairs dipped a little under my weight. I ducked

into the cabin. The steward backed off to my right, and on my left another guy in uniform squeezed out of the cockpit and said, "Welcome aboard, sir. You have an all–Air Force crew today, and we'll get you there in no time at all."

I said, "Get me where?"

"To your destination." The guy crammed himself back in his seat next to his copilot and they both got busy checking dials. I followed the steward and found a cabin full of butterscotch leather and walnut veneer. I was the only passenger. I picked an armchair at random. The steward hauled the steps up and sealed the door and sat down on a jump seat behind the pilots' shoulders. Thirty seconds later we were in the air, climbing hard.

Chapter 2

I figured we turned east out of McChord. Not that there was much of a choice. West was Russia and Japan and China, and I doubted such a small plane had that kind of range. I asked the steward where we were going, and he said he hadn't seen the flight plan. Which was obvious bullshit. But I didn't push it. He turned out to be a chatty guy on every other subject. He told me the plane was a Gulfstream IV, confiscated from a bent hedge fund during a federal proceeding, and reissued to the Air Force for VIP transportation. In which case Air Force VIPs were lucky people. The plane was terrific. It was quiet and solid, and the armchairs were sensational. They adjusted every which way. And there was coffee in the galley. A proper drip machine. I told the guy to keep it going, but that I would go back and forth myself, for refills. He appreciated that. I think he took it as a mark of respect. He wasn't really a steward, obviously. He was some kind of a security escort, tough enough to get the job, and proud I knew it.

I watched out the window, first at the Rockies, which had dark green trees low down and blinding white snow high up. Then came the tawny agricultural plains, in tiny mosaic fragments, plowed and sowed and harvested, over and over again, and not rained on much. By the look of the land I figured we clipped the corner of South Dakota and saw a bit of Nebraska before setting out over Iowa. Which because of the geometric complexities of high altitude flight meant we were likely aiming some ways south. A Great Circle route. Weird on a flat paper map, but just right for a spherical planet. We were going to Kentucky, or Tennessee, or the Carolinas. Georgia, even.

We droned on, hour after hour, two full pots of coffee, and then the ground got a little closer. At first I thought it was Virginia, but then I figured it was North Carolina. I saw two towns that could only be Winston-Salem and Greensboro. They were on the left, and receding a little. Which meant we were heading southeast. No towns until Fayetteville. But just before that came Fort Bragg. Which was where Special Forces HQ was located. Which was Tom O'Day's natural economic habitat.

Wrong again. Or right, technically, but in name only. We landed in the evening dark at what used to be Pope Air Force Base, which had since been given away to the army. Now it was just Pope Field, just a small corner of an ever-bigger Fort Bragg. Reforms. Politicians will do anything to save a buck.

We taxied a long time, tiny on tarmac big enough

for airlift squadrons. Eventually we stopped near a small administrative building. I saw a sign that said *47th Logistics, Tactical Support Command.* The engines shut down and the steward opened the hatch and lowered the steps.

"Which door?" I said.

"The red one," he said.

I went down and walked ahead through the dark. There was only one red door. It opened when I was six feet from it. A young woman in a black skirt suit came out. Dark nylons. Good shoes. A very young woman. She had to be still in her twenties. She had blonde hair and green eyes and a heart-shaped face. Which had a big warm welcoming smile on it.

She said, "I'm Casey Nice."

I said, "Casey what?"

"Nice."

"I'm Jack Reacher."

"I know. I work for the State Department."

"In D.C.?"

"No, here," she said.

Which made some kind of sense. Special Forces were the armed wing of the CIA, which was the hands-on wing of the State Department, and some decisions would require all three fingers in the same pie all at once. Hence her presence on the base, young as she was. Maybe she was a policy genius. Some kind of a prodigy. I said, "Is Shoemaker here?"

She said, "Let's go inside."

She led me to a small room with a wired glass window. It had three armchairs in it, none of them matching, all of them a little sad and abandoned. She said, "Let's sit down."

I said, "Why am I here?"

She said, "First you must understand everything you hear from this point onward is a classified secret. There will be a severe penalty for a breach of security."

"Why would you trust me with secrets? You never met me before. You know nothing about me."

"Your file has been circulated. You had a security clearance. It was never revoked. You're still bound by it."

"Am I free to leave?"

"We'd prefer you to stay."

"Why?"

"We want to talk to you."

"The State Department?"

"Did you agree to the part about classified secrets?"

I nodded. "What does the State Department want with me?"

"We have certain obligations."

"In what respect?"

"Someone took a shot at the president of France."

"In Paris."

"The French have appealed for international cooperation. To find the perpetrator."

"It wasn't me. I was in LA."

"We know it wasn't you. You're not on the list."

"There's a list?"

She didn't answer that, except to reach high up between her jacket and her blouse and pull out a folded sheet of paper, which she handed to me. It was warm from her body, and slightly curved. But it wasn't a list. It was a summary report from our embassy in Paris. From the CIA Head of Station, presumably. The nuts and bolts of the thing.

The range had been exceptional. An apartment balcony fourteen hundred yards away had been identified as the rifleman's hide. Fourteen hundred yards was more than three-quarters of a mile. The French president had been at an open-air podium behind wings of thick bulletproof glass. Some kind of a new improved material. No one had seen the shot except the president himself. He had seen an impossibly distant muzzle flash, small and high and far to his left, and then more than three whole perceptible seconds later a tiny white star had appeared on the glass, like a pale insect alighting. A long, long shot. But the glass had held, and the sound of the bullet's impact against it had triggered an instant reaction, and the president had been buried under a scrum of security people. Later enough bullet fragments had been found to guess at a fifty-caliber armor-piercing round.

I said, "I'm not on the list because I'm not good enough. Fourteen hundred yards is a very long way, against a head-sized target. The bullet is in the air three whole seconds. Like dropping a stone down a very deep well."

Casey Nice nodded and said, "The list is very short. Which is why the French are worried."

They hadn't been worried immediately. That was clear. According to the summary report they had spent the first twenty-four hours congratulating themselves on having enforced such a distant perimeter, and on the quality of their bulletproof glass. Then reality had set in, and they had lit up the long-distance phones. Who knew a sniper that good?

"Bullshit," I said.

Casey Nice said, "What part?"

"You don't care about the French. Not this much. Maybe you would make some appropriate noises and get a couple of interns to write a term paper. But this thing crossed Tom O'Day's desk. For five seconds, at least. Which makes it important. And then you had a SEAL on my ass inside twenty-eight minutes, and then you flew me across the continent in a private jet. Obviously both the SEAL and the jet were standing by, but equally obviously you had no idea where I was or when I would call, so you must have had a whole bunch of SEALs and a whole bunch of jets standing by, here, there, and everywhere, all over the country, day and night. Just in case. And if it's me, it's others, too. This is a full-court press."

"It would complicate things if it was an American shooter."

"Why would it be?"

"We hope it isn't."

"What can I do for you that's worth a private jet?"

Her phone rang in her pocket. She answered and listened and put it back. She said, "General O'Day will explain. He's ready to see you now."

Chapter 3

Casey Nice led me to a room one floor up. The building was worn and the contents looked temporary. Which I was sure they were. A guy like O'Day moved around. A month here, a month there, in nondescript accommodations behind meaningless signs, like *47th Logistics, Tactical Support Command.* In case someone was watching. Or *because* someone was watching, he would say. Someone was always watching. He had survived a long time.

He was behind a desk, with Shoemaker in a chair off to one side, like a good second-in-command should be. Shoemaker had aged twenty years, which was to be expected, because it was twenty years since I had last seen him. He had put on weight, and his sandy hair had dulled down to sandy gray. His face was red and pouched. He was in ACU fatigues, with his star proudly displayed.

O'Day had not aged at all. He still looked a hundred. He was wearing the same thing he had always worn, which was a faded black blazer over a V-neck sweater, which was also black, and which had been darned so many times there was more darn than sweater. Which led me to believe Mrs. O'Day was still alive and well, because I couldn't imagine anyone else taking up needle and yarn for him.

His gray lantern jaw flapped up and down and he stared out at me with dead eyes under overhanging brows and he said, "It's good to see you again, Reacher."

I said, "You're lucky I didn't have a pressing engagement. Or I'd be complaining."

He didn't answer. I sat down, on a metal chair I guessed was Navy issue, and Casey Nice sat down on a similar chair beside me.

O'Day asked, "Did she tell you all this is secret?"

I said, "Yes," and beside me Casey Nice nodded emphatically, as if very anxious to confirm she had followed her orders by so doing. O'Day had that effect on people.

He asked me, "Did you see the summary report?"

I said, "Yes," and Casey Nice nodded again.

He said, "What do you make of it?"

I said, "I think the guy's a good shooter."

"So do I," O'Day said. "Has to be, to sell a guaranteed one-for-one at fourteen hundred yards."

Which was typical of O'Day. Socratic, they call it in college. All kinds of back and forth, designed to elicit truths implicitly known by all rational beings. I said, "It wasn't a guaranteed one-for-one. It was a guaranteed two-for-two. The first round was supposed to break the glass. The second round was supposed to kill the guy. The first bullet was always going to shatter. Or deflect, best case. He was ready to fire again, if the glass had broken. A split-second yes-or-no decision. Fire again, or walk away. Which is impressive. Was it an armor-piercing round?"

O'Day nodded. "They put the fragments in a gas chromatograph."

"Do we have that kind of glass for our president?"

"We will by tomorrow."

"Was it fifty-caliber?"

"They collected enough weight to make it likely."

"Which all makes it more than impressive. That's a big ugly rifle."

"Which has been known to hit at a mile out. A mile and a half, once, in Afghanistan. So maybe fourteen hundred yards isn't such a big deal."

Socratic.

I said, "I think hitting twice at fourteen hundred yards is harder than hitting once at a mile or more. It's all about repeatability. I think this guy has talent."

"So do I," O'Day said. "Do you think he's been in the service somewhere?"

"Of course he has. No other way to get that good."

"Do you think he's still in the service somewhere?"

"No. He would have no freedom of movement."

"I agree."

I said, "Are we sure he was selling?"

"What are the odds a citizen with a grievance was also once upon a time a world-class sniper? More likely the citizen with a grievance has spent some money on the open market. Maybe a small group of citizens with a grievance. A faction, in other words. Which would increase the spending potential."

"Why do we care? The target was French."

"The bullet was American."

"How do we know?"

"The gas chromatograph. There was an agreement. Some years ago. Not widely publicized. Not publicized at all, actually. Every manufacturer blends the alloy differently. Only slightly. But enough. Like a signature."

"Lots of the world buys American."

"This guy is new on the scene, Reacher. This profile has never been seen before. This was his first job. He's making his name here. And it's a hell of an ask. He has to hit twice, and fast, with a fifty-caliber cannon from fourteen hundred yards. If he makes it, he's in the Major Leagues for the rest of his life. If he misses, he's bush league forever. That's too big of a gamble. The stakes are way too high. But he shoots anyway. Which means he *knew* he was going to hit. He had to know. For certain, twice, at fourteen hundred yards, with total confidence. How many snipers that good are there?"

Which was a very good question. I said, "Honestly? For us? That good? I think in every generation we'd be lucky to have one in the SEALs, and two in the Marines, and two in the army. Total of five in the service at any one time."

"But you just agreed he isn't in the service."

"Plus therefore an additional matching five from the previous generation, not long retired, old enough to be at loose ends, but still young enough to function. Which is who you should be looking at."

"Those would be your candidates? The previous generation?"

"I don't see who else would qualify."

"How many significant countries are there, in that line of work?"

"Maybe five of us."

"Times an average of five eligible candidates in each country is twenty-five shooters in the world. Agreed?"

"Ballpark."

"More than ballpark, actually. Twenty-five happens to be the exact dead-on number of retired elite snipers known to intelligence communities around the world. Do you think their governments keep careful track of them?"

"I'm sure they do."

"And therefore how many of them do you think would turn out to have rock-solid alibis on any random day?"

Given that they would be surveilled very carefully, I said, "Twenty?"

"Twenty-one," O'Day said. "We're down to four guys. And that's the diplomatic problem here. We're like four guys in a room, all staring at each other. I don't need that bullet to be American."

"One of ours is not accounted for?"

"Not completely."

"Who?"

"How many snipers that good do you know?"

"None," I said. "I don't hang out with snipers."

"How many did you ever know?"

"One," I said. "But it's obviously not him."

"And you know this because?"

"He's in prison."

"And you know this because?"

"I put him there."

"He got a fifteen-year sentence, correct?"

"As I recall," I said.

"When?"

Socratic. I did the math in my head. A lot of years. A lot of water over the dam. A lot of different places, a lot of different people. I said, "Shit."

O'Day nodded.

"Sixteen years ago," he said. "Doesn't time fly when you're having fun?"

"He's out?"

"He's been out for a year."

"Where is he?"

"Not at home."

Chapter 4

John Kott was the first son of two Czech emigrants who escaped the old Communist regime and settled in Arkansas. He had a kind of wiry Iron Curtain look that blended well with the local hardscrabble youth, and he grew up as one of them. Apart from his name and his cheekbones he could have been a cousin going back hundreds of years. At sixteen he could shoot squirrels out of trees too far away for most folks to see. At seventeen he killed his parents. At least, the county sheriff thought he did. There was no actual proof, but there was plenty of suspicion. None of which seemed to matter much, a year later, to the army recruiter who signed him up.

Unusually for a thin wiry guy he was immensely calm and still. He could drop his heart rate to the low thirties, and he could lie inert for many hours. He had superhuman eyesight. In other words, he was a born sniper. Even the army recognized it. He was sent to a succession of specialist schools, and then he was funneled straight to Delta. Where he matched his talents with unrelenting hard work and made himself a star, in a shadowy, black-ops kind of a way.

But unusually for a Special Forces soldier the seal between the on-duty part of his head and the off-duty part was not a hundred percent watertight. To drop a guy at a thousand yards needs more than talent and athletic ability. It needs permission, from deep down in the ancient part of the brain, where fundamental inhibitions are either enforced or relaxed. It needs the shooter to really, really, truly believe: *This is OK. This is your enemy. You're better than him. You're the best in the world. Anyone who challenges you deserves to die.* Most guys have an off switch. But Kott's didn't close all the way.

I met him three weeks after a guy was found with his throat cut, in the weeds behind a faraway bar in Colombia, South America. The dead guy was a U.S. Army sergeant, from the Rangers. The bar was a hangout for a CIA-directed Special Forces unit, who were using it for downtime when they weren't out in the jungle, shooting cartel members. Which made the suspect pool both very small and completely silent. I was with the 99th MP at the time, and I got the job. Only because the dead guy was American military. A local civilian, the Pentagon would have saved the airfare.

No one talked, but they all said plenty. I knew who had been in the bar, and I made them all describe it, and they all told me some little thing. I built up a picture. One guy was doing this, another guy was doing that. This guy left at eleven, that guy left at midnight.

The other guy was sitting next to the first guy, who was drinking rum not beer. And so on and so forth. I got the choreography straight in my head, and I revised it over and over until it ran smooth and coherent.

Except for Kott, who was nothing more than a hole in the air.

No one had said anything much about him. Not where he was sitting, or what he was doing, or who he was talking to. He was more or less completely undescribed. Which could be for a number of reasons, one of which was, just possibly, that although no one in his unit was going to actively rat him out, no one was going to make stuff up for him, either. Some kind of ethics. Or lack of imagination. A wise choice, either way. Invention always unravels. Better to say nothing. As in, just possibly, hypothetically, a long fierce argument with the dead guy might become . . . nothing. Just a hole in the air.

It was a weak case, involving a lot of circular theory and a star player and a clandestine operation, but to its credit the army looked at it. And quite correctly said we were going nowhere without a confession.

They let me bring Kott in.

Most of asking questions is listening to the answers, and I listened to Kott for a good long time before I concluded that deep down the guy had an arrogant streak as wide as his head. And as hard. He wasn't making the distinction. *Anyone who challenges you deserves to die* is battlefield bullshit, not a way to live.

But I had known people like that all my life. I was the product of people like that. They want to tell you about it. They want you to understand. They want you to approve. OK, so maybe some stupid temporary pettifogging regulation was technically against them at one point, but they were more important than that. Weren't they? Right?

I let him talk, and then I backed him up and pretty much made him admit that, yes, at one point he was talking to the dead guy. After which it was downhill all the way. Although an uphill metaphor would be better. The process felt like lighting a fire under a kettle, or pumping a bicycle tire.

Two hours later he was signing a long and detailed account. The dead guy had called him a pussy, basically. That was the bottom line. Trash-talking, that had then gotten completely out of hand. Some response was called for. Some things couldn't be excused. Could they? Right?

Because he was a star player and it was a clandestine operation they gave him a plea deal. Some variant of murder two for fifteen years. I was fine with it. Because there was no court martial I snuck the extra week in Fiji and met an Australian girl I still remember. I wasn't about to complain.

O'Day said, "We shouldn't make unexamined assumptions. There's no evidence he ever even looked at a gun again."

"But he's on the list?"

"He has to be."

"What would be the odds?"

"One in four, obviously."

"Would you put your money on?"

"I'm not saying he's our boy. I'm saying we have

to face the fact there's a one-in-four possibility he might be."

"Who else is on the list?"

"One Russian, one Israeli, one Brit."

I said, "Kott's been in prison fifteen years."

O'Day nodded and said, "Let's start with what that would do to him."

Which was another very good question. What exactly would fifteen years in prison do to a sniper? Good shooting is about a lot of different things. Muscle control might suffer. Good shooting is about being soft and hard at the same time. Soft enough to keep tiny jitters out, hard enough to control a violent explosion. General athletic condition might suffer, which was important, too, because a low heart rate and good breathing were all part of the deal.

But in the end I said, "Eyesight."

O'Day said, "Because?"

"Everything he's seen for fifteen years has been pretty close. Walls, basically. Even the exercise yard. His eyes haven't focused long since he was a young man." Which all sounded good to me. I liked the mental image. Kott, gone soft, maybe a little trembly now, wearing glasses, stooping even though he was small to start with.

Then O'Day read out the prison discharge report.

Kott's heritage was rooted in Czechoslovakia or Arkansas or probably both, but he had mapped his fifteen years of jail time like a mystical sage from the east. He had taken up yoga and meditation. He had worked out very lightly, once a day, to maintain core strength and flexibility, and he had been still for many hours, hardly breathing, all the time with a blank thousand-yard stare he said he needed to practice.

O'Day said, "I asked around. The girls who work here, mostly. They say Kott's type of yoga is all about stillness and relaxed power. You fade, and fade, and fade, and then bang, you go to the next position. The same with the meditation. Empty your mind. Visualize your success."

"You saying he got out of prison better than he went in?"

"He worked hard for fifteen years. In a very single-minded manner. And after all, a gun is just a metal tool. Success is all about the mind and the body."

"How would he get to Paris? Does he have a passport?"

"Think about the factions. Think about their spending power. A passport is the least of their problems."

"Last time I saw him, he was signing the paper. Over sixteen years ago, apparently. I don't see how I can help you now."

"We have to cover all the bases."

"Which base could I possibly cover?"

"You caught him once," O'Day said. "If needs be, you can catch him again."

Chapter 5

Shoemaker got involved at that point, as if the overview was completed, and it was time for the details. A lot hinged on the motive for the attack. Certain factions would never hire an Israeli, which would increase the odds to one in three, except that apparently the Israeli looked kind of Irish and had a neutral code name. Maybe the factions didn't know. Which would confuse the issue. But in the end the quest for motive had been abandoned. The State Department's list of people mad at the French was long. Therefore all four suspects were being treated equally. No profiling was allowed.

I turned to Casey Nice and said, "This is still bullshit."

Once again she said, "What part?"

"Same part. This is way too much. You wouldn't piss on the French if they were on fire. Yet here you are. You're reacting like this was Pearl Harbor. Why? What is France going to do to you? Stop sending cheese?"

"We can't be seen to drag our feet."

"You can't be seen at all. You're moving from place to place and hiding behind phony signs. Which is good. No watcher out of any embassy is going to figure out who you are or what you're doing. Not even the French embassy. They can't know if you're helping or not. So why bother?"

"It's a matter of reputation."

"There's a one-in-four chance a convicted American felon is freelancing somewhere in the world. He wouldn't be the first and he won't be the last. Our reputation could stand that kind of tiny hit. Especially because the French guy is still alive. No harm, no foul."

O'Day stirred and said, "We don't make the policy rules."

"The last time you listened to the Congress, Abraham Lincoln was in short pants."

"But who *do* I listen to?"

I said, "The president," and stopped.

O'Day said, "Everyone's mad at the French, which is ultimately the same thing as no one's mad at them. No one had a particular reason to shoot the guy. Not this year. Not more than usual. Therefore right now the smart money says this was an audition. Our boy was making his bones, ahead of a bigger proposition. Which would be who? No one knows, but they're all betting it's them. And why wouldn't they? They're all the most important person in the world. They've got an EU meeting coming up, all the heads of government, and then there's the G8 and the G20. That's twenty world leaders right there. Including ours. All posing for a group photograph. Standing still and smiling. On the steps of a public building, probably. They don't want a guy on the loose who can shoot more than three-quarters of a mile."

"So this is politicians covering their ass?"

"Literally. All over the world."

"Including our guy?"

"Doesn't matter what he thinks personally. The Secret Service is freaking out enough for both of them."

"Hence a private jet for me."

"Money no object."

"But not just me, right? Please tell me you're not relying on one guy here."

O'Day said, "We have all the help we need."

I said, "It's likely not Kott."

"It's definitely not three of them. You want to roll the dice or do the work?"

I didn't answer that. Shoemaker told me I would be billeted in quarters nearby, and that I was restricted to that part of the base. If questioned either officially or casually I was to say I was a civilian contractor with an expertise in pallet loading. If pressed I was to say I was working with the 47th Logistics on a problem in Turkey. Which made some kind of sense. As soon as I said Turkey, the questioners would assume missiles, and the good guys would back off, and the bad guys would be misinformed. Which in O'Day's opinion was an outcome devoutly to be desired.

I said, "Who's looking for the other three?"

O'Day said, "Their own people, in their own countries."

"Not the French in France?"

"They assume he's gone home to lay up."

"Maybe he's an ex-pat. A Russian who lives in France. Or an Israeli, or a guy from Great Britain. In an old farmhouse, or a villa by the sea."

"They may not have considered that."

"Did Kott go to live in France?"

O'Day shook his head and said, "He went back to Arkansas."

"And?"

"We put a surveillance drone over his house a couple of times in the first month. We saw nothing to worry about. Then the drone was needed elsewhere, and he went on the back burner."

"And now?"

"We got the drone back. His house is empty. No sign of life."

Casey Nice walked me over to the quarters Shoemaker had mentioned, which turned out to be an improvised little village made up of separate prefabricated and transportable living units adapted from fifty-three-foot steel shipping containers. Eight feet high, eight feet wide, with windows and doors cut into them, and AC, and water lines and power lines all hooked up. Mine was painted sand yellow, probably shipped back from Iraq. I had lived in worse places. It was a pleasant night. Spring, in North Carolina. Too early in the year to be hot, too late to be cold. There were stars out in the sky, and ghostly wisps of cloud.

We stopped at my metal door and I said, "Are you in one of these things?"

Casey Nice pointed to the next row. "The white one," she said. If she was on First Street, then I was on Second. I said, "Is this what you signed up for?"

"This is where the rubber meets the road," she said. "I'm happy enough."

"It's likely not Kott," I said again. "Statistically when it comes to snipers the Russians produce the most and the best. And the Israelis love fifty-caliber rounds. It's likely one of those two."

"But it's the yoga that worries us. Clearly Kott had an aim in life. He was planning to get out and take up where he left off." Then she nodded to herself, as if her job was done, and she walked away and left me there. I opened my door and went inside.

Inside looked exactly like a fifty-three-foot shipping container, all corrugated metal, painted glossy white all around, with a living area and a kitchen and a bathroom and a bedroom all in a line. Like an old-fashioned railroad apartment. The windows had blast covers that dropped down inside to make work surfaces. There was a plywood floor. I unpacked, which consisted of taking my clip-together toothbrush from my pocket, assembling it, and propping it in a bathroom glass. I thought about taking a shower, but I never got to it, because there was a knock at my door. I hiked back through the narrow cramped rectangle and opened up.

Another woman in a black skirt suit and dark nylons and good shoes. This one was closer to my own age. She had an air of command and seniority. Her hair was silvery black, neatly cut but not styled or colored. Her face had been pretty once, and was handsome now. She said, "Mr. Reacher? I'm Joan Scarangello."

She stuck out her hand. I took it and shook it. It felt slim but strong. Plain nails, cut short and square. Clear polish. No rings. I said, "CIA?"

She smiled and said, "It's not supposed to be *that* obvious."

"I already met State and Special Forces. I figured the third wheel would come rolling down the pike pretty soon."

"May I come in?"

My living area was eight feet high and eight feet wide and about thirteen feet long. Adequate for two, but only just. The furniture was bolted to the floor, a short sofa and two small chairs, all arranged in a tight little grouping. Like an RV, or maybe a design study for a new Gulfstream cabin. I sat on the sofa and Joan Scarangello sat in a chair, and we adjusted our relative angles until we were looking at each other face to face.

She said, "We very much appreciate your help."

I said, "I haven't done anything yet."

"But I'm sure you will, if necessary."

"Did the FBI go out of business? Isn't finding American citizens in America normally their job?"

"Kott might not be in America. Not currently."

"Then he's your job."

"And we're doing it. Which includes getting the best help we can. Anything else would be negligent. You know the man."

"I busted him sixteen years ago. Apart from that I know nothing about him."

"The EU, then the G8, and then the G20," she said. "The European Union, then the world's eight largest economies, and then the world's twenty largest economies. Heads of state, all in the same place at the same time. By definition all but one of them on unfamiliar turf. If one of them goes down, it's a disaster. If more than one goes down, it's a catastrophe. And as I believe you pointed out, the Paris shooter was ready to fire twice. And why would he stop at two? Imagine if three or four went down. We'd have paralysis. Markets would crash, and we'd be back in recession. People would starve. Wars might start. The whole world could fall apart."

"Maybe they should cancel their meetings."

"Same result. The world has to be governed. They can't do it all by phone."

"They could for a month or two."

"But who's going to propose that? Who's going to blink first? Us, in front of the Russians? The Russians, in front of us? The Chinese, in front of anybody?"

"So this is all a testosterone thing?"

Joan Scarangello said, "What isn't?"

I said, "Speaking of governing the world, I don't even have a phone."

She said, "Would you like one?"

"My point is, John Kott is a guy I met for one day, sixteen years ago. I have no resources, no communications, no databases, no systems, no nothing."

"We have all of that. We'll give you what leads we have."

"And then send me out to get him?"

She didn't answer.

I said, "Here's the thing, Ms. Scarangello. I know I only just got here, but I wasn't born yesterday. I didn't just fall off the turnip truck. If Kott's the guy, you want me out there blundering around because whoever is bankrolling him will want to stop me. Whatever faction, as O'Day likes to say. I'm supposed to bring them out in the open. That's all. All I am is bait."

She didn't answer.

I said, "Or maybe you want Kott to come for me himself. He's plenty mad at me, after all. I put him away for fifteen years. I'm sure that put a crimp in his lifetime plans. He's probably nursing an appropriate degree of resentment. Maybe all that yoga was for me personally, not general career advancement."

"No one is thinking in terms of bait."

"Bullshit. Tom O'Day thinks of everything, and chooses the easiest and most effective."

"Are you scared?"

"You know any infantrymen?"

"This base has plenty."

"Talk to them. The infantry puts up with a world of shit. They live in holes in the ground, cold, wet, muddy, hungry, with incoming mortars and artillery and rockets, and bombs and gas, and air assault and missiles, and they have nothing ahead of them except barbed wire and machine gun nests, but you know what they hate most of all?"

"Snipers," she said.

"Correct," I said. "Random death, out of nowhere, anytime, anyplace, no notice, no warning. Every minute of every day. No relief. The stress becomes unbearable. It sends some of them mad, literally. And I can understand why. Right now I'm sitting in a little metal box and I'm already liking it more than I should."

"I met your brother once," Scarangello said.

"Really?"

She nodded. "Joe Reacher. I was a young case officer and he was with military intelligence. We worked together on a thing."

"And now you're going to tell me he spoke well of me and said I was the baddest son of a bitch in the valley. You're going to leverage a dead man."

"I'm sorry he died. But he did speak well of you."

"If Joe was here he'd tell me to run away from this thing as far and as fast as I can. There's a clue in the title. Military, and intelligence. He knew Tom O'Day, too."

"You don't like O'Day, do you?"

"I think someone should give him a medal and a bullet in the head and name a bridge after him."

"Maybe this wasn't a good idea."

"I'm surprised he's still in business."

"This kind of thing keeps him in business. Now more than ever. He's front and center."

I said nothing.

Scarangello said, "We can't make you stay."

I shrugged.

"I owe Rick Shoemaker a favor," I said. "I'll stick around."

Predictable.

Chapter 6

Scarangello left after that, leaving a faint perfumed scent in the air, and I took my shower and went to bed. O'Day liked to start every morning with a conference, and I planned to be there, right after breakfast. Which I couldn't find. The dawn light showed we were stuck in a remote corner of Pope Field, which was vast. I figured I was a mile or more from the nearest mess hall. Maybe five miles. And my movements were restricted. Walking around Fort Bragg unauthorized wasn't the smartest thing to do. Not under the current circumstances. Not under any circumstances, really.

So I headed back to the red door and found Casey Nice in a room with a table. The table was loaded with muffins and pastries on plates, and big catering boxes of coffee. Dunkin' Donuts, not army issue. Private catering. Reforms. Anything to save a buck.

Casey Nice said, "Comfortable quarters?"

I said, "Better than sleeping in a hollow log."

"Is that what you normally do?"

"Figure of speech," I said.

"But you slept well?"

"Terrific."

"Did you meet anyone last night?"

"I met a woman named Joan Scarangello."

"Good."

"Who is she exactly?"

"A deputy to the deputy director of operations."

Which sounded junior, but wasn't. In CIA-speak a D-DDO was part of a tiny circle at the very top. One of the three or four most plugged-in people on the planet. Her natural habitat would be a Langley office about eight times the size of my shipping container, probably with more phones on the desk than I had seen in my entire life. I said, "They're really taking this seriously, aren't they?"

"They have to, don't you think?"

I didn't answer that, and then Scarangello herself came in. She nodded a greeting and took a muffin and a cup of coffee. Then she left again. I took two muffins and an empty cup and a whole box of coffee. I figured I could prop it on the edge of the conference table with the spigot facing toward me. Refills as and when required. Like an alcoholic behind a bar.

The morning conference was in a room next to O'Day's upstairs office. Nothing fancy. Just four plain tables pushed together in a square, and eight chairs for the five of us. Shoemaker and O'Day and Scarangello were already in their places. Casey Nice sat down next to Scarangello and I chose a spot with an empty chair on either side. I got the coffee set up and bit the head off a muffin.

Shoemaker went first. He was in fatigues again, with his star, which was not surprising, but his opening analysis was informed enough to suggest he might have been worth it, which was. He said, "The Polish government looks set to announce a snap election, and the Greeks too, probably. Which looks like democracy in action, but if you drill down into the European Union constitution you find a provision that allows heads-of-state pow-wows to be postponed if two or more member states are at the polls. In other words, they're running for the hills. The EU meeting ain't going to happen. Which moves us on to the G8 in three weeks. Those plans are still intact. Which gives us both the time and the target."

I took a breath to speak but O'Day shot out a lengthy arm, with his palm toward me, like he was telling a dog to stay, and he said, "You're about to warn us we're making a massive assumption here, and that the real target could be anything. Which is correct, but please understand we don't care about any other target. If something else gets hit, we'll be dancing jigs and reels. Until then, for operational purposes, we're assuming an assassination attempt against a world leader is already a proven fact."

I said, "I was going to ask who's in the G8."

Which must have been a dumb question, because they all started fidgeting and no one answered. Eventually Casey Nice said, "Ourselves and Canada, the UK and France, Germany and Italy, and Japan and Russia."

I said, "Those aren't the eight largest economies."

"They were once," Joan Scarangello said. "Some things get set in stone."

"So if this is personal or nationalist it could be any one of them. But if it's some big terrorist statement, then with all due respect, it's probably not Italy. I mean, who would notice? Those guys change every three weeks anyway. Or Canada. You wouldn't recognize the guy if you saw him in the grocery store. Japan, the same. And France. The UK, too. Some posh boy goes facedown, it's not going to destabilize the world. Germany is possibly a slight problem."

Scarangello nodded. "Europe's largest economy, the region's only fiscal grown-up, and a whole new psyche that absolutely depends on politicians *not* getting shot. Things could unravel. And rock bottom is a long way down in Germany."

"So it's ourselves and Russia and Germany. Which is easy. Just keep those three guys under wraps. No fresh air for them. Let the other five walk about. Or send the vice presidents, too, for the photo ops. Which could be spun. We're so ballsy we'll send both of them."

O'Day nodded. "That's Plan B, and it's already drafted. Plan A is to find John Kott. And to hope that London and Moscow and Tel Aviv meet with similar success."

"Do we know anything about their guys?"

"We know all about them. The Brit is an ex–SAS operator named Carson. In uniform he had more than fifty kills around the world, not that anyone will admit it, one of them at two thousand yards, documented and verified. The Russian is a guy called Datsev. His first instructor was at Stalingrad, which was a hard school. The Israeli is called Rozan. Best they ever saw with a fifty-caliber Barrett, which is really saying something, for the IDF."

"They all sound better than Kott."

"No, they sound about as good as. Fourteen hundred yards was nothing to Kott. Pure routine. Until you busted him, that is."

"You sound like you think I shouldn't have."

"He was worth more to us than the grunt he killed."

I said, "Where is the G8 meeting?"

"London," O'Day said. "Technically just outside. A stately home, or an old castle. Something like that."

"Does it have a moat?"

"I'm not sure."

"Maybe they should start digging one."

"The idea is not to let it get that far."

"I can't help you there anyway. My passport is expired."

O'Day said, "You should speak to the State Department about that." Then he looked up, and Casey Nice put her hand under her jacket again, the same way she had when she showed me the embassy report, and she came out with a slim blue booklet, which she slid across to me. It was warm, like before.

It was a passport, with my name and my face in it, dated yesterday, good for ten years.

Chapter 7

After the conference ended, I was asked to go to Rick Shoemaker's office, where he asked me to start detailed tactical planning for a trip to Arkansas. Which was ridiculous. Arkansas didn't need detailed tactical planning. And it was the wrong direction. I said, "He'll have stayed in Europe, surely. He's probably already in London. If it's him at all."

Shoemaker said, "Joan Scarangello told us you fully understand your role."

All I am is bait.

I said, "Are you serious?"

He said, "It's no big deal. As you point out, if Kott's the guy, he's unlikely to be there himself. But if he is the guy, then they might have someone there to monitor our progress. It's an obvious first stop. It's one we should make anyway. We need to confirm he took up shooting again. If he didn't, we're home and dry. Yoga and meditation get you only so far. You need some trigger time, too. They might be expecting us to check.

They'll be low-grade people. No problem for you. But we might get something out of them."

"If it's him."

"And if it isn't, you've got even less to worry about."

"Why me? There are plenty of federal agents in the world. They would work as bait. Better than me, probably. They could show up with lights and sirens."

"You know how many Americans have top secret security clearances now?"

"No idea."

"Nearly a million, and half of them are civilians. Executives and businesspeople and contractors and subcontractors. And best case, out of any million people a couple hundred will be seriously bent."

"That's O'Day talking."

"He's usually right."

"And always paranoid."

"OK, cut it in half. We've got a hundred traitors with top secret security clearances. National security is completely out of control. It has been for a decade. Therefore right now this is a closely held project. This information is not being widely distributed. At the moment General O'Day prefers people he knows he can trust."

"I can't even rent a car. I don't have a driver's license or a credit card."

"Casey Nice will go with you," Shoemaker said. "She's old enough to drive."

"Then she'll be bait, too."

"She knows what she signed up for. And she's tougher than she looks."

* * *

In the end the detailed tactical planning came down to grabbing my toothbrush from my bathroom, and copying down Kott's last known address, which was a rented place miles from anywhere in the bottom left corner of the state, where Arkansas becomes either Oklahoma or Texas or Louisiana. Casey Nice went into her white box wearing her black skirt suit and came out again five minutes later wearing blue jeans and a brown leather jacket. Which I agreed was better for the bottom left corner of Arkansas.

They gave us the same plane. Same crew. I let Casey Nice precede me up the steps, which was the only rational thing to do when one of you is a twenty-something girl in jeans, and one of you isn't. I sat in the same chair, and she sat opposite. This time the steward knew all about where we were going, which was Texarkana. A civilian field, with car rental. Not a Great Circle route. Just west and south, over Georgia and Alabama and Mississippi. One pot of coffee would do it, probably, unless Casey Nice wanted a cup.

I said to her, "Shoemaker told me you know what you signed up for."

She said, "I think I do."

"Which is what?"

"It's a theory they have. You've seen how it is. We're all working together. The theory is in the future we'll merge completely. Behind the scenes, that is. So we have to get exposure. Which is fine. I need to be ready. Most of my career is in the future."

"What kind of exposure have you gotten so far?"

"I'm not worried about this, if that's what you mean."

"Good to know," I said.

"Should I be?"

"You ever been in a hotel with one of those real big beds? About seven feet long? If we're ever out in the open, that's how far you should be from me. Because best case here is Kott has nothing to do with any of this, and he was away on a fishing trip when your drones came over, and now he's back home again, with a long straight driveway and a loaded gun by his kitchen window. Depending on how excited he gets, the first shot might miss by six feet. But it won't miss by seven."

"I don't think he's home. I think he's in London."

"Why him? The others sound better."

"Datsev was Red Army as a very young man, and then Russian Army. Until five years ago. He left the state's employ. Rozan has been out of the IDF even longer. Carson the Brit has been out of the SAS longer still. But Paris was a brand new profile. Why would Datsev or Rozan or Carson wait so long before going into business? This feels like a guy who just spent a year tuning up ahead of hanging out a shingle. A guy whose retirement only just began."

"You should still stay seven feet away. Datsev and Rozan and Carson could have been otherwise employed. Private armies or security, or maybe they were running organic bookstores, but times went bad. Or maybe their pensions just ran out. Or maybe they just got out of jail for unconnected offenses. Kott could have been on the freelance market longer than any of them, even if it was only a year."

"Then they'd pick him first, because he's the most experienced. He's in London. I'm sure of it. I'm not worried about Arkansas."

Neither was I, at first.

Chapter 8

We landed in Texarkana and found rental cars at the end of a long line of establishments all connected with the aviation business. Casey Nice came out with a perfectly standard Maryland driver's license, and I caught a glimpse of her date of birth, and I worked out she was twenty-eight years old. She accompanied the license with a Visa card from a Maryland bank. In exchange she got a whole bunch of forms to sign, and then the key to a Ford F-150 pickup truck, which seemed to be what people wanted at the Texarkana airport.

The truck was red and had a navigation device connected to the cigarette lighter. She put in the address we had. The thing scrolled like it was summoning up vast reserves of local knowledge, and then it told us the trip was going to be fifty miles. I looked back at the airport as we left. I could see our plane. Ahead were narrow winding roads and new leaves on the trees.

I said, "We should stop for lunch."

She said, "Shouldn't we do the job first?"

"Eat when you can. That's the golden rule."

"Where?"

"First place we see."

Which turned out not to be the kind of rural diner I was hoping for. Instead we rolled through a neat little crossroads town and came upon a crisp little commercial development with a Shell station at one end and a family restaurant at the other. In between were budget establishments selling life's necessities at low prices, including a pharmacy and a clothing store. The restaurant had plain wood tables and mismatched plates, but it had good solid fare on the menu. I caught up on breakfast, with coffee and pancakes and eggs and bacon. Casey Nice ordered a salad, and drank plain water. She paid, on O'Day's budget, presumably.

Then I detoured to the clothing store and hunted around at the khaki end of the color spectrum and the low end of the price list, and I picked out underwear and socks, and pants, and a shirt, and a jacket that might have been intended for golf in the rain. I didn't find any shoes better than the pair I had on. As always I changed in the cubicle and left my old stuff in the trash. As always Casey Nice was interested in the process. She said, "I heard about this at the briefing, but I wasn't sure whether to believe it."

I said, "You had a briefing about me?"

"General O'Day calls you Sherlock Homeless."

"He should think about buying a new sweater himself."

We got back in the red truck and moved on, north and west, skirting the corner of Texas, heading for the

Oklahoma line. The navigation device showed our destination as a black and white checkered flag, like the end of an auto race, and it seemed to be out in the middle of absolutely nowhere. I hoped more roads would show up on the screen when we got closer.

An hour later more roads had indeed shown up, all thin and gray and twisting. There were lakes and streams and rivers too, oriented in a way that suggested a landscape scarred by ravines. Which a glance ahead at the real world confirmed. Low wooded hills, one behind the other, running left to right, like a washboard. Casey Nice pulled over a mile short of the checkered flag and took out her phone, but she couldn't get a signal for whatever it was she wanted. A satellite view, maybe. So we were stuck with the navigation device, which had the checkered flag planted half a mile north of the road we were on, all alone in a sea of green.

"A long driveway," I said.

"Let's hope it's not straight," she said.

We rolled on, slower, until finally we saw the mouth of the driveway up ahead on the right. It was just a stony track through the trees, starting out between token gateposts made of piled rocks, and then winding quickly out of sight behind the new green leaves. There was a mailbox on the shoulder, all rusted, with no name on it. And directly opposite, on the left side of the road, clearly visible, was a house. Kott's nearest neighbor, presumably.

I said, "Let's start there."

The neighbor's house was nothing fancy, but it was

a halfway decent place. It was long and low and made of brown boards. It had a gravel patch out front, with a pick-up truck parked on it. Out back it looked like there might be a small garden. On one side was a TV dish as big as a family car, and on the other side was a washing machine all streaked with rust, with its hoses hanging down in the dirt, all pale and perished.

I put a knuckle on the bell button and heard suburban chimes behind the door. There was no response. Then we heard footsteps and a guy came around from the back of the house, on the washing machine side. He was maybe forty, with close-cropped hair and a beard the same length, and a thick neck, and skeptical eyes, and a face that would have been unremarkable except for a missing front tooth, just left of center in his upper jaw.

He spoke in a neutral tone and said, "Help you?"

Which in my experience are two words that can precede anything from genuine wholehearted cooperation to a bullet in the face. I said, "We're looking for John Kott."

He said, "Not me."

"Do you know where he lives?"

The guy pointed through his thin hedge, across the road, to the driveway mouth beyond.

I said, "Is he home?"

"Who's asking?"

"He's a buddy of mine."

"From where?"

"Prison," I said.

"Why don't you drive on up and see for yourself?"

"We're in a rental. They make you pay now, if you blow a tire. And that track looks pretty bad."

The guy said, "I don't know if he's home."

"How long has he lived there?"

"About a year."

"Is he working?"

"I don't think so."

"Then how does he pay the rent?"

"I have no idea."

"Do you see him coming and going?"

"If I happen to be watching."

"When was the last time you saw him?"

"Can't say for sure."

"Today? Yesterday?"

"Can't say. I don't spend a lot of time watching."

"A month ago? Two months?"

"Can't say."

I asked, "What does he drive?"

"An old blue pick-up truck," the guy said. "A Ford, from way back long ago."

"You ever hear shooting up there?"

"Up where?"

"In the woods. Or the hills."

"This is Arkansas," the guy said.

"Does Mr. Kott get visitors?"

"Can't say."

"Any strange people hanging around?"

"What kind of strange people?"

"Strange foreign people, maybe."

"You're the first I've seen in a long time."

I said, "I'm not a strange foreign person. I'm neither of those things."

He asked, "Where were you born?"

To which there was no good answer. He could tell

by my voice I wasn't born in the South. And New York or Chicago or Los Angeles would be all the same to him. So I told him the truth. I said, "West Berlin."

He didn't reply.

"Marine family," I said.

"I was Air Force," he said. "I don't like the Marines. Bunch of showboating glory hunters, in my opinion."

"No offense taken," I said.

The guy turned away and looked at Casey Nice, top to bottom, bottom to top, quite slowly, and he said, "I'm guessing you were never in prison."

She said, "Only because they're not smart enough to catch me."

The guy smiled and ran his tongue out through the gap in his teeth. He said, "Catch you doing what, little missy?"

Casey Nice said, "You should get that tooth fixed. You'd have a nice smile, if you did. And you should take the washing machine out of the yard. I don't think it's compulsory."

"Are you making fun of me?" The guy stepped up and stared at her, and then he glanced at me, and I gave him a blank-eyed look, like I had a fifth of a second to decide whether to leave him limping for a week, or in a wheelchair for the rest of his life. He paused a beat, and then he said, "Well, I hope y'all have a nice visit with your buddy," and he walked away, around the back of his house again, but this time on the dish side. We stood for a second in the weak spring sun, and then we got back in the rented truck and aimed it across the two-lane's hump, straight at the mouth of Kott's stony track.

Chapter 9

The track was little better than a dry riverbed, but at least it wasn't straight. Not at first. It came in off the two-lane at a shallow angle, and then it turned sharp right, to climb up a bank, before it curved left again, to align itself with the ravine it was following. Then it was going to hairpin right. And beyond that we couldn't see. Casey Nice was hunched forward, fighting the wheel, which was writhing and bucking in her hands.

I said, "You need to sit back. In fact you need to push your chair back."

"Why?"

"Because when the shooting starts, you need to get down in the foot well. I don't know if the engine in this thing is iron or aluminum, but either one is good protection. If you're not killed instantly, that is."

"He's in London."

"One of them is. The other three aren't."

"He's the pick of the litter."

"He's been in prison fifteen years."

"With a plan. Either it worked or it didn't. If it did, he's as good as he ever was. Which is plenty good enough for Paris. Or he might even be better than he ever was. Have you thought of that? Which would be superhuman, basically."

"Is that the State Department's official in-house analysis? You guys should stick to passports and visas."

We crawled on up, toward the blind hairpin turn. We saw no surveillance. No one was monitoring our progress. The ravine we were following would look small from the air, like a scratch on a lover's back, but up close and personal, on a human scale, it was plenty impressive. It was maybe thirty feet deep, like a long gash from a raked claw, and the bottom was filled with broken and tumbled rocks, so that not much grew there except small hardy weeds and bushes. The trees restarted at the tops of the banks, and their leaves were out, still curled and half-sized, but numerous enough to block the view.

I said, "Maybe we should walk from here."

"Seven feet apart?"

"At least."

She slowed the truck and came to a bouncing stop. There was nowhere to pull off. The track was about one truck wide. Which was good. I said, "If he's out at the grocery store we'll hear him get back. He's going to honk his horn when he finds this thing here."

"He's in London."

"Stay with the truck, if you want."

"I don't want."

"Then you go first. Like you were selling encyclopedias. He won't shoot you."

"You sure?"

"You haven't challenged him yet."

"See? You do know something about him."

"I'll be about twenty yards behind. Holler if there's a problem."

I watched her go. She stepped neatly from rock to rock in the center of the track, and carefully, as if the streambed had water in it, and she needed to keep her feet dry. I followed twenty yards back, stepping longer but slower, planting my feet like climbing a hill, even though the slope was gradual. She paused before the hairpin and looked back, and I shrugged, and she moved on out of sight. I stopped for a moment and listened hard, but heard nothing except the click of stones under her feet, so I moved on after her, a little faster, aiming to close the gap to what it had been before.

After the hairpin turn there was a long straight stretch along the uphill side of the ravine, and then a suggestion of a clearing in the trees, and maybe a house made of the same dark boards as its neighbor. And maybe a wink of dull blue paint, to the left, behind distant leaves. Maybe a parked pick-up truck, from way back long ago. Total distance from me to there was about a hundred yards.

Up ahead Casey Nice had moved over to the edge of the track. Slower going, but I guess she felt better there. As did I. I crabbed over to the opposite edge.

No point in presenting a single linear target. No point in her getting killed by a miss aimed at me, and no point in me getting killed by a miss aimed at her.

We moved on, in diagonal lock step, until she reached the edge of the clearing, where she paused and looked back. I gestured *hold still,* a standard infantry hand signal from way back in basic, but she got it and pulled back a step into the trees. I crossed the track, three long strides, and I joined her. She said, "Want me to go knock on the door?"

I said, "I think you're going to have to."

"Does he have a dog?"

"It would have barked already."

She nodded and took a breath and stepped out. I heard the sound change under her feet, from clicking stones to crunching gravel. I heard her knock on the door. No bell. Just a loud *tap-tap-tap* from her knuckles on the wood, which might have sounded urgent in the city, but which seemed appropriate in the countryside, where people can be busy faraway.

There was no response.

No tread or creak inside the house, no scuffle or crunch around it.

Nothing.

She knocked again.

Tap-tap-tap.

Silence. No response. No one home, no watchers, no surveillance.

I stepped out and hiked across and joined her. Most of the windows in the house had closed drapes behind them, and what few peeks in we got showed us nothing much except plain rooms furnished cheaply some years ago. The house was a long low ranch, very similar in style to the neighbor's below. Maybe built by the same people, at the same time. It was solid. The clearing where it stood was beaten earth half-heartedly sown with gravel. Last year's weeds were coming back, thinner by the front door, because of foot traffic, and equally by the back door, and equally along informal curving paths that led from both doors to where the blue truck was parked.

The blue truck was indeed a Ford, and ancient. A hundred bucks in cash, probably. Perfect for a guy just out of Leavenworth. It was stone cold and looked like it hadn't been moved in a while, but who could tell with a truck that old?

Casey Nice was looking for places to hide a spare key. Of which there was a notable lack. No flowerpots by the door, no statues, no stone lions. She said, "Should we break in?"

I saw a third path. Nothing more than a long shallow depression, and damaged weeds coming back differently, smaller in size, with dark bruised leaves. The path led beyond the old truck, and up toward the next ravine.

I said, "Let's check this out first."

She followed me single file, into the woods, right and left, and we found ourselves at the eastern end of another ravine. It was very like the one we had already seen, a gouge in the earth, maybe thirty feet deep, shaped like a bathtub of tremendous length. Some old geological event. Glaciation, possibly, a million years ago, giant sharp boulders embedded in a trillion tons of ice, grinding slow but certain, like plows in a field.

Like its twin it had broken rocks in the bottom, with not much growing there. Either side the trees grew tall, emphasizing the trench's depth, and exaggerating its length.

Three trees had blown over. Right at the eastern end of the hole. Three pines, straight and true. Two had come down parallel, about ten feet from each other, spanning the drop like the outer frame of a bridge. The third had been chainsawed into ten-foot lengths, which had been lashed across the gap between the fallen trunks to make a solid platform. The platform's upper face was an eight-by-four plywood board, exterior grade, nailed down hard.

Casey Nice said, "For what?"

We climbed onto the platform, inching out, using overhanging branches for support, unsteady for a second, and then we stood still on the board and looked all around. Behind us were trees. To our left and our right were trees. In front of us the ravine ran away west, into the far distance, straight and narrow. What little that grew in it was way down below us. The far end was almost out of sight. There was a smudge of gray there, an interruption, as if the trench was stopping shorter than it wanted to, maybe because of an unrelated rock fall eons later.

I looked down at the plywood and saw two vague oval shapes, close together, each one of them about the size of an ostrich egg, or a quarter-size football, side by side, like footprints from a person standing still. The shapes were gray, or slightly silvery, the way plywood gets when rubbed with metal, and there was graphite, too, from lubricating grease, as well as plain old dirt from the air, because deep down at a microscopic level the grease would always be sticky.

I squatted down and traced the shapes with my finger. I said, "A rifle that size has biped legs coming down off the front of the forestock. They can lock up or down. He put a little grease on the hinges, to protect them, like a cautious man should, and he wiped the excess with a cloth, and then he rubbed the cloth on the biped legs, against corrosion, especially the feet, which are the only parts that touch the world, after all, and then he came out here to practice so many times and in so many slightly different positions he left marks this big."

"Sherlock Homeless," she said.

I stared down the length of the ravine. I said, "Suppose those rocks make a kind of shelf or table? Suppose that's where he put his targets?"

She said, "What rocks?"

We paced it out, exactly parallel in the woods, staying straight, compensating for dodged trees, with me stepping a comfortable yard every time, with her counting, silently at first, and then when we got to twelve hundred and fifty she started counting out loud, initially in a low mutter, pure routine, and then she started to speak with more clarity and excitement as the numbers grew larger and larger, only to end with a low quizzical tone as I stepped absolutely level with the last of the tumbled gray rocks and she said, "Fourteen hundred yards."

Chapter 10

The rocks were indeed the result of an ancient fall, as far as I could tell, and they did indeed make a kind of shelf or table. Only twelve inches deep and four feet wide at its flattest. But apparently that was enough for a whole bunch of beer cans and bottles. There were shreds of metal and powdered glass everywhere. Shreds of white, too, as if he had rigged paper targets from time to time. Behind the shelf the rocks themselves were chipped and cratered all over. They were seriously blasted. Hundreds and hundreds of rounds had been fired. Maybe even thousands.

I said, "We need a container."

Casey Nice said, "What kind?"

"Just some little thing." I pointed below the chipped and cratered rocks. "We should take some dust with us. For the gas chromatograph. We need to know if they're the same bullets."

She patted her pockets, and I saw her hit a possibility, and discount it, and then come back to it when she ran out of alternatives. She looked at me, a little embarrassed.

I said, "What?"

She said, "I have a pill bottle."

"That should work."

She put her hand in her pocket and took out a small orange bottle with a label. She popped the top and spilled a bunch of pills into her palm. She shoveled the pills back in her pocket loose, and she put the top back on the empty bottle, and she tossed it to me.

"Thanks," I said. I brushed dust and grit and dirt into piles, and pinched it all up with finger and thumb, and dropped it in the bottle, over and over again, a little at a time. I had no real idea what a gas chromatograph was, except I was sure it was very sophisticated and could work with the tiniest of samples, but we needed lead fragments, and I wanted to increase the odds. So I kept on pinching and dropping until the bottle was more than half full, and then I put the top back on, and I put the bottle in my pocket, and I said, "OK, *now* we'll go break into his house."

Which we did by kicking down the door. Which was easy enough. A question of force, obviously, which is the product of mass times velocity squared, and that *squared* part puts a premium on speed, not weight. Bulking up by twenty pounds at the gym is good, because it throws an extra twenty pounds in the mix, but moving your foot twenty percent faster is better. It does you four hundred percent of a favor. Because it gets squared. Which means multiplied by itself. Money for nothing. Like in baseball. You can swing a heavy bat slow or a light bat fast, and the slow heavy bat gets you a high fly to the warning track, and the light fast bat puts the ball in the bleachers. A principle too often forgotten. People treat doors with too much respect. They eye them warily and shuffle close and then do little more than press their soles against the wood.

Not me. We chose the rear door over the front, because it looked one category down in certain respects, like the thickness and the hinges and the lock, and the run-up would be longer back there. I needed three clear strides. Which I took at a comfortable walk. Nothing dramatic was required. As long as I was moving, then my upper leg could move faster, and my lower leg faster still, and my foot even faster, and then my heel could punch through the lock like it wasn't even there.

Which is what happened. I caught the door on the bounce and Casey Nice stepped in ahead of me. To a kitchen. I stepped in behind her and saw countertops and cabinets, and a metal sink, and a refrigerator the color of an avocado pear, and a range made of pressed metal, all curved and swooping, like a 1950s car. The countertops were dull, and the cabinets were painted a miserable color that might have been green or brown or anywhere in between.

The air was still, and it smelled dry, and there were no real kitchen odors. No onions, no garbage. Just a kind of neutral, inorganic nothing.

The air smelled old.

Casey Nice moved toward the hallway door and said, "Ready?"

"Wait," I said. I wanted to listen, for the low vibration any living thing gives out. But I heard none. The house was silent and empty. Forlorn, even, as if it had been empty for a good long time.

I said, "I'll check the living room. You check the bedrooms."

She went first, out into a hallway, which was paneled with plywood stained a dark sludge color, and she glanced around and headed left, so I went right, and found a living room with an L-shaped dining nook. It was a well-built room, and graceful in its proportions, but it was heavy with dark wood, and what wasn't dark wood was covered in bland vinyl wallpaper, like a mid-priced hotel. The furniture was a sofa and an ottoman and two armchairs, all in brown corduroy, all well used. There were two side tables, and no television. No newspapers, either, or magazines. Or books. There was no telephone. No old sweater dumped over the arm of a chair, no dried-up beer glass, no half-full ashtray. Nothing personal at all. No real sign of life, except the wear and tear and the permanent slumped impressions in the sofa.

From the far end of the house Casey Nice called out, "Reacher?"

I called back, "What?"

"You really need to see this."

Something in her voice.

I said, "What is it?"

"You need to see it."

So I headed for the sound of her voice, and stepped into a room, and came face to face with myself.

Chapter 11

It was a photograph, obviously. Black and white, of my face. But it had been blown up life size. In a commercial photocopier, probably. Almost to the edges of a sheet of letter size paper. Which had been pinned to the wall with thumbtacks. Six feet five inches from the floor. Below it more sheets of paper had been pinned to the wall, like tiles, overlapping in places, shaping a neck, shoulders, a torso, arms, legs, and on them the rest of me had been sketched in by hand, with a black permanent marker, to match the sooty tone of the Xerox of my face. A life-size human, right there, standing still, head up, thumbs forward, solidly planted in shoes drawn to the last detail, even the laces.

It was a pretty good impression, overall. Wouldn't have fooled my mother, but it was close enough.

It had a knife in the chest. About where my heart would be. A big kitchen item, maybe ten inches long, buried five inches in the wall board.

Casey Nice said, "There's more."

She was standing in an alcove, maybe meant for a bed. I stepped over and found the back wall covered with papers. All about me. At the top was the same photograph, life size. Below it was where it had come from. Which was the bio page from my army personnel file, with my thumbnail headshot glued in the top right corner, crisply Xeroxed. Below the bio page were dozens of other pages, all Xeroxed, all pinned up, packed close together, ordered in some way.

Chosen in some way.

They were my failures. They were after-action reports, mostly, admitting missed clues, and missed connections, and risks gone bad. Thirty whole pages were about Dominique Kohl.

My failures.

Casey Nice asked, "Who was she?"

I said, "She worked for me. I sent her to arrest a guy. She was captured, mutilated, and killed. I should have gone myself."

"I'm sorry."

"So am I."

She studied the pages for a minute and said, "You couldn't have known."

I said, "She was exactly your age."

She said, "There's more, I'm afraid."

She led me to another room, where I saw on a table what I guessed was a homemade rack, good for pinning paper targets on, good for propping on a rocky shelf fourteen hundred yards from the rifle. Admirable initiative, except the paper targets were my photograph. Same deal. Life size. There were two stacks. One used, one not. The unused examples were what I had seen. My face, a sooty Xerox, right to the limits of letter size paper. The used examples were even less pretty. A lot of them were more or less completely shredded, either by the massive trauma of the fifty-caliber round, or by fragments blasted back from the cratered rocks behind, or by both. But some examples had held up better. One was unmarked except for a neat half-inch hole just below my right cheekbone. Another had a hole on the right corner of my mouth.

From fourteen hundred yards. Left and a little low, but still, good shooting.

He got better.

Further down the pile, again, many were completely destroyed, but the good ones were pretty damn good, including three with the hole right between my eyes, one fractionally left, one fractionally right, the last dead center.

From fourteen hundred yards.

More than three-quarters of a mile.

Casey Nice asked, "How old is the photograph?"

I said, "Could be twenty years."

"So he could have had the file before he went to jail."

I shook my head. "Some of those bad things happened after he went away. He got the file when he came out."

"He seems really mad at you."

"You think?"

"He's in London."

"Maybe not," I said. "Why would he be? If he's this mad at me, why would he take time out overseas?"

"Lots of reasons. First is money, because this thing is going to be a real big payday, believe me. But second is he can't find you. You're a hard man to pin down. He could look forever. He didn't think that far ahead."

"Maybe. But right now he doesn't need to find me. I showed up at his door. And the odds are three-in-four he's here."

"He could have shot us a dozen times. But he hasn't. Because he isn't here."

"Was he ever? Where's his stuff?"

"I'm guessing he doesn't have stuff. Maybe a bed-roll and a backpack. A monkish existence, or whatever they call people who meditate. He packed it up and took it with him to Paris. And then to London."

Which made some kind of sense. I nodded. Kott had nothing for fifteen years. Maybe he had gotten used to it. I took a good long look at the target with the dead-center hole, right between my eyes, and then I said, "Let's go."

The walk back to the red truck felt better than I thought it might. Because of the trees. It was geometrically impossible to hit a long-range target through a forest. There would always be a tree in the way, to stop the bullet, or deflect it uncontrollably. Safe enough.

There was no width to turn the truck around, and we didn't want to back all the way down, so we drove on up to the house again and U-turned on the gravel patch, and came back facing the right way. We saw nothing and no one on the track, and the two-lane road was empty. We told the navigation device to take us back to the airport, and it set about doing so. The same fifty miles, in reverse.

I said, "I apologize."

She said, "For what?"

"I made a category error. I took you to be a State Department person loaned out to the CIA for exposure and experience. And therefore maybe a little out of your depth. But it's the other way around, isn't it? You're a CIA agent loaned out to the State Department. For exposure and experience. Of passports and visas and all kinds of forms. Therefore not out of your depth at all."

"What gave me away?"

"A couple of things. The infantry hand signal. You knew that."

She nodded. "Lots of time at Fort Benning."

"And you were all business."

"Didn't Shoemaker tell you I'm tougher than I look?"

"I thought he was trying to justify a crazy risk."

"And by the way, the State Department does way more than passports and visas. It does all kinds of things. Including it supervises operations like these."

"How? This operation is O'Day and two CIA people. You and Scarangello. The State Department isn't involved."

"I'm the State Department. Like you said. Temporarily. And theoretically."

"Are you keeping your temporary and theoretical boss in the loop?"

"Not completely."

"Why not?"

"Because this is too important for the State Department. If it's the Brit or the Russian or the Israeli, then sure, we'll let State take the victory lap, but until we know that for certain, this remains a closely held project."

"Is that what you call it now?"

"Top secret was already taken."

"It's headline news. How top secret can it be?"

"Tomorrow it will be yesterday's news. The French are going to make an arrest. That should calm things down."

"Who are they going to arrest?"

"Some patsy or other. They'll find some guy willing to play a wild-eyed terrorist for three weeks. In exchange for favors elsewhere. I imagine they're casting the role right now. Which will give us time and space to work."

"It's fourteen hundred yards," I said. "That's what matters. Not which one is shooting. They need a perimeter. Call it at least a mile."

"Or they could hide in holes in the ground. Which they might have to, sooner or later. But until then we prefer a proactive approach. We need John Kott in custody. Certainly we don't want to be the only one who doesn't get his guy."

"How are the others doing?"

"You heard what O'Day said this morning. They have names and photographs and histories."

"Is that all?"

"They've got what we've got. It's a level playing field so far."

We drove on, and eventually returned the truck and hiked over to a wire gate in a wire fence, and then a golf cart picked us up and drove us to our plane. Two hours later we were back at Pope, where we found out the playing field wasn't level anymore.

Chapter 12

The playing field wasn't level anymore because the Israelis had found their guy. Mr. Rozan had been located. He had been on vacation. The Red Sea. The watchers had missed his departure. But now he was back. His movements had been traced and all kinds of bar staff and restaurant workers had confirmed his story. It was watertight. He had not been in Paris. He was not a possibility. He was off the list.

"Which makes our task slightly more urgent," O'Day said. He liked afternoon conferences, too. We were all in the same upstairs room again, with the pushed-together tables. O'Day, Shoemaker, and Scarangello, all in position, with me and Casey Nice as late arrivals, jet whine still whistling in our ears. We told them what we had found in Arkansas, and we gave them the dust and the grit, in an evidence bag, not the pill bottle. Shoemaker was disappointed there had been no just-in-case surveillance. He had wanted the bait ploy to work. And then O'Day said he figured Kott's obsession with me was understandable.

I said, "I'd like to know how he got my file."

He said, "A friend in the bureaucracy, presumably. It's a routine file in routine storage in Missouri."

"He has no friends in the bureaucracy. He didn't even have friends in his unit. None of them would lie for him."

"Then he bought the file."

"With what? He was just out of Leavenworth. And then he went out in his back yard and fired about a thousand fifty-caliber rounds, which can be five bucks a pop. Even in Arkansas. Where did he get that kind of money?"

"We'll look into it."

"How? You're not equipped. Enough with the national security bullshit. This is a police inquiry now. He had a fourteen-hundred-yard practice range and a fourteen-hundred-yard money shot. Is that a coincidence? Or was that apartment balcony in Paris selected long ago? Did he train for it specifically? In which case this could be a conspiracy already dating back most of a year. We need data. As in, for a start, who owns that apartment in Paris?"

"Are you volunteering to be our policeman?"

"I thought I was bait."

"You could be both."

"I never volunteer for anything. Soldier's basic rule."

"Maybe you should. You won't rest easy. Not after seeing what you saw."

"There could be a dozen people in the world still

real mad at me. Why would I care? None of them is ever going to find me."

"We found you."

"That's different. You think I would answer an ad from Kott?"

"You'd leave him out there?"

Socratic.

I said, "I'm not his parole officer."

He said, "You're in pretty good shape for your age, Reacher. No doubt because your chosen lifestyle gives you plenty of opportunity for exercise. Walking, mostly, I suppose. Which is the best kind of exercise, they tell me. But my guess is it's not really a chore. It's part of the appeal, isn't it? Open roads, sunny days, far horizons. Or the city, with noises and lights, and hustle and bustle, and a freak show everywhere you look. You like walking. You enjoy the freedom."

I said, "What's your point?"

"It's not the same with a sniper out there."

Joan Scarangello looked straight at me, daring me to disagree.

O'Day said, "Especially with a sniper so batshit crazy he does yoga for fifteen years and then draws a picture on his bedroom wall."

I said nothing.

He said, "What type of police inquiries would you make?"

"He left his truck at home. Therefore he was picked up. Not by a car service, because he has no phone and there's no cell signal. It was prearranged. As was everything, obviously, which means people have been up and down that driveway for months. Someone must have seen something."

"The neighbor didn't."

"So he says now. He's been paid off. And coached."

"You think?"

I nodded. "He had to admit knowing his neighbor. Too weird not to, for Arkansas. But he was told to clam up about the comings and goings. As soon as I asked about foreigners hanging around, he changed the subject. He insulted the Marine Corps and started leering at Ms. Nice."

O'Day turned to Casey Nice and said, "Is that what happened?"

She said, "I dealt with it."

"What did he say about the Marines?".

"Showboating glory hunters."

"Was he a Navy man?"

"Air Force."

O'Day nodded sagely and turned back to me. He said, "Conclusion?"

I said, "The neighbor's got a bag of cash in the back of his closet."

"Untraceable."

"Maybe, maybe not. But he knows who gave it to him. And more of the same cash is in some ammo dealer's register. Who will remember selling a thousand fifty-caliber rounds. That's a big order."

"Could be he went to many different dealers."

"Exactly. And it could be many different folks made the buys, to keep it clean. And the more guys, the more flights in and out of Little Rock and Texarkana, and the more car rentals, and the more gas bought at the local stations, and maybe speeding tickets and parking tickets and video in cop car dashboards, and the more breakfasts and lunches and dinners bought in the local restaurants, and the more nights spent in the local motels. All these things should be checked out. As well as what the neighbor knows."

O'Day worked his mouth, opening it and closing it like he was rehearsing different answers, but in the end all he said was, "OK."

I said, "I can't go do it. I have no status. No one would talk to me."

"The FBI will do it."

"I thought this thing was top secret. Or closely held."

"Divide and conquer," O'Day said. "They can all have a small piece of it. As long as no one has enough to see the whole."

"Then I recommend they start yesterday."

"Tomorrow's the best I can do." He made a note on a piece of paper. He said, "The Russians are getting nowhere. Comrade Datsev has disappeared completely. The British think their boy Carson is traveling on a passport recently and fraudulently acquired. So they're looking at people with brand-new passports who traveled to Paris during the relevant time frame. Trains, planes, automobiles, and boats. They have nearly a thousand names."

"Where was Carson last seen?"

"At home, a month ago. A routine drive-by, by Special Branch."

"What about Datsev?"

"Similar, in Moscow. About a month ago. The difference is neither one has been traced to a fourteen-hundred-yard practice range. I have a bad feeling this one is down to us."

"Carson or Datsev could have trained overseas. They wouldn't need as long as Kott. He had catching up to do. Maybe they all got together somewhere. Maybe there was an audition before the audition. Maybe there was a three-way competition, winner gets the job."

O'Day said, "Maybe a lot of things."

I said, "Do we have photographs?"

He opened a red file folder and took out four head shots, all color. He slipped one out of the pile and discarded it. A curly-haired guy, with a tan and a guileless smile. Rozan, presumably, the Israeli, no longer a suspect. He skimmed the remaining three across the table, in my direction. First up was a shaven-headed guy of about fifty, with a face as blank as a two-by-four, and dark eyes that tilted slightly at the outer corners. Mongolian blood in there somewhere.

"Fyodor Datsev," O'Day said. "Fifty-two years old. Born in Siberia."

Then came a guy who might have started out pale, but who had gotten lined and darkened by sun and wind. Short brown hair, a watchful gaze, a busted nose, and a half-smile that was either ironic or threatening, depending on how you chose to look at it.

"William Carson," O'Day said. "Born in London, forty-eight years old."

Last up was John Kott. Some people got bigger with age, bloated and doughy, like Shoemaker for instance, but Kott had gotten smaller, wirier, boiled down to muscle and sinew. His Czech cheekbones were prominent, and his mouth was a tight line. Only his eyes had gotten bigger. They blazed out at me.

O'Day said, "That's his prison release picture. The most recent we have."

An unsavory trio. I butted the photographs into a stack and slid them back.

I said, "How are the Brits doing with their moat?"

Scarangello said, "They're not going to enforce a mile perimeter. You know how densely populated Great Britain is. It would be like emptying Manhattan. It's not going to happen."

"So what next?"

O'Day said, "You go to Paris."

"When?"

"Now."

"As bait or a cop?"

"Both. But mostly we need eyeballs on the crime scene. In case something was missed."

"Why would they show me anything? I'm nobody."

"Your name will get you in anywhere. I called ahead. Anything they'd show me, they'll show you. Such is the power of O'Day. Especially now."

I said nothing.

Shoemaker said, "You speak French, am I right?"

I said, "Yes."

"And English."

"A little."

"Russian?"

"Why?"

"The Brits and the Russians are sending people,

too. You're bound to meet. Get what you can from them, but don't give anything away."

"Maybe they've been given the same instructions."

O'Day said, "We need a CIA presence," and Casey Nice sat forward in her chair.

Joan Scarangello said, "I'll go."

Chapter 13

They gave us the same plane, but a fresh crew. Two new guys in the cockpit, and a new flight attendant, this one a woman, all of them in Air Force fatigues. I got on board straight out of the shower, in my new clothes from Arkansas, and Scarangello followed me five minutes later, showered too, in another black skirt suit. She had a small wheeled suitcase with her, and a purse. It was going to be an overnight flight, seven hours in the air plus six time zones, which would get us in at nine in the morning, French time. My usual armchair had been laid flat and butted up against the armchair opposite, which had also been laid flat, to make a couch. The same thing had been done to the pair of chairs on the other side of the cabin. There were pillows and sheets and blankets. Two long thin beds, separated by a narrow aisle. Which worked for me. Scarangello didn't look so sure. She was a woman of a certain age and a certain type. I think she might have appreciated a little more privacy.

But first we had to sit on regular chairs, at a table, for takeoff, and then we stayed there, because the flight attendant told us there were meals to be eaten. Which didn't match the surroundings. They were not the culinary equivalents of butterscotch leather and walnut veneer. They were not army issue, either. Or Air Force. They were burgers, in cardboard clamshell boxes, reheated in the on-board microwave, unrecognizable and off-brand, presumably bought from a shack near Pope's main gate. Maybe right next to the Dunkin' Donuts.

I ate mine, and then half of Scarangello's, after she left it. Then she started working out how to get herself into bed without embarrassment. I saw her eyes darting all around, checking angles, looking at the lighting, figuring out where I would be and what I might see.

I said, "I'll go first."

The bathroom was through the galley, all the way in back, ahead of the luggage hold, where they had stashed her bag. I used the head and brushed my teeth, and walked back to the bedroom area, and chose the bed on the starboard side. I took off my shoes and socks, because I sleep better that way, and I lay down on top of the blanket, and I rolled on my side and faced the wall.

Scarangello took the hint. I heard her go, all stiff swishing from wool and nylon, and then later I heard her pad back, softer, probably in cotton, and I heard her get in bed and arrange the sheets. She made a little sound, somewhere halfway between a sleepy murmur and a cough, which I took to be an announcement, like *OK, thanks, I'm all set now,* so I rolled on my back and looked up at the bulkhead above me.

She said, "Do you always sleep outside the covers?"

I said, "When it's warm."

"Do you always sleep in your clothes?"

"No choice, in a situation like this."

"Because you have no pajamas. No home, no bags, no possessions. We had a briefing about you."

I said, "Casey Nice told me that." I rolled back toward the wall a little, adjusting my position for comfort, and something dug into my hip. Something in my pocket. Not my toothbrush, which was in my other pocket. I lifted up and checked.

The pill bottle. I cupped it in my palm, and looked at the label, in the dim light, purely out of interest. I guess I was expecting allergy medicine, perhaps carried in anticipation of spring pollens in the woods of Arkansas, or else painkillers, perhaps carried after dental work or a muscle strain. But the label said Zoloft, which I was pretty sure was for neither allergies nor pain. I was pretty sure Zoloft was for stress. Or for anxiety. Or for depression or panic attacks, or PTSD, or OCD. Heavy duty, and prescription only.

But it wasn't Casey Nice's prescription. The name on the label wasn't hers. It was a man's name: Antonio Luna.

Scarangello said, "What did you think of our Ms. Nice?"

I put the bottle back in my pocket.

I said, "Nice by name, nice by nature."

"Too nice?"

"You worried about that?"

"Potentially."

"She did fine in Arkansas. The neighbor didn't get · to her."

"How would she have done if you hadn't been there?"

"The same, probably. Different dynamic, similar result."

"That's good to know."

"Is she your protégée?"

Scarangello said, "I never met her before. And I wouldn't necessarily have chosen her. But she was who we had at State, so she fit the bill."

I said, "These world leader guys risk getting shot all the time. It's the cost of doing business. And protection is better than ever now. I don't understand the big panic."

"Our briefing indicated you're a competent mathematician."

"Then your briefing was incorrect. High school arithmetic was as far as I got."

"Area of a circle with a fourteen-hundred-yard radius?"

I smiled in the dark. *Pi* times the radius squared. I said, "Very nearly two square miles."

"Average population density in major Western city centers?"

Which was neither math nor arithmetic, but general knowledge. I said, "Forty thousand people per square mile?"

"You're behind the times. Closer to fifty thousand now, plus or minus. Parts of London and Paris are already seventy thousand. On average they'd have to lock down tens of thousands of rooftops and windows and a hundred thousand people. Can't be done. A gifted long-range rifleman is their worst nightmare."

"Except for the bulletproof glass."

Scarangello nodded in the dark. I heard her head move on her pillow. She said, "It protects the flanks, but not the front or the rear. And politicians don't like it. It makes them look scared. Which they are. But they don't want people to know that."

It's not the same with a sniper out there.

I asked, "Did anyone know for sure the glass would work?"

Scarangello said, "The manufacturer claimed it would. Some experts were skeptical."

My turn to nod in the dark. I would have been skeptical. Fifty-caliber rounds are very powerful. They were developed for the Browning machine gun, which can fell trees. I said, "Sleep well."

Scarangello said, "Fat chance."

We landed in bright spring sunshine at Le Bourget, which the flight attendant told us was the busiest private airfield in Europe. The plane taxied toward two black cars parked on their own. Citroëns, I thought. Not limousines exactly, but certainly long and low and shiny. Five men were standing near them, all a little windblown and huddled and flinching from the noise. Two were obviously drivers, and two were gendarmes in uniform, and the last was a silver-haired gentleman in a fine suit. The plane rolled on and then stopped, and a minute later the engines shut down, and the five guys straightened up and stepped forward in anticipation. The flight attendant got busy with the door, and Scarangello stood up in the aisle and handed me a cell phone.

"Call me if you need me," she said.

"On what number?" I said.

"It's in there."

"Are we going different places?"

"Of course we are," she said. "You're looking at the crime scene and I'm going to the DGSE."

I nodded. The *Direction Générale de la Sécurité Extérieure.* The French version of the CIA. No better, no worse, overall. A competent organization. A courtesy call on Scarangello's part, presumably, and probably a high-level exchange of information as well. Or lack thereof.

"Plus I'm bait," I said.

"Only incidentally," she said.

"Casey Nice came with me to Arkansas."

"Seven feet away."

I nodded again. "Which is harder in apartment doorways."

"He's in London," Scarangello said. "Whichever one it is."

The plane door opened and morning air blew in, cool and fresh, lightly scented with jet fuel. The attendant stood back out of the way, and Scarangello went first, pausing a second on the top step, every inch the visiting dignitary. Then she continued down, and I followed her. The silver-haired guy in the suit greeted her. They obviously knew each other. Maybe he was her exact equivalent. Maybe they had done business

before. They got in the back of the first Citroën together, and one of the drivers got in the front and
drove them away. Then the two gendarmes in uniform stepped up in front of me and waited, politely
and expectantly. I fished my stiff new passport out of
my pocket and handed it over. One guy thumbed it
open and they both glanced at the printed name, and
the photograph, and my face, and then the guy gave it
back, two-handed, like a ceremonial offering. Neither
one of them actually bowed or clicked his heels, but a
casual observer would have sworn both of them did.
Such was the power of O'Day.

The second driver opened the door for me and I
slid into the back of the second Citroën. He drove me
away, through black mesh gates, past a terminal building, and out to the road.

Le Bourget is closer to downtown, but the giant civilian Charles de Gaulle airport is farther out on the
same road, northeast of the city, so traffic was bad.
There was a crawling nose-to-tail stream of cars and
taxis, all of them heading for town. Most of the taxi
drivers looked Vietnamese, many of them women,
some of them with lone passengers in the back, some
of them with groups fresh from joyful reunions at the
arrivals door. Straddling the road were overhead electronic signs warning of congestion, and advising *attention aux vents en rafales,* which meant beware of
some kind of wind, but I couldn't remember what *rafales* meant exactly, until from time to time I saw cars
suddenly rocking on the road and flags suddenly

snapping on the buildings, and I recalled it meant *gusts*.

My driver asked, "Sir, do you have everything you need?"

Which in an existential sense was a very big question, but I had no immediate requirements, so I just nodded in the mirror and stayed quiet. In fact I was hungry and short on coffee, but I figured those problems would resolve themselves fast enough. I figured the morning flights from London would get in a little after me, and the morning flights from Moscow later still, and that the Paris cops wouldn't want to schedule three separate dog-and-pony shows at the crime scene, so we would all go there together, which meant I would likely have time for a decent breakfast before my Russian and British counterparts showed up. I would be taken to a hotel to wait, no doubt, something suitable for a police department budget, and there would be cafes nearby, all of them pleasant. Paris was a pleasant city, in my opinion. I was looking forward to the day ahead.

Then it arrived.

Chapter 14

We crossed the Périphérique, which is Paris's version of D.C.'s Beltway, where the city changes from a Eurotrash mess outside to a vast living museum inside, all tree-lined streets and grand preserved buildings and ornate ironmongery. We came down the Rue de Flandre, and onward, aiming for the gap between the Gare du Nord and the Gare de l'Est railroad stations. Once there the driver went into full-on urban mode and dodged left and right through tiny side streets, before coming to a stop at a green door in a narrow alley off a road named Rue Monsigny, which I figured by dead reckoning was about halfway between the back of the Louvre and the front of the Opéra. The green door had a small brass plaque next to it which said *Pension Pelletier*. A *pension* is a modest hotel, somewhere between a rooming house and a bed-and-breakfast. Suitable for a police department budget.

My driver said, "They're expecting you, *monsieur*."

I said, "Thanks," and opened the door and climbed out to the sidewalk. The sun was weak and the air was neither warm nor cold. The car drove away. I ignored the green door for the time being and stepped back out of the alley to Rue Monsigny. Directly opposite me another narrow street came in at a tight angle, creating a small triangle of surplus sidewalk, and like all such unconsidered spaces in Paris it had been colonized by a cafe, with tables and chairs set out under umbrellas, and like all such Paris cafes at that time of the morning it was about a third full of patrons, most of them inert behind newspapers, and empty cups, and plates dusted with croissant flakes. I stepped over and sat down at a vacant table, and a minute later an elderly waiter in a white shirt and a black bow tie and a long white apron came over, and I ordered an extensive breakfast, anchored by a large pot of coffee, accompanied by a *croque madame,* which is ham and cheese on toast with a fried egg on top, and two *pains au chocolat,* which are rectangular croissants with sticks of bitter chocolate in them. Tough duty, but someone had to do it.

Two tables away a guy was reading the inside of his morning paper, leaving the front page facing me, and I saw from the headline that the assassination panic was indeed over, like Casey Nice had said it would be. *Tomorrow it will be yesterday's news.* An arrest had been made, the perp was in custody, the matter was resolved, the world could relax. I was too far away to read on into the fine print, but I was sure the story would be all about a lone fanatic with an unfamiliar North African name, an amateur, a crackpot, no connections, no need to worry. *That should calm things down. Which will give us time and space to work.*

I ate my food and drank my coffee and watched the mouth of the alley. The *vents en rafales* kept on coming, periodically, the umbrella above my table flapping furiously for a second, and then subsiding. Plenty of people passed by on foot, on their way to work or from the store, carrying sticks of bread, or walking tiny dogs, or delivering mail or packages. The waiter cleared my plates and brought me more coffee. Then eventually a black Citroën similar to my own nosed into the alley and stopped at the green door. The passenger in the back paused a beat, no doubt being told *They're expecting you, monsieur,* and then he climbed out and stood still on the sidewalk. He was a guy of average size, maybe fifty years old, with a fresh shave and short salt-and-pepper hair neatly combed, and he was wearing a plaid muffler and a tan Burberry trench coat, below which were pant legs of fine gray cloth, probably part of a Savile Row suit, below which were English shoes the color of horse chestnuts, buffed up to a gleaming shine.

Which made him the Russian, I thought. No Brit operative would dress that way, unless he was trying out for a part in a James Bond movie. And the new Moscow had plenty of luxury apparel stores. Apparatchiks had never had it better. His car backed up and drove away. He looked at the green door for a moment, and then just as I had done he turned away from it and headed out toward the cafe, checking its patrons as he walked, his eyes moving left and right and resting on each person less than a split second before moving on to the next. Quick and dirty assessments, but evidently accurate, because he walked straight up to me and said in English, "Are you the American?"

I nodded and said, "I figured the Brit would get in before you."

"I didn't," the guy said. "Because I left in the middle of the damn night." Then he stuck out his hand and said, "Yevgeniy Khenkin. Pleased to meet you, sir. You can call me Eugene. Which would be the direct translation. Gene, for short, if you like."

I shook his hand and said, "Jack Reacher."

He sat down on my left side and said, "So what do you make of all this shit?"

His diction was good, and his accent was neutral. Not really British, not really American. Some kind of an all-purpose international sound. But very fluent. I said, "I think either you or I or the Brit has a serious problem."

"Are you CIA?"

I shook my head. "Retired military. I busted our guy once. Are you FSB or SVR?"

"SVR," he said, which means *Sluzhba Vneshney Razvedki,* which was their foreign intelligence service. Like the CIA, or the DGSE, or MI6 in Britain. Then he said, "But we're all still KGB really. Old wine, new bottles."

"Do you know your guy Datsev?"

"You could say that."

"How well?"

"I was his handler."

"He was KGB? I was told he was army. Red, and then Russian."

"I suppose he was, technically. Maybe that's what it said on his pay checks. On the rare occasions there were pay checks. But a guy who shoots that well? Better employed elsewhere."

"Doing what?"

"Shooting the people we wanted shot."

"But not anymore?"

Khenkin said, "Do you follow soccer?"

"A little," I said.

"The best players get big offers. One week they're dirt poor in some little village, the next week they're millionaires in Barcelona or Madrid or London or Manchester."

"And Datsev got an offer like that?"

"He claimed to have a vest pocket full of them. He got mad at me when I wouldn't match them. And then he disappeared. And now here we are."

"How good is he?"

"Supernatural."

"Does he like fifty-caliber rounds?"

"Horses for courses. At that range, sure."

I said nothing.

Khenkin said, "But I don't think it's him."

"Why not?"

"He wouldn't agree to an audition. He has nothing to prove."

"So who do you think it is?"

"I think it's your guy. He has something to prove. He was in prison fifteen years."

I heard a cell phone ring, and I waited for Khenkin

to dig in his pocket to answer it, but he didn't, and I realized the ringing was in my own pocket. The phone Scarangello had given me. I hauled it out and checked the screen. *Blocked,* it said. I pressed the green button and said, "Yes?"

It was Scarangello. She said, "Are you alone?"

I said, "No."

"Are we being overheard?"

"By three separate governments, probably."

"Not on this phone," she said. "Don't worry about that."

"What can I do for you?"

"I just heard from O'Day. The chromatograph tests are in on the fragments you brought back from Arkansas."

"And?"

"They're not the same bullets. Not armor piercing. They were match grade. Cast and machined for improved accuracy."

"American made?"

"Unfortunately."

"Those things are six bucks each. Is O'Day following the money?"

"The FBI is on it. But this is good, right? Overall?"

"Could be worse," I said, and she clicked off, and I put the phone back in my pocket. Khenkin asked me, "What's American made and six bucks each?"

I said, "That sounds like the start of a joke."

"What's the punchline?"

I didn't answer, and then the same elderly waiter came by and Khenkin ordered coffee and white rolls, with butter and apricot jam. He spoke in French, again fluent but not rooted in any physical part of the world. After the waiter left again Khenkin turned back to me and said, "And how is General O'Day?"

I said, "You know him?"

"Of him. We learned all about him. Studied him, in fact. Literally, in the classroom. He was a KGB role model."

"I'm not surprised. He's doing OK. He's the same as he ever was."

"I'm glad he's back. I'm sure you are, too."

"Did he ever leave?"

Khenkin made a face, not *yes*, not *no*. He said, "We understood his star was fading. Periods of relative stability are bad for an old warhorse like him. A thing like this reminds people. There's always a silver lining."

Then another black Citroën nosed through the pedestrian chaos and turned into the alley. Driver in the front, passenger in the back. It stopped at the green door, and waited a beat. *They're expecting you, monsieur.* The passenger climbed out. He was a solid guy, maybe forty or forty-five, a little sunburned, with cropped fair hair and a blunt, square face. He was wearing blue denim jeans, and a sweater, and a short canvas jacket. He had tan suede boots on his feet. Maybe British army desert issue. His car drove away, and he glanced at the green door once, and then he turned away from it and scanned ahead, left, right, and he crossed Rue Monsigny and came straight toward us.

He said, "Reacher and Khenkin, is it?"

"You're well informed," Khenkin said. "To already know our names, I mean."

"We try our best," the guy said. He sounded Welsh to me, way back. A little sing-song. He stuck out his hand and said, "Bennett. Pleased to meet you. No point in trying my first name. You wouldn't be able to pronounce it."

"What is it?" I asked.

He answered with a guttural sound, like he was a coal miner with a lung disease. I said, "OK, Bennett it is. You MI6?"

"I can be if you want. They paid for my ticket. But it's all pretty fluid at the moment."

"You know your guy Carson?"

"We met many times."

"Where?"

"Here and there. Like I said, it's all pretty fluid now."

"You think it's him?"

"Not really."

"Why not?"

"Because the Frenchman is still alive. I think it's your guy." Bennett sat down, on my right side, face-on to Khenkin on my left. The waiter showed up with Khenkin's order, and Bennett asked him for the same thing. I asked for more coffee. The old guy looked happy. The tab was building. I hoped either Khenkin or Bennett had a wad of local currency. I didn't.

Khenkin looked across at Bennett and asked, "Do you know the G8 venue?"

Bennett nodded. "By conventional standards it's pretty safe. Maybe not so much, with Kott on the loose."

I said, "It might not be Kott. You need to keep an open mind. Preconceptions are the enemy here."

"My mind is open so wide my brains are about to fall out. I still don't think it's Carson. Datsev, maybe."

Khenkin said, "Then it wasn't an audition, and we're wasting our time on all this theoretical shit. Datsev wouldn't audition. He's too arrogant. If it was Datsev shooting, then it was what it was, which was a hit on the Frenchman, which failed, because of the glass, which also means we're wasting our time, because the trail went cold days ago."

The waiter came back, with Bennett's coffee and bread, and a third pot of coffee for me, and across the street a minivan painted up in police department colors eased into the alley and stopped at the green door. A lone cop got out, in a blue uniform and a *képi* hat, and he knocked on the green door and waited. A minute later a woman in a housedress opened up, and there followed a brief and confused conversation. *I've come for the three guys,* probably. *They haven't checked in yet,* presumably. The cop stepped back and looked all around, up and down the alley, across Rue Monsigny, and he tipped his hat forward and scratched the back of his head, and then his eyes came back to us in a kind of long-delayed slow-motion double take, and he thanked the woman in the housedress and set off toward us. I saw him make up his mind to pretend not to have been confused at all, to take the chance we were who he thought we were, and he stepped up to our table and said, "We have to go to the police station first." He said it in French, in a guttersnipe Paris accent the equivalent of a Brooklyn accent in old New York, or a Cockney accent in London, but without the charm, just a sulky put-upon whine, like the weight of an unfair world was pressing down on his shoulders.

Bennett said, "He says we have to go to the police station first."

"I know," Khenkin said.

I said nothing.

In the end Khenkin paid our tab, from a roll of crisp new Euros that might have been genuine, or not. We all stood up and stretched and brushed crumbs from our clothes, and then we followed the cop across the street to the van. The sun was climbing higher in the morning sky, which was as blue as a robin's egg, and I felt a little warmth, until the gusting wind snapped in again, like a cold hand on my shoulder. Khenkin's expensive coat flapped around his knees, and then the gust died just as suddenly and the warmth came back, until we stepped into the shadow of the alley.

We climbed in the van, Bennett first, then Khenkin, then me, light-hearted at that point, the way you load up for transport off-post, to a bar or a club or somewhere you know women are waiting.

Chapter 15

The police station we were taken to was not really a police station at all. Not the kind of place a member of the public would go to report a missing cat or a lost wallet. It was more like an intelligence bunker, entered through an anonymous gray door set among the row of government buildings on the left bank of the river, near the *Assemblée Nationale,* which is France's version of the Capitol Building, or the Houses of Parliament. The gray door led to a flight of stairs, which led two stories underground to a low-ceilinged warren with gray paint on the walls and gray linoleum on the floors. A DGSE facility, I figured, and I hoped the money they were saving on decor was being spent on results.

We were led to a kind of conference room. All the chairs had been taken out, and the table was loaded with a long line of twelve laptop computers. All of them were open to the exact same angle, and all the screens were showing the exact same things, which were animated *Police Nationale* screensavers, moving slowly but purposefully around the screens, all in lock step, bouncing off tops and bottoms and sides, like an arcade ping pong game from way back when. A woman came in behind us, petite but all grown up, maybe forty-five years old, with soft dark hair and wise dark eyes. Under other circumstances I might have asked her to lunch. As it was she ignored me completely and spoke to no one in particular and said, "All our files are digital now. Start on the left and work to the right and you'll know what we know."

So Bennett and Khenkin and I crowded together in front of the first screen, and Khenkin tapped the touchpad with a manicured nail, and the screensaver disappeared, and a video recording took its place, and started rolling. French network television, I guessed, broadcasting the president's speech. It had been an evening event. The guy was at a podium in front of some wide marble steps, all lit up. There were French flags behind him. The bulletproof glass shields either side of him were barely visible. His microphones were small black buds on the end of black swan-neck stems coming up out of the podium desktop. By the sound of them they were highly directional, aimed at the guy's chest and throat and mouth, and not picking up a whole lot else. But clearly the TV people had mixed in some ambient sound from microphones elsewhere, because we could hear a quiet hubbub from the crowd, and some street sounds. The guy was giving a lot of guff about how progress was still possible, and how the twenty-first century could still be France's, given the right policies, which by chance happened to be his. At one point he stumbled over a word and glanced high to his left, almost pensively, and then he turned back and dug in again. Three seconds later he glanced left again, this time at something much closer, and he stumbled again, and then a couple of seconds after that he was knocked down and buried under a scrum of guys in dark suits and earpieces, who spirited him away along the floor like a giant turtle moving fast.

Khenkin used his nail again and rewound the coverage, to the president's first stumble, to the glance high and left. He said, "That's the muzzle flash. Has to be." Then three seconds later, at the second glance: "And that's the bullet hitting the glass."

We couldn't make out the sound of the gunshot. Maybe some big-time digital expert could have isolated a spike on the soundtrack, but it wouldn't have told us anything. Everyone already knew a gun had been fired.

"Seen enough?" Khenkin asked.

Bennett nodded and I said nothing, and Khenkin clicked the mouse and a street map of Paris popped up. It had a red arrowhead marked *A* on the front steps of Les Invalides, and another red arrowhead marked *B* some distance away, amid a thicket of small streets near the Boulevard Saint Germain. The two red arrowheads were joined by a thin red line, which was marked *1273 meters,* which was fourteen hundred yards in real money.

Bennett said, "Les Invalides is the old military hospital."

"I know," Khenkin said. "A monument now. Quite grand."

And a logical place for a big political speech. An emotionally significant location, an open area in front, big enough for a decent crowd, small enough not to be embarrassing if not many people showed up, spacious enough for media trucks and satellite dishes. The Boulevard Saint Germain location would be the apartment house. A long, long shot, more or less due west, over low-rise buildings and plenty of open space, nearly parallel with the river, and not more than a thousand yards from where we were right then. Very close to home, for anyone with anything to do with the government.

Khenkin clicked on a symbol and the next picture we got was an after-action photograph of the president's podium and its bulletproof glass shields. The podium was a sturdy affair, presumably designed for quick assembly and disassembly and storage in between, and the glass shields were half-invisible panels, each maybe seven feet tall and four feet wide, and possibly five inches thick, standing parallel with each other, boxing in the podium at a discreet distance, like the sides of a spacious phone booth.

"OK?" Khenkin said.

Bennett nodded and I said nothing and Khenkin clicked onward, to a close-up photograph of the spot where the bullet had hit the glass. It was nothing more than a tiny white chip, with thin cracks maybe an inch long, running away like spider legs. Khenkin clicked through a series of ever-enlarging close-ups, all the way to a shot through an electron microscope that made the pit look like the Grand Canyon, even though the embedded data said it was less than two millimeters deep. The last picture went back to normal size, the same as the first picture, but it was set up to animate, with the same kind of video technology they use on TV sports shows, where they freeze the action and then spin it around to examine it from a different angle. Accordingly the photograph rotated until we were looking at the glass shield more or less directly from the side, and then the viewpoint elevated slightly until we were looking at it a little from above. The shooter's-eye view, I figured, through his sniper scope, from the apartment balcony fourteen hundred yards away.

At normal size the tiny white chip was barely visible, but then a bright red dot appeared, to mark it, and then thin red lines sprouted from it, measuring its distance from the perimeter of the shield. It was a little over five hundred millimeters in from the left, and a little over seven hundred millimeters down from the top.

Khenkin looked upset about those measurements.

He leaned in and stared and said, "Do you see what I see?"

Bennett said nothing, and I said, "I don't know what you see."

Khenkin turned around and glanced left and right until he saw the dark-haired woman, and he said, "Can we go to the apartment now?"

The woman said, "Don't you want to see the rest of the presentation?"

"What's in it?"

"Forensics, trace evidence, ballistics, metallurgy, things like that."

"Do they tell us who the shooter is?"

"Not precisely."

"Then no," Khenkin said. "We don't want to see that shit. We want to see the apartment."

Chapter 16

We went to see the apartment in the same police department minivan, driven by the same whiny cop. The dark-haired woman came with us, with two of her laptops, and a senior *Police Nationale* guy came too, an old gray veteran in a blue battledress uniform. The drive was short and easy, from the Seventh *Arrondissement* to the Sixth, on the Boulevard Saint Germain all the way, and then into the back streets off Rue Bonaparte, to a fine old building that stood blank and quiet in a row of similar places. It was a solid Beaux Arts pile, with double-height carriage doors on the street, which would lead past a concierge's hutch to an interior courtyard, which would have staircases and rickety old iron elevators in each corner. I had been in such buildings before. There would be the smell of dust and cooking and floor wax, maybe the muffled tinkle of a grand piano somewhere, and a child's sudden laugh, and then grand but faded apartments, with gilt and cherry wood, and threadbare Aubusson carpets, and old Empire furniture lovingly polished.

The driver roused the concierge, who opened the double doors, and we drove in and parked in the courtyard. We used the stairs in the back left corner and walked up five flights to a door that was closed and locked but otherwise unmarked. No police tape, no prosecutor's seal, no official crime scene notice.

I asked, "Who owns this place?"

The old *Police Nationale* guy said, "She died two years ago."

"Someone must own it."

"Of course. But there were no heirs. So it's complicated."

"How did the shooter get in?"

"Presumably there were keys in circulation."

"The concierge didn't see anything?"

The old guy shook his head. "Nor the neighbors."

"Are there cameras on the street?"

"Inconclusive."

"And no one saw the shooter getting out again?"

"I think everyone was watching the mayhem on television." The guy took out a key that looked freshly cut and jiggled it in the lock until the door swung open. We stepped into a tall formal lobby, and onward into a tall formal hallway. The floors out there were black and white marble, worn dull and undulating by the passage of thousands of feet. The air was cold and still. There were double doors here and there, all of them eleven or twelve feet tall, some of them standing half open, with dim rooms beyond. The old guy led us into a salon and through it into a dining room about forty feet long. There was an immense mahogany table, partly covered with an old white sheet, and twenty chairs, ranged ten to a side, and a tiled fireplace fit for a castle, and spotty old mirrors, and marble busts, and dark landscape paintings in heavy gold frames. The end wall had three floor-to-ceiling French windows, all inward-opening, all facing west. The huge dining table was lined up with the center window, and the other two windows had marble-topped buffet tables near them. Classic old style, calm, restful, symmetrical, pleasing to the eye.

Outside the windows was the balcony.

It ran the whole depth of the room, and was about eight feet front to back, with a flagstone floor and a low stone balustrade. There was a long line of stone planters filled with powdery dirt and the dried-up remains of dead geraniums. There were two iron cafe tables, each with two iron chairs, set against the outside walls between the windows.

Beyond the balustrade, in the far, far distance, was a side view of Les Invalides' front steps. Three-quarters of a mile. Barely visible at all.

Bennett asked, "How did you trace this location?"

The old guy said, "The president saw the muzzle flash, which gave us the general direction. After that it was a simple ballistics calculation, which gave us four potential possibilities, all of them neighboring properties in this building. Three of them were occupied by innocent families. This one was empty. And there were fresh disturbances in the dust here. We're completely confident this is the scene."

The dark-haired woman said, "It's all explained in the presentation. You should have watched it."

Khenkin nodded, half apologetic, half impatient. He asked, "Where exactly do you think he fired from?"

The woman said, "We worked backward from the electron microscope. Armor-piercing rounds have a super-hard tip, so we could see the exact angle of impact, right down at the molecular level. We calculated velocity, which gave us the range, and we calculated the drop, which gave us the precise location. We believe he fired from the center of the balcony, from a seated position, with the rifle's bipod feet resting in the dirt in the middle planter. There were marks in the dirt, and scuffs on the flagstones."

Khenkin nodded again.

"Let's take a look," he said.

So we all trooped out and took a look. We were five stories up, and the air was fresh and the view was magnificent. The planter in the center of the row was a solid affair, heavy, rock steady, not tall but relatively wide, carved like an ancient Greek relic, smooth and mossy with age. It was a very plausible set-up spot. Given the slight downward angle to the target, a seated rifleman of average height would have been perfectly comfortable behind it. He would have been aiming through the balustrade itself, between two of the fat mossy urns that propped up the parapet.

I asked, "How tall is Datsev?"

Khenkin said, "A meter seventy, a meter seventy-five."

Which was about five feet eight inches, which was about average.

I looked at Bennett and asked, "And Carson?"

"Five nine," Bennett said.

Also average. As was Kott himself, at about five seven, the last time I saw him, sixteen years previously.

Khenkin sat down cross-legged, behind the planter, oblivious to his fine tailoring, and he closed one eye and squinted. He asked, "Do you have photographs taken from here? With the glass and the podium still in place?"

The dark-haired woman said, "Of course we do. They're in the presentation. You should have watched it."

"I'm sorry," Khenkin said. "Did you happen to bring them with you?"

"As a matter of fact I did." The woman fired up one of her laptops, and she clicked and scrolled, and then she laid the computer in the planter dirt right in front of Khenkin's face. She said, "That simulates the view through the scope, we think."

And it did, more or less. I ducked down to share a look, and saw the podium in the center of the screen, reasonably close, reasonably large, with the nearside glass shield barely visible but clearly in the way. The podium looked forlorn and abandoned, amid a scene obviously evacuated in a hurry and locked down afterward.

Khenkin said, "I can't see the little chip."

The woman squeezed between us. I caught the scent of Chanel. She clicked the mouse, and the red dot reappeared on the glass, five hundred millimeters from the left, seven hundred millimeters from the top.

Khenkin asked, "How big is your president exactly?"

The woman clicked again, and a figure appeared behind the screen, behind the podium, not the president of France, but a stand-in, presumably the same height and weight. A cop, maybe, or a security guy.

The red dot was six inches left of his throat.

"See?" Khenkin said. "I knew it. He was going to miss. Left and a little low."

He struggled to his feet and brushed grit off his Burberry and stepped right up to the balustrade. He stared out over the gray Paris rooftops, toward Les Invalides. Bennett joined him, shoulder to shoulder on his right, and I joined him, shoulder to shoulder on his left. I saw the Boulevard Raspail, and wide streets, and cars and people, and neat lines of pollarded trees, and open green spaces, and quiet honey buildings with black ironwork and slate roofs and limp flags, and ornate street lights, and the vague white bulk of the old hospital, and way beyond it in the far distance the top of the Eiffel Tower.

Then three things happened, in a neat deadly preordained rhythm as slow as the tick of an old clock, *one, and two, and three,* first a tiny pinprick of sudden light in the far distance, and then the snap of flags everywhere as a gust of wind blew by, and then Khenkin's head blew apart, right next to my shoulder.

Chapter 17

I was on the deck even before Khenkin's lifeless body made it there. His shattered head hit me on the way down and left a red and gray slick on the shoulder of my jacket. I remember thinking *Damn, that was brand new,* and then Bennett landed next to me, and then he disappeared, like a magic trick. One second he was right there on the terrace flagstones, and the next second he was gone, like a good covert operative should be. They have a saying in Britain: *No names, no pack drill.* Better not to be in the record at all.

The woman with the computers was on her knees, groaning rather than screaming, scrabbling her way back inside to the dining room, head down. The old cop in the blue battledress uniform was standing stock still, exactly where he had been all along, exposed from the waist up. Which I thought was OK, because I was sure the rifleman wasn't about to stick around for any length of time. Not in the center of

Paris. I knelt up and peered over the parapet and tried to fix where I had seen the muzzle flash. I closed my eyes and saw it again, just left of the old hospital, therefore even further away, in a roof window maybe six flights up.

I opened my eyes and checked. Either the Boulevard de la Tour Maubourg, or a small street behind it, a gray mansard roof, and what would inevitably be an oval Beaux Arts window, intricately framed with stone. Sixteen hundred yards away, maybe. Close to a mile. A seventeen-minute walk, at normal speed. I spun around and got up and hurdled the computer woman, who was still on her knees, and I hustled through the dining room and the salon and the hallway and the lobby, and down all the stairs to the courtyard, and out to the street.

I didn't head for Les Invalides. No point. I figured the shooter had already left, and for every minute I spent getting there, he would have the same minute to get further away. I heard sirens in the distance, the staid and plaintive *beep boop* the French still used, lots of them. So where was the guy heading? Not north, I thought. And not in a car. Because of the sirens. The river bridges were bottlenecks. No way off them, except the water. And the police had boats, too. So he would come on foot, south, or west of south. Not east of south, because the Gare Montparnasse railroad station lay in that direction, and public transportation was the second thing the cops would flood, right after the bridges. For the same reason the guy would avoid the Metro. He was on surface streets, on foot, by now a couple hundred yards into it, alongside the École Militaire, maybe, which would put him on either the Avenue de la Motte Picquet, or the Avenue Lowendal.

I used the Rue de Sèvres, not running, because passing cops would be jumpy, but certainly striding out with pace and determination. Much faster than the other guy would be going, for sure. He would be sauntering, no hurry, no particular place to go, the picture of innocence. But carrying what? No proven fifty-caliber sniper rifle broke down into separate components. Not without a saw and a blowtorch. Most were about five feet long and weighed north of thirty pounds. A Persian carpet? A bolt of cloth? Or had he hidden it somewhere?

I turned onto Boulevard Garibaldi, and figured by that point the guy must be about three hundred yards ahead of me, crossing my path in the far distance, so I pushed on hard, three fast minutes, until I came to the Rue de la Croix-Nivert, which was the continuation of the Avenue Lowendal, which meant a long block ahead was the Rue du Commerce, which was the continuation of the Avenue de la Motte Picquet. The guy must have gone down one of them, southwest, into the heart of the Fifteenth Arrondissement, where all was safe and comfortable.

I chose the first turn, because in the end I figured Lowendal would have felt better than the Motte Picquet, because it put the bulk of the École Militaire between the guy and the loudest sirens, which would have been the fast-response crews coming from the Eiffel Tower. So I turned and accelerated and stared ahead into the gray distance and cannoned into a small guy hurrying in the opposite direction. I caught a glimpse of him before I slammed into him and got the impression he was Asian, maybe Vietnamese, much older than expected from his lively pace, and then on impact he felt wiry and solid and surprisingly heavy.

I slowed a step to let him bounce off, hoping he would stay on his feet, whereupon I could just beg his pardon and move on with minimum delay. But he didn't bounce off. He clung on tight, folds of my jacket clenched in his hands, pulling downward, like he was weak in the knees. I staggered forward a step, bent over a little, trying not to tread on his feet, and he pulled me in a counterclockwise part-circle, and then he kind of leaned on me and started pushing me toward the curb.

Then he hit me.

He detached his right hand from my jacket and drew it back and folded his fingers into a classic rabbit-punch shape and aimed it down toward my groin. Which could have been a major problem, except that I flinched fast enough and the blow caught me just inboard of my hip bone, which was a sensitive spot in its own right. It spiked some kind of a nerve jolt down my leg, and my foot went numb for a second, and the guy must have sensed it, because he started shoving me toward the curb with all his strength, which was not inconsiderable. Behind me I could hear traffic, real close. A narrow Paris street, average speed about forty, nine drivers out of ten on their cell phones.

Enough.

I caught the guy by the throat, one-handed, and I pushed him away, arm's length, further than he could reach with his fists. He could have kicked me, but then, I could have been squeezing harder, and he seemed to understand that. I started to march him backward.

Which is when the cops showed up.

Chapter 18

There were two of them, both young, just regular street cops in a small car, in cheap blue uniforms not very different from the sanitation workers or the street sweepers. But their badges were real, and their guns were real. And the scenario unfolding right in front of them was indisputable. A giant white man was choking a small Asian senior and frog-marching him backward across the sidewalk. Which was what politicians would call bad optics. So I stopped walking, obviously, and I let the guy go.

The guy ran away.

He dodged left, and dodged right, and was lost to sight. The cops didn't go after him. Which made sense. He was the victim, not the perpetrator. The perpetrator was right there in front of them. They didn't need the victim's evidence, because they themselves had been actual eyewitnesses. Done deal, right there. I had a fifth of a second to make up my mind. Should I stay or should I go? In the end I figured the power of O'Day would protect me either way, and just as fast. And by that point the rifleman was long gone for sure. And staying would avoid getting all out of breath. So I stayed.

They arrested me there and then, on the sidewalk outside a tobacconist's store, for what seemed to be a variety of offenses, including assault, battery, hate crimes, and elder abuse. They crammed me in the back of their car and drove me to a station house on the Rue Lecourbe. The desk people searched me and took away Scarangello's cell phone, and my new passport, and my toothbrush, and my bank card, and all my American cash, and Casey Nice's empty pill bottle. Then they put me in a holding cell with two other guys. One was drunk and the other was high. I made the drunk guy give up his spot on the bench. Better to establish the pecking order early. It would save him trouble in the long term. I sat down in his place, and I leaned against the wall, and I waited. I figured I would be in the system inside twenty minutes, and I was sure Scarangello would be looking hard by then.

It took her an hour to find me. She came with the silver-haired guy in the good suit, who seemed to be a known quantity in those parts. All the cops in the place leapt to attention. A minute later I had my stuff back in my pockets, and a minute after that we were out on the sidewalk. I was free and clear. Such was the power of O'Day. Scarangello got in the back of the same black Citroën she had used from Le Bourget, and I climbed in after her, and the guy in the suit stayed on the sidewalk and closed the door on us, and he called out to the driver in French and said, "Take them straight to the airport." The car took off fast and I craned around and saw the guy watch us go for a second, and then duck back inside the station house.

Scarangello said, "Why did you run?"

I said, "I didn't run. I don't like running. I walked."

"Why?"

"I'm here as your cop. I was looking for the guy. That's what cops do."

"You were nowhere near. You were in the wrong neighborhood entirely."

"I figured he hadn't stuck around."

"You were wrong."

"So what happened?"

"They got him. And his rifle."

"They *got* him?"

"He waited right there."

"Which one was it?"

"None of them. It was a Vietnamese kid about twenty years of age."

"And what was the rifle?"

"An AK-47."

"That's bullshit."

She said, "In your opinion."

I started to say something, but she held up her hand. She said, "Don't tell me anything. I don't want the raw data. There could be subpoenas flying around by tomorrow. Safer for me not to know. I'm going to wait for the official statement."

I said, "I was going to ask if you mind if we take a little detour."

"The plane is waiting."

"It can't leave without us."

"Where do you want to go?"

I leaned forward and said to the driver in French, "Head for the Bastille and turn right."

The guy thought for a second and said, "On Roquette?"

"All the way to the end," I said. "Then wait at the gate."

"Yes, sir," he said.

Scarangello turned to quiz me again, but her focus fell short, on the shoulder of my jacket. The red and gray slick, now dark brown and purple, and on closer examination flecked with fine shards of white bone. She said, "What's that?"

I said, "Just a guy I used to know."

"That's disgusting."

"It's raw data."

"You need a new jacket."

"This is a new jacket."

"You have to get rid of it. We'll go buy you another one. Right now."

"The plane is waiting."

"How long can it take?"

"This is France," I said. "Nothing in the stores is going to fit me."

She said, "Where are we going?"

"Something I want to do before we leave."

"What?"

"I want to take a walk."

"Where?"

"You'll see."

We crossed the Seine on the Pont d'Austerlitz, and hooked a left on the Boulevard de la Bastille, and headed up toward the monument itself, fast and fluent through the traffic, as if the driver was using lights and siren, although he wasn't. The monument was the hub of a crazy traffic circle, called the Place de la Bastille, just as bad as all the others in Paris, and the fourth of its ten exits was the Rue de la Roquette, which led basically east, straight to the cemetery gate.

"Père Lachaise," Scarangello said. "Chopin is buried here. And Molière."

"And Edith Piaf and Jim Morrison," I said. "From the Doors."

"We don't have time for tourism."

"Won't take long," I said.

The driver parked at the gate and I got out. Scarangello came with me. There was a wooden booth that sold maps to all the famous graves. Like Hollywood, with the stars' homes. We walked in, on a wide gritty path, and turned left and right past elaborate mausoleums and white marble headstones. I navigated by memory, from a sullen gray winter morning many years previously. I walked slow, pausing occasionally, checking, until I found the right place, which was now a strip of lawn, green with new spring grass, studded with headstones, broad and low. I found the right one. It was pale, and barely weathered at all, with two lines of inscription still crisp and precise: *Josephine Moutier Reacher, 1930–1990.* A life, sixty years long. I had arrived exactly halfway through it. I stood there, hands by my sides, with another man's blood and brains on my jacket.

"Family?" Scarangello asked.

"My mother," I said.

"Why is she buried here?"

"Born in Paris, died in Paris."

"Is that how you know the city so well?"

I nodded. "We came here from time to time. And then she lived here after my father died. On the Avenue Rapp. The other side of Les Invalides. I visited when I could."

Scarangello nodded and went quiet for a spell, maybe out of respect. She stood next to me, shoulder to shoulder. She asked, "What was she like?"

I said, "Petite, dark haired but blue eyed, very feminine, very obstinate. But generally happy. She made the best of things. She would walk into some dumpy Marine quarters somewhere and laugh and smile and say, *'Ome sweet 'ome.* She couldn't say the letter *H* because of her accent."

Scarangello said, "Sixty is not very old. I'm sorry."

"We get what we get," I said. "She didn't complain."

"What was it?"

"Lung cancer. She smoked a lot. She was French."

"This is Père Lachaise."

"I know."

"I mean, not everyone gets buried here."

"Obviously," I said. "It would get pretty crowded."

"I mean, it's like an honor."

"War service."

Scarangello looked at the headstone again. "Which war?"

"World War Two."

"She was fifteen when it ended."

"They were desperate times."

"What did she do?"

"Resistance work. Allied airmen shot down in Holland or Belgium were funneled south through Paris. There was a network. Her part was to escort them from one railroad station to the next, and send them on their way."

"When?"

"Most of 1943. Eighty trips, they say."

"She was thirteen years old."

"Desperate times," I said again. "A schoolgirl was good cover. She was trained to say the airmen were her uncles or brothers, visiting from out of town. Generally they were disguised like peasants or clerks."

"She was risking her life. And her family's life."

"Every day. But she took care of business."

Scarangello said, "This information wasn't in your file."

"No one knew. She didn't talk about it. I'm not even sure my father knew. After she died we found a medal. Then an old guy came to the funeral and told us the story. He was her handler. I assume he's dead now, too. I haven't been back since we buried her. This is the first time I've seen the stone. I guess my brother organized it."

"He chose well."

I nodded. A modest memorial, for a modest woman.

I closed my eyes and remembered the last time I had seen her alive. Breakfast, with her two grown sons, in her apartment on the Avenue Rapp. The Berlin Wall was coming down. She was very sick by that point, but had summoned the will to dress well and act normal. We drank coffee and ate croissants. Or at least my brother and I did, while she hid her lack of appetite behind talking. She chattered about all kinds of things, people we had known, places we had been, things that had happened there. Then she had gone quiet for a spell, and then she had given us a pair of final messages, which were the same messages she had always given us. Like a motherly ritual. She had done it a thousand times. She struggled up out of her chair and stepped over and put her hands on my brother Joe's shoulders, from behind, which was all part of the choreography, and she had bent and kissed his cheek from the side, like she always did, and she had asked him, "What don't you need to do, Joe?"

Joe hadn't answered, because our silence was part of the ritual. She had said, "You don't need to solve *all* the world's problems. Only some of them. There are enough to go around."

She had kissed him again, and then she had struggled around behind me, and kissed my cheek in turn, and measured the width of my shoulders with her small hands, and felt the hard muscles, as always, still fascinated by the way her tiny newborn had grown so big, and even though I was close to thirty by then she said, "You've got the strength of two normal boys. What are you going to do with it?"

I hadn't replied. Our silence was part of the ritual.

She answered for me. She said, "You're going to do the right thing."

And I had tried, mostly, which had sometimes caused me trouble, and sometimes won me medals of my own. As a small tribute I had buried my Silver Star with her. It was right there under my feet, right then, in the Paris dirt, six feet down. I imagined the ribbon was all rotted away, but I guessed the metal was still bright.

I opened my eyes, and I stepped back, and I looked at Scarangello, and I said, "OK, we can go now."

Chapter 19

The airplane cabin was warm, so out of deference to Scarangello's injured sensibilities I took off my ruined jacket and folded it inside out and dumped it on an unoccupied chair. We were out of French airspace after forty minutes, and then we crossed Great Britain diagonally, eight miles high, and then we started on the long haul over the far North Atlantic. A Great Circle route. We ate stuff the crew had picked up at Le Bourget, and then we stretched out in reclined chairs, on opposite sides of the aisle, head to toe, close, but not too close.

I asked her, "Who exactly was the guy in the suit?"

She said, "DGSE's head of counterterrorism."

"Was the Vietnamese kid his? With the AK-47?"

"His?"

"Was he another patsy? For the newspapers?"

"No, he was for real. Still there, at an attic window."

I said nothing.

She said, "What?"

"You don't want me to tell you anything."

"Is this something O'Day will figure out?"

"I'm sure he already has."

"Then you can give me the deep background."

"What do you remember about the Soviets?"

"Lots of things."

I said, "Above all they were realistic, especially about human nature, and the quality of their own personnel. They had a very big army, which meant their average grunt was lazy, incompetent, and not blessed with any kind of discernible talent. They understood that, and they knew there wasn't a whole lot they could do about it. So instead of trying to train their people upward toward the standard of available modern weaponry, they designed their available modern weaponry downward toward the standard of their people. Which was a truly radical approach."

"OK."

"Hence the AK-47. For instance, one example, what does a panicky grunt do under fire? He grabs his rifle and hits the fire selector and pulls the trigger. Our guns go from safe to single shot to full auto, which is nice and linear and logical, but they knew that would mean ninety-nine times in a hundred their guys would panic and ram the selector all the way home, and thereby fire off a whole magazine on the first hasty and unaimed shot. Which would leave them with an empty weapon right at the start of a firefight. Which is not helpful. So the AK selector goes safe, then full auto, then single shot. Not linear, not logical, but certainly practical. Single shot is a kind of default setting, and full auto is a deliberate choice."

"OK."

"And they knew the rifle wouldn't get any kind of care or maintenance in the field, so they made it reliable under practically any circumstances. When the trigger is pulled, the weapon will fire. We saw AK-47s that had been buried in the ground for years, with the woodwork all eaten away by insects, and they still worked just fine."

"OK."

"And they knew their average grunt couldn't hit anything further than a couple hundred feet anyway. Probably couldn't *see* further than a couple of hundred feet. So why spend money on accuracy? The AK-47 is reliable first, second, and third, and accurate nowhere. It's a close-quarters weapon. Practically like a handgun. Across the street, or a city block, or one riverbank to the other."

"You saying it couldn't have made the shot?"

"Not a hope in hell. You could give Kott or Carson or Datsev the best AK-47 ever made, and they'd be useless beyond about four hundred yards. But the shot that killed Khenkin was about sixteen hundred. Four times as long. They wouldn't even have hit the right building. Plus, the round is puny. It would have barely gotten there at all. They'd have had to launch it upward about thirty degrees, like dropping a big fat curveball over the plate. Up and down, like a ballistic missile. Which is an impossible shot. And even if they had made it, the bullet would have arrived with so little energy you could have swatted it aside with a ping pong paddle. It would have bounced off Khenkin's hair gel. But it didn't. It blew his head right off his shoulders."

"So?"

"It wasn't any twenty-year-old Vietnamese kid with an AK-47."

"Then why was he there?"

"I'm guessing he was a part of a package deal. Kott or Carson or Datsev or whoever hired some local support. Which in Paris might well be Vietnamese. There's a big community. I'm sure most of them are on the up and up, driving taxis or whatever, working hard, but equally I'm sure some of them are gangbangers. They put maybe ten or a dozen on the street, as a rolling cordon around the guy, to protect the escape. No doubt the old man who stopped me was one of them. He was running interference. And they put the kid in the attic, as a decoy. They're blooding him. He's making his bones. Get arrested, stay quiet, hang in there, and he's a made man. I bet there was no firing pin in his gun. Just so they can be sure of getting him off on the technicality."

Scarangello was quiet for a spell, and then she said, "It has to be Datsev, right? What would Kott or Carson have against Khenkin?"

I said, "I'm sure O'Day has all kinds of theories about that."

But it turned out the Socratic method had its limitations. O'Day and Shoemaker and Nice had gone through plenty of back and forth, but had elicited no truths implicitly known by all rational beings. They had collected detailed briefings from Paris, and Moscow, and London, and diagrams, and photographs, and video and after-action reports, and they had been through the data many times over, but they had reached no conclusions. They were waiting to see what I had to say.

We landed at Pope Field in the late afternoon, less than a day after we left it, having gained back the six hours we lost on the way out. Scarangello wanted to shower before we all sat down and got into it, which seemed reasonable, so O'Day gave us thirty minutes, which I spent in the shower, too, first rinsing Khenkin off my coat, which was easy enough, because the fabric was waterproof, so the gunk sluiced right off. I kept it going until the remaining beads of water showed up clean, and then I patted it dry with a towel. Then I hosed myself down, and used the shampoo, and used the soap, and then dressed again fast enough to hit the buffet room before the conference started. There wasn't much on the tables, but at least there was coffee, so I took a cup and headed upstairs.

O'Day was in his customary spot, and Shoemaker was right there next to him. Casey Nice greeted me with her smile, and I sat down, and Scarangello came in after me, glowing from the hot water, hair still wet, in another black skirt suit.

O'Day said, "First let's dispose of the Vietnamese."

I said, "There's a first time for everything."

He didn't smile. I guessed he had looked only about eighty years old during that ancient conflict, and had been in charge of some of the strategy, possibly, and was therefore still a little sensitive about it. Casey Nice filled the awkward silence. She said, "We're assuming the rifleman or his paymasters hired a local criminal element for local support. Or as a way of getting permission to operate on their turf. Or both."

"Likely," I said. "Unless the paymasters *are* the Vietnamese. Maybe it's a government thing. Maybe they're going to invade Russia."

"Are you serious?"

"Not very," I said. "I agree with you. It was local support."

"In which case as a matter of pride and discipline they won't spill anything meaningful. Which leaves us with absolutely nothing except our own interpretation of a very confusing and incomplete scenario."

"Nothing incomplete about it. Not from Khenkin's point of view, anyway."

"We think he traveled to Paris anxious to convince us and the Brits that Datsev wasn't involved. Do you agree?"

I nodded. "He said it was beneath Datsev to audition."

"And the DGSE tells us Khenkin seemed obsessed with showing the shot was going to miss. Which it was, apparently. Left and a little low. Moscow says Datsev never misses. And left and a little low happens to be Kott's signature from Arkansas. With those paper targets we saw."

I said, "It wasn't Kott on that apartment balcony."

O'Day looked up. "And you know this how?"

"The DGSE lady figured the shooter was seated behind a planter. But Kott trained for a year lying down prone. It's like sleeping. Everyone has a natural position. And sitting behind a planter isn't Kott's."

O'Day nodded.

He said, "Good to know."

Casey Nice said, "But Khenkin couldn't have known that. All he could have claimed is that Datsev wouldn't have missed. So he was a happy camper, until he got shot. Which is where it gets confusing. As in, it wasn't Datsev, and then suddenly it was. Because there was history between Datsev and Khenkin, and presumably no history between either Kott or Carson and Khenkin."

I said, "Stand up."

She said, "What?"

"Stand up and take off your shoe."

"Why?"

"Just do it."

She did it. She stood up, and she said, "Which shoe?"

"Either one," I said. I stood up too. She bent and slipped off her left shoe. I crossed the room to the door. Like every other door in the place it was a painted wood rectangle about six feet six inches high and two feet six inches wide. I said, "Suppose this was a glass panel. Suppose you knew it was pretty tough. Suppose I gave you one chance to shatter it with the heel of your shoe. A good solid blow. Show me where you would hit it."

She paused a beat, and then she limped and padded toward me. She reversed the shoe in her hand and held it like a weapon. She stopped. She said, "I don't know enough about it. This is ceramics technology. This is the science of strong materials."

"Datsev and Kott and Carson aren't scientists either. Do it by instinct."

I saw her glance at one spot after another. She raised the shoe, tentatively, and moved it a little, as if involuntarily, as she rehearsed different alternatives in her mind. I said, "Talk me through it."

She said, "Nowhere close to the edge. I think it would just chip, nothing more, like a small bite out of a large cookie."

"OK."

"Not dead center, either. I feel the shock of the impact would kind of spread out uniformly, and equally, and then maybe bounce back internally, off the edges, and kind of cancel itself out. It might just flex, like a drum skin, if I hit it in the center."

"So where?"

"Somewhere off-center but not too far off-center. So the shock would be kind of asymmetrical. So the internal stresses would help."

"Show me."

She gave it one last look, and raised the shoe, and mimed a big swing, and ended up with the heel on the paint just inside the upper left quadrant, such that if the size of the door was scaled up to the size of the bulletproof shield in Paris, then the spot she was marking would be a little over five hundred millimeters in from the left, and a little over seven hundred millimeters down from the top.

I said, "The second shot was supposed to kill the

guy. Not the first. The first shot was supposed to break the glass. That's all. Therefore it wasn't a miss. It was dead on target."

Casey Nice hopped around near the door and got her shoe back on, and then we sat down again. I said, "I think Khenkin understood all this from the start. What the DGSE had figured out made it more likely it was Datsev, not less. He came to Paris hoping his boy was in the clear, but everything he saw told him he wasn't."

Shoemaker said, "Any one of the three could have made that shot."

"But what about the next shot? I think that's what was on Khenkin's mind. Because whoever was shooting had to jump his aiming point about six inches up and to the right to get the guy. Real fast, too. Which is a hell of a thing to do, on the fly, from fourteen hundred yards. It meant the muzzle would have to move about seven *thousandths* of an inch. Not more, not less, and fluently, and fluidly, and very precisely, but also calmly. There was no time to settle and check and breathe. If the glass had shattered, the French guy would have been in the wind more or less immediately. At least he would have been hopping around like crazy. As it was he was buried in agents about two seconds later. Think about it. You shoot, you move the muzzle seven thousandths of an inch, and you shoot again, all way faster than I can even say it. That would have taken supernatural skill. And Datsev was supernatural, according to Khenkin."

O'Day said, "OK, we're making progress here. The shooter was Datsev."

I said, "Khenkin certainly thought so. I was watching him. He was a tough nut, but there was a soft side to him. He was grumpy in the morning, because he had gotten up too early. But he was happy, too. At that point it was just a fun day out in Paris. It was someone else's problem. Mine, probably. He paid for my breakfast, even. Then the chips started to fall, and then it wasn't such a fun day after all. Because now it was his problem. He was going to have to go home and break the bad news. He didn't want to do that. There was a bit of the bureaucrat in him."

"But then Datsev shot him and saved him the trouble."

"No," I said. "Datsev didn't shoot him."

Chapter 20

I said, "You have to think about that second shot. And you don't have to take my word for it. Get on the phone and call our five best snipers. The Recon Marines, the SEALs, Delta Force, wherever. I'm sure you could do that. I'm sure you've got them all on speed dial. I'm sure they all work for you, really, the same way Datsev worked for the KGB."

Shoemaker said, "The KGB was history a long time ago. Now it's the SVR."

"Old wine, new bottles."

"What's your point?"

"Ask our best guys about that second shot. Ask them about two trigger pulls, like a fast double tap, with nothing in between except a six-inch deflection at fourteen hundred yards. All with a rifle over five feet long, that weighs more than an iron bar."

"What would they tell me?"

"They'd tell you hell yes sir, they could make that shot blindfolded."

"So what's the problem?"

"Problem is, then you'd say, stop with the rah-rah bullshit, soldier, and tell me the truth, and to a man they'd swear that shot was impossible."

"Apparently Khenkin didn't think so."

"He believed his own hype. Datsev is human, just like you or me. Well, me, anyway. He couldn't have made that shot. No one on earth could have made that shot."

"So what are you saying?"

"There were two shooters."

The room went quiet at that point, and I used the time to finish my coffee. I said, "One of them was either Datsev or Carson, and the other one was John Kott."

O'Day raised his head, slowly, like an old gray turtle coming up out of the sand, and he said, "You just told us quite emphatically that Kott wasn't there."

"I said he wasn't on the balcony. He was in the dining room, prone on the dining table, the end part of which was about the size of an eight-by-four sheet of plywood. He was aiming over his partner's head. Think about it. Two snipers. One is cross-legged behind the planter. The other is prone on the table. They've been there thirty minutes. They're in the zone. They're breathing slow. They're just floating along. The French doors are open. The one behind the planter is set up on the glass shield. He's chambered with an armor-piercing round. He's chosen the exact same aiming point Ms. Nice did. Purely by instinct. Above and behind him, the one on the table is chambered with a match grade bullet. He's set up on the French guy. On his temple, probably.

Maybe the guy's wearing body armor under his suit. Not much of an impediment, probably, but why risk an unknown factor? The head is better. So it's right there in the scope. He's just waiting for the glass to break."

"But it didn't."

"So they beat feet and get the hell out of Dodge. But Kott stays in Paris. He'd prefer to stop the investigation right there. He camps out and watches that balcony, day after day. Or maybe he's tipped off by the French. You should check. But whichever, finally he gets his chance. Three investigators show up. When he saw me in his scope he must have thought he'd won the lottery. His little heart must have gone pit-a-pat. Then he calmed down and pulled the trigger."

"And hit Khenkin by mistake?"

"Not by mistake. He got me center mass, a dead-on bull's-eye, a no doubter, an Olympic gold medal right there. I was a dead man from the moment he pulled the trigger. But the bullet was in the air nearly four seconds. And there was a gust of wind. I remember seeing it. I remember the muzzle flash, and then the snap of a flag, and then Khenkin got hit. Because the wind moved the bullet. Only about a foot and a half, over sixteen hundred yards. It nudged it just a little, right to left as it flew, from my chest to his head."

"You can't prove that."

"I can," I said. "If it was Datsev aiming at Khenkin, then Bennett would have been killed. He was next in line. You can't argue with the wind. It was right there. The flags went crazy, and then stopped just as fast. It was gusty all morning. Check it out."

O'Day was quiet for a spell. Then he said, "Two

shooters. Jesus." Then he said, "We have to give this theory to London and Moscow. If we're all behind it, that is. Rick?"

Shoemaker paused a beat, and nodded.

"I'm in," he said.

"Joan?"

Scarangello said, "Better to think two if it's really one, than one if it's really two. We should err on the side of caution."

O'Day didn't ask Casey Nice.

I said, "I'm going to London now."

O'Day said, "Now?"

"I don't mind about the picture in his bedroom. I don't even mind that the little runt just took a shot at me. That's an occupational hazard, for a cop. But he was careless and he missed. He shouldn't have tried on a windy day. He killed an innocent man. That's different. That was a mistake. And like you said, I caught him once. I can catch him again."

"And then what?"

"I'm going to twist his arm out of his shoulder socket and beat him to death with his own right hand."

"Negative," O'Day said. "You'll go to London when I tell you to. This is a complex business. Preparations must be made."

"You can't give me orders. I'm a civilian."

"Helping his country. Let's do it right."

I said nothing.

He said, "Khenkin wasn't an innocent man. He was KGB. He did bad things."

I said nothing.

He said, "I told you so."

"Told me what?"

"It's not the same with a sniper out there."

Scarangello asked, "Will they work together in London, too?"

"Probably," I said. "It's a target-rich environment. It would double their firepower."

"So who's in the frame for the second spot? Carson or Datsev?"

"I'm not a gambling man."

"If you were?"

"Then Carson. Khenkin said Datsev wouldn't audition. I didn't read that as hype. It felt authentic to me."

"Wait until we're ready," O'Day said. "Then you can go to London."

Chapter 21

The conference ended and I headed downstairs and out the red door, aiming for my corrugated quarters, but Casey Nice caught up to me steps later and said, "You want to go get some dinner?" Which sounded like a fine idea to me. The last hot food I had eaten was the *croque madame,* in Paris, paid for by Yevgeniy Khenkin himself.

I said, "Where?"

"Off post," she said. "Barbecue or something."

"You have a car?"

"More or less."

"What does that mean?"

"You'll see."

"Deal," I said.

"I should change," she said. She was in a black skirt suit. Dark nylons, good shoes. Perfect for D.C. or Virginia, maybe not so much in a country shack outside of Fayetteville.

I said, "I'm happy to wait."

"Five minutes," she said.

Which turned out closer to ten. But it was worth the delay. She knocked on my door and I opened up and found her in a pony tail and a version of her Arkansas outfit. The same brown leather jacket, over a white T-shirt, with different jeans. Same color, but lower cut. And all scraped and sanded and beat up. *Distressed,* I believed they called it, which to me meant *upset,* which just didn't compute. Was there a finer place to be, than where those jeans were?

She had car keys dangling from her finger, and she held them up to show me, and she said, "I apologize in advance."

"For what?"

"You'll see."

And I did, about two hundred yards later, in a fenced lot near Pope Field's perimeter road. The lot was full of everything I had expected to see, which was pick-up trucks and domestic muscle cars about twenty years old, and beat-up Mercedes and BMWs brought home from deployments in Germany. I kept my eye out for anomalies, and I saw a tiny Mini Cooper the color of lavender, and then further on a VW new-style Beetle, yellow, half-hidden behind some hideous old farm vehicle. I figured hers was the Beetle, if she was already apologizing. Maybe it was a graduation present. Maybe she had a daisy in the vase on the dash, to match the paint.

But it wasn't the Beetle. It was the hideous old

farm vehicle next to it. I said, "What the hell *is* this thing?"

She said, "Some of it's an old Ford Bronco. The rest of it is metal sheets welded on, as and when the original parts fell off. The brown coloration is equal parts rust and mud. I was advised not to wash the mud off. For corrosion protection and added strength."

"Where did you get it?"

"A guy at Fort Benning sold it to me."

"For how much?"

"Twenty-two dollars."

"Outstanding."

"Climb aboard. It's open. I never lock it. I mean, why would I?"

The passenger door hinge was more rust than mud, and I had to put some strength into it. I squealed it open just wide enough to slide in sideways, and I saw Casey Nice was doing the exact same thing on her side, like we were limbo dancing toward each other. There were no seat belts. No seats at all, really. Just a green canvas sling fraying its way off a tubular metal frame.

But the engine started, eventually, after a bunch of popping and churning, and then it idled, wet and lumpy. The transmission was slower than the postal service. She rattled the selector into reverse, and all the mechanical parts inside called the roll and counted a quorum and set about deciding what to do. Which required a lengthy debate, apparently, because it was whole seconds before the truck lurched backward. She turned the wheel, which looked like hard work, and then she jammed the selector into a forward gear, and first of all the reversing committee wound up its business and approved its minutes and exited the room, and then the forward crew signed on and got comfortable, and a motion was tabled and seconded and discussed. More whole seconds passed, and then the truck slouched forward, slow and stuttering at first, before picking up its pace and rolling implacably toward the exit gate.

I said, "You should have stolen John Kott's old blue pick-up truck. It would have been a significant upgrade."

She said, "This thing gets me from A to B."

"What happens if you're heading for C or D?"

"It's a beautiful evening. And walking is good for you."

We rolled out through one of Fort Bragg's many sub-gates, into the real world, or at least a version of it, on a plain North Carolina two-lane road lined on both sides with establishments geared exclusively to the tastes and economic capabilities of military men and women. I saw loan shops and fast food shacks and used car dealerships, and no-contract cell phones and dollar stores and video game exchanges, and bars and lounges of every description. Then a slow mile later such places started thinning out, in favor of vacant lots and piney woods, and a sense of empty vastness ahead.

The truck kept on going. Not fast, and accompanied by the smell of burnt oil, but forward progress was maintained. We turned right, deeper into the emptiness, clearly heading for somewhere Casey Nice knew, and she said, "Does it bother you that Kott has been gloating over your failures?"

"Not really," I said. "They're in the public record."

"It would bother me."

"Head to head I'm one-zip in front. He should gloat over that."

"Thanks to a gust of wind."

"I was born lucky."

"Plus you stood upwind of the others."

"That, too."

"Deliberate?"

"Ingrained. Which is a form of deliberate, I suppose." Up ahead I saw lights strung through the trees, and then a clearing in the woods, with a tumbledown shack in the center, and tables and chairs set out all around it on gravel and dirt. The shack had a chimney, and I could see heat and smoke coming up out of it. I could smell slow-cooked meat.

Casey Nice said, "OK?"

I said, "My kind of place."

She began the process of slowing the truck, which involved stamping hard on the brake pedal and then pumping it like crazy. She turned the wheel and bumped into the lot and came to a stop. She switched off and pulled the key. The engine ran on for a whole minute, and then shuddered and died. We squeezed our way out and found a table. The place had no name. And no menu, really. There was a choice of meat, with either Wonder bread or baked beans on the side, and three kinds of canned soda to drink. Polystyrene plates, plastic forks, paper napkins, no credit cards accepted, and a waitress who looked about eleven years old. All good.

We ordered, ribs and bread for her, pork and beans

for me, with two Cokes. The sky was clear and the stars were out. The air was crisp, but not cold. The place was about half full. I dug in my pocket and took out the pill bottle. I put it on the table, with the label facing away. I said, "You should have this back. Eating lint from your pocket can't be doing you any good."

She left it where it was for a moment. Then she dug in her own pocket and came out with her pills cupped in her hand. Seven of them. Fewer than before. She blew dust off them, and picked up the bottle, and popped the lid with her thumb, and shoveled the pills back inside.

I said, "Who is Antonio Luna?"

"A friend of mine," she said. "I call him Tony Moon."

"A co-worker?"

"Just a guy I know."

"Who had an empty bottle just when you needed one?"

She didn't answer.

"Or who fakes some symptoms and then gives you the prescriptions he gets, all because you can't talk to your company doctor?"

She said, "Is this any of your business?"

I said, "None at all."

She put the bottle in her pocket.

She said, "There's nothing wrong with me."

I said, "Good to know."

Then our food arrived, and I forgot all about pills, legit or otherwise. The beans were beans, and the Coke was Coke, but the meat was sensational. Just a no-name clearing in the North Carolina backwoods, but right then there was nowhere I would have rather been. Casey Nice looked like she shared my opinion. She was sucking the meat off her ribs and smiling and licking her lips. All good, until her phone rang.

She wiped her fingers and answered and listened and hung up. She said, "We have to go back. Something just happened in London."

Chapter 22

What had happened in London was that someone had died. Which was not news in itself. London's population was about eight million, and the UK's death rate was over nine per thousand per year, so on any given day a couple hundred Londoners would breathe their last. Old age, overdoses, degenerative illnesses, cancers of every kind, car wrecks, fires, accidents, suicides, heart attacks, thromboses, and strokes. All normal.

Getting shot in the head by a high-powered rifle, not so much.

We chugged back to Bragg in the ancient patched-up Bronco, and we found O'Day and Shoemaker and Scarangello waiting for us in the upstairs room. Shoemaker gave us the facts. There was a big-deal Albanian gang leader in London, name of Karel Libor, very rich, very brutal, very successful, running drugs and girls and guns. Like most very rich and very successful big-deal gang leaders, he was also very paranoid.

He had a lot of guys looking after him, and would go nowhere unless his destination had been checked and secured. Even the trip from his door to his car was protected. But apparently not from a fifty-caliber round fired from a thousand yards away. Mr. Libor's head had exploded and splashed all over the armored Range Rover he was trying to get into.

"Conclusions?" O'Day asked.

Shoemaker sat back, as if the question wasn't aimed at him, and Scarangello glanced at Casey Nice, who shrugged and said nothing. I said, "Kott and Carson are in London already. They're hiring local support. But not with money. Apparently the help wanted payment in kind this time. As in, the elimination of a rival."

O'Day nodded. "A rival otherwise very difficult to get to, at street level. But raise your eyes, and London's skyline is densely developed now. Lots of opportunities at a thousand yards, one imagines. And a thousand yards is nothing to Kott. Practically point-blank range."

"Or Carson," I said.

"Or Datsev," he said. "Carson is only your opinion. We must keep an open mind."

"Did anything like this happen in Paris?"

O'Day nodded again. "I think it did. Not that we ever put two and two together, because there was no rifle involved. About a week before the attempt on the president, an Algerian gang leader was knifed to death in Montmartre. A very big cheese, as the French might say. And looking back at it now, you'd have to say the Vietnamese were plausible beneficiaries."

Casey Nice asked, "Who benefits in London?"

"I'm awaiting a definitive report," O'Day said. "But

ballpark estimates put two in the frame. A Serbian outfit in the west of London, and an old-fashioned English gang in the east. Karel Libor was a thorn in both their sides, according to MI5."

I said, "Where exactly is the G8 location?"

"In the east of London."

"Then if local really means local, they're palling up with the old-fashioned Brits."

"For what exactly?" Scarangello asked.

Shoemaker said, "Part of the payment in kind would be considered an old-fashioned tribute, to be allowed to operate there at all. Like a toll or a tax, almost. The rest will be for logistics, places to stay, places to hide, and then on the day itself, sentries and other security close up, and a cordon out at a distance. Like we just saw in Paris."

"That makes it harder for us."

I shook my head.

"It makes it easier," I said. "We're not looking for two guys anymore. We're looking for about fifty-two guys. They say local support, I say breadcrumbs."

O'Day said, "You were right about Kott's neighbor, by the way. The FBI found most of ten thousand dollars in cash. But not in the back of his closet."

"Where, then?"

"In the washing machine in his front yard."

"Smart," I said. "I should have checked. Who gave it to him?"

"He won't say. And waterboarding is out of fashion at the moment."

"He's too scared to say. Which might be significant."

"And the French found the bullet that killed Khenkin. From this morning. Badly deformed against the wall of the apartment house, but the chemistry is the same as the fragments you brought back from Arkansas. The same batch, quite possibly."

I nodded. "Which raises questions about travel. He didn't fly commercial, or you'd have a paper trail. He couldn't check a fifty-caliber rifle and a box of bullets without someone noticing."

"Two possibilities," Shoemaker said. "A cargo ship out of Mobile or Galveston, or a private plane out of practically anywhere. Customs checks at private fields in Europe are basically non-existent."

"Private plane for sure," O'Day said. "These people are throwing money around. I mean, ten grand for a toothless hillbilly in Arkansas? That's way over the odds. The guy would have been happy with a couple hundred, surely. They're not looking for value. They're looking for easy solutions, and they have the budget to make them happen."

Casey Nice asked, "How did they get to London today?"

Scarangello said, "Train, probably. Through the tunnel. There's a passport check in Paris, but apart from that it's fast and easy, city center to city center."

"How did they transport their rifles?"

"Golf bags, maybe. Or ski bags. Lots of people carry weird luggage."

"How did they know who to hook up with in London, in terms of local support?"

"Prior research, I assume. Prior negotiation, perhaps."

"We'll know more in the morning," O'Day said. "Take the rest of the evening off, and we'll reconvene at breakfast tomorrow."

I went down the stairs and headed out the red door, but once again I heard the click of good shoes and the swish of dark nylons behind me. I turned around and found Joan Scarangello coming after me. She was looking at me with some kind of bleak emotion in her eyes. She said, "We need to talk."

I said, "About what?"

"You."

"What about me?"

"I don't want to talk out here."

"Where, then?"

"Your quarters. They feel unoccupied. Like neutral space."

So we walked over together and I opened up and we sat like we had before, with me on the sofa and her in a chair, with our angles adjusted, so that we were looking at each other face to face. She asked, "Did you enjoy your dinner?"

"Not bad," I said. "You?"

"I spent it arguing with Generals O'Day and Shoemaker."

"About the quality of the food?"

"No, about your role in London."

"What about it?"

"London won't be the same as Paris. The Brits are different. They'll be running their own show. They'll accept advice and information, but they won't let us actually do anything. Not on their turf. And we have to respect that. They're important to us in many ways."

"So?"

"My position is you should go as an acknowledged asset."

"But O'Day argued against that, because then I wouldn't be able to do anything."

Scarangello nodded. "He wants you there as a private citizen. Not acknowledged by us. Which means if you get caught choking some random senior on the sidewalk, there will be absolutely nothing we can do to help you."

"I'll be careful."

"I'm serious," she said. "General O'Day is talking about things that are blatantly illegal. Your being there in the first place will be blatantly illegal. A very dim view is taken of unacknowledged assets inside an ally's jurisdiction. If you screw up, you'll be a common criminal, nothing more. Worse than that, in fact. The Embassy checks up on common criminals, but no one will check up on you. They'll run a mile in the opposite direction. Because we'll tell them to."

"I'll be careful," I said again.

She said, "I read the John Kott file."

I said, "And?"

"You did a very nice job with the interrogation."

"Thank you."

"You gave him the rope and he hung himself. He was arrogant, and he couldn't bear to be challenged."

I nodded. "That was about the gist of it."

She said, "I think you're just as bad as he was."

I said nothing.

She said, "This is where you tell me you never cut anyone's throat."

"I would if I could."

"I think it's too big of a risk to send you to London in any capacity."

"Then don't."

"Meaning you'll get yourself there anyway?"

"Free country."

"I could take your passport back."

"It's right here in my pocket. Come and get it."

"I could cancel it in the computer. You'd be arrested at the airport."

"Your decision," I said. "No skin off my nose. Kott will come home sooner or later. I'll get him then. Amid all the paralysis, and the crashing markets, and the recession, and the people starving, and the wars starting, and the whole world falling apart. None of which will bother me in the least. I can look after myself. And I don't have a real big portfolio."

She said nothing.

I said, "You need the best help you can get. Anything else would be negligent. I seem to remember those words from somewhere."

"And you're the best help?"

"That remains to be seen. Either someone will get the job done, or not. That someone might be me, or not. The future's not ours to see. But my track record is reasonable, and I don't see how I could hurt."

"You could hurt by getting arrested inside the first five minutes. Then we've got a diplomatic incident on top of a security emergency. I'm not sure I can trust you."

"Then come with me," I said. "You could sign off on my every move. We could confer, shoulder to shoulder. Not seven feet apart."

She nodded. "That's the compromise I agreed to with O'Day."

"Really?"

"Not me," she said. "Casey Nice will go with you. Unacknowledged. She's not on their radar. She's far too junior. And right now she's not CIA, anyway. She's State Department."

"Rules of engagement?"

"You do exactly what she tells you."

Scarangello left after that, leaving the scent of soap and warm skin in the air, and I waited a minute and then headed out too, back to the red door. I went up the stairs to Shoemaker's office, and found him at his desk. I said, "Scarangello told me about your dinner conversation."

He said, "Happy?"

"Yeah, I'm turning cartwheels."

"Look on the bright side. You'll need updates and intelligence. We'll give them to Nice, she'll give them to you. You'd be in the dark without her."

"Has she operated overseas before?"

"No."

"Has she operated anywhere before?"

"Not as such."

"Do you think this is a good idea?"

"It's a necessary compromise. It gets you there. You don't have to listen to what she says."

"But I have to take care of her."

"She knows what she signed up for. And she's tougher than she looks."

"You said that before."

"Was I wrong?"

I thought about her pal Tony Moon, and I said nothing.

Shoemaker said, "Walk away if you want to, Reacher. You don't owe me shit. The statute of limitations ran out years ago. It was O'Day's idea to take that route. A psychological insight, he called it. He said it was the only thing likely to work."

"Was he wrong?"

"Walk away if you want," he said again. "There are hundreds of people working on this. And the Brits are taking it very seriously. I mean, they already were. It's a G8 meeting. If you're in the security business, then that's your Super Bowl right there. So they're on it. So you won't be missed. You're one guy. What difference could you make?"

"Is this another psychological insight?"

"I want you there, sure. I want everyone there. A human wall, if necessary. Whatever it takes. Because if an American shooter turns the G8 into the G4, we're in real big trouble as a nation."

"Is *that* a psychological insight? As in, I'm a patriot, right? What is this, Manipulation 101?"

"Go talk to O'Day," he said.

Which I did, immediately afterward, by walking past the conference room to the office next to it. O'Day was at his desk, in his black blazer and his black sweater. His head was bent, and when he looked up at me he did it with his eyes only, as if his neck hurt to move.

I said, "This is right up there with the worst ideas of all time."

He said, "But even so, it's your best chance to get John Kott. I'll be feeding Ms. Nice everything I know. You'll have the power of the whole government behind you. And you need to finish this now. You won't sleep at night until he's gone."

"I'm sleeping just fine."

"Then get over yourself. We all read your file, obviously. Those pages on Kott's bedroom wall? We know what they say. Our Ms. Nice is exactly the same age as one Dominique Kohl, who got her breasts cut off with a kitchen knife, because you sent her to arrest a maniac."

"Yes," I said. "That's what those pages say."

"What are you, superstitious? Everyone is twenty-eight sooner or later. There's no connection. And you won't be sending her to arrest anyone. Because no arrests are going to be made. I want you in there, and only you, up close and personal, and I want you to bring me their ears to prove it."

"Why me? There are hundreds of people on this."

"And if it's easy, no doubt one of them will do the job. But it won't be easy. That's the truth of it. It might slide right past all of them. That's what I'm afraid of. I need a backstop. I need someone I can trust."

Which was another psychological insight, presumably.

Chapter 23

I met with Casey Nice the following morning. She had been told. She was all aglow. She explained the procedures. She said, "There's GPS in our cell phones, so they'll be watching over us every step of the way. I'll be getting real-time information by voice, text, and e-mail. We have each other's numbers pre-programmed in, plus Generals O'Day and Shoemaker, for emergencies. All calls will be encrypted and untraceable."

I said, "Did they tell you the rules of engagement?"

"Yes, they did."

"Who told you?"

"All of them."

"Separately or together?"

"Separately."

"Did they all say the same thing?"

"No, they didn't."

"So which one of them are you listening to?"

She said, "General O'Day."

* * *

Shoemaker gave us the practical stuff. Chargers for our cell phones, credit cards, a wad of English cash money, hotel reservations, and airplane tickets from Atlanta to London Heathrow, on Delta. The company Gulfstream would fly us down to Georgia, but after that we were strictly commercial, just like regular citizens.

Then we all met in the conference room, because O'Day had two items of late information for us. First up was a photograph. It was a still taken from the security video system at the Gare du Nord railroad station in Paris. It was time-stamped fifty minutes after the shot that killed Khenkin. The focus was off and there was a little blur, but it was clear enough. It showed a guy, average height, wiry, all muscle and sinew. He was turned half away from the camera, lost in a crowd, but his cheekbones gave him away. It was John Kott. His eyes were cast down and his mouth was a tight line. Hard to say from a literal snapshot, but his body language and his facial expression made me feel he was uneasy in the hustle and bustle. Which would be understandable. Fifteen years in Leavenworth, then another in the Arkansas backwoods. The Gare du Nord was one of the busiest railroad terminals in the world. A big change of pace.

O'Day said, "That's the concourse just ahead of the Eurostar tracks. The London train pulled out ten minutes later. We should assume he was on it."

Casey Nice said, "Why isn't Carson with him?"

O'Day said, "We should assume they traveled separately. Much safer that way. They wouldn't risk both getting nailed, by the same piece of bad luck."

Then he opened a file and pulled out a bunch of paper. The gang analysis from MI5 in London. He said, "They're sure it's the local English guys. They own the streets around the target, and they moved in on Karel Libor's operations very fast. Too fast for the news of Mr. Libor's demise to have reached them through conventional channels. They knew it was going to happen beforehand. Because they set it up."

He read out a list of four names, a top boy and three trusted lieutenants, White, Miller, Thompson, and Green, like a law firm, and then he described an inner circle of thirty more, supplemented when and where necessary by contract labor anxious to prove its worth. He said collectively they were known as the Romford Boys, and always had been, because they were based in a place called Romford, which was on the eastern edge of the city, north of the river, just inside the orbital highway. He said they were largely white and largely native born. He described their business activities, which were drugs, girls, and guns, the same as Libor's activities, with protection rackets and loan sharking as the icing on the cake. He had no lurid tales to tell us, of gruesome murders and horrific punishments and sadistic tortures. He said over the years their many and various victims had simply disappeared into thin air, and were never seen again.

Casey Nice went to pack, and I showered again and dressed again and put my toothbrush in my pocket.

We met in the Gulfstream's cabin. She was wearing her Arkansas outfit. She said, "General O'Day told me you're dubious about all of this."

I said nothing.

She said, "Working with me, I mean."

I said nothing.

She said, "What happened to Dominique Kohl was not your fault."

"O'Day showed you the file?"

"I had already read it, on Kott's bedroom wall. It wasn't your fault. You couldn't have known."

I said nothing.

She said, "I'm not going to arrest anyone. I'm going to hang way back. It's not going to happen again."

"I agree," I said. "These things are generally the exception, not the rule."

"It could be over before we get there. The Brits must be busting a gut."

"I'm sure they are."

"We'll have all their data a minute after O'Day gets it. We'll be OK."

"Now *you* sound dubious."

"I'm not quite sure what to expect."

I said, "Neither am I. No one ever is. On either side. Which is a good thing. It means the game goes to the fastest thinker. That's all you need to be."

"We can't both be the fastest."

"I agree," I said again. "I might slip into second place. In which case someone is going to start shooting at me with a rifle. So you better stay seven feet away."

"Suppose I'm in second place and they start shooting at me?"

"Same thing. Seven feet away. At least I'll get a sporting chance."

The Atlanta airport was so big we had to catch a cab from the General Aviation offices to the passenger terminals. Casey Nice checked in at a thing that looked like an ATM, but I went to the desk instead, where a glance at my new passport got me a boarding pass made of old-fashioned pasteboard. We were in premium coach, which struck me as an oxymoron. Nice said it meant extra leg room. She explained a long and complicated algorithm by which the government saved taxpayer money. Everyone started out in regular coach, unless and until there were compelling reasons why not. The only box we checked was that we were expected to start work immediately after disembarkation. Which got us the leg room.

Which turned out to be not very much. We went through security, shoeless and coatless and with empty pockets, and then we wandered through what looked like a shopping mall, to the gate area, via a coffee cart for me and a juice bar for her. She had a small suitcase with wheels, and a thing about halfway between a handbag and a shopping bag. She fit in better than I did, as a regular citizen. We sat on thinly padded chairs and waited, and then eventually we got on the plane, after the rows with the regular leg room had all filled up first. Our chairs were the usual kind of thing, and the extra space in front of them was clearly going to work for her, but not for me. If I jammed the bony structure in the small of my back hard against the seat, then I could bend my knees a little more than ninety degrees, but that was about as good as it got.

The pilot said the flight time was going to be six hours and forty minutes.

Two hours later we had eaten and drunk, and the cabin staff turned up the heat so we would all fall asleep and leave them alone. Coshing, I had heard them call it, in conversations among themselves. But it was fine with me. I had slept in worse positions. My headrest had little wings that moved, so I clamped my head like I was wearing a medical device, and I closed my eyes.

Casey Nice said, "I take the pills because I get anxious."

I opened my eyes.

I said, "Do they work?"

"Yes, they do."

"How many do you have left?"

"Five."

"You had seven last night, at dinner."

"You counted?"

"Not really. I noticed, is all. It's a description. They were yellow, they were small, they were in your pocket, there were seven of them."

"I took one last night and one this morning."

"Because you were anxious?"

"Yes."

"What were you anxious about?"

"Mastering the brief, and executing the mission."

"Are you anxious now?"

"No."

"Because of this morning's pill?"

"It already wore off. But I feel OK."

"That's good," I said. "Because this is the easy part."

"I know."

"Doesn't Tony Moon's doctor worry about him never getting better?"

"People take these things for years. All their lives, some of them."

"Is that what you're going to do?"

"I don't know."

"What else makes you anxious?"

She didn't answer at first. Then she said, "The stakes, I guess. Just the stakes. They're so high. We can't let it happen again."

"Can't let what happen again?"

"September eleventh."

"How old were you, anyway?"

"Formative years."

"Is that when you decided to join the CIA?"

"I knew I wanted to do something. The decision was made for me, in the end. I was recruited out of college."

"Where did you go?"

"Yale."

I nodded inside my medical brace. Yale was pretty much a CIA kindergarten. Like Cambridge University in England, for MI6. All a terrorist needed to do was work his way through the alumni rolls. Or bomb a reunion dinner. I said, "You must be smart, to have gotten into Yale."

She didn't answer.

I said, "Do you work hard?"

She said, "I try my best."

"Do you pay attention?"

"Always."

"And you paid twenty-two bucks for vehicular transportation."

"What's that got to do with anything?"

"It means you're just a little bit unconventional. Which is the fourth of the four things you need to be. All of which you are. Which is all we'll ever need. Smart people, working hard, paying attention, thinking laterally."

"We had those on September tenth."

"No, we didn't," I said. "We really didn't. Like we didn't have much of an army in 1941. It had been a long time since we had needed one. We had out-of-date people doing out-of-date things. But we got better real quick. Just like you did. It's not going to happen again."

"You can't say that."

"I just did."

"You can't know it."

"It's not worth taking a pill for. Just work hard, pay attention, and keep on thinking. That's all you can do. And it's not just you, anyway. There are thousands of you, just as good, working just as hard, paying just as much attention."

"We could still fail."

"Relax," I said. "At least for a couple of weeks. This thing isn't September eleventh. I know Scarangello is full of doom and gloom, but suppose she's wrong? Some politician gets whacked, exactly half his country will be throwing a street party. They'll be buying beer and flags. Could spark an economic miracle."

"I'm sure that possibility was investigated. But I think Deputy Deputy Scarangello's position represents the majority view."

"Is that what you call her?"

"That's what she is."

I asked, "Is your gun waiting at the hotel?"

She said, "What hotel?"

"Where we're staying. Or do you pick it up someplace else?"

"There is no gun. I'm unacknowledged. The government can't arm me. You either."

"So what are we supposed to do?"

She said, "Standard procedure would be to supply ourselves locally, by foraging."

I forced my head left and right, to push back the wings on my headrest. I said, "Which might be easy enough to do, because presumably the Romford Boys are being vigilant, on behalf of Kott and Carson, and sooner or later we're going to touch their outer cordon, like tweaking the edge of a spider's web, and presumably the outer cordon is armed, which means we're about to be, because we're going to take the guy's weapon away."

"I think that's one possibility they would want us to consider. Plus General Shoemaker thinks contact with Romford's outer cordon is a good tactic in its own right. In the form of an invented approach on a business matter, he suggested. If we get past one layer, we can triangulate against the second layer and get a sense of where the center is. Where Kott and Carson are, in other words."

"If I ask you a question, will I get an honest answer?"

"Depends."

"How many other unacknowledged assets is the United States sending?"

"Seven."

"How many undercover Brits?"

"Last I heard, thirteen."

"And what about the other six countries?"

"They'll send two each, except for Russia, who will match us with seven."

"When will they all arrive?"

"Ahead of us, probably. We might be late to the party."

"And how busy are these boys in Romford?"

"Busy doing what?"

"Doing deals. With suppliers and wholesalers and retailers and stuff like that."

"I have no idea."

"At least moderately busy, right? Drugs and girls and guns is all about buying and selling. And there's always some new face on the scene with a better price, at one end of the deal or the other. So from time to time they talk to unknown people. They're somewhat accustomed to it. So if some stranger shows up dressed like a tough guy with a bullshit deal, they won't think too much about it. Maybe not with the second guy, even. But you just counted thirty-seven people who are all going to have the same idea as Rick Shoemaker did. After the third or the fourth the cordon is going to start shooting on sight. So we're not going to do the spider web thing. We're going to do something else."

"What else?"

"I'll explain it later," I said, because at that point I was drawing a blank, and she had only five pills left.

Chapter 24

I slept for maybe three hours, bolt upright, head clamped, and then about ninety minutes before arrival the lights came on and a whole lot of crashing and banging started up in the galleys. Casey Nice had the look of a person who hadn't slept at all. She was a little pale and shiny and feverish. The joys of all-night travel. She said, "Have you been to London before?"

"A few times," I said.

"What do I need to know?"

"You haven't been before?"

"Not for work."

"This isn't work. We're unacknowledged, remember?"

"Exactly," she said. "I'm about to walk into a foreign country and break about a hundred laws and treaties. They take a dim view of that."

"Scarangello told me."

"She was right."

"In which case the airport will be your biggest

problem. We should assume they're on heightened alert. And they're paranoid anyway. They have cameras and one-way glass everywhere. They'll be watching us from the minute we step out of the plane. From the jet bridge onward, literally. Us and everyone else. They're looking for nervous or furtive behavior. Because this is their first and best chance to catch people. And it doesn't help us if we're turned away at the border or locked up for questioning. So don't look nervous or furtive. Don't think about the hundred laws or treaties. Think about something else entirely."

"Like what?"

"What would you most like to do in London? Like a secret desire. As stupid as you want."

"You really want to know?"

"I want you to imagine you're doing it. Or heading straight for it. That's why you're here. You're going to catch a cab and go right there."

"OK."

"And then after the airport it gets much easier. Except that every square inch of every public space has a camera on it. Plus most private spaces, too. London has a quarter of the whole world's supply of closed circuit cameras, all in one city. It's not possible to avoid them. We have to accept it and move on. We're making a movie, whether we want to or not, and the only thing we can do about it is get out real fast afterward, before they start to look at the tapes."

"If we find Kott and Carson, we won't need to get out fast. We'll be invited to Buckingham Palace to get a medal."

"Depends what we do with them after we find

them. And how well we do it. I'm sure the Brits like a nice clean job just as much as we do, but if it's not clean, they'll sell us out in a heartbeat. They'll get questions in their Parliament, and there are all kinds of hostile newspapers there, so it will take them about a second and a half to come out swinging. They'll claim they wanted a legal arrest and a Miranda warning and a fair trial all along. They'll call us illegal foreign mercenaries. Murderers, in fact. We'll be denounced. And if necessary we'll be sacrificed. So all in all I like the fast exit strategy better. Plus I have no desire to go to Buckingham Palace anyway."

"Wouldn't you like to meet the Queen?"

"Not really. She's just a person. We're all equal. Has she expressed any interest in meeting me?"

"Don't think like that in the airport. You'll be arrested for sure. They'll think you've come to blow her up."

Mornings over Heathrow were busy times of day, in terms of air traffic, and we circled for more than forty minutes, in long lazy loops over the center of London, with some passengers uptight about the so-near-and-yet-so-far feel of it all, and others happy just to watch the view out the window, of the snaking river and the huge, sprawling, spreading city, and the famous buildings strewn all around, tiny in the vertical distance, but impossibly detailed. Then we got serious and lined up on approach, and the wheels came down, and we waddled in, low and slow, to a smooth landing and a fast taxi.

Disembarking took a good long time, with people standing and stretching, and re-establishing contact with their cellular networks, and retrieving their luggage, and looking under their seats for the things they had lost. So we entered the terminal as part of a ragged linear crowd, ones and twos and threes, all separated but clearly associated, all heading the same way at roughly the same speed, which was about halfway between impatient and fatigued. I saw no furtive behavior in the passengers ahead of me. I didn't look behind, in case I looked furtive myself.

We had no problem at the passport desk, after a long wait in a long line. Casey Nice went first, with her paperwork neatly filled out, and I lip-read a question about why she was visiting, and I saw her say, "Vacation," and then add, "I mean a holiday," like a bilingual person. I went next, and was asked no questions. My new passport got its first stamp, and I rejoined Nice beyond the podiums, and we headed out through the baggage hall, to Her Majesty's Customs. Who were not a problem either. They were heavily invested in the hidden surveillance thing. We walked past about an acre of one-way windows, and no visible humans at all.

Then came crowds of people waiting to greet folks other than us, and cold morning air blowing in through the curbside doors, and overhead signs listing our onward transportation options, which were railroad or subway or bus or taxi. Heathrow was way west, and our hotel was way east, which was a long enough ride to be easily memorable by a taxi driver, as his best fare of the week. Plus the wads of money handed over by Shoemaker, while generous, were not infinite.

So we opted for the subway, for the experience, more than anything, and because I believe you can best sense the mood of a city in its tunnels. The reverberant acoustic amplifies feelings of fear or tension, or reveals their absence.

It was a long ride, on hard benches, with two connections, rushing and slamming through tubes barely wider than the cars themselves. I felt no special edge in the air. Plenty of normal workaday angst and worry, but nothing more than that. We got out at a place called Barking, into mid-morning sunlight. Casey Nice looked like an abandoned waif, standing on the sidewalk outside the station with her rolling suitcase, tired and a little disheveled. She figured our hotel was still some ways away. A long walk. I saw no cruising cabs. Too far from the center. She said, "We really need a Town Car."

I said, "I don't think they have them here."

But they seemed to have a rough equivalent. I saw a couple of battered sedans outside a whitewashed storefront labeled *Barking Minicabs.* We walked over there and I went in alone. There was a guy behind a high plywood counter. I asked him for a car. He said street hails were not allowed. Pre-booked only.

I said, "I'm not hailing anything. I'm talking in a normal voice. And I'm not on the street."

He said, "Pre-booked only. We could lose our license."

"Do I look like a government inspector to you? Do I look like a cop?"

He said, "You have to book by telephone." He

pointed to a large sign on the wall, which said *Pre-booked Only,* with a telephone number below.

I said, "Really?"

He said, "We could lose our license."

I was about to contemplate alternative methods, but then I remembered I had a phone in my pocket. Scarangello had given it to me, in Paris. O'Day had fitted it with a GPS chip, for the mission. I took it out and dialed the number on the sign. There was silence at first, while a whole lot of location services and international assistance kicked in. Then a desk phone rang, about a yard from my elbow. The guy picked it up.

I said, "I need a car."

The guy said, "Certainly, sir. When would you like it?"

"Thirty seconds from now."

"Picking up where?"

"Right here."

"Destination?"

I named the hotel.

"Number of passengers?"

"Two."

The guy said, "Your driver will be with you in a minute."

Which was technically twice as long as I had asked for, but I didn't make any trouble about it. I just clicked off the call and rejoined Casey Nice on the sidewalk. I told her what had happened, and she said, "You shouldn't have pushed it. They'll remember you. And a place like that is probably paying protection money to the Romford Boys. They'll trade gossip for sure."

* * *

The car was worn out and filthy and not very spacious, but it got us where we were going, which was a budget hotel with a parking lot, trapped in a mixed line of various enterprises in a neighborhood that way back long ago had been a remote and distant village. It still looked like one in certain hidden corners. There was old brickwork in places, and an inappropriately grand old house, now boxed in tight by much smaller suburban structures. An old manor, presumably, fat and happy two hundred years ago, the city just a folk tale, a whole day's ride away. But then came the railroad, and maybe the manor lost a ten-acre field, and then another, and then came the buses and the cars, and the manor lost its orchard, and then its garden, and then everything except a flagstone square in front, big enough for two cars, if both of them were careful.

The hotel was purpose built, with an eye on efficiency. They could have taken a crane and stacked up the units at Pope Field four stories high, and the result would have been similar. We checked in and got our keys, and Nice wanted to go up to dump her bags, so I went to find my own room, which was severely plain, but had everything I needed, and nothing I didn't. I washed up and combed my hair with my fingers, and then I headed back downstairs, where I found Nice ready and waiting for me.

She said, "So what's the plan?"

I said, "We'll go take a look."

"At what?"

"The G8 venue."

Chapter 25

The guy at the hotel desk called a minicab for us, properly pre-booked on the telephone, and it showed up surprisingly quickly. Nice gave the driver the address, and we headed what felt north and east to me, through streets that felt suburban, but compressed somehow, as if they were all just a little busier and narrower and faster than they really wanted to be. We passed a sign that said we were in Romford. But we stayed west of the center and then looped around above it, on a small road, into a sudden expanse of green parkland, shaped like a slice of pizza, broadening out as it ran away from us, until it was bounded at its far end by the thrashing traffic on the orbital highway. Or on the M25 motorway, as the local signs called it.

In the middle of the wedge of green was a fine brick house, with bays and gables and chimneys, and steep-pitched roofs, and hundreds of glittering leaded windows. Elizabethan, possibly, or an elaborate Victorian fake. All around it was raked golden gravel, and all around the gravel was plain green lawn, very simple and mannered, but ultimately more corporate than Zen.

All around the lawn was a high brick wall, laid out in a giant rectangle. It boxed the house in completely, left side, right side, back, front, but at a very generous distance. The lawns were broad and deep. It was a well-judged calculation. The wall was indisputably related to the house, definitely part of the architecture, but from the inside the gardens would have felt extremely spacious. Beyond the wall was a slim remnant of the pie-shaped slice of green, and then London started up again, on both sides, as if exerting inward pressure.

I said, "Is this it?"

Casey Nice said, "Yes. It's called Wallace Court. Home of the Darby family for many centuries. The house is from the fifteen hundreds and the wall is Victorian. It's a conference center now."

I nodded. Another old manor, also fat and happy two centuries ago, but maybe luckier for longer. The Victorian owner must have seen something coming. Maybe he was an investor in the railroad. So he built the wall, to keep the world at bay. And I guessed that it had, in a tolerable way, for another hundred years or more, until the motorway was built, and the noise made living there impossible. So at long last the family had given up and moved out, and a home had become a business center, where maybe the noise made people feel plugged in and energetic.

I said, "This can't be a typical location for a G8 meeting."

Casey Nice said, "No, it was controversial. Normally they want somewhere far more rural and isolated. But the Brits insisted. Because it's near where the Olympics were, or something. I don't think anyone's real clear about the reason."

We stayed in the minicab for a long moment after it stopped. *It's not the same with a sniper out there.* Then we took a deep breath and climbed out for a closer look. The wall was about nine feet high, and thick, and ornamented, and buttressed. It must have cost a fortune. There must have been a billion bricks in it. Whole towns could have been built. I thought again about the Victorian guy. Mr. Darby, from way back long ago. Probably wore a beard or muttonchop whiskers. He must have been colossally obstinate. Better to up sticks and go buy an island.

The wall had just one gate in it, at the front, ornate iron painted black, with gold leaf here and there. It was exactly symmetrical with the house's front door, all the way down at the other end of the long straight driveway. Which all made the place not such a terrible spot. Untypical and controversial, maybe, but not suicidal. Bring in the army, put the infantry all around the outer face of the wall, fully armed, in battledress, maybe ten yards apart, put a big security apparatus around the single gate, and you've taken care of ninety-nine percent of conventional threats right there. An up-armored Humvee might be able to burst through the bricks, or maybe not, but anything smaller certainly couldn't. So I could see why eight secret services had signed off on it. They thought the place was adequate.

Until.

The G8 was still the best part of three weeks away, but preparations were already being made. That was clear. There were panel vans unloading in the distance. And there was a policeman at the gate. And he was watching us carefully. Not a polite bobby in a pointed hat, but a squat tough guy with a Kevlar vest and a Heckler and Koch submachine gun.

Casey Nice whispered, "He's seen us."

I said, "That's his job."

"We can't just walk away again. That's suspicious behavior."

"So let's go talk to him."

I strolled over, and stopped, not too close, with the kind of body language we have all learned to use: *Don't give the man with the gun a reason to worry about you.* I said, "We were hoping to get in here."

The man with the gun said, "Were you, sir?"

His accent was local, and his tone was flat, and the way he said *sir* was deliberately neutral, as if he was really saying *I'm obliged to use this word, but I don't mean it.*

I said, "I might have been misled, I suppose. My guidebook is very old."

He said, "What guidebook?"

"My father gave it to me. I think his gave it to him, before that. It's kind of a family heirloom, I suppose. It says certain days of the year you can get in here and see the house and the gardens for sixpence."

"You should take that book to the antique dealer."

"I figured the sixpence might have gone up with inflation."

"This place hasn't been a private house for thirty years. And at the moment it's closed anyway. So I would appreciate it if you would move along now."

"OK," I said, and we did, slowly, with long and detailed glances, to the left, to the right, behind us, eye level, upward, at trees, and row houses, and two-family houses, and squat, square apartment houses, and gas stations, and convenience stores, and traffic, and sky. Our minicab had gone, so we kept on walking. Casey Nice said, "What next?"

She looked tired, so I said, "We go back to the hotel and take naps."

Which we didn't get, because of a phone call from O'Day, which among other things made me wish I was a gambling man. Scarangello had asked, *Who's in the frame for the second spot?* I had said Carson, which turned out to be right. Because Datsev had been found. Arrested, in fact. The news was just in from Moscow. More than three weeks earlier he had been hidden in the trunk of a car in a garage under a nightclub, and driven out of town, to a private air-field, and flown four thousand miles east, where he had set up and waited patiently, like snipers do. When the time was right he had fired a single round through the head of a guy who owned a bauxite smelting op-eration. Twelve hundred yards, O'Day said. Business as usual, in the world of privatized natural resources. With one pull of the trigger Datsev's paymaster had become the second-biggest aluminum guy on the scene.

Which wasn't quite enough, unfortunately. The biggest guy naturally felt threatened, and naturally saw an opportunity for further consolidation, and he had friends in high places, all bought and paid for. So law enforcement made an uncharacteristic attempt to enforce the law. Which was helped by the weather. Spring in the far east of Russia was not the same thing as spring in North Carolina or Paris or London. There were freezing temperatures and late snow. The newly-second-biggest guy's plane had been grounded. His entourage had all been found holed up in a local hotel. Datsev was with them. A spell of old-wine-in-new-bottles KGB-style interrogation had gotten to the heart of the matter fairly quickly, and Datsev was in custody. O'Day figured he would be given a choice: go back to work for the SVR, no bitching and moaning, or go to jail. Which was really no choice at all, he said, for anyone with a working knowledge of the Russian prison system. He had already moved Datsev's file out of the freelance column and into the employed. What the future would bring, he didn't know, but he was clear about the past: Datsev hadn't been in Paris on either occasion, and wasn't in London now.

We clicked off the call. We were still in our hotel lobby. Casey Nice said, "It just got harder. Because Carson is local, and Kott speaks English, too."

"Want coffee?" I said.

"No," she said.

"Hot tea?"

"Decaf, maybe."

So we left the hotel again in favor of a bare-bones cafe on the other side of the street, and a little ways down the block. Not an international chain. Nothing like the coffee shop in Seattle. Just a traditional London place, with chilly fluorescent light and damp laminate tables. I got coffee, and she got decaf, and I said, "Close your eyes."

She smiled and said, "Shoes on or off?"

"Think about what we saw, walking away from Wallace Court. Picture it. Tell me the first thing that pops into your head."

She closed her eyes and said, "Sky."

I said, "Me, too. It was a low-built environment. Some three-story row houses, some four- and five-story apartment houses, but mostly regular two-story two-family houses, some of them with attic bump-outs."

"Which adds up to about ten thousand upper-story windows within a three-quarter-mile radius."

"Not ten thousand. It ain't Manhattan or Hong Kong. It's Romford. But a few thousand, sure. Of which a few hundred might be really good choices. What would you do, if you were in charge of security?"

She said, "I'd have to defer to the Secret Service."

"Suppose you were in charge of the Secret Service?"

"I wouldn't change anything. I'd tell them to keep on doing what they're doing."

"Which is what? Have you seen the president arrive somewhere?"

"Of course I have. An armored limousine drives into a closed street, and then into a large white tent attached to the destination building. The flap of the tent is closed behind it. The president is never exposed. He's safe in the armored car, and he's safe in the tent. From a sniper, at least. The sniper doesn't know exactly where or exactly when the president is getting out of the car. He can't see, because of the tent. He could fire randomly, I suppose, but what are the odds? Best guess in the world would miss by twenty feet and two seconds."

I said, "And the Secret Service will bring that system, right? They always do. Their own armored limousine and their own tent, in an Air Force cargo plane. Doesn't matter what the Brits say about running their own show. If you want the President of the United States at your party, the Secret Service tells you how things are going to be. You're going to have a tent on the side of your house, whether you like it or not. And the president is not going to say the others can't use it. He's not going to say, sorry guys, but you have to go to the tradesmen's entrance."

"They don't all have their own armored limousines."

"Doesn't really matter. A couple of Mercedes sedans would work. With dark windows. Which one is the prime minister in? Which one has the aides and the staffers? It's the same principle as the tent."

"So what are you saying?"

"If I'm John Kott, I'm not liking it. Or William Carson. Against me I've got obvious and infallible security precautions that will inevitably be used, and a low-built environment, and a very flat trajectory, and prime firing positions numbered only in the low hundreds. I mean, if the Brits broke open the overtime

budget they could put a copper in every single bedroom."

"You think an attack is not possible?"

"Where could it be? The limousine drives into the
tent."

She said, "You're forgetting the photograph."

Chapter 26

I asked Casey Nice about the photograph, and she gave me a detailed explanation. She said like everything else to do with politics and diplomacy it was a bigger deal than it appeared to be. It was much more than a ritual formality. It was freighted with subtext. It was about image, and collegiality, and an opportunity for the little guys to stand next to the big guys, on an equal footing, literally. It was about status and worth and the newspapers back home. In other words it was about exposure, both metaphorical and real. An open-air background was considered important. It was about being seen out there in the world with your peers, talking, joking, joshing, rubbing shoulders, doing deals, being just as important as everyone else.

And Nice said they would all be outside for more than just the photograph. They would walk on the lawns from time to time, in twos and threes. If the guy from Italy had a problem about the debt or the Euro, he had to be seen strolling with the German, deep in private conversation. Maybe they would only be talking about their kids or soccer, but the image would count in Rome. Likewise our president would be seen with the Russian guy, and the British guy and the French guy would get together, and the Japanese guy would talk to the Canadian. The potential combinations and recombinations were endless. Plus they all got on each other's nerves on a regular basis, and some were still secret smokers, so breaks were always necessary.

Nice said, "Kott and Carson are going to have visible targets, believe me."

I asked, "Is there an option to cancel the meeting?"

She said, "No."

Through the steamy cafe window I saw a black panel van pull up outside our hotel.

I asked, "Can't the photograph be taken inside?"

She said, "Theoretically, but not under these circumstances."

"Reasonable prudence is not acceptable?"

"Not if it looks like cowardice."

"That's crazy."

"That's politics. The world needs to see them taking care of business. And some of them have elections coming up. This kind of coverage is important."

Across the street the black panel van waited at the curb. No one got out. No one got in.

I said, "What about if it's raining?"

She said, "They'll wait until it stops."

"It might never stop. This is England."

"It's not raining now. Want me to look up the weather report?"

I shook my head. I said, "Hope for the best, plan for the worst. Is the outside location for the photograph fixed in advance?"

She said, "The back patio. There are shallow steps. The short guys like to use them."

"The back of the house faces the highway. Better than facing the city."

"Plenty of structures either side."

"Are they using bulletproof glass?"

"No point," she said. "Those panels work with one guy at a microphone. They don't work with eight people milling around."

I nodded. I pictured the eight people in my mind, milling around. Presumably they would come out of some kind of a patio door, all of them faking bewilderment at the way they had so suddenly to pivot between high-minded seriousness and the sordid demands of the press. *Gosh, really? We have to do this now? Well, let's be quick about it and get back to work.* So there would be plenty of faux-sheepish grins, and plenty of good-natured jostling for the back of the line. Which would all take place within a very tight little group, I guessed, because of the demands of collegiality and equality and reflected glory. Certainly none of them would want to get separated. A leaked picture with a group of seven on one side of the frame and a lone figure on the other wouldn't look good. The headlines back home would write themselves. *Out of touch, ignored, shunned, aloof, doesn't play well with others.*

So they would stay tight, and then when they figured the news outlets had enough goofy stuff in the can, they would line up on the steps, and they would puff out their chests, and they would stand absolutely still.

With no blindfolds.

Across the street the black panel van was still there.

I said, "How are you doing with the pills?"

She said, "I still have five."

"So you're feeling OK?"

She nodded. "Pretty good."

"Because the brief is mastered, and our initial execution has been satisfactory?"

"Because I can see a way through this now. I feel like the problem is narrowing itself down. Kott and Carson will want to see the back patio, and the back lawn, maybe. Which takes about sixty percent of the buildings right out of the picture. We know where we'll find them. Roughly, I mean. Ballpark, at least."

Across the street the black panel van was still there.

I said, "Suppose we hit a roadblock along the way?"

She said, "What kind?"

"Something unexpected. Will you be OK?"

"I think that would depend."

"On what?"

She was quiet for a long moment. She was giving the question her serious attention. She said, "I would be OK if it didn't knock us off our stride."

"You mean, if we get a problem, we should deal with it fast and decisively?"

"Yes," she said. "If it's a roadblock, we have to

get through it and keep on going. We can't afford to get sidetracked. I can see a way through now, and I don't want it to close up again."

The black panel van was still there.

"OK," I said. "Let's go back to the hotel."

Chapter 27

The van at the curb was facing away from us as we walked toward it. It was about the size of a small SUV, and about the same shape, but it was all sheet metal at the back. A windshield, and a driver's window, and a passenger's window, and nothing else. It was painted black, with no writing on it, as far as I could see. And it was very clean. It was waxed and polished, like a mirror. Like the SEAL car in Seattle. Which was a good question, right there. Who uses large black vehicles and keeps them immaculately clean? Only two answers. Limousine companies, and law enforcement. And limousine companies didn't use panel vans. Small buses, maybe, but passengers like windows.

Except this was London, and what did I know? Maybe a cultural revolution was underway, involving a sudden new enthusiasm for automotive cleanliness. Maybe it would hit America six months later, like Beatlemania. Although every other vehicle I had seen was filthy.

Casey Nice said, "Are they cops?"

I said, "I'm sure they'll make it clear, one way or the other."

We crossed the street and we walked on, toward the van, all the way, and the front doors opened, both together, fast and smooth, unlatched when we were close, and then opened when we were closer still. Two guys climbed out. The one on the sidewalk pivoted slowly, while his partner hustled around the hood. Same sweep, different speeds. Some kind of a synchronized move, no doubt perfected by long practice.

Both guys were in dark suits under black raincoats. Both were white. Or pink, to be accurate. Chapped, like they'd had a long hard winter. Both were shorter than me, but not much lighter. Both had big, knuckley hands, and cords of muscle in their necks.

They blocked our way.

"Help you?" I said, like the neighbor in Arkansas.

The guy who had taken the shorter pivot said, "I'm going to put my hand in my pocket very slowly and show you a government identification document. Do you understand?"

Which was a neat trick, potentially, in that we would be staring at the guy's moving hand, inching its way into his pocket, pausing there, inching back out, and meanwhile the other guy could have been doing anything at all. He could have been assembling a brand new Heckler and Koch from a kit of parts.

But then, if they thought they needed weapons, they would have come out of the van holding them.

I said, "I understand."

The guy glanced at Casey Nice and said, "Miss?"

She said, "Go ahead."

So he did, slowly, and he came out with a leather ID wallet. It was black, and it looked old and worn. He opened it, finger and thumb. It had two plastic windows, a little yellowed, face to face. Behind one was a version of the Metropolitan Police badge. Sculpted and shiny and very impressive on their pointed helmets, not so much when printed on paper. Behind the other plastic window was an ID card.

The guy held out the wallet.

His thumb was over the picture.

I said, "Your thumb is over the picture."

"I'm sorry," he said.

He moved his thumb off the picture.

The picture was him.

Above his face was printed: *Metropolitan Police.*

He said, "We need to ask you some questions."

I said, "What questions?"

"We need you to get in the van."

"Where will you sit?"

The guy missed a beat, and said, "We need you to get in the back of the van."

I said, "I don't like the dark."

"There's a wire screen at the front. You'll get plenty of light."

"OK," I said.

Which seemed to surprise him a little. He missed another beat. Then he nodded and stepped forward, and his partner came with him, and we stepped backward, and half turned, and stepped off the curb into the road, and then we hung back and waited politely for one of them to open the doors.

The one who had hustled around the hood did it, first by turning the handle, then by pulling the right-hand panel, and propping it, then by pulling the left-hand panel, and propping it, too, both doors standing open more than ninety degrees, so that together they made a chute. The load area inside was completely empty, and completely unmarked, and every bit as clean as the outside. All bare metal, all painted black, all waxed and polished. The interior walls were stamped and pressed for strength. The floor was ribbed. And as promised there was a thick wire grille welded full-width and full-height behind the passenger compartment.

There were no handles on the inside of the doors.

The guy turned back from the left-hand door, coming up a little, because he had stooped to operate the prop, and I launched off my back foot and jerked at the waist and smashed my elbow into the bridge of his nose, a clubbing blow, slightly downward. His knees crumpled and his head snapped back and bounced off the door with a metallic boom, but I didn't see what happened to him next, because by that point I had already twisted counterclockwise and knocked Casey Nice out of the way and launched the same elbow at the first guy, who was a big strong man, but clearly not much of a fighter. Maybe he had gotten too comfortable with getting by on appearance and reputation alone. Maybe it was years since he had been involved in an actual scuffle. The only way to deal with a sudden incoming elbow was to twist and drive forward and take it on the meat of the upper arm, which is always painful and sometimes numbing, but generally you stay on your feet. But the guy went the other way. He chose the wrong option. He reared up and back, chin high, hoping to dodge the blow, which didn't work at all, and never really could. The elbow caught him full in the throat, perfectly horizontal, like an iron bar moving close to thirty miles an hour. Speed matters, like in baseball and busting down doors. And the human throat is full of all kinds of vulnerable gristle and small bones. I felt my elbow crush a lot of it, and then I whipped back to the other guy, but he didn't need a follow-up question. He was sitting on his ass, propped against the open door, blood streaming from his nose, out for an eight count. So I turned back again and saw the guy I had hit in the throat flat on his back in the gutter. He was whooping and wheezing and pawing at his windpipe.

I knelt next to him and patted him down. No gun. No knife. I went back to the guy on his ass. No gun. No knife. Not in broad daylight, I guessed. Not in London.

Casey Nice staggered back into view. She looked very pale. She said, "What the hell are you doing?"

I said, "Talk later. We're in public here. Get them in the van first."

The guy in the gutter was barely breathing. I bunched the front of his raincoat in my hands and lifted him up and turned him around and got his head and shoulders into the load space, and then I shoveled the rest of him inside, and then I did the same thing with the other guy, but with his collar from behind, and the back of his belt, because he was bleeding badly all down his front, and I didn't want to get marked or sticky. I kicked the props and closed the doors on them, and checked the handle.

Secure.

Casey Nice said, "Why did you do that?"

I said, "You didn't want to be sidetracked."

"They're *cops,* for God's sake."

"Get in the front. We need to dump this thing somewhere."

"You're crazy."

I looked all around, and saw some cars and people, but they all seemed to be going about their normal business. No big crowd was gathering. No one was standing with a flat hand over an open mouth, or fumbling for a cell phone. We were being ignored. Almost consciously. The same the world over. People look away.

I said, "You told me if we get a problem, we should deal with it fast and decisively."

I stepped back up on the sidewalk and tracked around to the driver's door. I got in and pushed the seat back as far as it would go, which wasn't very far, because of the wire screen. I was going to be driving with my knees up around my ears, on the left side of the road, with a stick shift and a diesel engine, none of which I was used to.

Casey Nice got in next to me. She was still pale. The key was still in the ignition. I started the motor and pressed the clutch and waggled the stick. There seemed to be a whole lot of gears in there. At least seven of them, including reverse. I took an educated guess and shoved the stick left, and up, and looked for the stalk that would work the turn signals.

Casey Nice said, "I meant different problems than cops."

I said, "Cops are the same problem as anything else. Worse, in fact. They can take us back to the airport in handcuffs. No one else can do that."

"Which they will now. For sure. They'll hunt us down with a vengeance. You just assaulted two police officers. We're on the run, as of this minute. You just made things a thousand times harder. A million times harder. You just made things impossible."

I clicked the turn signal and checked the door mirror. I moved off, with a lurch, because of a clumsy left foot.

I said, "Except they weren't police officers."

I changed gear, once, twice, three times, a little smoother as I went along, and I got straight and centered in the left-hand lane.

She said, "We saw his badge."

"I bet it was done on a home computer."

"You *bet*? What does that even mean? You're going to assault a hundred cops just in case one of them isn't?"

I changed gear again and sped up a little, to blend in.

I said, "No cop on earth would call his badge a government identification document. Cops don't work for the government. Not in their minds. They work for their department. For each other. For the whole worldwide brotherhood. For the city, just maybe, at the very best. But not the government. They hate the government. The government is their worst enemy, at every level. National, county, local, no one understands cops and everyone makes their lives more and more miserable with an endless stream of bullshit. A cop wouldn't use the word."

"This is a different country."

"Cops are the same the world over. I know, because I was one, and I met plenty of others. Including here. This is not a different country when it comes to cops."

"Maybe that's what they call their ID here."

"I think they call it a warrant card."

"Which he knew we wouldn't understand. So he used different words."

"He would have said, I'm a police officer, and I'm going to put my hand in my pocket very slowly and show you ID. Or my ID. Or identification. Or credentials. Or something. But the word *police* would have been in there somewhere, for damn sure, and the word *government* would not have been, equally for damn sure."

She said nothing for a minute, and then she bagged out her seat belt and squirmed around and knelt up for a look through the grille.

She said, "Reacher, one of them isn't breathing."

Chapter 28

I glanced back, but I couldn't keep my eyes off the road long enough to be sure. Maybe he was just breathing very slowly. Casey Nice said, "Reacher, you have to do something."

I said, "What am I, a doctor?"

"We have to find a hospital."

"Hospitals have the cops on speed dial."

"We could dump the truck at the door, and run."

I drove on, with no real idea where I was headed, taking the easy option at every junction, going with the flow, on roads that seemed endlessly long but never straight. I guessed we were aiming basically north, away from the river. I guessed Romford was somewhere on our right. We passed all kinds of places, including every kind of no-name fast food, kebabs, fried chicken, pizza, hamburgers, and every kind of insurance bureau, and phone shops, and carpet shops. No hospitals. If the guy had stopped breathing, he had died minutes ago.

I pulled off into a lumpy blacktop rectangle boxed

in on two sides by two rows of single-car garages. The space between them was empty, but for a broken and rusted bicycle. No people. No activity. I stopped the van and fumbled the shift into neutral and turned around.

And looked.

And waited.

The guy wasn't breathing.

The other guy was staring at me. The bottom part of his face was a mask of red. The top part was pale. Now he *was* white. His nose was badly busted. His eyes were wide open. I said to him, "I'm going to come around and open up. You mess with me in any way at all, I'll do to you what I did to him."

He didn't answer.

I said, "Do you understand?"

He said, "Yes."

Little bubbles of blood formed at the corners of his mouth.

I opened the door and climbed out and walked around. Casey Nice did the same thing on her side. I turned the rear handle and opened up. The guy who was breathing was on the left, and the guy who wasn't was on the right. I put my arm in, as a test. No reaction. So I found a wrist on the right and checked for a pulse.

Nothing there.

I leaned right in and knelt up and felt for the neck. The guy was still warm. I pulled his collar down a little and got my fingers in behind the point of his jaw. I kept them there a good long time, just in case. I looked here and there, waiting. The guy had a twice-pierced ear. And a small tattoo on his neck, just peeking out from under his collar. It looked like a leaf twisting in the wind.

He was dead.

I said, "We should search his pockets. We should search both of them."

I stepped sideways, to start in on the live guy.

She said, "I can't do that."

I said, "Do what?"

"Search a dead man."

"Why not?"

"Too creepy."

"Want to swap?"

"Could you do both?"

"Sure," I said. So I did. The live guy had suspiciously little in his pockets. And what he had was a little suspicious. By the time I had finished with his pants I was sure he wasn't a cop. He had too much cash money, for one thing. Hundreds and hundreds of British pounds, maybe even thousands, in a huge greasy roll. Cops are public servants, which doesn't make them paupers, but they live lives of payments and budgets and credit cards bending under the strain. Added to which the guy had no communication device. Nothing at all. Nowhere. No cell phone, no radio. Which was unthinkable, for a cop during work hours.

I kept his money and passed his ID wallet to Nice and said, "Check it out."

Then I started in on the dead guy, and came away with an identical haul. Cash money, and an ID wallet. I kept the money and gave the wallet to Nice. She had the first one in pieces. She said, "I guess you were right.

This is phony. The plastic is deliberately scratched, and I think the yellowing is a highlighter pen. The ID card is a Word document, and the shield is a low-resolution image printed off a web site, I imagine."

I looked back at the dead guy's tattoo. Maybe it wasn't a twisted leaf. Because why would a big tough guy want a twisted leaf? Or any kind of a leaf? Unless he was a conservationist, which I was sure he wasn't.

Maybe it was something else.

I said, "Watch this."

I leaned in and untied the guy's tie, and snaked it out of his collar, and ripped open the first four buttons on his shirt, and folded it back like a guy at a disco way back in the day.

The tattoo was not a leaf. It was a curlicue, a little decorative flourish adorning the top left corner of a letter of the alphabet, a capital, which started the first word of a two-word name or label, written in a curve high on his chest, where a woman would wear a necklace.

Romford Boys.

"In case they go to prison," I said. "The other guys leave them alone."

I closed the doors again and checked the handle.

Secure.

Casey Nice said nothing.

"What?" I said.

"It was too big of a risk. Suppose you were wrong? It was only words."

"It was people looking away. Because they know what's good for them. Maybe they're used to it. Maybe those black vans mean only one thing in that neighborhood. Maybe that's how people disappear, never to be seen again."

She said nothing.

"And there were only two of them. If we were being chased up as unacknowledged foreign assets, they'd have given the job to Special Branch, who need to justify their enormous budget, plus they love drama anyway, so they'd have brought half a dozen SWAT teams, with tear gas. We'd have been outnumbered fifty to one. It would have been a war zone. It's not like the movies anymore. They don't walk around town wearing trench coats."

"When did you know?"

"They should have used a sedan. And they should have said they were MI5. You expect all kinds of bullshit from those guys."

We got back in the front of the van and I leaned over and checked the glove box. There were two cell phones in there, both pre-paid burners with a set number of pre-paid minutes, both still in their drugstore packaging, effectively untraceable if bought with cash, which I was sure they had been. Diligent security, overall. Clearly the Romford Boys ran a tight ship. Any kind of operation was a point of vulnerability. Even picking up two unsuspecting strangers outside a cheap hotel. Anything could have happened. We might have struggled, and an unbribed cop might have driven by, at exactly the wrong moment. Hence no guns, and no knives, and no used phones. Less latitude for the prosecutor, less data for the files.

I waggled the stick, left, and up, and bumped across the blacktop, back to the road.

* * *

We drove south a mile, and then turned east for Romford. I like trash talk as much as the next guy, and I wanted to find the best place for a statement. I wanted the van found after a day of worry, and I wanted to see who did the finding, and I wanted to see it from a safe and secure location. So we put those three moving parts in play and cruised around until we found a spot that checked the boxes. Which was a cracked concrete parking lot behind a small supermarket. In turn behind the lot was the back of a guest house. The guest house was carved out of two old townhouses made into one, and it had plenty of windows. Casey Nice got a map on her phone and checked the area. It was satisfactory. The guest house was on a major north-south road, and there were turns east and west close by.

She said, "But they'll have eyes in there, surely. Obviously they did in the minicab company. In exchange for a discount on their protection money, probably. Maybe a big discount. The guy who took us to Wallace Court must have phoned it in immediately."

"Because Wallace Court was on their radar," I said. "This place isn't. And they think they've got us now, anyway. They won't start looking again until they find this van. So we're OK for the time being."

We circled once more and pulled up a hundred yards short of the parking lot entrance. I told Casey Nice I would meet her on the corner. She said, "There might be a camera in the parking lot."

I said, "I'll keep my head down."

"Not enough. You're very distinctive."

"We'll be out of the country before they look at the tapes."

She didn't answer. Just got out and walked away. I knew exactly what we had touched, and I wiped it all with the dead guy's tie, exterior handles, interior handles, steering wheel, shifter, column stalks, seat latch, seat belt latch, glove box latch. I dumped the tie in the gutter and shrugged my coat down off my shoulders and pulled the sleeves down over my hands, and I drove like that through the last short stretch and parked in a random slot near the supermarket's loading door. I stopped the engine, and pulled the key, and blipped the lock, and walked away, bent at the neck and staring at the concrete beneath my feet.

Nice was waiting on the corner, and we walked another block and turned again, on a road that was wider and busier than most, with four lanes, with buses and trucks and bumper-to-bumper traffic. We found the guest house's front door, exactly where it should have been. We went in, and found a lobby that might have been fresh and clean about thirty years ago, but wasn't anymore. We asked for a room on the back. We said we were worried about noise from the road. We said the airline had lost our bags, and was supposed to bring them over. I paid in cash from the dead guy's roll, and we got a big brass key, and we headed upstairs.

The room was cold, and a little damp, but the window was big, and we got an excellent view. The lot was right there, about forty-five degrees below us. The van was clearly visible, its back to us. Casey Nice sat on the bed, and I used a chair from a dressing table, set far from the window. I didn't want someone to glance up and see two pale ovals pressed against the glass. Always better to be well back in the dark, like John Kott in Paris, on the dining room table.

We waited, like I had many times before. Waiting was a big part of law enforcement, and a big part of army life generally. *Long slow periods of nothing much, with occasional bursts of something.* I was good at it, and Casey Nice turned out to be good at it, too. She stayed awake, which was the main thing. She rested easy, not staring intently, but keeping her gaze where she would notice movement. At one point she used the bathroom, and I wondered about pills, but I didn't say anything.

Then she asked the inevitable question. She said, "Do you feel bad about the guy?"

I said, "What guy?"

"The guy who died."

"You mean the guy I killed in cold blood?"

"I suppose."

"Some tough guy he was."

"Do you feel bad?"

"No," I said.

"Really?"

"Do you?"

"A little."

"You didn't do anything to him."

"Even so."

"He had a choice," I said. "He could have spent his days helping old ladies across the street. He could have volunteered in the library. I expect they have a library here. He could have raised funds for Africa, or wherever they need funds these days. He could have done a whole lot of good things. But he didn't. He chose not to. He chose to spend his days extorting money and hurting people. Then finally he opened the wrong door, and what came out at him was his problem, not mine. Plus he was useless. A waste of good food. Too stupid to live."

"Stupidity isn't a capital crime. And there's no death penalty here, anyway."

"There is now."

She didn't reply to that, and we lapsed back into silence. The afternoon light faded, and a yellow vapor lamp came on in the parking lot below us. It was up on a tall pole, and it caught most of the black panel van. Other cars came and parked and went away again. Every one of their drivers glanced at the van, and then looked away. At first I thought it was because they must know whose van it was, and were therefore unsettled. Then I realized there must be another reason.

I said, "The other guy must be banging and hollering."

Which was a mistake on my part. I should have told him not to. Or made sure he couldn't. It was going to screw up my time line. I wasn't going to drop a day of worry on them. Couple hours, at most. Although initially there seemed to be a marked lack of enthusiasm among the population of Romford for playing the Good Samaritan. No one did a damn thing for the guy. They all just glanced away and got out of the lot as fast as they could. Proof once again, I supposed, that tyrants inspire no love or loyalty.

Casey Nice said, "I'm hungry."

I said, "I'm sure there's food on the block. Kebabs, fried chicken, pizza, hamburgers, whatever you want. This place seems to be the fast food capital of the world."

"Should we get something?"

"Eat when you can. That's the golden rule."

"Are you hungry?"

"A little."

"What would you prefer?"

"Pizza," I said. "Plain cheese. Smaller chance of rats and pigeons among the ingredients. Or cats and dogs."

"Something to drink?"

"Whatever was made in a factory and comes in a sealed container."

"Will I be safe?"

"Depends what you order."

"I mean, walking around here."

"You worried about getting mugged?"

"I'm worried about getting spotted by a Romford Boy."

"They aren't looking for us. They think they've got us."

"There's a difference between actively looking for us and accidentally spotting us."

"If you had seven words to describe yourself, what would you say?"

"You mean physically or psychologically?"

"I mean, suppose you were the minicab driver, diming us out."

"I'm not sure."

"Female, average height, pony tail, brown leather jacket. That's what he said. Nothing you can do about your height or your gender, but you can take out your pony tail and lose your jacket. Then you're just a twenty-something woman in jeans and a T-shirt. Of which there are a hundred thousand around here. Safe as houses."

So she reached up behind her and pulled out whatever elastic band she had in there, and she shook her head, and her hair fell loose. She slipped the jacket off one shoulder, and then the other, and she pulled it down over her arms, and she laid it on the bed, and she turned back to face me.

Did she look like Dominique Kohl? Yes and no. Not really, in that she shaded toward the Scandinavian end of the gene pool, and Kohl was closer to the Mediterranean. Kohl had darker skin, and darker hair, and darker eyes. The weeks I had known her had been exceptionally hot, even for D.C. in the summer, and she had gotten browner and dustier as the days went by. She had worn shorts most of the time, and a T-shirt. And it was the T-shirt that connected her to Nice. Kohl's had been olive green, and Nice's was white, but under those flimsy garments were young, fit women in the peak of condition, lean, smooth, somehow flexible and fluent and elastic, somehow identical. Outwardly, at least. Inwardly was different. Where Nice was diffident, Kohl had been bolder, completely sure of her capabilities, notably self-confident, absolutely ready to beat the world.

It hadn't saved her.

I said, "Take care."

Nice said, "I'll be back in ten."

She left, and I heard her footsteps fade in the hallway. I ducked away from the window for a second and put my hand in her jacket pocket. I pulled out the orange plastic bottle.

She had three pills left.

Chapter 29

I sat alone and watched the little supermarket's parking lot, and I saw the same things repeated over and over again. Drivers would park their cars, and get out, and glance at the black van, suddenly startled and unsure, and then they would avert their eyes and hustle inside the store. They would come out again minutes later and drive away as fast as they could.

Ten minutes passed, and Casey Nice didn't come back.

The sky behind the light on the pole went full dark, and a little night mist came down, and a scrim of dew formed on the black van, which rocked and bounced from time to time. The live guy inside must have been getting desperate. Maybe he needed the bathroom.

Fifteen minutes gone, and Casey Nice didn't come back.

Then finally a driver parked his car, and got out, and glanced at the black van, and didn't walk away. He was a young guy, maybe twenty, with a pudding-bowl haircut all slicked down with grease. He took a cautious step toward the van and cocked his head and listened. He took another step and peered in through the driver's window, from the side, and then he craned his neck and peered in through the windshield, from the front.

He took his cell phone out of his pocket. Contract labor, maybe, anxious to prove his worth. He listened again, presumably to the live guy inside, dictating a number, and he dialed.

Behind me a key turned in the lock and Casey Nice walked in the room. She had two stacked pizza boxes balanced on spread fingers, and a thin plastic bag in her other hand, with wet soda cans in it.

"OK?" I said.

She said, "So far so good."

I nodded toward the window. "Some kid just made a call."

She put our dinner on the dressing table and took a look. The young guy was talking on his phone. He bent down and read out the van's license plate. Then he held the phone away from his mouth, and shouted a question through the seal between the driver's door and the pillar, and then he put his ear close to the same crack and listened to the answer. The live guy's name, presumably, which the young guy repeated into his phone.

Casey Nice asked, "Why doesn't he break the window or force the door?"

I said, "You think he knows how?"

"I'm sure he does. Looking at him, I mean. Not that I should rely on stereotypes."

"I'm guessing the guy on the phone is telling him not to. This is a hard world. These are not conquering heroes. They screwed up. They're not worth damaging a vehicle for. Someone will bring a spare key."

"How soon?"

"Five minutes," I said. "Maybe ten. Quick enough, anyway. They don't care about their guys, but they'll want to hear the story."

I got up off my chair and opened a pizza box. Plain cheese, white dough, a little bubbled and blackened here and there by the oven, and smaller than the giant hubcaps sold in America. I said, "Thank you for my dinner," like my mother had taught me to.

She said, "You're very welcome," and she took hers, and we both ate a slice. The soda was Coke, and it was ice cold. In the lot below us the young guy was off the phone, stumping around, waiting. For congratulations, without a doubt. Definitely contract labor, racking up the bonus points.

Casey Nice's phone dinged, like a tiny bell.

"Incoming text," she said. She checked. "From General O'Day. He wants to know why we're static."

I said, "Tell him we're resting."

"He knows we're not at our hotel. Because of the GPS."

"Tell him we're at the movies. Or the theater. Or in a museum. Tell him we're furthering our cultural education. Or getting our nails done. Tell him we're at the spa."

"He knows we're not. He'll have checked Google Maps, surely. Street View, probably. He knows where we are."

"Then why ask?"

"He wants to know why we're not mobile."

"Tell him to relax. Micromanaging from three thousand miles away is pointless."

"I can't. He's updating us, and I'm supposed to update him. That's the only way this thing is going to work."

I looked down at the scene below. No change. The van, inert. The kid, waiting. I said, "OK, tell him we're acting on Shoemaker's suggestion. Tell him we're attempting contact with the outer cordon."

"I'll have to tell him how, I'm afraid. As in, not with a phony business proposal."

"Go ahead. He won't mind."

"He might. They were worried about you."

"Scarangello was. Shoemaker might have been. But O'Day won't get all bent out of shape."

"Are you sure?"

"Try it," I said. "Tell him exactly what happened."

So she swiped and dabbed at her screen with dancing thumbs and I glanced back at what was happening out the window. Which wasn't much. The light, the mist, the van, the kid. I looked away again and saw her finish up and put her phone on the bed and take a second slice of pizza. I chewed cheese and sipped Coke and waited. Below us the young guy was watching the road, and ducking back to the van every few minutes, laying his hand on it and calling through the door seal, with reassurances, probably. *Yes, I called, they said they were coming, they'll be here in a minute.*

Nice's phone dinged again. O'Day's reply. She

checked it twice and told me, "He sends his sincere congratulations and says keep it up."

I nodded. "Human life means nothing to him. All he cares about is the result."

Nice didn't reply.

I said, "Ask him for the intel he got from MI5, about these Romford people. Pictures, histories, rap sheets, everything he's got. We should know exactly who we're dealing with here."

She started texting again. Below us the young guy was talking through the door seal again. His body language was placatory. He was squirming and patting the air and glancing hopefully toward the road. *They're coming, I promise.*

And then they came.

Two cars drove into the lot, both of them black, both with dark windows, the first a four-door Jaguar sedan, the second a big two-door coupe, long and low and imposing. A Bentley, I thought. They came in fast and slammed to a stop, right in the middle of the space. All four of the Jaguar's doors opened wide and four men climbed out, all of them white, all of them in dark suits. They formed up like a perimeter, facing outward, heads up, hands loose by their sides. The kid with the greasy hair hung back. The Bentley's driver got out. He was another guy in a suit, just like the first four. He checked all around, left, right, front, rear, and then he walked a wide circle to the passenger door and opened it, like a chauffeur should.

And a giant climbed out.

He led with a bent head and a bent back, folded at the waist, folded at the knees, and then he straightened up in stages, like a complex mechanism, like a child's toy that starts out as a squat dump truck and then clicks open, one component after another, to reveal an action figure. He was huge. His arms were longer than most people's legs, and his hands were bigger than shovels, and his torso was the size of an oil drum, tightly encased in a tubular three-button suit coat that would have been ankle-length on an average human. His feet were the size of river barges, and his neck was a foot wide, and his shoulders were a yard wide, and his head was bigger than a basketball. He had big ears sticking straight out, and an overhanging brow, and pronounced cheekbones, and tiny eyes buried deep, and a receding simian chin. He looked like a Neanderthal waxwork in a natural history museum, except that he was pale and sandy, not dark, and he was at least twice the size of any ancient hominid. He could have been seven feet tall, and three hundred pounds. Maybe more. He moved with a kind of loose-limbed rawboned ranginess, four or five feet with a single enormous stride, his huge shoulders rolling, his immense hands swinging free.

Casey Nice said, "Jesus Christ."

"I don't think so," I said. "No beard. No sandals."

The guy stepped up close to the back of the van, two paces, where a normal guy might have needed four, and he flapped his hand toward it, a gesture like a big white swan taking off, and his chauffeur dug in a pocket and came out with a key. The big guy stood back a pace, four feet right there, and the chauffeur jammed the key in the lock and turned it and pulled the doors, first the right, and then the left. The four guys from the Jaguar shifted position, moving the perimeter tighter, turning to face inward, making a half-circle, enclosing the space like bystanders watching a street fight.

They all waited.

The live guy scrambled out, sliding on his front, feet first, slow and stiff and hurting. He steadied himself against the lip of the load floor, and straightened up, and turned around to face the music. The gush of blood down his front looked black in the vapor light. His skin looked yellow. The giant stepped forward again and stared past him into the dark interior. At that point I couldn't see his face, but he seemed to ask a short question. Probably: *What the hell happened?*

The live guy didn't really answer. He just shook his head and breathed out and held his hands out from his sides, palms upward, like a helpless shrug. The question was repeated. This time the live guy answered, just a mumble, his bloodied mouth barely moving at all, three or four syllables, nothing more. Maybe *he jumped us,* or *they jumped us,* or *they got away,* or *we didn't get 'em.*

The giant processed the information, his huge head going down a degree, then coming back up, as if swallowing the bad news, physically. He was quiet for a minute. Then he started talking again, his body language exaggeratedly amiable, which meant he had to be taunting the guy, because there was no more pertinent information to be gotten. *There were two of you, right? And two of them? One of which was a girl?*

Was it her who hit you? And so on and so forth, sarcastic and humiliating. From my angle I could see the live guy's face, which was looking more and more miserable. And apprehensive. And terrified. As if he knew what was coming.

And then it came.

The giant moved with astonishing speed for one so big. His right hand bunched into a fist the size of a bowling ball, and his waist and his shoulders twitched, and he smashed a straight drive into the center of the live guy's ruined face, and the guy smashed backward against the truck's left-hand door, and bounced off, and went straight down on the concrete, face first.

"Charming," I said. "Not the kind of leadership skills they teach you at West Point."

The guy on the ground lay still. The kid with the greasy hair stared at him, with his mouth wide open. Casey Nice stared, too, with her mouth open. Then her phone dinged again. Another text. She looked away from the window. She said, "General O'Day is e-mailing the data from MI5. We should have it in a minute." She swiped to another screen and waited.

Below us the giant stood still for a second, and then he jerked his enormous head toward the Bentley, and his chauffeur scurried back and held the door. The big guy strode over and lined himself up and started re-folding himself to fit. The action figure became a dump truck again. He bent his knees, and bent at his waist, and tucked in his elbows, and hunched his shoulders, and ducked his head, and backed butt-first into his seat. The chauffeur closed the door on him, and looped around the hood to his own place.

The car backed up and turned around and drove away.

Two guys got back in the Jaguar and followed the Bentley, and the other two rolled the live guy over, and picked him up off the concrete, armpits and knees, and shoved him back in the rear of the van. They closed the doors on him again, and locked the handle, and pulled the key. One of them came out with a decent-sized pink banknote, fifty British pounds, I thought, and gave it to the kid. Then they got in the front of the van together and backed up and turned and followed the Jaguar. The kid was left standing alone in the pool of light, holding the money, looking like he had wanted more, maybe a nod or a clap on the shoulder or a promise of future inclusion. He looked disappointed, as if by an anticlimax, as if he was thinking: *I could have gotten fifty lousy pounds by mugging an old lady.*

Casey Nice's phone made a different sound, like a tiny muted *clang.* She said, "The e-mail from General O'Day."

Which was blank except for a link to an attachment. She touched it and a dense document slid sideways into view. We sat together on the bed, thigh to thigh, and she held the phone between us, and we read. The header was a dry, academic, multi-line sentence about organized crime activity in and around Romford, Essex, written in a manner I presumed reflected the British clandestine services' house style. Very University of Cambridge. Like Yale, but different. Nothing like West Point. Nothing like the real world, either.

The opening paragraph was first a disclaimer, and then a reassurance. Nothing had been proved, and there were no criminal convictions, but all information contained therein was believed to be solid. It went on to say there was no proof and there had been no convictions because of presumed witness intimidation, and because of other factors that weren't exactly specified, which I took to mean bribery of local law enforcement officials.

The second paragraph opened with a bald statement that organized crime activity in Romford, Essex, was entirely dominated by a structured association of local inhabitants who had long been called the Romford Boys. The tone was slightly apologetic, as if University of Cambridge types were embarrassed to repeat a name that belonged so clearly on the street, rather than in the classroom. Then the paragraph continued with an overview of the Boys' activities, which, as O'Day had already told us, covered the importation and sale of illegal narcotics, and illegal firearms, and the control of prostitution, which involved human trafficking, and the operation of protection rackets, which were believed to extend through the majority of commercial enterprises in the locality, and loan sharking at fantastic rates of interest. The gross value of the activities was put as many tens of millions of British pounds annually.

The biographies started in the third paragraph.

The boss was one Charles Albert White, known as Charlie. He was seventy-seven years old, born on a local street, and educated at public expense until the age of fifteen. He had no third-party employment records, owned a home unencumbered by mortgages or other kinds of loans, and was married with four adult children, all of whom lived elsewhere in London and were believed to be uninvolved in their father's activities.

A clandestine surveillance shot laid into the document showed Charlie White to be a bulky, round-shouldered old man with sparse gray hair and a plain face dominated by a bulbous nose.

Below Charlie in the pecking order was a kind of executive council made up of three men, first Thomas Miller, known as Tommy, sixty-five years of age, and then William Thompson, known as Billy, sixty-four, and finally, a much younger man at just thirty-eight, was Joseph Green, known as Little Joey.

Little Joey was the giant. No question about it. His photo was cropped a whole inch longer than the others. He was listed as six feet eleven, and twenty-two stone, which as far as I understood foreign weights and measures came out to exactly three hundred and eight pounds. He was their enforcer. Again MI5 was scrupulous about mentioning the lack of proof or convictions, but Little Joey's swift rise to parity with men old enough to be his father could only be explained by extreme efficiency. He was in MI5's books for eleven certain homicides, and too many beatings to count. *Grievous bodily harm* was the legal phrase used, which seemed appropriate.

Casey Nice said, "Why do they call him little?"

"Because they're British," I said. "They're into irony. If they called him Big Joey, he'd be a dwarf."

She scrolled onward, but the document ended right

there. Little Joey was the last item. I said, "We need more than this. We need the spear carriers, and locations, and addresses. You better get back to O'Day."

"Now?"

"Sooner the better. Data is king. And get what he has about the Serbians in the west."

"Why?"

"We need guns. Elephant guns, for preference, having seen Little Joey in action. And I doubt if the Romford Boys will be keen to sell us any. So we need to make contact elsewhere."

"We don't have time for all of that now. This hotel is paying protection money, almost certainly. And we can be sure right about now the Romford Boys are starting to call around for information."

I nodded. "OK, finish your pizza and we'll move right along."

"I lost my appetite. We should get going immediately."

She closed the document and swiped her phone back to its home screen, as if to underline her point.

I said, "Where do you want to go?"

She said, "We can't go back to our own hotel. They were there once already. That's the first place they'll look."

"Your stuff is there."

She didn't reply.

I said, "We could risk five minutes. In and out, real quick, to get it."

"No," she said.

"Can you live without it?"

"You don't have stuff."

"I'm used to it."

"Maybe I could get used to it, too. The Sherlock Homeless method. I mean, how bad can it be? We could stop by somewhere and I could get a tooth-brush."

I said, "You never put on clean clothes in the morn-ing. That's about the worst of it."

"Right now that sounds better than the alternative."

"And no pajamas."

"I can live with that."

"OK," I said. "We'll head downtown. The center of London. The Ritz, maybe. Or the Savoy. We've got plenty of money, thanks to them. And they won't have eyes in places like that."

"How do we get there? We can't call a cab."

"We'll take the bus," I said. "I doubt if the London transportation system is paying protection money."

So we left the room, with nothing in our hands, and we dumped the key at the desk, and we let our-selves out into the night.

Chapter 30

There were big red buses running both ways on the road outside, and we elected to go south, aiming to change at the next big crossroads and head west for the center. All our money was in big bills, which we figured wouldn't be welcome on a bus, so we ducked into a convenience store and bought travel cards named after bivalve mollusks. Then we located the nearest bus stop and hung back in the shadows until we saw what we wanted lumbering through the traffic toward us. It was after seven in the evening, and I was tired, and Nice looked completely done in. She hadn't slept in about a day and a half.

The outer hinterland of London felt vast, and the bus was slow, so we took a chance and got out again back in Barking, where we knew we could get the subway, which we figured would be faster. We checked the map at the station and used the District Line, which had a stop at a place called St. James's Park, which sounded like it might be near some fancy places. Which it was. We came up into the night air and saw signs to Westminster Abbey in one direction and Buckingham Palace in the other. And there was a big hotel right across the street. Five stars. Not the Ritz, not the Savoy, but a shiny international chain that looked adequate in every respect.

We went in, and the guy at the check-in desk took a little advantage of our fatigue by claiming only top-tier rooms were available that night, at prices that would have rented a house with a pool for a month outside of Pope Field, but the Romford Boys were paying, so we didn't really care. I counted off the huge sum from one of the greasy rolls, and in return we got key cards and all kinds of information about room service and restaurants and club floors and business centers and wifi passwords. Casey Nice bought a toothbrush in the lobby shop, and we rode up in the elevator. I saw her to her door, and waited until it locked behind her, and then I continued on to my own room, which justified its top-tier status not by being notably large, but by having its bed more or less completely hidden under fat chintzy pillows. I swept them all to the floor, and threw my clothes after them, and climbed under the covers, and went straight to sleep.

I was woken up eleven hours later by Casey Nice on the room phone. She sounded bright and cheerful. Whether that was due to eleven hours of sleep or better living through chemistry, I didn't know. She said, "Do you want to get breakfast?"

The clock in my head was showing just after eight in the morning, and there was bright daylight outside my window. I said, "Sure, come knock on my door when you're ready."

Which she did, about ten minutes after I was showered and dressed. She was in the same outfit as the day before, obviously, but she didn't seem unduly perturbed by it. We rode down to the restaurant, and got a table for two in the far corner. The place was full of sleek types discussing agendas and doing deals, some of them face to face, some of them on cell phones. I ordered British food, heavy on fat and sugar, but with coffee, not tea. Casey Nice chose lighter fare, and laid her phone next to her napkin, for easy reference.

She said, "According to General O'Day, as of this morning neither MI5 nor the local police department know anything about a casualty among the Romford Boys. Seems like Charlie White is playing it close to his vest."

I nodded. Par for the course. Standard procedure. The dead guy would have gone into a car crusher in a back street or a pig trough in a local Essex farm about the same time I was going to sleep.

She said, "And General O'Day says so far six out of the eight nations have attempted undercover contact with the outer cordon, and they've all failed."

I nodded again. A no brainer. The Romford Boys would be erring on the side of caution. They would take the small risk of missing a genuine deal, in order to protect their mission.

She said, "We'll get a full roster of names later today. And locations, but that data is difficult. There are lots of potential locations, including remote rural places. Plus we assume by now they're already exploiting Karel Libor's infrastructure. Which would give them more options."

I nodded for a third time. Kott and Carson were needles in one of about a hundred unknown haystacks, and they would stay that way for the time being.

She said, "And the best approach to the Serbians is through a pawn shop in a place called Ealing. Which is an outer suburb, to the west, a little less than halfway back to the airport. I looked it up on the map."

"You've been busy. I hope you slept."

"I did," she said. "I feel great."

I didn't ask about pills.

She said, "You knew the minicab company was bent. Didn't you? Right at the beginning."

I said, "Educated guess."

"You used them to attract attention. Like having them pick us up at the hotel and take us to Wallace Court. Which was the plan you made on the plane. You decided to make the cordon come to us."

Which was giving me more credit than I was due. Largely because of the word *plan.* I said, "I wasn't sure what to expect. No one ever is. It's all about reacting."

She paused a beat. "Are you saying you don't have a plan?"

"I have an overall strategic objective."

"Which is what?"

"To get out of here before they check the tapes."

She said, "Let's go to Ealing."

We started back at the St. James's Park subway station, where the map showed us the same District Line we had come in on then continued westward, all the way to a station called Ealing Broadway, which Casey Nice's phone showed was the one we wanted, which we figured was extremely convenient. So we waited in the station, which was literally tubular, like the local name, the Tube, and we got on the train, and we settled in for the long journey. I said, "Talk to me."

She said, "What do you want me to say?"

"Tell me where you were born. Where you grew up. The name of your pony."

"I didn't have a pony."

"Did you have a dog?"

"Most of the time. Sometimes more than one."

"With names?"

"Why do you want to know?"

"I want to hear you say it."

She said, "I was born in downstate Illinois. I grew up in downstate Illinois. On a farm. The dogs were usually named after presidents from the Democratic party."

I said, "Where was I born?"

"West Berlin. You told that guy in Arkansas."

"Where did I grow up?"

"All over the world, according to your file."

"Could you tell that by the sound of my voice?"

"You sound like you don't really come from anywhere."

"Therefore you're going to do the talking in the pawn shop. Your accent is better than mine. Presumably these Serbian guys worry about entrapment, so any British accent would be an alarm bell. The person could be an undercover cop. Being foreign is better. And you sound really American. Assuming the Serbian ear can tell the difference."

"OK," she said, cheerful enough. Pills or no pills, she was doing fine so far.

We clattered onward, rocking a little with the motion, and then the train came out from under the ground and rode along on the surface, through the daylight, slow and stately, like any other local service. We got out at the Ealing Broadway terminal, which looked like any other regular aboveground railroad facility, and we stepped out to the street. Ealing looked like the places we had seen equally far to the east, once remote rural settlements, then swallowed up, and looking a little awkward about it. There was a long commercial strip, and some big public buildings, and some small parades of mom-and-pop stores, one of them with its window whitewashed over and a sign saying *Ealing Minicabs* on it, and right next to that was a place where either mom or pop or both were in the business of lending money against small and valuable securities, because there were iron bars on the windows and a sign saying *Ealing Cash Loans.* I had been expecting to see an arrangement of three golden spheres hanging on a black gallows, which I understood was the traditional British symbol for a pawn shop, but I had to make do with a small neon replica high in the window. Which was otherwise full of abandoned securities, some of them small, some of them valuable, some of them both, some of them neither.

"Ready?" I asked.

"As I'll ever be," she answered.

I opened the door, and let her step in past me, and I followed her into a place that looked nothing like it would in the movies. It was a bland, rectangular space, mostly dirty white, with laminate everywhere, and fluorescent tubes on the ceiling. Operationally it was laid out like a horseshoe, with waist-high counters running around three sides, with glass panels in the counters, showing artless displays inside, of yet more abandoned pledges.

There was a guy behind the counter, at the eleven o'clock position, a medium-size man maybe forty or fifty years old, very dark and unshaven, wearing a rust-colored sweater that must have been knitted with fat wooden needles. He was bent over, polishing something small, a bracelet maybe, with a rag held between his thumbs. He turned his head sideways, like a swimmer, and looked at us, in a way that was neither hostile nor interested. After a long minute we realized the stare was all the greeting we were going to get, so I hung back and Casey Nice stepped up, and she said, "Do you mind if I browse?"

Which focused all the guy's attention on her, because of the singular pronoun. *I*, not *we*. Clearly I was not a potential browser. I was nobody. Her driver, maybe. The guy behind the counter said nothing, but he nodded, a single upward jerk of his head, which because of his position came out sideways, which seemed appropriate in the low-ceilinged space, and partly encouraging, as if to say, *have at it,* but also partly discouraging, as if to say, *but what you see is all we got.*

I stood where I was, and Nice moved around, peering down, occasionally laying a fingertip on the glass, as if to isolate something for closer consideration, and then moving on, as yet unsatisfied. She went left to right, and then all the way back again, right to left, before straightening up and saying, "I don't see the kind of thing I'm looking for."

The guy in the sweater didn't answer.

She said, "My friend in Chicago told me this is where she came."

The guy in the sweater said, "For what?"

He wasn't English. That was for sure. He wasn't French or Dutch or German. Or Russian or Ukrainian or Polish. Serbian was entirely plausible.

Casey Nice said, "My friend had concerns about her personal safety. You know, in a foreign city for the first time. Without the precautions she would be legally entitled to take at home."

The guy in the sweater said, "Are you from America?"

"Yes, from Chicago."

"This is not a gymnasium, lady. We don't teach self-defense here."

"My friend said you have certain items for sale."

"You want a gold watch? Take two or three. Use them to bargain for your life."

"My friend didn't buy a watch."

"What did she buy?"

Nice put her hand out, low down, away from her side, slightly behind her. She clicked her fingers. My cue, I supposed. The driver. Or the help. Or the bagman. I stepped forward and took out the dead guy's cash roll, and held it lightly between thumb and index finger, and I tapped it end-on against the glass counter, and I held it there, upright, a fat greasy cylinder as big as a whisky glass, sour and dense with paper money. The guy took a good long look at it, and then he glanced at me, and then he turned back to Casey Nice.

He said, "Who is he?"

"My bodyguard," she said. "But he couldn't get his gun through the X-ray machine."

"There are laws here."

"There are laws everywhere. But the same thing gets past them all."

The guy looked back at the money.

He said, "Go wait in the minicab office. Next door. Someone will drive you."

"Drive me where?"

"We don't keep those items here. Too many police. They search us all the time. There are laws."

"Where do you keep them?"

The guy didn't answer. He took out his phone and dialed. He said a short sentence in a low tone and a fast foreign language. Not French or Dutch or German. Or Russian or Ukrainian or Polish. Serbian was still top of the list. The guy clicked off his call and shooed us away and said, "Go. They will drive you."

Chapter 31

We went, and they drove us. In the minicab office there was a guy already on his way around the
counter as we stepped inside. He was a version of
the guy in the pawn shop next door, a little younger,
a little straighter, a little heavier, but just as dark and
unshaven. A cousin, possibly, or just a guy from the
same little village in the old country. He showed us to
a Skoda sedan at the curb. A taxi. We got in the back,
he got in the front. Behind the wheel. He started it up,
and hit the gas, and we took off, and we heard the
click of the locks, as we passed a certain pre-set speed.

There was no point asking where we were going.
No way would we get an answer. A silent driver was
all part of the theater. Not that it mattered, anyway.
We knew generically, if not specifically. We were heading north, clearly. We didn't need the exact name of
the next-but-one overrun manor that lay in that direction, as long as we could picture it. Or picture part of
it. The important part. A storage unit, possibly, in a

bland and deserted business park on the dismal edge of a blighted part of town, or a barn-like structure on open land near a tangle of streets, or maybe a real barn, way out in the country, an hour or more north of town. Maybe we were in for a long trip. By the sound of it the Skoda had a diesel engine. Which would be economical. I leaned forward and checked the gas. It was full.

Outside the window the traffic was slow and the view stayed suburban for a good long time, and then I saw the arch of the big soccer stadium, which meant we had made it to a place called Wembley. Still heading north. But we didn't settle in for a long trip out of town. We turned pretty soon, and looped around a little, almost back on ourselves, and I saw a sign to a place called Wormwood Scrubs. Which was the name of a famous London prison, I thought, which gave me a clue about the kind of neighborhood we were headed for.

But we didn't go all the way to the prison. The streets we passed got a little darker and gloomier, but we turned off the main drag some ways short of the worst of it. We took a sudden left, and then another, through a gate in a brick wall, and then straight inside a large brick building that could have been a streetcar depot a hundred years before, or a factory, back when people made things in cities, other than noise and money. Now the place was being used as an auto repair shop, by the look of it specializing in fast and dirty fixes for the minicab trade. There were piles of part-worn tires, all gray and dusty, and every car I saw was similar to the Skoda we were riding in. Battered sedans everywhere, one of them up on a hoist, some of them with dented panels cut away, all of them presumably being brought back to whatever kind of code was demanded of telephone cars. *We could lose our license,* the guy in Barking had said, and I guessed there were more ways of losing it than just taking the wrong kind of booking.

We came to a stop in an empty workshop bay, as if we wanted our oil changed or our tracking checked. The sound of our engine was loud against the walls. Behind us a guy came out of the shadows and walked across the floor and hit a big green button. A chain-driven security shutter started clattering down over the opening we had driven through. The daylight was sliced thinner and thinner until it disappeared completely, leaving us with nothing but the dim glow of electric bulbs, in fixtures slung from the rafters high above our heads.

The guy who had driven us turned off the motor and climbed out, and he opened Casey Nice's door for her, either because of some old-world Balkan courtesy, or because he was impatient. Nice got out, and I got out on my side, and I stepped over tools and air hoses into clear space at the rear of the car. The guy who had closed the roller door came back, and two more guys came out of a boxed-off room, and we ended up in an informal little cluster, outnumbered four to two. They were all of a kind, not young, not old, all dark and unshaven, all a useful size, all silent and wary. There were no mechanics at work. No men with wrenches, in oil-stained overalls. Sent away, I guessed, temporarily, while the secret business was done.

One of the two from the boxed-off room seemed to be the main man. He looked us up and down, and said, "We need to know who you are."

Casey Nice said, "We're Americans, with money, who want to buy something from you."

"How much money do you have?"

"Enough, I'm sure."

"You're very trusting," the guy said. "To come here, I mean. We could take your money from you for nothing."

"You could try."

"Are you wearing wires?"

"No."

"Can you prove that?"

"You want me to take my shirt off? Because that ain't going to happen."

The guy said nothing in reply to that, but his mouth got a little wet and mobile, as if he thought making her take her shirt off would be an excellent idea. I said, "You can take a look at our passports, and you can figure out how likely it is that the British authorities would employ foreign citizens for an undercover sting, and then you can take a look at the money, and then we'll take a look at the merchandise. That's how it's going to go."

"Is it?" the guy said.

"Pretty much," I said.

He looked at me, hard, and I looked right back at him. The first staring contest of his day, probably, but one he was destined to lose. Staring isn't difficult. I can do it all day long. Without blinking, if I want to, which is sometimes painful, but always useful. The trick is to not really look at them, but to focus ten yards beyond, on nothing, which produces a glassy effect, which makes them worry, mostly about what's going on behind your empty eyes.

The guy said, "OK, show me your passports."

I went first, with my stiff blue booklet, very new, but indisputably genuine. The guy flicked back and forth through it, and felt the paper, and checked the photograph. And the printed data too, apparently, because he looked up at me and said, "You weren't born in America."

I said, "Only technically. Children of serving military are considered born in America for all legal and constitutional purposes."

"Serving military?"

"You remember us, I'm sure. We came and kicked your ass in Kosovo."

The guy paused a beat, and said, "And now you're a bodyguard?"

I nodded.

I said, "You better believe it."

He handed my passport back. He didn't look at Casey Nice's. One was enough. He said, "Come in the room and we'll talk."

The room was a semi-tight fifteen-by-fifteen space, walled off from the workshop many decades previously, in a fairly arbitrary position, to do with power lines, possibly. The walls looked like single-skin brick, plastered smooth and painted with shiny institutional paint, dull green in color, like pea soup. There was a window with a metal frame, with a desk under it, and three armchairs. No gun cabinets. No closets. Just a place for doing business, like a salesman's office behind a lot full of ten-year-old cars.

The guy said, "Please take a seat," and when we didn't he took one himself, going first, perhaps as an example, or a reassurance.

We took a seat.

The guy said, "What are you looking for?"

I said, "What have you got?"

"Handgun?"

"Two. We both carry. People don't expect that."

"What do you like?"

"Anything that works. And that you've got ammunition for."

"Mostly we have nine-millimeter. It's easy to get in Europe."

"Works for me."

"You like Glock?"

"Is that what you've got?"

"It's what we've got most of. Glock 17s, brand new, if you want a matching pair."

"And a hundred rounds each."

The guy paused a beat, and then he nodded, and he said, "I'll go get you a price."

He got up out of his chair, and stepped out of the room.

He closed the door behind him.

And locked it.

Chapter 32

For a second I took the snick of the lock to be normal, somehow consistent with the whole cloak-and-dagger drama queen bullshit we had seen since the beginning, starting with the gnome behind the pawn shop counter. Exaggerated lock-and-key precautions at the warehouse end of the operation might be seen as authentic, by some buyers, and maybe exciting, somehow suggestive of other locks and keys, perhaps to whole storerooms stacked with boxes, each one full of weapons still dewy with oil.

Then in the second second I dismissed that theory, because it was a lock too far. At that point we were still equal parties to a negotiation, both sides on best behavior, properly wary and skeptical, for sure, like buying a used car, but at least polite.

No one locks customers in a room. Not so early in the game.

Therefore the third second was spent understanding something was seriously wrong, a familiar chill stabbing my face and my neck and my chest, and then I was glancing at Casey Nice, which upped the stakes, because she was glancing back at me, and then I was mentally listing the factors we had to deal with, purely on autopilot in the back of my brain, *walls, a door, a window, four guys outside,* and then in the fourth second the *who* and the *why* hit me, which made the whole thing worse.

Because as far as the Serbians were concerned, we were customers, nothing more. Just possibly conceivably some kind of a weird student exchange program whereby FBI agents from America were moonlighting in London, maybe with London coppers doing the same thing in New York or LA or Chicago. But probably not. So we were customers, no different from a junkie talking to one of their dealers, or a john hiring one of their hookers. And customers get service, not a locked door. Or an enterprise goes out of business, pretty damn quick.

So why? Only two possibilities. The first of which I hashed through during the fifth second. Maybe the Romford Boys were in such a state they had put out a general alert, like a price on our heads, with descriptions, all across the network. Maybe Charlie White had a red telephone on his desk, like in the Oval Office, for pride-swallowing calls between bosses. Maybe on this occasion he was willing to take help from anyone who would sell it.

Or, during the sixth second, the second possibility, which was right there in O'Day's own words, at the conference after the aborted barbecue dinner. *A Serbian outfit in the west of London, and an old-fashioned*

English gang in the east. Karel Libor was a thorn in both their sides, according to MI5.

In *both* their sides. Which might make this whole thing a co-production. A joint venture. An alliance, just for the duration. A one-time truce. Shared aims, shared benefits, shared duties, shared information. Kott and Carson completely safe, the whole of London covered, from east to west, like the District Line. What would that cost? A steady hand and a steady eye and a fifty-caliber round, obviously, but money too, probably. A lot of money. Again, O'Day's own words. *These people are throwing money around. They're not looking for value. They're looking for easy solutions, and they have the budget to make them happen.*

But whichever, hired hands or co-equal partners, they had locked us in for a purpose. And that purpose was to keep us there, ahead of some kind of an upcoming predetermined event. Which would almost certainly be the arrival of a third party. The claimant. The vested interest. The prisoner escort. Little Joey, for sure, mob handed, with a whole crowd of guys at his back. He would come in his Bentley, and there would be other cars, more Jaguars maybe, and at least one plain black van.

For us.

Not good.

Nice said, "We walked right into it, didn't we?"

I said, "We've got some time."

"How much?"

"Not sure. But London is big and traffic is slow and we're all the way on the other side of town. They've got to get a little convoy together. That's ten minutes, right there, even if they're all on the ball. Then they'll have to loop all the way north in a big wide circle, or come all the way through the center of the city. The East End, Westminster, Paddington. Could be we have an hour. Or more than an hour. Could be we have nearer to ninety minutes."

"To do what?"

"Whatever needs doing."

"Can you kick down the door?"

The door was a stout wooden item, hardened with age, well fitted in its frame.

"I could from the outside," I said. "Probably. But not from the inside."

"Can we break the window?"

The window was not a Victorian original. It was 1930s pattern, I thought, a replacement, enhanced by the benefits of science. Low maintenance, because it was made of aluminum or some kind of galvanized metal. Which was evidently strong enough to support large panes of glass, for extra daylight. Large enough panes for an average person to climb out. The glass looked perfectly normal. I said, "I think we're going to have to break it, yes."

"Where does it lead?" She answered her own question by peering out, close up, nose against the glass, left and right. There was nothing ahead except a blank brick wall. She said, "It's an alley. Fairly long and narrow. I think it's closed off at both ends. We'd be trapped in it. Unless we could get in some other building's back window. And then out their front door."

I said, "Don't worry about all that now."

"So when should I worry about it?"

"First we wait. Five minutes. We could be wrong. Maybe it was just an excess of enthusiasm. Maybe he'll come back with a price."

We waited. Five minutes. The guy didn't come back with a price. On the other side of the door the workshop was quiet. There was no automotive maintenance underway. Which was a situation I had misinterpreted completely. I thought the grease monkeys had been sent away so the gun deal would stay private. But it was our capture that was supposed to stay private.

Missed clues, missed connections, risks gone bad.

My failures.

Dominique Kohl.

I said, "We need a complete inventory of this room."

Casey Nice said, "What are we looking for?"

"Everything. When we know what we've got, we'll decide how to use it."

We didn't have much. In terms of large items easily visible, we had three armchairs, a desk, and a desk chair. The armchairs were the kind of thing you might have seen thirty years before in a corporate waiting area. Danish, possibly, or Swedish. Stubby wooden legs, under a simple upholstered shape, with knobby fabric gone flat and greasy with wear. The desk was even older. It was made of oak, in a traditional shape and style, with a kneehole drawer and three more in either pedestal, the bottom pair deep enough for files. The desk chair looked like a dining chair. Or a kitchen chair. No casters, no arms, no reclining mechanism.

No lumbar support, no ergonomics. Just four sturdy legs, and a hard seat with a vague butt-shaped molding carved into it, and a straight back.

No phone, no desk light, nothing on the walls, no knives and forks left over after hasty working lunches. No electrical cords, no phone chargers, no letter openers, no paperweights. The desk's kneehole drawer held three forgotten paperclips, all dull with age, and a lone shaving from a sharpened pencil, and dust and grit trapped in the corners, and nothing else. Five of the six other drawers were similarly barren, but the deep drawer on the left had a sweater in it, a malodorous old item maybe dumped one warm day and never retrieved. It was off-white wool, with thin denim panels applied at the shoulders and the elbows. Its size was medium, and its manufacturer was someone I had never heard of.

We stood back.

Casey Nice said, "What were you hoping to find?"

I said, "An armored division would have been nice. Failing that, a couple of Heckler and Koch MP5s with a dozen spare magazines would have been convenient. Or even a book of matches would have been useful."

"We've got nothing."

"We've got what we've got."

"What are we going to do?"

So I told her what, and we rehearsed it carefully, over and over again, and then we started doing it.

Chapter 33

I picked up an armchair, fingers and thumbs dug hard into the soft upholstery, and I hoisted it in front of my face, holding it upside down at a forty-five degree angle, leading with the stubby wooden legs, and I took two long strides and flung it at the window. The legs shattered the glass, very noisily, and the bulk of the thing bounced off the center spine of the frame and fell back on the desk and ended up on its side on the floor. Noise, noise, noise.

Casey Nice stepped over close to the window, and I picked up the desk chair and went to the door to wait.

No point in us getting out the window, I had said. *The alley leads nowhere. We need to bring the four guys back in the room.*

And they came. Human nature. A sudden loud crash, obviously the window glass shattering, what else were they going to do? They were going to burst in, look around, hustle to the broken window, stick their heads out the hole, and look left and right.

The lock clicked, the door opened fast, and the first guy got partway in. He was the main man, who had done all the talking. I got my right hand on the back of his neck and helped him along, with a vicious backhand shove that sent him skittering toward Nice at the window. *I can deal with numbers two, three, and four,* I had said. *But number one is yours. Get the best jagged splinter you can find, wrap your hand in the old sweater, and stick the splinter in his eye.*

Which I sincerely hoped she was doing, but I wasn't watching, because at that point I was smashing the desk chair into the second guy's head. Into it, not over it. Not like a saloon brawl in an old Western movie. Like a lion tamer in the circus. Because jabbing is better, like a punch, your whole moving bodyweight concentrated through the inch-square end of a leg. Mass and velocity, just like baseball, just like everything. I was aiming for a broken skull at the minimum, and instantaneous brain death at the maximum. I was hoping for an inch-square shard of bone punched right through into the soft tissue beyond. Which I might well have gotten. I couldn't tell immediately. That would be a question for the autopsy. But either way, killed or just stunned, the guy went down like a sack. He was the guy who had driven us in the Skoda. I dropped the chair and ran right over him to get at the next two.

Two against one is never a problem, I had said. *Don't worry about me. Just look after the first guy. If the splinter doesn't finish the job, slam him with the desk drawer, edge on, bridge of his nose, hard, and keep on slamming him until he goes quiet.*

The third guy had slowed up dramatically, after seeing the fate of the first two unfold right in front of his eyes, and the fourth guy had crashed into him from behind, but the slapstick ended right there. The surprise was over, and they were not idiots. They reversed direction instantly, retreating and regrouping like they should. Neither one had a gun in his hand, which was a risk gone good. London was different. Guns were for special occasions, not routine. I was more worried about knives, because I don't like them much, and Londoners do, apparently, but neither one had a knife out either. Not yet, anyway. No way of knowing what was still in their pockets.

The workshop floor was a cluttered space bigger than a basketball court, littered with tools and hoses, blocked here and there by cars and hoists, still lit by nothing more than electricity. The security shutter was still closed. The two guys ahead of me fanned out twenty feet, and then stopped and turned, and cast about, the third guy ducking left and picking up a tire iron, the fourth guy ducking right and scooping a wrench off a bench. The third guy was one of the pair who had come out of the boxed-in room. The fourth guy was the one who had stepped out of the shadows and closed the security gate. They came back a step toward me, in unison, balanced easy, up on their toes, arms out, eyes on me, blank and unwavering. Not the worst I had ever seen. Tough lives, and perpetual conflict in their ancestral DNA, and maybe some military service, and maybe some guerilla activity, and certainly the guts to muscle in on folks like Charlie White and Karel Libor and make a shady living in a foreign capital. They weren't going to fall down in a dead faint if I shouted *Boo*.

In my mind's eye I could see Little Joey's Bentley nosing through the traffic, but I figured I still had plenty of time. And there was no sense in rushing. Always better to let them come to you. Let them commit. Let them show you their moves, which shows you their weaknesses.

We stood there for most of a minute, which felt like a good long time, locked together in a silent unchanging triangle, all of us tense, all of us rocking a little, staying loose, staying limber, their eyes on me, my eyes between them, relying on peripheral vision only, while learning the territory, and judging angles, and mapping routes. The Skoda we had arrived in was on my left, and beyond it was a car up on a ramp, all black and dirty on its underside, and then there was an empty bay, and then there was a dusty sedan parked in a corner, with soft tires and a front wing missing, and on the other side of the space were racks of components in soiled cardboard boxes, and tires, some new and stickered, most not, and a wheel-balancing machine, and oil funnels, and drums full of old rags, and a sad stack of corroded mufflers waiting for disposal. Behind me was more of the same, plus the boxed-in room, where I heard a sudden soft whimper. Male or female, I couldn't tell, and I didn't look back.

The fourth guy moved. His wrench was a big handsome thing, dull steel, maybe a foot and a half long, with jaws each end two inches wide. For some kind of a big heavy-duty component, I guessed. A suspension bush, perhaps. Whatever that was. I knew nothing about cars. I knew some of the words, but not what they meant. The guy was holding the wrench like a hammer, and he raised it up, and he took a step forward. Whereupon the other guy should have rushed me, while I was distracted, but he didn't. Maybe teamwork wasn't on their agenda. Every man for himself. Which suited me fine. Two against one is never a problem, but no one likes to work harder than he needs to.

The guy took another step. The wrench was still raised like a hammer. I took a step forward in turn, because I wanted my subconscious mind to know for sure what was behind me, which had to be empty space if I had just stepped out of it. And because moving up is always better than moving back. It unsettles the other guy, just a little. He had a wrench, and he was holding it like a hammer, and he was advancing, so why wasn't I retreating?

Come right ahead and find out, pal, I thought.

He kept on coming, with just a trace of uncertainty in his face, and beyond him his partner started moving too, just a step. Show time. I watched the guy with the wrench, watched his hips and his waist, waiting for the first small sign of imminent action, and I saw it coming, his legs bracing, his elbow rising an inch, his intention as plain as day. He was going to launch himself at me with the wrench raised high, and he was going to bring it down like a tomahawk, ideally on the top of my head, but no big deal if he missed, because he still had a target about a yard wide to aim at, my left shoulder, my head, my right shoulder. A busted collar bone would have worked for him just fine, at that point.

So I went for him first, a long, fast, skipping stride, like a boxer aiming to finish a helpless opponent, and in the space of a split second all his previous certainty disappeared, and he crashed out of an offensive mode into a defensive panic, his back arching a little, his elbow rising even higher, as if he felt now he needed to land an even more enormous blow. Which was his weakness. Blunt instruments require a back-swing, which is purely wasted motion. At the critical time his weapon was moving in exactly the wrong direction.

I got the flat of my left palm on the underside of his elbow and pushed hard, exploiting his own momentum, forcing the backswing way further than he intended, bringing his upper arm past vertical, bringing the weight of the wrench scything down behind his back until it was about to hit him in the ass, whereupon I reached around behind him with my right hand and grabbed the wrench and twisted it and tore it clean out of his grasp. Which was not wasted motion. Taking the wrench away from him was the same thing as my own backswing. I swung it right back in immediately, high and hard and flat, and I caught him in the side of his jaw, just below his cheekbone, which must have smashed his upper back molars, assuming he had any, and the hinge of his jaw, and which must have jerked his brain around inside his skull like a jellyfish in a bell jar.

He went down sideways, like a tree, on his right shoulder, and I heard the breath *oomph* out of him, and I heard his right temple hit the floor. By which point I was already double-timing it over to his partner, pretty sure the guy wasn't going to do the only thing that could have saved him. And he didn't.

He didn't throw the tire iron at me. He held on to it, in a sudden defensive panic just like his friend, rearing back, arching away.

Game over, right there. One on one, me against him. I slipped the wrench through my hand until one end was tight in my palm, and I jabbed it at him like a sword, my arm now about five feet long, effectively. You could have scoured every rainforest in the world and found the lankiest baboon or orangutan ever born, and he would have had a shorter reach than me. The guy could flail away with his tire iron to his heart's content, and he wasn't going to get it near me.

I said, "Where are Kott and Carson?"

He didn't answer.

"The two men the Romford Boys are hiding," I said. "Where are they?"

He didn't answer.

I jabbed him with the wrench, in the chest, in and out real fast. The open jaws were sharp, evidently. He yelped and backed off a yard. I stepped forward a yard. I said, "Where are they?"

He didn't know what I was talking about. That was clear. His eyes were truly blank. No evasion there. Maybe the two outfits were cooperating to a limited extent, but important information was still compartmentalized.

I said, "Where are the guns?"

He didn't answer. But now there *was* evasion in his

eyes. And resolve. He knew, but he wasn't going to tell me.

Behind me I heard the same soft whimper and Casey Nice called out, "Reacher, hurry."

So I did. I jabbed the guy with the wrench again, and he swung his tire iron to fend it off, with a jarring *clang,* and I jabbed again, and he parried again, by that point putting all his focus on our respective above-the-waist activities, which was exactly where I wanted it, because it meant I was able to step in and kick him in the nuts with absolutely no impediment at all.

And it was a good kick. Mass and velocity, like baseball, like everything. The guy dropped his tire iron, and folded forward and down, and tipped onto his knees, gasping and retching, hanging his head, kneeling there right in front of me. Which gave me plenty of time and space to pick my spot. I tapped him hard on the side of the head with the wrench, serious but not deadly, like a tennis player just warming up, and he rolled over on his side and lay still.

Then I hustled back to the boxed-off room, to see how Casey Nice was doing.

Chapter 34

The first guy was lying mostly on his back with a foot-long shard of glass in his eye. Dead, for sure. I could tell by the limp shapelessness of his body. Unmistakable. Life had recently departed. There wasn't much blood. Just a slow trickle, now stopped, hanging on his cheek like a fat red worm. Plus a thick clear liquid, which might have been the inside of his eyeball.

It was the second guy who was whimpering. The guy I had hit with the chair. He was on the floor in the doorway. His hair was all matted with blood, and there was a decent pool of it under his head. His eyes were closed. I didn't think he was about to get up and give us any trouble. Not anytime soon, anyway.

Casey Nice was backed up against the desk, looking somewhere halfway between shaky and resolute. I had asked Shoemaker, *Has she operated overseas before? Has she operated anywhere before?*

She had now.

I said, "You OK?"

She said, "I think so."

"You did a good job."

She didn't answer.

I said, "We need to search this place."

She said, "We need to call an ambulance."

"We will. After we search. We need guns. That's what we came for."

"They won't be here. It was a decoy."

"How many secure locations do they have? I think the guns are here. I asked the last guy, and he got all worried."

"We don't have time."

I thought about Little Joey, in his Bentley. Nosing through the traffic. Red lights and gridlock. Or maybe not. I said, "We'll be quick."

She said, "We better be."

We started by searching the main man's pockets. I figured if he had a key, then we might be able to tell what kind of a lock we were looking for, and therefore where we might find it. A safe key would look different from a door key, which would look different from a locker key. And so on, and so forth. But all he had was a car key. It was a grimy old item on a creased leather fob that had *Ealing Taxis* printed on it in flaking gold leaf. Possibly one of the battered sedans in the shop was his. He had cash money too, spoils of war, which I added to our treasury. And a cell phone, which I put in my pocket. But he had nothing else of interest.

We had already searched the boxed-off room, so

we moved out to the main workshop floor. There was a toilet in the far corner, with nothing in it except basic facilities and about a trillion bacteria. It was like a huge three-dimensional petri dish. But it was hiding nothing except contagious disease. It had no hidden panels, and no opening sections in the walls, and no trapdoor in the floor.

The rest of the space was one big open area, full of cars and clutter, as we had seen. Complete visual chaos, but conspicuously lacking in obvious hiding places. There were no doors in any of the walls, no closets, no large square boxes, no locked compartments. There was nothing thrust down the centers of the stacks of tires.

"No guns here," Nice said. "It's an auto repair shop. What you see is what you get."

I didn't answer.

She said, "We have to go."

I thought about Little Joey, in his Bentley. Already through the city center, by that point, probably. Out the other side, going fast on a wide road heading west.

"We have to go," she said again.

In his Bentley.

"Wait," I said.

"For what?"

No large square boxes, no locked compartments.
Bullshit.

I said, "The main man wouldn't drive a rent-a-wreck. Why would he? Karel Libor had a Range Rover. The Romford Boys use premium brands. Wouldn't the Serbians, too? They wouldn't want to look like poor relations."

"So?"

"Why was the guy carrying the key to a clunker?"

"Because they fix clunkers here. That's their job. Or their cover."

"It's not the boss man's job to look after the keys." I went back to the boxed-off room, to the guy's pocket, and came back with the key. It had a metal shaft and a plastic head, but not a big bulbous thing like a modern car has. No battery, no transponder, no security device. Just a key.

I looked around. I started with the dusty sedan parked in the corner, with the soft tires and the missing front wing. Because why would a car stay in the shop long enough to get soft tires? That was no kind of an efficient business practice. A car needed to be on the road, earning its keep. If it was unfixable it needed to be towed away and crushed. Because the workshop needed to earn its keep, too. Every square foot had to turn a profit.

I looked at the car's trunk. It was a large square box, and a locked compartment, right there. Hiding in plain sight.

I tried the key.

It didn't fit.

Nice said, "Reacher, we have to go."

I tried the next car, and the next. The key didn't fit. I tried the Skoda we had arrived in, even though I knew it would be hopeless. And it was. I went from car to car. The key didn't fit any of them.

Nice said, "We're out of time."

I looked around, and gave it up.

"OK," I said.

I went back to the boxed-in room's doorway, and knelt over the guy lying there. He had stopped whimpering, but he was still alive. He must have had a skull like concrete. I found the Skoda key in his pocket. I tossed it to Nice and said, "Start the car. I'll get the roller door."

The roller door had a palm-sized button on a switch box, which was connected to its winding mechanism by a long swan-neck metal conduit. I pressed the button hard, and the motor jerked to life, and the slack was pulled out of the chain, and the door rattled and started to rise. The daylight came back, inch by inch. It spread across the floor, and up the wall on the other side of the space. I saw Casey Nice in the Skoda's driver's seat. I saw her looking down at the controls. I saw a puff of black smoke as the engine started.

I saw another palm-sized button on another switch box. And another. And another. On the hoists. Hydraulic mechanisms, up and down. The hoists were empty, all but one. Which had a car raised high, its underside all black and dirty, its trunk way up there, above head height. Out of sight and out of mind. Some cop I was.

I hustled back and gave Nice a wait sign. I hit the button. There was a grinding noise and the hoist came down, slowly, slowly, past my eye line, and onward. The car on the hoist was a boxy old thing, covered in dust. With soft tires. The hoist slowed and settled, and the car rocked once, and went still, and the grinding noise stopped, and at the same time the roller door at the entrance hit the top of its travel, and its noise stopped, too, leaving only the heavy diesel beat of the Skoda's idling engine.

I stepped up to the dusty car's trunk lid. Which was less dusty than the car itself. It had finger marks all over it near the lock, and palm prints all over it near the lip. It had been raised and lowered about a hundred times since the passenger doors had last been opened.

The key fit.

The lid came up, on a noisy spring.

The car was a decent-sized sedan, and its trunk was pretty deep and wide and long, big enough for a bunch of suitcases, or two or three golf bags, or whatever else a person might want to transport. And it was full.

But not with suitcases or golf bags.

It was full of handguns, and boxes of ammunition.

The handguns were all Glocks, at first sight, all brand new, all wrapped in plastic, neatly stacked, mostly 17s, the original classic, some 17Ls, with longer barrels, and some 19s, with shorter barrels. All nine-millimeter, which matched the Parabellum ammunition stacked alongside, in boxes of a hundred.

Casey Nice got out of the Skoda. She took a look, and she said, "Sherlock Homeless."

I said, "The 19 will fit your hand better. You OK with the short barrel?"

She paused a beat and said, "Sure."

So I unwrapped a 19, and a regular 17 for myself, and I loaded them from one box of ammunition, and took two more boxes unopened. We left the hoist down and the trunk lid up, and we got in the Skoda, with Nice driving. We backed up and turned and headed for the exit.

"Wait one," I said.

She braked, and came to rest with the hood in the bar of daylight coming in the door. I said, "Where are we?"

She said, "Wormwood Scrubs."

"Which is like where else, comparatively?"

"The South Bronx, probably."

"But the British version. Where they don't hear gunshots every day."

"Probably not."

"In fact when they do, they still call the cops. Who show up with SWAT and armored vehicles and about a hundred detectives."

"Probably."

"And I never trust a weapon I can't be sure will work."

"What?"

"We need to test-fire the Glocks."

"Where?"

"Well, if we did it here, the cops would come, and they would get ambulances for those who need them, and then they would gather enough red-hot evidence to put a serious dent in this whole Serbian thing they seem to have out here. Which all in all might be considered a public service."

"Are you nuts?"

"Aim for the cars. I always wanted to do that. Two rounds each, and then get the hell out."

Which is what we did. We wound down our windows, and we got our shoulders out, and we aimed behind us, and we fired four spaced shots, crashingly loud, through four separate windshields, and before the last echo came back off the bricks we started rolling, slow and sedate, completely ordinary, just a local minicab, properly booked by phone.

We found the main road in from the west, and we headed for the center of town. Less than a mile into it, we were passed on the opposite side by a fast little convoy, led by a big black Bentley coupe, which was followed by four black Jaguar sedans, and bringing up the rear was a small black panel van.

Chapter 35

We parked in a no-parking zone in a side street near the Paddington railroad station. The plan was to lock the car and walk away. It was a very busy area. There were plenty of onward transportation options. There were buses, and black cabs, and two subway stations nearby, and the regular trains. On foot we could head south to Hyde Park, or north through Maida Vale to St. John's Wood. We would be caught on camera, for sure, no doubt many times, but it would take hundreds of hours of patient viewing to figure out who we were, and where we had come from, and where we had gone, and why.

I checked my appearance, to make sure I was fit for public consumption. My jacket was made of thin, stretchy material, no doubt good for all kinds of freedom of movement on the golf course, but it clung to the shape of whatever I had in my pockets. Which might have been OK with golf balls, but which wasn't OK with the Glock. I wanted it on the right, and it barely fit. Mostly because there was something else in there already.

It was the main man's cell phone. It was a drug-store burner, pretty much the same as the pair we had found in the Romford Boys' glove compartment. I passed it to Casey Nice and said, "See if you can find the call log."

She did something with arrows and a menu, and she scrolled up and down, and she said, "He made a thirty-second call to what looks like a local cellular number, and three minutes later the same number called him back, for one minute. That's the last of the activity."

I nodded. "Probably the APB on us went out in the middle of the night, and all the bad guys in London got briefed first thing this morning, so the Serbian guy called Romford and said, hey, those people you're looking for? I've got them locked in a room. But maybe he was only talking to a lieutenant at that point, who said we'll call you back, and who then went to tell Charlie White the news, and Charlie White called back himself, and made the arrangements."

"Would a minute be long enough for arrangements?"

"All they needed was an address. I'm sure Bentleys have satellite navigation. Even our pick-up truck in Arkansas had satellite navigation."

"OK."

"Although I didn't hear the phone ring."

She used the menu again, and the arrows.

She said, "It's set on silent."

I nodded again. "So that's what happened."

"I should give this Romford number to General O'Day. Don't you think? MI5 could trace it."

"To a cash payment in Boots the Chemist. Doesn't help."

"What's Boots the Chemist?"

"Their pharmacy chain. Like CVS. John Boot set it up, in the middle of the nineteenth century. He probably looked just like the guy who built the wall around Wallace Court. It started out as an herbal medicine store, in a place called Nottingham, which is way north of here."

"MI5 could track the phone to a physical location."

"Only if it's switched on. Which it won't be much longer. They'll trash it as soon as they hear the news from Wormwood Scrubs. They'll know their number was captured."

"They probably already heard."

I took the phone back from her.

I said, "Let's find out."

I peered at the buttons and found one marked *redial*. I pressed it with my thumbnail, and I watched the number spool across the screen, and I pressed the green call button, and I raised the phone to my ear.

I got a ring tone. The classic British two-beat purr. More urgent than the languorous American sound. I waited. Three rings, four, five, six.

Then the call was answered. By someone who had spent the six-ring delay checking his own screen and identifying the incoming number, clearly, because he had his first question all set and ready to go. A deep London voice asked, "What the hell is going on there? About a hundred filth have come past us already."

Filth meant cops. London slang. I said, "Where?"

The voice said, "We're parked three streets away."

I said, "Little Joey?"

He said, "Who is this?"

"I'm the guy who offed your guy. Last night, in the van. I saw your little tantrum."

"Where are you?"

"Right behind you."

I heard him move.

"Kidding," I said.

"Who are you?"

"I'd call myself a challenger, Joey, but I'd be selling myself short."

"No, you're a dead man."

"Not so far. You're confusing me with your boys. Or the Serbians. They took some casualties. That's for damn sure."

"They told me they had you locked up."

"Nothing lasts forever."

"What do you want?"

"John Kott," I said. "And William Carson. And I'm going to get them. Best bet is for you to stay out of my way. Or I'll run right over you."

"You have no idea."

"About what?"

"You have no idea the trouble you're in."

"Really? Truth is I feel pretty good right now. I'm not the one losing men left and right. That would be you, Joey. So this is a time for common sense and mature judgment, don't you think? Cut Kott and Carson loose, and I'll leave you alone. They already did Libor for you, and I'm guessing you already got your money. So what's in it for you now?"

"No one messes with me."

"As statements go, that's not entirely accurate, is it? I'm already messing with you. And I'm going to keep on messing with you, until you cut Kott and Carson loose. Your choice, pal."

"You're a dead man."

"You said that already. Wishing doesn't make it so."

No answer. The call ended. The phone went silent. I pictured the activity, on Little Joey's end. A minion, dispatched. The battery in one trash can, the phone body in a second can, the SIM card cracked with a thumbnail into four separate pieces, and dumped in a third can. A burner, burned.

On my end I wiped the phone on my shirt and tossed it on the back seat. Casey Nice said, "Will he listen? Will he cut them loose?"

I said, "I doubt it. Clearly he's used to getting his own way. Backing down would make his head explode."

I shoved my Glock deep in my pocket. It fit pretty well, without the competition. Nice watched me and did the same. Smaller pocket, but a smaller gun. I heard its stubby barrel click against her pill bottle.

I said, "Keep your pills in your other pocket. You don't want to get all snagged up."

She paused a beat. She didn't want to take the bottle out. She didn't want to show me.

I said, "How many left?"

She said, "Two."

"You took one this morning?"

She nodded and said nothing.

"And now you want to take another?"

She nodded and said nothing.

"Don't," I said.

"Why not?"

"They're the wrong pills. You have no reason to be anxious. You're performing very well. You're a natural. You were superb this morning. From the pawn shop onward. All the way to the splinter of glass."

Which was possibly one sentence too far. I saw her hand move, as if involuntarily, as if cupping itself around the dirty sweater padding the jagged edge. She was reliving the experience. And not liking it. Her eyes closed and her chest started to heave and she burst into tears. Tension, shock, horror, it all came out. She shook and howled. She opened her streaming eyes and looked up, and down, and left, and right. I turned to her and she collapsed against me, and I held her tight, in a strange chaste embrace, still in our separate seats, bent toward each other from our waists. She buried her head in the fold of my shoulder, and her tears soaked my jacket, right where Yevgeniy Khenkin's brains had been.

Eventually she started breathing slower, and she said, "I'm sorry," all muffled against my coat.

I said, "Don't be."

"I killed a man."

"Not really," I said. "You saved yourself. And me. Think about it like that."

"He was still a human being."

"Not really," I said again. "My grandfather once told me a story. He lived in Paris, where he made wooden legs for a living, but he was on vacation in the south of France, sitting on a hillside near a vineyard, eating a picnic, and he had his pocket knife out, to lever open a walnut, and he saw a snake coming toward him, real fast, and he stabbed it with the pocket knife, dead on through the center of its head, and pinned it to the ground, about six inches from his ankle. That's the same as you did. The guy was a snake. Or worse than a snake. A snake doesn't know it's a snake. It can't help itself. But that guy knew what he was choosing. Just like the other guy, yesterday, who wasn't helping old ladies across the street, or volunteering in the library, or raising funds for Africa."

She rubbed her head against my arm. Nodding agreement, maybe. Or not, perhaps. Maybe just wiping her eyes. She said, "Doesn't make me feel better."

"Shoemaker told me you knew what you signed up for."

"I did, in theory. Actually doing it feels different."

"There's a first time for everything."

"Are you going to tell me it gets easier?"

I didn't answer. I said, "Save the pills. You don't need them. And even if you do, save them anyway. This is only the beginning. It's going to get harder later."

"That's hardly reassuring."

"You have nothing to worry about. You're doing well. We're both doing well. We're going to win."

She didn't answer that. She hung on for a moment longer, and then she eased away from me, and we both retreated to our own spaces, and we sat up straight. She huffed and sniffed and wiped her face with her leather sleeve. She said, "Can we go back to the hotel? I want to take a shower."

I said, "We'll find a new hotel."

"Why?"

"Rule one, change locations every day."

"My new toothbrush is still there."

"Rule two, keep your toothbrush in your pocket at all times."

"I'll have to buy another."

"Maybe I'll get a new one, too."

"And I want to buy clothes."

"We can do that."

"I don't have a bag anymore."

"No big deal. I've never had a bag. All part of the experience. You change in the store."

"No, I mean, how do we carry the boxes of ammunition?"

"In our other pockets."

"Won't fit."

She was right. I tried. The box stuck half in, half out. And my pocket was bigger than hers to begin with. I said, "But this is London. Who's going to recognize it for what it is?"

She said, "One person in a thousand, maybe. But what happens if that one person is a cop, like at Wallace Court, with a bulletproof vest and a submachine gun? We can't be seen walking around town with boxes full of live ammunition."

I nodded. I said, "OK, we'll get a temporary bag." I looked all around, in front, behind, both sides of the street. "Although I don't see any bag stores here."

She pointed half-left. "There's a convenience store

on the corner. Like a miniature supermarket. One of their chains, I think. Go buy something. Gum, or candy."

"Their bags are thin plastic. I've seen them. You put the Coke in one last night. It was practically transparent. As bad as our pockets."

"They have big sturdy bags, too."

"They won't give me a big sturdy bag for gum or candy."

"They won't *give* you any kind of bag. You have to buy them here. Which means you can choose whatever kind you want."

"You have to buy the stuff *and* the bag it goes in?"

"I read about it in a magazine."

"What kind of country is this?"

"Environmental. You're supposed to buy a durable bag and use it over and over again."

I said nothing, but I got out of the car and walked up to the corner. The store was a bare-bones version of a big supermarket. Daily necessities, lunch items, six-packs, and soft drinks. And bags, just like Nice had predicted. There was a whole bunch of them near the checkout lanes. I picked one out. It was brown. It looked about as environmental as you could get. Like it had been woven out of recycled hemp fibers by one-eyed virgins in Guatemala. It had the supermarket's name screen printed on it, faintly, probably with all kinds of vegetable dye. Carrots, mainly, I thought. Like the writing would all disappear in a shower of rain. But as a bag it was OK. It had rope handles, and it opened out into a boxy shape.

I didn't really want gum or candy, so I asked the

woman at the register whether I could buy the bag on its own. She didn't answer directly. She just looked at me like I was a moron and slid the bag's tag across her scanner, with an electronic *pop,* and she said, "Two pounds."

Which I figured was OK. It would have been fifty bucks in a West Coast boutique. The Romford Boys paid for it, and I put their change in my back pocket, and I walked back to the parked Skoda.

It wasn't there.

Chapter 36

I put my hand on the Glock in my pocket, and the back part of my brain told the front part, *seventeen in the magazine plus one in the chamber minus two fired in the Serbian garage equals sixteen rounds available,* and it pulled me back against a real estate broker's window, to cut 360 degrees of vulnerability to 180, but mostly it screamed at me: *Dominique Kohl.*

I took a breath and looked left and right. There was no traffic cop to be seen. Which would have been logical. Nice would have taken off in a heartbeat if she had spotted one. Digital information in a camera system could be erased at the touch of a button, but Nice's face and the Skoda's plate in the same human memory at the same time couldn't be managed so easily. Grander schemes had unraveled for less. But there was no cop on the block. There was no uniformed individual sauntering along, with notebook in hand.

And there were no members of the public staring

open-mouthed at the empty length of blacktop, either, as if after some big commotion. And Nice wouldn't have gone down easy, not for the Romford Boys, not for the Serbians, not for anyone. She had doors that locked and a loaded gun in her pocket. Sixteen rounds available, the same as me. The street was far from quiet, but it was humming with nothing more than normal city activity. No big incident had taken place. That seemed clear.

I slid along the broker's window and stepped back into a doorway, for ninety degrees of exposure, like I had only a baseball diamond ahead of me. Traffic on the street was one-way, from my right to my left. There was a steady flow. Small hatchback cars, black taxis, an occasional larger sedan, delivery vans. No drivers peering left and right, no shotgun passengers searching faces. No one looking for me. I stepped out a pace and checked the corners. No one waiting there.

She knows what she signed up for. And she's tougher than she looks.

She was captured, mutilated, and killed. I should have gone myself.

I'm going to hang way back. It's not going to happen again.

I stepped out of my doorway and walked against the flow of traffic. There were people on both sidewalks, hurrying in both directions, in cheap suits and thin raincoats, carrying small furled umbrellas, like British people do, just in case, and briefcases and shopping bags and backpacks, no one doing anything other than just hustling along. No furtive behavior.

No black vans idling at the curb, no big guys looking around, no cop cars.

I took out the phone Scarangello had given me, and I found Nice's number in the directory, and I called it. There was a long pause, nothing but scratchy silence, maybe waiting for network access, maybe waiting for an encryption protocol to lock in, and then I heard a ring tone, a long soft American purr in the heart of London, and another, and more, for a total of six.

No answer.

I clicked off.

Hope for the best, plan for the worst. Maybe she was driving, and couldn't talk. Maybe something had spooked her off the curb, and she was circling the block. Some innocent reason. Left, and left again, and again, as many times as it took for me to finish my business in the convenience store. Eventually she would see me standing on the sidewalk, and she would swoop in and pick me up.

I watched the corner ahead of me.

She didn't come.

Or worst case, her phone was in some other guy's hand, who would have a calculating gleam in his eye, as he watched the screen and saw my name there. Maybe they would stop, and try to reel me in. Right there and then. A two-for-one special. An improvised plan. Some kind of a trap, nearby. Casey Nice as bait, and some kind of an ambush.

I watched my own screen.

No one called me back.

Plan for the worst. The only other number in the directory was O'Day's. *There's GPS in our cell phones,*

so they'll be watching over us every step of the way.
He could lead me to her. Literally step by step. Until
they ditched her phone, at least. I dialed, and heard
the scratchy silence again.

Then I clicked off the call, because up ahead of me
the Skoda was coming around the corner.

Nice was driving, but she wasn't alone. Behind her
in the back seat was another figure, solid but insubstantial in the shadows, tilted somehow, as if watching over her shoulder. Then the car got closer and I
recognized the guy. Maybe forty or forty-five years
old, a little sunburned, with cropped fair hair and a
blunt, square face, wearing a sweater and a short canvas jacket. With blue denim jeans, no doubt, and tan
suede boots, maybe British army desert issue.

Bennett, the Welshman with the unpronounceable
first name. Last seen disappearing in Paris. The MI6
agent. Or MI5. Or something in between. Or something else entirely. *It's all pretty fluid at the moment,*
he had said, in his sing-song voice.

The Skoda swooped to the curb and braked hard in
front of me. Both Nice and Bennett looked up at me,
necks craned under the windshield rail, eyes a little
wide, appealing somehow, Nice more so than Bennett, as if she was saying, *pretend this is normal.*

I got in. I opened the passenger door, and dumped
myself in the seat, and got my feet in, and closed the
door again. I held the environmental bag in my lap.
Nice hit the gas and turned the wheel and took off

again. She said, "This gentleman's name is Mr. Bennett."

"I remember," I said.

"We've met," Bennett said, to her, not to me. "In Paris, where a gust of wind saved his ass."

I said, "Now you admit to being there?"

"Not in writing."

"Why did you hijack my ride? I was worried there, for a second."

"There's a traffic warden two streets away. They use photo tickets now. Better if you don't get caught up in that kind of complication."

"What do you want?"

"Pull over," he said. "Any place you like. We'll move again if we see anyone coming."

Nice slowed the car, and hunted for a space at the curb, and ended up half in and half out of a bus stop. Technically illegal, no doubt, but Bennett showed no great concern. I asked him again, "What do you want?"

He said, "I want to ride along for a day or two."

"With us?"

"Obviously."

"Why?"

"I have a roving brief at the moment. Which I interpret to mean I should keep an eye on the other thirty-six undercover operators in London and latch on with whoever's furthest ahead."

"We're not ahead."

"Neither is anyone else, I'm sorry to say. But at least you're having fun."

"Not so far."

"But you're making some kind of progress."

"Are we?"

"Don't be so modest."

"Are you wearing a wire?"

"Want to search me?"

"I will," Nice said, over her shoulder. "If I have to. There are rules."

"Says the unacknowledged asset, operating inside an ally's territory, with two recent homicides in her slipstream."

I said, "You can look at me for both of those."

"Implausible," Bennett said. "How do you explain Wormwood Scrubs? You took one and she took three? I don't think so. You should have moved the bodies a bit. The pattern was too clear. I think the splinter of glass was down to Ms. Nice alone. I'll give you yesterday's caved-in throat, though. So I'd say it's a one-all draw at the moment. A tie, as you would call it."

"What do you want?" I said, for the third time.

"Don't worry," he said. "There are no wires for NHI cases."

Casey Nice said, "Which are what?"

"No humans involved. We're not very interested. But they are. That's the problem. That's the downside. Now you've got two gangs after you."

"How interested is not very?"

"On our part? We'll take notes, but we won't actually do anything with them."

"Paper records?"

"Inevitable, I'm afraid."

"In which case we weren't there."

He said, "Where?"

I said, "Anywhere."

"Technology says otherwise. We watch where you go, you know. And GPS is a wonderful thing. How else could I find you, just now for instance, parked miles from the scene of the crime, in a stolen car no less, and all at a moment's notice?"

I said, "Our phones are encrypted."

He just smiled and said, "Oh, please."

"Please what?"

"Think about why you people put up with us. As in, why us and not Germany now? What do we bring to the table?"

"GCHQ," I said.

He nodded. "Our version of the NSA. Our listening post. But so much better than the NSA, it's embarrassing. You need us. That's why you put up with us."

"You're eavesdropping."

"No, we're facilitating," he said. "We're gathering things up and passing things along. Occasionally we might test for intelligibility. On a purely technical level."

"Surely CIA transmissions are unbreakable."

"The CIA certainly thinks so."

"You've broken their code?"

"I think we sold them their code. Not directly, of course. I'm sure it was a complicated sting."

"I'm sure you're not supposed to do that kind of thing."

"And I'm sure it was all a long time ago."

"So did we do a public service? With the Serbians?"

"You hurt them. But you didn't kill them. Like cutting an arm off an octopus. Not that we're ungrateful, you understand. Seven arms are easier to fight than eight. If only marginally."

"You want more."

"They're both coming after you. Which presents opportunities, perhaps. In my opinion a few more casualties would not be frowned upon, in certain circles."

"With you riding along?"

"Purely as an observer. Some of these people are British citizens. And as Ms. Nice pointed out, there are rules."

"Are you going to give us help?"

"Do you need any?"

"We asked for a list of locations."

Bennett nodded. "We saw that transmission."

"We haven't had an answer."

"Locations are difficult. More than ever now, because we have to figure in Karel Libor's portfolio, and the Serbians too, as of this morning. Because if the Serbians really are cooperating with Romford, then logic says they might have put Kott in one place and Carson in another, or vice versa, far from each other. Safer that way. And logic also suggests they'd be using remote addresses. And the land around London is pretty flat. Rolling, at best. Not the kind of terrain for approaching distant isolated farmhouses suspected of containing either one or two of the four best freelance snipers in the world."

I said, "I would still like the list."

"OK, we'll release it today. You'll get it just as soon as it bounces off O'Day."

"But you're betting on remote farmhouses? Well separated?"

"Not necessarily. There are different possibilities."

"Such as what?"

"They have safe houses, and there are plenty of houses they rent out, and therefore plenty of tenants just delighted to get out of town for a week or two. And there are plenty of people who owe them money, who would love to earn a rebate by feeding a stranger three times a day, and giving him a bed for the night, and then saying nothing at all about it."

"But you think far from prying eyes would be better?"

"At first sight much better. But ultimately it's a trade-off, isn't it? They have to assume we have a plan for shutting down access to the center of town. Like a post 9-11 thing. I'm sure every big city does. And they wouldn't want to get caught on the outside of a thing like that. Not when they've got a big rifle to bring through the cordon. So all in all I think they'll move in sooner rather than later. They might already be here."

"We saw a few hundred viable locations overlooking Wallace Court."

"Which we're searching very carefully. But what if they're in viable locations we didn't see?"

"*Do* you have a plan for shutting London down?"

"Of course we do."

"Then why aren't you using it?"

"Because we remain optimistic."

"Which is a politician talking."

"The aim is to wrap this up quickly."

"Which also sounds like a politician talking."

"Politicians sign our paychecks."

"So what kind of help will you give us?"

"We'll show you where Little Joey lives. Nothing happens without him. You can watch the comings and the goings, and you can see if you can figure things out."

"Are you saying you can't?"

"The movements we have so far observed have shown no coherent pattern."

"Then maybe Little Joey isn't the guy."

"Charlie White is far too old and far too grand to be running around, and Tommy Miller and Billy Thompson are only ten years younger, and they're nothing more than bureaucrats now, anyway. Which is what gangs are all about these days. Tax strategies, and legal investments, and things like that. Little Joey Green is the only one who actually does anything. Trust me on that. If they're rotating the guards in and out, or sending food and women, then it's all coming through Little Joey's driveway."

"Except you haven't observed it."

"Not as yet."

"How long have we got, before the politicians panic?"

"Not long."

"Do they have a Plan B?"

"It would help me if we didn't get that far."

"So now we're helping you?"

"We're both helping each other. That's how it's supposed to work, isn't it?"

"Do you listen to the hot line between Downing Street and the Oval Office?"

"Why do you want to know?"

"Personal interest."

"By tradition we leave that one alone."

"Good to know."

He said, "Let's go find you a new hotel. You should have some down time. I'll text you when we're ready to go out to Little Joey's place."

I said, "You have our phone numbers?"

He didn't answer.

"Silly question," I said.

Bennett swapped places with Nice and drove us south, to the Bayswater Road, which was the northern limit of Hyde Park, and then east to Marble Arch, and then south again on Park Lane, into Mayfair, which was rich enough to be neutral territory. No gangs there, at least of any type I would recognize. We drove past the Grosvenor House Hotel, and the Dorchester, and we pulled in at the Hilton. Bennett said, "They won't look for you here. For the money you've taken, they'll figure you went somewhere fancier. Somewhere with a bigger name, like Brown's or Claridges, or the Ritz, or the Savoy."

I said, "How do you know about the money we've taken?"

"It was in Ms. Nice's report to O'Day."

"Which you happened to test for intelligibility."

"The choice of test sample is a random procedure. Purely a lottery. Driven by engineering. Something to do with the mean time between failures."

"We should throw our phones away."

Casey Nice said, "We can't."

Bennett said, "I agree. You can't. You need to check in with O'Day on a regular basis. That's the deal he made with Scarangello. If you go to radio silence now, then the deal is off, and you're disowned by all concerned, in which case you better be out of the country within an hour, or you're going to be hunted down like common fugitives."

"You know about Scarangello, too?"

"Try to remember, anything that ends up in the state of Maryland goes through the county of Gloucestershire first. And in reverse."

"You must be listening to the whole world."

"Pretty much."

"So who's bankrolling this thing? Have you figured that out yet?"

"Not exactly."

"And you're the A team, right? With the big brains? So much better than the rubes at Fort Meade?"

"Normally we do pretty well."

"But not this time, apparently. So now you want to dump it all on us. You want us to keep on communicating with O'Day, so you can listen in while we take all the risks."

"We didn't rule the world by being nice."

"The Welsh ruled the world?"

"The British ruled the world. And the Welsh are

British. Just as much as the Scots. Just as much as the English, even."

I didn't answer. Nice passed me the ammunition boxes, and I put them in the environmental shopping bag, and we got out of the car, and we walked into the hotel lobby.

Chapter 37

The Hilton was more than adequate for our needs. A generic name, but they had maxed out the fanciness in honor of the Park Lane location. And the prices. And the snootiness. They started out a little dubious about our lack of luggage. All we had was the bag of bullets. And they started out equally sniffy about taking cash, but then they saw our many thick rolls of bills, and instantly upgraded us in their minds from budget tourists to eccentric oligarchs. Not Russians, probably, because of our accents, so Texans, maybe, but in either case they became extremely polite. The bell boys were especially disappointed we had no other bags to carry. They were smelling fifty-pound tips.

Our rooms were on different floors, but we headed together to Nice's first, for a safety check, and because I felt she should have a box of ammunition with her. A lone last stand in a hotel room was highly unlikely, but highly unlikely things can happen, in which case

116 would be a much more interesting number than plain old 16 straight.

Her room was empty and unthreatening. It had the same basic architecture as a thousand motel rooms I had seen, but it was prettied up to a far higher standard, including literally, in that it was twenty floors from the ground with a view of the park. I put her box of a hundred Parabellums on her night stand, and glanced around one more time, and headed back toward the door.

She said, "I've still got two left. I feel good now."

I said, "Tell me about when Bennett got in the car."

"That's what he did. He just got in the car. I saw him on the opposite sidewalk, dialing his phone, and then listening, like people do, and at that point he was just some guy, but then my phone started ringing, so I answered, and it was him. He crossed the street and got in right behind me. He told me General O'Day had given him my number, and that General Shoemaker had confirmed it, and that we should move off the curb and drive around the block because we were in a no-parking zone and there was a traffic cop behind us."

"So you moved off?"

"He was clearly legitimate. I thought to know the names of both generals showed he was on our side."

"What do you think now?"

"Not entirely legitimate, but still on our side."

I nodded. "That's what I thought, too. Did you believe the things he said?"

"I think there were some exaggerations. Unless he was being suicidally candid about a program that must still be deeply classified. On the British side, certainly. Who would react, surely, if their biggest secrets were being talked about in the open."

"Some guys can be suicidally candid. They grow to hate the bullshit. There's no reaction because it doesn't really matter anyway. People like that are not security risks. Having everything out there is the exact same thing as having nothing out there. The Brits are hacking our signals. The Brits are not hacking our signals. Both things are up there under the spotlight. Which doesn't help us know which one is true."

"So are they hacking our signals?"

"Think about the things he didn't exaggerate."

"Which were what?"

"He came right out and said they were getting nowhere with the activity at Little Joey's house, and nowhere with tracking down the paymasters on-line."

"So?"

"Poor performance."

"No one bats a thousand."

"But the Brits are very good at this. They invented most of it. I'm not buying the big gap between them and the NSA, but they're at least equal. We have to admit that. Maybe a little better. They're a subtle people, deep down. In the best sense of the word. Good card players, generally. And they're tough, when they need to be. Ultimately they always do what it takes. But they're getting nowhere."

"It's a tough case."

"Tough enough that neither the NSA nor GCHQ can get a foot in the door?"

"I guess."

"So how likely is it a rookie analyst and a retired military cop are going to provide the vital breakthrough? What are we going to see that they haven't seen?"

"There might be something."

"There's nothing. Because Bennett is now thinking the same way O'Day was thinking. A few days late. Bennett was in Paris. He knows Kott was aiming at me. Now he knows Kott is in London. He thinks he can shake something loose by pushing us out there, front and center. As targets. It's a Hail Mary pass. And it's all about him. He doesn't care what happens to us. He's watching for the muzzle flash. That's all he wants. Before the politicians panic."

"I'm sure you planned to be front and center all along."

"Not as a target."

"Does it matter what someone else calls you?"

"Exactly. We have to do it anyway. We don't get a choice. Same with the phones. We have to update O'Day. Bennett gets what he wants, both ways."

"Only because we get what we want, too. First, in fact. So it doesn't really matter."

"It makes a total of two governments thinking of us as nothing but bait. Which is one government too many. We're depending on them in a lot of ways. What they feed us depends on what they think of us. Subconsciously, I mean. They can develop a bias. We have to be ready to recognize it."

"And do what?"

"We need to think strictly for ourselves. There may be orders we need to ignore."

She looked away and said nothing, but then eventually she nodded, in a way that could have been deeply contemplative, or ruefully determined, or somewhere in between. It was hard to tell.

I said, "Still feeling good?"

She said, "We have to do it anyway."

"Not what I asked."

"Should I still be feeling good?"

"No need to feel anxious, anyway. Not about which agency will betray you, and which won't. Because they all will, sooner or later."

"That's really going to cheer me up."

"I'm not trying to cheer you up. I'm trying to get us on the same wavelength. Which is where we need to be."

"No one is going to betray us."

"You would bet your life on them?"

"Some of the people I know, yes."

"But not all of them."

"No."

"Same thing."

She said, "Which bothers you."

I said, "Which bothers you more."

"Shouldn't it?"

"You know what your biggest mistake was?"

"I'm sure you're going to tell me."

"You should have joined the army, not the CIA."

"Why?"

"Because this whole stress thing you've got going on is because you think national security is on your shoulders alone. Which is an unreasonable burden. But you think it because you don't trust your colleagues. Not all of them. You don't believe in them. Which leaves you isolated. It's all down to you. But the army is different. Whatever else is wrong with it, you can trust your brother soldiers. And believe in them. That's all there is. You'd have been much happier."

She was quiet for a beat, and then she said, "I went to Yale."

"You could switch right now. I'll take you to the recruiting office."

"Right now we're in London. Waiting for a text from Mr. Bennett."

"When we get back. You should think about it."

She said, "Maybe I will."

The text from Bennett came through two hours later. I was alone in my own room, which was the same as Nice's, but on a higher floor, and facing in the opposite direction. My view was of Mayfair's prosperous rooftops, all gray slate and red tile and ornate chimneys. The American Embassy was close by, somewhere just north of me, but I couldn't see it. I was on the bed, and my phone was charging on the night stand, and it buzzed once and the screen lit up: *Lobby 10 minutes.* I called Nice on the house phone, and she said she had gotten the same message, so I laid back down for five more minutes, and then I put my reloaded Glock in my coat pocket, and I headed out to the elevator.

Nice was already in the lobby, and Bennett was already in a car at the door. The car was a local General

Motors product, called a Vauxhall, new and washed, midnight blue, so completely anonymous it could only be a law enforcement car. I guessed the Skoda had already been wiped and dumped, or set on fire. It was early in the evening, and the sun was very low over the park.

I got in the back seat, and Nice sat up front next to Bennett, who hit the gas and launched out into the traffic. I asked him, "Where are we going?"

He didn't answer for a long moment, because he had to get off Park Lane heading south and back on Park Lane heading north, which involved a high-speed 360 all the way around Hyde Park Corner, which was a hub just as crazy as the Place de la Bastille. Then he said, "Chigwell."

"Which is what?"

"The next place north and west of Romford. Where you go when you get a little money. Some of it is very suburban. Big houses, and plenty of space between them. Walls, and gates, and things like that. Some trees, and open spaces."

"And Little Joey lives there?"

"In a house of his own design."

We saw plenty of houses and plenty of designs before we saw Joey's. The trip was slow. Traffic was bad, because we were heading basically out of town, along with about a million other people trying to get home. Every light and every corner had a traffic jam. But Bennett didn't seem worried about time. I guessed he was happy to wait for the sun to go down.

We made it through some historic districts, and then out into the further reaches, heading always a little east of north. We drove a short stretch on a motorway, one ramp to the next, and then we were in Chigwell, and we soon saw streets that would have melted the iciest heart, with the setting sun golden behind them, with substantial houses all in glowing red brick, some with iron fences, or walls and gates, like miniature Wallace Courts, most with trees and shrubberies, all with expensive late-model automobiles on their driveways, their chrome ornaments flashing bright wherever the sun escaped the shadows.

I said, "Are we driving right up to his door?"

Bennett said, "No, it's a lot more complicated than that."

And it was, at least geographically. We parked the car in a lot made of crushed grit, behind a pub, but we didn't enter the establishment. We walked right by it. Maybe there was an arrangement with the owner. Nothing said, nothing asked, nothing offered, but a clear understanding all the same. *Don't call the tow truck, and don't ask questions.* Then we made a left and a right through leafy streets, no doubt closely observed from behind lace curtains, but the British are cautious people, and we fell squarely on the right side of the benefit of the doubt. Just three random people, taking a stroll. We watched the sun go down, finally, and the sky went dark, and we passed a long board fence, and then just before another started up there was a yard-wide gap, which was the entrance to some kind of a public footpath, long and straight and narrow, with trodden-down weeds and a meager scattering of black grit underfoot, and high board fences on either side, exactly a yard apart all the way. We walked single file, Bennett first, then Nice, then me, a hundred and fifty paces, until we came out in a grit clearing with a green garden shed in it, which up close was a decent size, and recently painted, with two words over the door picked out in white: *Bowling Club.* Behind it was an immense square of perfect lawn.

"Different kind of bowling," Nice said.

"Very popular sport," Bennett said.

"Hence the enormous building," I said. "But I guess they need to accommodate everyone at once. That would explain it. For the grudge matches."

"There are many other clubs," Bennett said. "All of them larger."

He bent down and took out a key from under a stone. The key looked freshly cut. He put it in the door. He had to jiggle it a little. But he got the job done. The door swung inward, and I saw gloom inside, and caught a musty smell, of wood and wool and cotton and leather, all stored too long in damp conditions. He held the door with spread fingers and used the other hand to motion us through.

I said, "What's in there?"

He said, "Check it out."

What was in there was a whole lot of bowling club stuff, but it was all piled to one side, leaving a clear lane in front of the windows, which looked out over the immaculate grass. Neatly spaced in the clear lane were three kitchen stools, each one set out behind a pair of huge night-vision binoculars, each pair mounted on a sturdy three-legged frame.

Bennett said, "We had gales last winter. Nothing very serious, but one fellow lost a panel out of his fence, and another lost a twenty-foot conifer. Which by chance opened up a direct line of sight from this shed to Little Joey's house. Which was lucky, because we can't get any closer. We assume his immediate neighbors are either working for him or loyal to him or scared of him."

"So this little shed is surveillance HQ for Joey?"

"You get what you get."

"You sit for hours with your back to the door?"

"Take it up with whichever carpenter died fifty years ago."

"With the key under a rock?"

"It's a budget issue. It's the sort of thing they suggest. Why not share a key instead of cutting ten? So they can buy a new computer."

"No video?"

"That kind of thing, they like to spend money on. Wireless upload straight out of the binoculars. All day and all night. High definition, but monochrome."

"Does the bowling club know you're here?"

"Not exactly."

"Good," I said. I figured swearing a busybody committee chairman to silence was like taking out an ad in the newspaper.

Nice said, "Suppose they come in to play a game of bowls?"

Bennett said, "We changed the lock. That one is ours, not theirs. They'll think there's something wrong with their keys. They'll call a meeting. They'll vote on whether to spend club funds on a locksmith. They'll make speeches for and against. By which time either it won't matter anymore, or we'll have changed the lock back again and gone home happy."

I said, "How well can we see from here?"

He said, "Take a look."

So I shuffled in, and sat down on the middle stool, and took a look.

Chapter 38

Clearly the binoculars had some kind of fantastic high technology in them, because the image was
spectacular. Not all green and grainy like I was used
to, but liquid and silvery and endlessly precise. I was
looking at a house about four hundred yards away, at
an angle of about forty-five degrees. I could see the
front, and all of one side, in large segments, through
the bays of an iron fence, which was built on a brick
knee wall, and divided into sections by occasional
brick pillars. The effect was reasonably grand, and I
was sure the expenditure had been saner than the lu-
natic scheme at Wallace Court.

The house itself was a large, solid thing, made of
brick, made to look Georgian or Palladian or whatever other kind of symmetrical style was currently in
vogue. It was completely conventional. It had a roof,
and windows, and doors, in the right numbers, in all
the right places. It was like a kid had been given paper
and crayons and told to draw a house. *Good, now add*

more rooms. It had an in-and-out driveway, through one electric gate and out the other. The driveway was made of blocks that looked silvery but might have been brick-colored. There was a small black sports car crouched near the door, parked at an angle, as if it had arrived in a hurry.

I sat back.

I said, "That's Little Joey's house?"

Bennett said, "Yes, it is."

"Great line of sight."

"We got lucky."

"He designed it himself?"

"One of his many talents."

"It looks like every other house."

Bennett said, "Guess again."

I sat forward. I took a second look. Roof tiles, bricks, windows, doors, rainwater gutters, all arranged in a boxy rectangular structure filling most of its lot. I said, "What am I looking for?"

Bennett said, "Start with the Bentley."

"I don't see it."

"It's right there by the door."

"No, that's something else. It's much smaller than the Bentley."

"No, the house is much bigger."

"Than a car?"

"Than a normal house. Little Joey is six feet eleven inches tall. Eight-foot ceilings don't appeal to him. Regular doorways make him stoop. That house is a normal house, except every dimension on every blueprint was increased by fifty percent. All in perfect proportion. Like it had swollen up, uniformly. The opposite of a doll's house. An exact replica, but bigger, not smaller. The doors are more than nine feet high. The ceilings are way up there."

I looked again, and focused on the car, and forced myself to see it for the size it really was, whereupon the house did exactly what Bennett had said. It swelled up, in perfect proportion. An exact replica, but bigger.

Not a doll's house. A giant's house.

I sat back.

I said, "What do regular people look like, when they go in and out?"

Bennett said, "Like dolls."

Casey Nice squeezed behind me, and sat on a stool, and took a look for herself.

I said, "Tell me what you've seen so far."

Bennett said, "First of all remember where we are. We're right next to the motorway up to East Anglia, and right next to the M25, where we can go either east or west, or we could go the other way, and be lost in the East End ten minutes from now. It's a plausible center for operations. That's why they all check in here. Not just because Joey is a control freak. He came to them. That's why he built his house here, I'm sure of it. He thinks a good boss is always on top of every detail."

"Who have you seen checking in here?"

"Lots of people. But we can explain them all."

"Talk me through it."

"We knew something was about to happen, because Joey suddenly doubled his personal guard. At the time we didn't know why, but now we guess that was when Kott and Carson made their initial contact, before the job in Paris. And now they're here, as promised, and they need guards of their own, and food, and entertainment, all of which would come through here."

"Even if they're hiding far away?"

"Far away for Joey Green means the other side of the M25. We're not talking about the highlands of Scotland. Thirty minutes from here is the remotest place Joey ever heard of."

"But you're not seeing it?"

Bennett shook his head, no. He said, "We would expect a consistent pattern, something extra, laid on top of their normal activity, but we're not getting it. There are occasional stray vehicles, and we track them as far as we can. We've even done computer simulations, based on which way they're heading. They never go anywhere useful."

Beside me Casey Nice said, "Maybe Kott and Carson went back to France, to wait. Much less vulnerability there, wouldn't you think? Because we're looking for them here. Maybe this is a just-in-time thing. Maybe they're planning a last-minute return. Which would explain what you're seeing. Or not seeing. People who aren't actually here at the moment wouldn't need feeding."

Bennett said, "Why would they risk the lockdown? That would be unprofessional."

I said, "Which Carson isn't, right?"

"Is Kott?"

"Kott would look at the lockdown like he looks at everything else. Distance, wind, elevation. All the data. He wouldn't risk it, because he couldn't predict it. Lockdowns are about emotion, not reason. I think Kott has been inside for days."

"So do we. But there's no pattern here. Just the normal comings and goings."

I said, "Is Joey home right now?"

"Of course he is. His car is outside."

I sat forward again, and looked. The immense door, dwarfing the car. The townhouse windows, as big as billiard tables. I said, "Maybe Kott and Carson are someplace where they don't need Joey's guys to bring them food. Maybe they're ordering out. For pizza, or chicken, or cheeseburgers. Or kebabs. This part of town seems to have plenty of choices. Or maybe they're both on a diet. And maybe they don't want hookers."

"Kott was in prison fifteen years. He's got a lot of catching up to do."

"Maybe the meditation straightened him out and made him pure of heart."

"They'd need guards, come what may. Partly because they need to rest and sleep, but also because Joey likes to put on a show. Four guys at a time, minimum, which is twelve guys a day. They'd rotate through here. No other way of doing it. For briefing, and debriefing. Joey is big on debriefing. The more he knows, the better he feels. Information is king. He'd want to know all their secrets. Might be useful in the future. The Karel Libor thing is going to start a fashion. They're all going to want their own pet sniper."

I said, "What does Joey do for food?"

"He's getting his deliveries as normal."

"Does he eat a lot?"

"Twice as much as me. He's twice the size. A van goes around the back to the kitchen. Sometimes twice a day. God forbid a gangster should have to go to the supermarket."

"Does he sample his hookers?"

"He's been known to give the fresh meat a run-out. But not often. He likes it rough. No good if his new stars are marked up for the first few weeks. So mostly he heads for the other end of the pipeline. He finishes off the used-up ones."

"Any recent increase in frequency?"

"There are always hills and valleys."

Beside me Casey Nice said, "Why haven't you arrested him?"

"The last time a witness spoke up against the Romford Boys was before you were born."

I kept my eyes on the binoculars. Nothing was happening. The scene was static. I said, "So what are your theories?"

"Some of us are thinking this cooperation with the Serbians might go back a month. Maybe that initial approach from Kott and Carson was a joint approach. In which case it would make sense to let the Serbians shelter them. Safer that way. We're all over east London, for obvious reasons, and meanwhile they're stashed way out in west London. Classic misdirection."

"Joey wouldn't get his debriefs."

"That's the main weakness in the theory. We think he could live with not knowing their secrets, because you don't miss what you never had. But he couldn't live with the Serbians getting them instead. Which emotion comes out on top? The behavioral psychology subcommittee is debating it now."

"The what?"

"The behavioral psychology subcommittee."

"Anything else?"

"The conventional in-house wisdom says we know there's a safe house somewhere, and the problem is solved the minute we find it. London is full of cameras and recognition software, and we have a mass of real-time traffic data, and we've got the programmers working hard, and the analysts harder still."

"Who are all smart people, right?"

"Very smart."

"Which is why you're better than the NSA, right?"

"And cheaper."

I sat back.

I said, "I'm wondering why you brought us here. You could have just told us. You could have said, Joey has a house and nothing happens there."

"We're sharing the data."

"You're overcomplicating the data. Or blowing smoke."

"How so?"

"To tell you that I would have to believe what you say."

"Why wouldn't you?"

"It's a simple chain of logic, but I have to trust each component."

"Why wouldn't you?" he said again.

"Those things you told us earlier. You have a no-humans-involved protocol, with different procedures.

You're hacking our phones right now, as individuals. You're hacking CIA communications generally. You could listen to the hot line into the Oval Office, if you wanted to, but you don't, simply because of good manners. If all of that is true, then all of it has to be classified. You talk about it, you get sent to the Tower of London. You get your head cut off. Or whatever the modern equivalent is. A life sentence for treason."

"I'm not going to jail."

"Because?"

"I wasn't telling you anything I got from inside the building."

"What building?"

"Any building."

"So what are you telling us?"

"You know how it is. There are a million stories and a million rumors. Most of them are bullshit. But there are always three or four that could be true. But they're all contradictory. So you use your hard-won skill and insider judgment and you decide which one to believe in."

"Why should you believe in any of them?"

"Because one of them is bound to be true."

"Hacking our phones is neither a story nor a rumor. It's a fact."

"It's a small fact. And the small facts we know can be indicative of the bigger facts we don't know. All part of the reasoning process. If we attack low level American assets, why wouldn't we attack high level American assets? It's all the same electricity in the same wires. And if we attack high level assets, why wouldn't we listen to the Oval Office?"

"Therefore the things you told us were merely theories you believe in."

"I can't prove them."

"But?"

"I know they're true."

"Because?"

"Human nature," he said. "You know how it is. Whatever your intentions, if you have the ability to do something, then you will do it, sooner or later. The temptation is always there, and it can't be resisted forever. Don't tell me you think any different."

"What about the other things you told us?"

"Like what?"

"You think Kott and Carson are definitely in London."

"Hundred percent certain."

"Based on your skill and insider judgment?"

"Everything I know says they're here."

"And they're being guarded, and fed, and entertained by the Romford Boys."

"It's how things are done. The courtesies are very elaborate."

"Hundred percent certain?"

He said, "More than."

"And the guards and the food and the entertainment would be quarterbacked by Joey himself."

"No question about that. Hundred percent."

"But no one is dashing back and forth between Joey's house and wherever."

"And that's not just my belief. That's a fact."

I said, "Ms. Nice and I had a conversation. The whole British government is getting nowhere. So how likely is it a rookie analyst and a retired military cop are going to provide the vital breakthrough?"

Bennett said nothing.

"But I guess you want it to look that way. You want it to be one of us who comes out and says it. So you can act all surprised. To ease your conscience a little."

He said nothing.

"A simple chain of logic," I said again. "Kott and Carson are in London, the Romford Boys are hiding them, but there's no traffic in and out of Little Joey's driveway."

Bennett said, "All true."

"Therefore Kott and Carson are inside Little Joey's house."

Bennett said nothing.

"Joey doubled his guard for a reason. He was expecting houseguests. I mean, where could be safer? The cops can't get near the place, and no civilian would dare to try. And if Joey wants to keep these guys close, maybe with an eye to the future, then there's no place like home for a thing like that. He'll let them hole up there as long as they want. They'll leave when the time is right. They could walk from here to Wallace Court, if they had to. They arrived inside one of those stray vehicles you saw. Maybe driven around the back. No use following the vehicle afterward, because it wasn't going anywhere. It had been hauling stuff in, not hauling it out. But aside from all of that, you're seeing exactly what you'd expect to see. Two teams of house guards rotating in and out, and lots of food coming in. Enough for three people."

Bennett didn't answer.

"Now you can say wow, you must be right, we had no idea, and we're so sorry for accidentally bringing you to a spot exactly four hundred yards from where two of the world's greatest riflemen are watching out the window."

"I am sorry," he said.

"But there's a silver lining, right? There always is. If you see a weapon discharged inside that house, you could order up all kinds of SWAT and armored vehicles. Job done, right there. If you see a weapon discharged. Which isn't a given. But which might become more likely if they had something to shoot at."

"Not my idea," he said.

"Whose, then?"

"Like I said before, they didn't rule the world by being nice."

"They?"

"We. But not me. Not personally."

"Don't apologize," I said. "This is exactly where I wanted to be."

Chapter 39

I stayed where I wanted to be for about thirty more minutes, with Casey Nice alongside me at her own pair of binoculars, both of us watching the static scene and trying to draw what conclusions we could from it. Bennett stood behind us, listing the activity they had already seen, and answering the few questions we had.

I asked him, "What kind of probable cause would get you in there?"

He said, "Apart from a muzzle flash?"

"Let's hope things don't go that far."

"A positive visual ID on either one of them would work."

"Which you haven't gotten yet."

"Not yet."

There were lights in some of the windows, both upstairs and down, behind what looked like semi-transparent roller shades. But there were no shadows cast, no figures, no movement. And no blue glow from a television set. Probably the occupied core of the house was in back, or on the far side, neither of which we could see. A kitchen and a family room, possibly, with guest bedrooms upstairs. Or a self-contained suite of their own. Like a pied-à-terre apartment, except fifty percent larger. Designed either for the present purpose, or for giant and incapacitated in-laws, twenty years in the future.

I asked, "You got an opinion on when exactly they'll move into position down at Wallace Court?"

Bennett said, "That's the big question, isn't it?"

"What's the big answer?"

"We'll be closing roads a day or two before it starts. I'm sure they're aware of that. And I'm sure they know a day or two means three or four, sometimes. So my guess is they'll move five days ahead."

"That gives them a long wait."

"Snipers love all that laying up bullshit. All part of the mystique."

"Can you catch them in transit?"

"We could if we knew what time on which day they're due to head out. We could engineer a traffic stop. A broken brake light, or something. But we don't know. So we'd have to stop everything of theirs that moves, for about a week or so, to be on the safe side. After the third or the fourth time, old Charlie White would start calling in favors. He owns some local politicians, and some local police, we think. Might be worth it, just for the entertainment value alone. We'd have half a dozen solid citizens swearing up and down that yeah, OK, old Charlie might be a pimp and a thief and a gun runner, but he's definitely not a terrorist."

I asked, "Who's the we? As in, we could, we'd have to, we think, we'd have?"

Bennett said, "It's all pretty fluid at the moment."

"Why?"

"We aim to wrap this up quickly."

"Says the politician."

"Who gives as well as gets. He removes certain barriers, at the stroke of a pen. He relaxes certain regulations. In fact he begs to. He's ready to repeal anything and everything, all the way back to the Magna Carta. An attack of this nature on British soil would be worse than catastrophic. It would be embarrassing."

"Why don't they cancel it?"

"That would be even more embarrassing."

I said, "How many viable locations did you count near Wallace Court?"

"Your thing in Paris changed our thinking a little bit. That was sixteen hundred yards, and dead on, apart from the gust of wind. So if we look at the back patio and the back lawn and a radius of sixteen hundred yards, then we figure about six hundred places."

Nice said, "Which means you'd have to search a hundred and twenty a day to be sure of finding them there. Can you do that?"

Bennett said, "Not a hope in hell. Plus we're worried about the M25 motorway. That would be the ultimate just-in-time delivery, wouldn't it? Imagine a high-sided commercial vehicle pulling over on the shoulder, with some kind of elevated shooting platform constructed in the interior, and an unobtrusive hole in the siding. And big scopes on the rifles. They could cover the whole of the patio and the whole of the lawn."

I said, "Can't you close the motorway?"

"The M25? Unacceptable. The whole southeast of England would be jammed solid. We're talking about closing the shoulder and the inside lane, for phony road repairs, but even that's a big ask. Traffic dynamics are very weird on that road. Like chaos theory. A butterfly flaps its wings in Dartford, two hundred people miss their flights at Heathrow, forty miles away."

I sat back from the binoculars. "So all in all you're saying we should nail them before they leave Joey's house."

"I think that would be a very favorable outcome."

"And according to your various closely held beliefs, they're going to be in there at least the next several days."

"That's only a best guess. Always better to strike while the iron is hot."

Beside me I heard Casey Nice breathe in.

"Not tonight," I said.

Bennett said, "Too soon?"

"Do it once, and do it right."

"When, then?"

"We'll text you. We've got your number."

Bennett locked up the Bowling Club's door, and put the key back under the stone, and we walked back the way we had come, out of the small grit clearing into the narrow straight path, and then onward through the silent streets, and back to the pub, and around behind it, where the Vauxhall was waiting patiently, exactly where we had left it, untouched, and not even boxed in.

"Where to?" Bennett asked.

I said, "An all-night pharmacy."

"Why?"

"We want to buy toothbrushes."

"And then?"

"The hotel."

"I thought Americans had a work ethic."

"First light," I said. "Be ready and waiting. You're going to drive us."

"Where?"

"Wallace Court."

"Why?"

"I want to stand on the back patio."

Bennett said, "Wallace Court doesn't matter. Not if we nail them before they leave the house."

"Hope for the best, plan for the worst. Could be the end game is all in the last five minutes, just before they pull the triggers. We need to know the lie of the land. We need to triage those six hundred places. I'd like a top ten. At least a top fifty."

"Those streets are full of Romford Boys."

"I certainly hope so. I want to be seen, still here, still poking around. I want that message to get back to John Kott, double quick."

"Wouldn't the opposite be better? You could take them by surprise."

I nodded. "Surprise is good. But sometimes it's better to unsettle them."

"They're not the kind of people who get unsettled."

"Doesn't take much to miss at sixteen hundred yards. A couple of beats per minute, maybe. He hates me because I sent him away. He hates himself because he let me break him down. There's a couple of beats per minute in either one of those. Both of them together, then two and two make five. I want him to know I'm coming, because that's the only way I'll survive long enough to get there."

He let us out in the Hilton's carriage circle, and we went in, and he drove away, and we arranged to meet in the famous top-floor restaurant, twenty minutes from then. A late dinner, just the two of us. I knew she wanted to shower, so I did too, and we got to the maitre d' lectern about a yard apart. She looked good, which I figured was partly being resolute, and partly being twenty-eight years old, and therefore still full of energy and resilience and even a certain amount of optimism.

We got a square table near a window, where we got a spectacular high-floor view of the twinkling city, interrupted only by the black of the park. The window glass was also reflective enough we could see most of the room behind us. Both picturesque and safe, all at once. A two-for-one deal. We ordered drinks, bottled water for her, black coffee for me. There was candlelight, and crystal, and a piano tinkling somewhere. She said, "This is very glamorous. It's just like the movies."

I said, "I guess it is."

"This is the scene where you try to get rid of me, isn't it?"

"Why would I do that?"

"Because now it gets hard."

"Which would argue for maintaining numbers, not reducing them."

"But you'll worry about me. You'll look at me and you'll see Dominique Kohl. That's worth two beats a minute."

"Suppose I say I won't worry about you?"

"Then I'll say you should. The only way to do this is go through Little Joey first. Who will be difficult to go through. Who likes rough sex with new hookers. If you get captured, you'll get a bullet in the head. If I get captured, I'll be begging for one."

"Suppose neither one of us gets captured. That's the more likely outcome. Joey needn't be difficult to go through. He's a big target. Lots of center mass."

"With a driver and four guards in a Jaguar, everywhere he goes."

"Until we make them all unemployed. Then they'll disappear. They won't fight on for free."

"You really want me there?"

I didn't answer. Dominique Kohl had asked: Will you let me make the arrest? Which was a question I wish I had answered differently. A waiter came over and took our order. I got a rib eye steak. Nice got duck, and when the waiter left she asked again, "You really want me there?"

"Not my decision," I said. "You're the boss. Joan Scarangello told me so."

"I think the strategy is sound."

"Me, too."

"But the execution will be complex."

"I'll take all the help I can get."

She said, "Suppose you had never picked up that newspaper? Where would you be now?"

"Seattle, probably. Or the next place."

"And all of this would be happening without you. Do you think about that?"

"Not really. Because I picked up the paper."

"Why did you call? Were you curious?"

"Not really," I said again. "I knew O'Day would be involved. And I prefer not to be curious about his line of work."

"So why did you call?"

"I owed Shoemaker a favor."

"From when?"

"About twenty years ago."

"What kind of favor?"

"He kept his mouth shut about something."

"Want to tell me?"

I said, "Personally, no."

"But?"

"It could be argued the nature of the incident has a bearing on the mission. In which case you're entitled to the information."

"Which is what?"

"Long story short, I shot a guy trying to escape."

"Is that a bad thing?"

"The trying to escape part was invented for the record. It was a routine execution. National security is a tricky thing. It's all about public image. Therefore sometimes retribution is public, and sometimes it isn't.

Some traitors get arrests and trials, and some don't. Some end up as tragic accidents, maybe shot to death by muggers, on street corners in weird parts of town."

"And General Shoemaker knew?"

"He was an accidental witness."

"Did he object?"

"Not in principle. He understood. He was in military intelligence. Ask around. The CIA was just the same. It was a pragmatic period."

"So how do you owe him a favor?"

"I shot the guy's friend, too."

"Why?"

"I got a bad vibe. Which ended up righteous, because the guy had a gun in his pocket, and his home address was a treasure trove. He turned out to be my guy's contact. As an espionage thing, they got a twofer out of it. More than that, in the end. They made arrests up and down the chain. But the inquiry panel wanted to be absolutely sure I had seen the gun first. Some legal thing. And the truth is, I hadn't. And Shoemaker didn't rat me out."

"So now you're going to fight his battle for him. That's a lot of payback. Seems out of proportion."

"That's how favors work. Like in the mob movies. Some guy says, one day I will call on you to perform a service. You don't get to pick and choose. And anyway, maybe it was Shoemaker's battle in the beginning, but it's mine now. Because O'Day was right. It's a big world, but I can't be looking over my shoulder all the time. So Kott gets a rematch."

"Do you want me with you?"

"Only if you want to be. On an ethical level, first.

The favor is a hint. Like a script for me to follow. O'Day wants an executioner. He doesn't want arrests and trials."

"On any level, do you want me with you?"

I said, "Where do you want to be?"

"I want to be part of it."

"You are part of it."

"Entering a phase not entirely suited to my skills."

"What's wrong with your skills?"

"I'm an average shot with no aptitude for hand-to-hand combat."

"Doesn't matter. We'll complement each other. Because the physical part is the least of it. The game goes to the fastest thinker. Which is what you're good at. Or at least, two heads are better than one."

She didn't answer.

I said, "We start again at seven o'clock in the morning. Take the rest of the night off."

We rode down in the elevator together, but I got out alone, on my floor, which was a couple above hers. The turn-down lady had been in my room. I reopened the drapes and looked out across the rooftops. I guessed most of what I was seeing was about a hundred yards away. The comfortable middle distance, in a crowded city. An easy angle, and some kind of default focus. I raised my eye line a little, and tried to guess double, for two hundred yards, and again, for four hundred, and again, for eight hundred, and then one last time, for sixteen hundred yards.

I was staring into the far, far distance. If Romford

was Mayfair, we'd be searching ten thousand locations.

Kohl had asked, Will you let me make the arrest?

I had said, I want you to.

As a reward, really. Or an acknowledgment. Or a compliment. Like a battlefield decoration. An earned privilege. She had done all the work. And had all the ideas, and made all the breakthroughs. Hence the reward. Which was substantial, in the coded language of the military, because we had a big enemy. Not physically. Not as I recall. I stuck a chisel in his brain, many years afterward, and I don't remember a big man. But he was big in terms of power. And prestige, and influence. A real long shot. Especially for a woman. Which was part of it. It was a long time ago. Recognition was important. And she deserved it. She did the work, and had the ideas, and made the breakthroughs. She was very thorough, and very smart.

Hadn't saved her.

I took my clothes off and got into bed, but I left the drapes open. I figured the city glow might comfort me, and the dawn might help me wake.

At one minute past seven the next morning we were on our way to Wallace Court, in Bennett's car, which was no longer an anonymous blue Vauxhall, but an anonymous silver Vauxhall. Otherwise identical. Like rental cars. We drove most of the same route, but faster, because the morning traffic was running the other way. Into town, not out. Rush hour, but not for us. Bennett looked tired. Casey Nice looked OK. We didn't talk.

Nothing to say. No doubt Bennett thought I was wasting his time. Which was possible. Or probable, even. But there's always a percentage chance of something. Maybe of not having to say *if I had known then what I know now*. Which phrase is used a lot. My mother said it all the time. In her case, she meant it most sincerely, but she said it like an elocution exercise, like a person learning a foreign language, which she was, with all her attention on the three cascading vowel sounds at the very end, and none at all on the consonants along the way: *If I 'ad known zen what I know now*.

I know now, like drumbeats. Portentous, and a little sinister, like tympani strikes at the start of a gloomy symphony. Shostakovich, maybe.

I know now.

I knew twenty minutes into the visit.

Chapter 40

When we got close I started to recognize some of what we had seen from the minicab, the second one, the one properly pre-booked on the telephone. I had seen some of the streets before, suburban but compressed, a little busier and narrower and faster than they really wanted to be. I remembered some of the stores, even. Carpets, cell phones, chickens, cheeseburgers, kebabs. And then the sudden green space, and the fine old house, and the crazy wall, still shouldering London aside after all these years.

The same squat tough guy was on duty at the gate, with his Kevlar vest and his submachine gun. Bennett nodded to him, and the guy took a step toward the gate, but his gaze fell on me, and he came back and said, "You're the gentleman with the guidebook. Sixpence to see the grounds. Welcome back, sir." Then he set off again and opened up. No radio check, no paperwork. No badge. Just a nod and a wink. The guy was in combat gear, basically, but it was blue, and it had *Metropolitan Police* on it here and there, embroidered on tapes and silk screened on Kevlar, subdued order, with black thread and black ink, plus monochrome versions of their helmet shields, like corporate branding, so I had no doubt the guy was a cop, but equally I had no doubt Bennett wasn't, yet Bennett was nodding and winking and the guy was hopping right to it.

It's all pretty fluid at the moment.

We drove the length of the driveway, and parked on the gravel near the door, where there was another armed policeman on duty. The house jutted in and out in places, where afterthought additions and extensions had been tacked on, but it was basically rectangular, much wider than it was deep. Not that it would be cramped from front to back. Far from it. I was sure it would be plenty spacious. But the proportions were dominated by the long, scattershot facade. No question about that. The place looked like four shoeboxes laid end to end. Maybe oak trunks long enough for front-to-back rafters were hard to find in Queen Elizabeth's time. Her dad had just built the Royal Navy. Lots of oak ships. Whole forests had been cut down.

We got out of the car, and Bennett nodded to the second cop, who nodded back, and then Bennett hustled us inside, impatiently, like he was embarrassed to be seen with us in public. Or maybe he was worried about rifle sights. Maybe he didn't want to stand next to me in the open. He had survived Paris, and he didn't want to get nailed in London.

The door was most of a tree, nearly five hundred

years old, banded with iron and studded with nail heads as big as golf balls. Inside I saw dark paneling, almost black with age, waxed and gleaming, a worn flagstone floor, and a huge limestone fireplace. There were oak settles and tapestry chairs, and electric bulbs in iron candelabra. There were oil portraits of solemn-faced men in Tudor costumes. Bennett took a right-hand corridor, and we followed him, ultimately into a room that had been modernized, with white paint and an acoustic ceiling. Beyond it was another room, similar, but smaller, with a large door in its end wall.

Bennett said, "That's the side entrance. That's where your president's tent will be. We imagine they'll all use it. From there they can come through here, with secure onward access to anywhere they need to be. Every room has natural light, but they're all big, and all seating is in the center, so in no case does anyone need to get close enough to the windows to be visible from outside. The impromptu walks on the lawn and the photograph are the only points of weakness."

We walked back the way we had come, but we took a right-hand turn well before we got to the hallway, into another corridor, this one with a creaky wide-plank floor, which led to a narrow room laid out left to right in front of us, which had nothing in its far wall except French doors, not at all correct for the period, all glass from top to bottom, with the patio beyond.

Bennett said, "They use this like an anteroom. They come in, they line up, they count heads, they make sure they're not leaving someone locked in the bathroom. Then they step out."

I stood there for a second, where they would, as if I was one of them, and I looked ahead through the glass. We were right of center, in terms of the building's symmetry, and the patio was built in a gentle curve, which meant we would be stepping out somewhat to the side of the deepest part. Which was OK. It would make the collegial cluster look geometrically authentic, rather than politically desperate. And it meant the shallow steps to the lawn were slightly closer, which would give the short guys less distance to hustle the tall guys. Presumably the photographers would be penned to the right, which meant the house would be at an angle in the background, which was better than a head-on brick wall, like a mug shot.

I put my hand on the handle, and I wondered if I had sold them short, by imagining their forced guffaws and their fake bewilderment, at having to change gears so quickly. Maybe it wasn't fake. In the tent, in the side door, through the secure access, not close to a window, these guys lived with close-order security every minute of their lives, maybe to the point where stepping out to an open-air patio was indeed a bewildering thing to do. Stepping out, shuffling slowly, head high, eyes nowhere except on some other guy equally scared, then standing still, facing front, chest out, smiling, not moving, a high sky above, and who knows what in the distance.

It's not the same with a sniper out there.

I opened the door, and I stepped out, and I stood still.

The early morning air was cold and a little damp. Underfoot the patio was made of mid-gray stone, which was worn with age and smoothed by rain. I walked to the exact center of the paved area, and I stood straight and faced front, and then I turned half left and stared in that direction, and then back to the right, and then I walked slowly forward to the lip of the steps to the lawn, like a diver at the edge of the board, and I stood with my hands behind me, chest out, head high, like I was in a photograph, or in front of a firing squad.

Ahead of me was a broad sweep of lawn, and then the back wall, and then a scrubby piece of common land, and then a safety fence, and then the M25 motorway, which could have been eight lanes at that point, rushing right and left in the far distance. And right there and then I abandoned Bennett's motorway idea. No just-in-time delivery. Not a viable location. Traffic was fast and heavy. Heavy in the sense of flow and per-minute density, and heavy literally. Some of the trucks were huge, and the biggest were in the inside lane, and they were all going fast, immense rushing bludgeons through the air. Trees far beyond the shoulder were thrashing about. A parked truck would be battered by slipstream. A platform built high inside would feel it badly. It would rock and judder, more or less continuously, with peaks and troughs at unpredictable intervals. Range would be about three quarters of a mile, which meant a rock or a judder worth the thickness of a dime would see them miss the house altogether. Not a smart spot. Dismissed.

But could a parked truck let two guys out, to make their own way forward?

No point. There were no viable firing positions anywhere between the house and the motorway. None at all, short of propping a ladder against the back wall, and aiming over it. Which would be discouraged, no doubt, probably by squat tough guys in Kevlar vests.

All safe dead ahead.

In which respect the pizza-slice shape of the site was a bonus. It meant the safe zone was not just dead ahead. It curved around sideways, and generously, both directions, to my left and my right, in a big, empty sweep, from maybe ten on a clock face all the way around to two.

The pizza-slice shape also meant the streets flanking us were not parallel. They ran away from us, one to the left and one to the right, like the spines in a fan. Which was good, at first glance. It meant the more distant the house, the more extremely oblique its line of sight would get, to the point where maybe we could eliminate some buildings altogether. A sniper could hardly hang out a window and aim more or less parallel to the glass, like riding sidesaddle.

But at second glance it was too good, because the angle exposed us to just as many side windows as front windows. You win some, and you lose some. I checked everything I could see, on the north side first, then the south, from about eight hundred yards out to sixteen hundred, which was thousands and thousands of windows, most of them winking the dawn sun back at me, in a ragged linear sequence, with moving spots of pink, first one street, and then a jump to the next, as if the neighborhood had been built by ancient astronomers for solar celebrations.

In the end I figured the south side was worse than the north. It was denser, and on balance it had taller buildings. I picked one out at random, about fifteen hundred yards away, most of a mile, a tiny thumbnail, a tall, narrow house, red brick and handsome, with a steeply pitched roof. It looked like it had all kinds of attic rooms. And maybe actual attics. A dislodged roof tile would work as well as an open window. I pictured John Kott, prone on a flattened bedroll, on a board laid across rafters above a top-floor plaster ceiling, with a chink of light ahead of him, where a tile had been slipped sideways, unnoticeable from the outside, too high, and just one of many. *We had gales last winter,* Bennett had said, in his sing-song voice.

I pictured Kott's eye, patient and unblinking behind the scope, the inch-wide crack in the roof giving him twenty yards side to side, at the far end of the deal. I pictured his finger on the trigger, relaxed but ready to squeeze, through the slack, pausing, then moving again, like clicking a tiny mechanical switch, the quiet tick of a precision component, causing an immense chemical explosion, the recoil bucking, the bullet launching on its long, long journey. More than three whole seconds in the air, *one thousand, two thousand, three thousand,* half an inch wide, like a human thumb, flying like a missile, straight and true, subject only to the immutable effects of gravity and elevation and temperature and humidity and wind and the curvature of the earth. I stared at the distant house and counted three long seconds in my head and tried to picture the bullet's flight. It seemed as if I should be able to see it coming. Straight at me. Like a tiny dot, getting bigger.

Flash *one thousand two thousand three thousand* game over.

Which is when I knew.

More than three whole seconds in the air.

Chapter 41

I was a lot faster getting back into the anteroom than I had been getting out of it. Bennett was watching me, and I asked him, "The bulletproof glass in Paris was new, right?"

"Yes," he said. "Improved, anyway."

"Do you know anything about it?"

"No," he said. "Other than it's glass, and, well, bulletproof."

"I need to know everything about it. Who designed it, who researched it, who funded it, who manufactured it, who tested it, and who signed off on it."

"We already thought of that."

"Thought of what?"

"Borrowing the shields and flying them in from Paris. Putting one either side. They're not very wide, but given the way the streets run, they would reduce the field of fire by about ten percent each. But we decided against it. Politicians are civilians. They'd cower behind the shields. Subconsciously, maybe, but it wouldn't look good. And they couldn't stay there forever. Which would give the bad guys the other eighty percent to aim at anyway. So all in all we thought it would be a net loss."

"That wasn't what I was thinking of. All I need is the information. On the quiet, if you can. No need to make a whole big thing out of it. Pretend it was just you and me. Like a private venture, outside of the mainstream. Like a hobby. But fast."

"How fast?"

"Fast as you can."

"What does the bulletproof glass have to do with anything? We're not going to use it. I told you that."

"Maybe I want to use it myself. Maybe I want to ask if they sell direct to the public."

"Are you serious?"

"It's a side venture, Mr. Bennett. Just a small inquiry. Nothing to do with anything. But fast, OK? And face to face only. Nothing on paper. Nothing up the chain. Understood? Like a hobby."

He nodded, and glanced back at the corridor, which presumably led to other corridors, and staircases, and rooms, and he said, "Do you need to see anything else?"

"No, we're done here," I said. "We're leaving, never to return. Like the Darby family, after all those years, when the motorway was built. No more Wallace Court for us."

"Why not?"

"Because it's never going to get this far."

"You sure?"

"Hundred percent."

He didn't answer.

"You said that would be a favorable outcome. You said we were supposed to help each other. You said that's how it's supposed to work."

He said, "It is."

"Then relax. Trust me. Crack a smile. It's never going to get this far."

He didn't crack a smile.

We drove back to the hotel, snarled all the way in traffic, maybe the peak of the morning rush, an hour or so after sunrise, or maybe just after the peak, but bad enough anyway. The immense sprawling city was still packing them in, but only just, and very slowly. We got back to Park Lane two hours after we left it, three quarters of which had been spent in the car. Worse than LA.

Bennett gave his keys to the valet, just like a regular person, and we all three rode up to the top-floor restaurant, where we figured the breakfast service would still be running. We got a booth behind a structural pillar. Worse view, but better privacy. Bennett spent a lot of time tapping on his phone. He said he was ordering stuff up for us, including large-scale government maps, and an architect's blueprint still held by the zoning authority, and three sets of aerial images, one taken from a space satellite, and another from an accidentally-on-purpose-off-course sightseeing helicopter, and a third from an unknown source, which he said had to mean an American drone, except officially there were no American drones in Britain, which was why it was labeled an unknown source. He said his people would load what we needed on a secure tablet computer, and bring it to the hotel.

Then he said, "We can't afford collateral damage. Not there. Some people on that street are innocent members of the public. Not many, but a few. Which is a shame. We could have taken care of this long ago. We could have planted a bomb and called it a gas leak."

Then he left, but Nice and I lingered a little, over coffee in my case, and small bites of toast in hers, and she asked, "Why are you all of a sudden so interested in the bulletproof glass?"

"Just a theory," I said.

"Something I should know about?"

"Not yet. It doesn't change what we have to do next."

"Will Bennett get that information for you?"

"I think so."

"Why? Does he owe you a favor now? Did I miss something?"

"It's a brother soldier thing. You should try it. You'd be happier."

"Is he British Army?"

"Think about that fluid thing he keeps talking about. It can only mean they've put special units together. The best of the best. All the different agencies, like an All-Star team. Who would lead such a thing?"

"They would all want to."

"Exactly. So much so their heads would explode if they didn't. But whose head would explode the worst?

Who's bringing the gun to the knife fight, in terms of exploding heads?"

"I don't know."

"The SAS. They don't like their own officers. They certainly aren't going to work for someone else's. Easiest just to put them in charge. Which is obviously what they did. Which was a good move. Because they know best anyway. Plus they think they have a dog in the fight. The renegade, Carson. Bennett wants him just as much as I want Kott."

"Bennett is SAS?"

"No question."

"What do we have to do next?"

"Get into Joey's house."

"Into it?"

"I'd prefer to make them come out. But that's hard to do. In fact it's a tactical question that has never really been answered. We studied it in the classroom. Easy enough to make sure they never come out, but that's not the issue. How do you make them come out of there voluntarily? No one knows. No one ever has. I remember my dad studying it, when we were kids. With stuff like that, he used to involve us. With questions afterward. My brother Joe came up with a huge machine like a gigantic subwoofer, blasting infrasonic waves at them, real low frequencies at a real high volume, because he said it was believed by some scientists that modern humans had a low tolerance for such a thing."

"What was your answer?"

"Bear in mind I was younger than him."

"What did you say?"

"I said set the house on fire. Because I was damn sure modern humans had a low tolerance for *that*. I figured they'd come on out, sooner or later."

"Are we going to set Joey's house on fire?"

"It's an option, obviously."

"What are our other options?"

"They all involve faking Joey out of there and dealing with him separately. Ahead of time. Before we do anything else. Because in that case, back at the ranch, we would see a leadership vacuum. Which we could exploit."

"As in, we would be fighting a less effective enemy."

"Exactly."

"But we would be fighting somebody."

"Nothing ventured, nothing gained."

"You said they wouldn't fight on for free. Because they're unemployed now. You said they would disappear."

"Hope for the best, plan for the worst."

"Which is it going to be?"

"It's going to be the same thing it always is."

"Which is what?"

"Somewhere in between."

The tablet computer showed up an hour later. Bennett's people brought it. The computer looked very modern, and the people looked the way such people have always looked, which was surprisingly normal, but not completely. One was a man and one was a woman, both of them a long way past their rookie years, both of them quiet and contained and competent, and neither one visibly unhappy with their short-straw courier assignment. Good team players, obviously. Only the best for the best. They said normally they would ask us to sign for the delivery, given the sensitivity of the contents, but on this occasion Mr. Bennett had waived the requirement. They said the computer required two passwords. They said the passwords were the name of the prisoner Mr. Reacher shot while attempting to escape, and Ms. Nice's mother's Social Security number. The passwords were case-sensitive, and could be entered one time only. No three-strikes-and-you're-out with British software.

Then they left.

We took the tablet to Nice's room. It was like half of a laptop computer. No keyboard. Just a screen. A blank screen. Nice said, "You remember his name, right?"

"I remember both their names," I said.

"But I assume the password is the first one. The main man."

"The target."

"Yes, him. Or was the other one attempting to escape also?"

"Actually he was the only one attempting to escape. The target was already down. He didn't see me coming."

"Which one were you investigated for?"

"The second one, technically."

"Did people talk about the case?"

"Not if they wanted to live. It was about the assassination of an American citizen on American soil."

"But if they had talked about it, what would they

have called it? The case as a whole, I mean, like the John Doe thing, or whatever."

"Definitely the first guy."

"Who was the target. And Mr. Bennett is British, and therefore ironic. Which means we can assume his mention of the escape was tongue-in-cheek. Which all focuses back to the target. Which was the first guy. Which is the name we should use."

"First or last?"

"Has to be last. This was the U.S. Army, correct?"

"Or code name?"

"He had a code name?"

"He had two. One from us, and one from the Iraqis."

She said, "Do you wake up in a sweat about it?"

"About what?"

"That operation."

"Not really," I said.

"But if you did, what name would you call him? Like, I shouldn't have done that bad thing to who-ever."

"You think it was a bad thing?"

"It wasn't helping old ladies across the street to the library in Africa."

"You're as bad as Scarangello. We need to get you out of there and into the army before it's too late."

"What was his name?"

I said, "Tell me about your mother."

"What about her?"

"You know her Social Security number?"

"I help her with her paperwork. She's sick at the moment."

"I'm sorry."

"She has a brain tumor. It won't go away. She can't think straight. I deal with insurance and disability and things like that. I know her details better than mine, probably."

"I'm sorry," I said again. "She must be young."

"Too young for this."

"Do you have brothers or sisters?"

"No," she said. "There's just me."

I said, "Would the average person know her mother's Social Security number?"

"I don't know. Did you know yours?"

"I don't think so. Do you visit your mother?"

"As often as I can."

"In downstate Illinois? That's a lot of flying."

"It keeps me busy."

"Plus you worry when you can't get there, I guess. Like now."

"Nothing I can do."

"When did she get the diagnosis?"

"Two years ago."

"I'm sorry," I said, for the third time.

She said, "It is what it is."

"When did Tony Moon start going to the doctor?"

"It's not connected."

"You absolutely sure about that?"

"My mother isn't here now."

"But you're thinking about her."

"A little."

"And therefore feeling a little anxious."

"Not about her. It's not connected."

I said nothing.

She said, "I have one pill left."

"You took one?"

"Last night. I had to sleep."

I said, "Do your bosses know about your mother?"

She nodded. "It's a requirement. Family situations must be reported. They've been very supportive about it. They keep me free on weekends whenever they can."

"So there's a human resources file somewhere at Langley, recording the fact that your mother is sick and you're taking care of business for her. Which has to be confidential. Because everything at the CIA is confidential. And there's another file somewhere in the Pentagon, recording the name of a guy I shot in the head twenty years ago. Which I know for damn sure is confidential. But somehow MI5 in London got access to both files, to come up with unbreakable passwords for us. They're like DNA, or fingerprints."

She nodded again. "Mr. Bennett's hacking theories might be true. In which case he's showing off."

"Unless O'Day showed him the files."

"Why would he do that?"

"That's a question we'll ask Bennett."

"What was your guy's name?"

"Archibald," I said.

"That's the kind of name you don't hear often."

"Lowland Scottish," I said. "Via Old French and Old High German. The third Earl of Douglas was called Archibald the Grim. No such romance in my case. My guy was called Archibald the worthless piece of shit."

She held down a button and the screen lit up with a dialog box. She dabbed it with a fingertip and a cursor started blinking on the line, and a picture of a keyboard came up below it. She typed *Archibald,* nine letters, with a capital *A* and the rest in lower case. She checked it for spelling, *A-r-c-h-i-b-a-l-d,* and then she looked at me with eyebrows raised, and I nodded a confirmation, and she touched *Submit,* and there was a pause, and then a green check mark appeared at the end of the typed name, and the dialog box rolled away, and was replaced by a second box that looked just the same. She dabbed a button that changed the keyboard letters to numbers, and she typed three digits, and a hyphen, and two more digits, and another hyphen, and then four more digits. She checked it over, and touched *Submit,* and the green check mark showed again, and the dialog box rolled away, and was replaced by ranks of thumbnail images.

Chapter 42

The local government maps would have been great if we wanted to fix a sewer line or lay fiber optic cable. They showed plenty of subterranean detail, under the sidewalks, and under the road itself. In the movies we would have found a storm drain, about as wide as my shoulders, that ran under Joey's kitchen floor, and I would have climbed down into it two streets away, and inched along, until a sudden thunderstorm threatened to drown me before I got where I was going. It would have been a tense sequence, but in reality there was no storm drain. There was nothing wider than my wrist. Gas line, phone line, electricity supply, water main, and sewer pipe. The house itself was shown as nothing more than the grateful recipient of those public utilities. It was drawn as a large blank rectangle, with no interior detail at all.

The leftover architect's blueprint from the zoning office was better. It was printed small, but Nice stroked her fingertips over the computer screen and made it bigger, and then moved it around, so we could examine each separate area in detail. Or we could pretend it was us moving, not the plan, and take miniature walks through the house, from room to room, and up and down the stairs. The plan was covered in the architect's handwriting. Which looked like every other architect's handwriting. Maybe handwriting was a required credit in architect school. But the words the guy had written were plain and simple. He was giving us the structural details. Wood, metal, brick, plaster, and glass. Which was good to know. Almost every component listed was custom made. Which made sense. If you need a three-foot door, you go to the store. Four feet six, you call whatever old guys are still in their workshops. The fifty-percent hike in dimensions must have put ten thousand percent on the tab.

The house had two levels only. No habitable attic, and no basement. There were bedrooms and bathrooms upstairs, plus a separate self-contained guest suite, which had bedrooms and bathrooms all its own, plus a living room attached. Downstairs had a kitchen, and a breakfast room, and a dining room, and many other rooms, variously labeled as living rooms, or nooks, or parlors, or libraries, or studies, or offices. At first sight the floor plan looked intimate, even cozy, until you remembered how big it all was. The nooks were as big as anyone else's living rooms. And half as tall again, presumably. Like museum halls, at night. Not vast, but not human scaled, either, and badly lit, and echoing.

Casey Nice said, "Do you see a way in?"

I said, "We don't have an armored vehicle. Therefore we're pretty much limited to the doors and the windows."

"Which will be wired for alarms."

"Which will be redundant. They won't need a bell on the roof to tell them we're there."

"Which is where, exactly? In a house with four remaining guards and two world-class killers? Who collectively outnumber us three to one? In a structure much easier to defend than attack?"

"Assuming those questions were rhetorical, I think that's a fair summary."

"How long would it take to build a giant subwoofer?"

"I should have bought cigarette lighters, when I bought that shopping bag."

She said, "Seriously. I spent time at Fort Benning. They'd tell us we need to rethink this thing from zero minus about a hundred hours."

"Who would?"

"The instructors."

"Who all lived long enough to become instructors by improvising every single step of the way. They know plans are useless."

"Reacher, we have to have a plan."

I said, "Let's take a look at the aerial photographs."

The aerial photographs were in one sense amazing, in that they were all pin sharp, rock solid, high-definition color images, whether taken from a satellite many miles above the earth, or a silent drone too high to be seen, or a lurching helicopter a thousand feet up. In another sense they were useless, because they showed us no more than we had seen for ourselves through the night-vision binoculars. The same nothing, but from a different angle. There was a note against the helicopter shots saying the house had not been the primary focus of the mission. The focus was supposed to have been a meeting over drinks in the garden. Those pictures were included, for reference, and showed nothing but three men throwing their arms up over their heads. But by accident the coverage of the house was the best of the three. We could see all four walls pretty well. Doors, windows, points of strength and weakness. Of which there was more strength than weakness, overall. It was not an easy target, even before worrying about who or what was inside.

I said, "We'll figure something out. We have plenty of time. We have to deal with Joey first anyway."

She said, "Do you have a plan for that, at least?"

"What I did last time worked pretty well. Imagine if we had been out there in that parking lot. Behind the little supermarket. In the shadows. We couldn't have missed."

"You want to do *that* again?"

"I don't *want* to. Feel free to come up with alternative ideas."

"Would it even work again?"

"Good point. Probably not with a guy the same level as before. Joey might smell a rat. We're going to have to invoke his elaborate courtesies. We need to find someone he can't stay away from."

"Like who?"

"Old Charlie White would be the favorite. But I imagine he's taking extra precautions. So I guess we should look at either Tommy Miller or Billy Thompson. Which might spark some kind of infighting, possibly. Some kind of internecine conflict, over the spoils. In which case maybe all three of the others would show up at the scene, just to keep an eye on each other. In which case we could give the Romford Boys a real serious leadership vacuum."

"Joey has to be the priority."

"He will be. But if there are targets of opportunity after he's down, we should be prepared to react accordingly."

"I should clear it with General O'Day."

"Go right ahead. But first text Bennett and ask him what kind of security Miller and Thompson use. As in, the same as Joey, or better, or worse? And explain why we're asking."

She found her phone, and her thumbs started dancing. I heard the sound of her first text leaving, a comic noise, like a cartoon character slipping on a banana skin, and then she continued typing, on and on. The update for O'Day, I was sure. Full and complete compliance. O'Day had that kind of effect on people. I started thinking about bulletproof glass again, and I asked her, "Did you tell O'Day we were headed for Wallace Court this morning?"

She said, "It's in the first paragraph here."

"No, I mean, did you tell him ahead of time, that we would be there in the future?"

She slowed her thumbs, and spoke slowly, too, talking and typing all at once. She said, "No, not ahead of time. I wasn't sure we would actually go. Because I wasn't sure why we would want to. So all in all I figured a retrospective report would work better."

"OK," I said. She sped up again, and I watched her. Eventually she stopped typing, and read it all through, and sent it, with the same banana-skin noise. I asked her, "Do we have addresses for Miller and Thompson?"

"They weren't in the bios," she said.

"Then text Bennett again. I'm sure he knows."

The next hour was mostly texting, back and forth with Bennett and O'Day, asking and answering questions, and stockpiling data. Miller and Thompson lived in Chigwell too, four streets from each other, and four streets from Joey. No operational reason. Simply that Chigwell was where you went when you made money in Romford. Their security arrangements were the same as Joey's too, at least on paper. They each had a driver and four bodyguards. Three rotations a day. Miller had a new-model Range Rover, black, and Thompson had a new-model Range Rover Sport, also black. As good as Bentleys, according to many. Three lieutenants, all treated the same. At least on paper. But Bennett said in fact the people assigned to Miller and Thompson were second-rate. Little Joey got the pick of the litter. Partly because he was Little Joey, and partly because Miller and Thompson were bureaucrats. Vital, but not at the heart of the action. Hence a whole different dynamic. As between the two of them, there was nothing to choose. Either one would be a target of equal softness.

"Comparatively, I suppose," Casey Nice said.

I said, "We need a vehicle."

"General Shoemaker gave us credit cards. We could rent one."

"Not a good idea. Too much paperwork."

"Maybe Mr. Bennett would lend us one."

"I'm sure his are all fitted with satellite trackers, in which case he'd be worried about subpoenas."

"So how?"

"Second choice would be steal one. But ideally we should find another pair of foot soldiers and take their panel van. That would buy us a couple of seconds, with Miller or Thompson. They wouldn't see the threat right away. We'd look like their own people. At least at first."

"So that's two attacks we're making, not one."

"With two more still to go," I said. "The foot soldiers, then Miller or Thompson, then Little Joey Green, then whoever is still holed up in his house."

"So we have to survive four separate times. How likely is that?"

"Like the World Series. A big ask, but someone does it every year."

"It's a total of eighteen people."

"Twenty. You're forgetting the drivers. Miller and Thompson have one, and Joey has one. But it's not twenty all at once. That's the good news here. Maximum of six at a time, when we get to the big names, with the driver each and the four bodyguards."

"Some of which are the pick of the litter, standing in front of a guy nearly seven feet tall."

"We can aim over their heads."

"This seems crazy to me."

"Because you aren't quite sure what to expect. To which I say what?"

She thought back, and repeated it straight up. She had a good memory for words. She said, "You say no one ever is sure what to expect. On either side. Which is a good thing. It means the game goes to the fastest thinker. That's all I need to be."

"Correct," I said. "Weird things are going to happen, and things are going to change, and the ground is going to move under our feet, but if we keep on thinking fast, we'll be OK."

"You sure?"

"Like you said before, it's all comparative. Bottom line, it's about thinking faster than Joey Green. And the data was in on that a long time ago. Modern humans outlasted Neanderthal Man."

"What did you mean when you said weird things are going to happen?"

"Just that nothing turns out like you think it will."

"It sounded like you meant something more specific. Do you know things you're not telling me?"

I didn't answer.

Then Bennett showed up again in person, and raised the stakes. We got a call in Nice's room that he was downstairs. He asked us to meet him in the restaurant. He said he would buy us lunch. Nice shut down the tablet computer, which locked his semi-useful pictures behind our twin passwords, and then we rode up in the elevator, and we found him at a table by the window, with our drinks already ordered, bottled water for Nice and black coffee for me, at which point I knew he was about to ask for some real big favor.

Which he did.

He said the behavioral psychology subcommittee had met again, to review the report he had submitted that morning. And apparently the subcommittee had exceeded its brief, by thinking for itself. It had started from the same feeling I had gotten about internecine strife. If Miller or Thompson went down, then depending on the exact distribution between Charlie White and his lieutenants, which was an unknown at that point, then somewhere between perhaps fifteen and twenty percent of the Romford Boys' net profit was up for grabs. Which would be interesting.

But not as interesting as it might perhaps become, if the stakes were somewhat higher still, and certainly more Oedipal. Suppose our initial attack was on Charlie White himself? That would cut the head off the octopus, not just an arm. And it would certainly bring all three lieutenants to the scene, and even if I didn't get them all there, then they might well take care of each other later, because there would be an immediate war of succession. The two old heads against the young usurper, for the whole enchilada. The old heads knew all the business details, and the young usurper was nearly seven feet tall, which would make their opening skirmishes lively, which might make them all forget for a minute that old Charlie paid his cops and his councilors weekly, which might lead to a brief bribe-free window, during which time arrests could be made and prosecutions sought.

So, what did we think?

I said, "How are you doing with my information about the bulletproof glass?"

Bennett said, "It's coming."

"When?"

"How urgent can it be?"

"I want it one minute after you get it. And I want you to get it soon."

He nodded. "So what are we going to do about Charlie White?"

"We?"

"OK, you."

I said, "Where does he live?"

"He's still in Romford. Born and bred. He fancies himself an authentic man of the people."

"Single-family house?"

"What does that mean?"

"Detached," Nice said, like a translator.

"Of course," Bennett said. "Normal size, but it has a wall just like Joey's. Or a fence, or whatever you want to call it. Brick and wrought iron. To keep the grateful proletariat out."

"Security?"

"Six guards and a driver."

"Pick of the litter?"

"Competitive."

"Does he go out much?"

Bennett said, "He's going out tonight, as a matter of fact."

"Where?"

"To meet with the Serbians. To express his condolences."

"Is that one of the elaborate courtesies?"

"One of the most fundamental. They're in business together, and the Serbians suffered a casualty. The same thing happened last night, but in reverse, because of the guy you hit in the throat."

"An hour from now, is the behavioral psychology subcommittee going to come back to us and say we have to take out the Serbians, too?"

"We would like nothing better, but realistically you shouldn't take them on all at once."

I said, "We haven't agreed to take them on at all."

"The committee asked me to point out that we might have understated the quality of the security details protecting Miller and Thompson. They're better than we said. The point being, it's not much of a step to go for White instead."

"Is any of that true?"

"No. It's a very big step."

"But they have to be psychological."

"Whatever works."

"Works better with prior insight. Have you seen our files?"

Bennett smiled and said, "You got my heavy hint? With the passwords? O'Day supplied your files."

"Why?"

"Because we asked."

"Back in the day he would have told you to get lost."

"He's not what he was. He's feeling his way back. His star was fading, for a couple of years."

"Khenkin said the same thing in Paris."

"We could help you, if you need it. Four of Charlie's guards will be in a separate car, obviously. We could pick it off. A traffic stop, or something. Then you'd only have two to deal with, plus the driver, plus Charlie himself."

"One guard in the front with the driver, and the other in the back next to Charlie?"

"That's how they do it."

"What kind of car?"

"A Rolls Royce."

"Black?"

"Of course."

"Armored, like Karel Libor's Range Rover?"

"Only the back doors and the back glass. And only against handguns. I guess they call it the anti-opportunistic assassination option. For the kind of customer who has enemies walking by."

"And the chase car is a Jaguar?"

"They have dozens of them."

I said nothing.

Bennett said, "Traffic stops are expensive. Not just in money. There's exposure, and risk, and liability. Suppose a pregnant lady couldn't get through to the hospital? Suppose an old man had a heart attack because of all the excitement? Questions would be asked. It's a tactic we couldn't justify unless there was a significant potential reward."

My turn to smile. I said, "You didn't rule the world by being nice, right? You're saying if we go after Charlie White, you'll handle the chase car for us. But not if we settle for Tommy Miller or Billy Thompson. So our choice is fight two of Charlie's guards, or four of theirs. Charlie's will be better, but probably not twice as good. Therefore, what we have here is an incentive. Proposed and recommended by the behavioral psychology subcommittee. Am I right?"

"We're here to help each other. That's how it's supposed to work."

"When am I going to get my information about the bulletproof glass?"

"One minute after I get it."

"Which will be when?"

"Very soon."

"What time will old Charlie start out for his condolence visit?"

"Late. The sun has to be down. It's some ethnic thing. They have their rituals, too. We have some details, including a likely route. And we think we've found a spot for the thing with the chase car. I'll send over what we've got, on another computer."

Then he left.

Casey Nice asked, "Is this one of the weird things that was going to happen?"

I said, "No, this part was predictable."

Chapter 43

The new computer arrived, with the same people as before. They said in Nice's case, her new password was the customer help line number at her mother's health insurance company, and in my case, my new password was the name of the other guy Shoemaker had seen me shoot. Then they left, and as before, we carried the computer up to Nice's room, and we entered the private information, and the screen opened up with a long list of files and folders.

Most of the data was deep and random background, painstakingly gathered over many years, and then crunched through computers, this way and that, in the hopes that the past could predict the future. As in, on all the east-west cross-town trips that Charlie White had ever taken, he had never used the M25 motorway, preferring instead the North Circular Road, which, with the South Circular Road, was part of a much earlier attempt at an orbital system, once way out there on the edge of the city, now hopelessly overrun by sprawl. Old Charlie had taken the slow boat eighty-five-point-seven percent of the time. The other fourteen-point-three percent he had been driven straight through the center. This was believed to show a strong preference. I believed it showed Sunday came but once a week. When the center was quiet, a straight line was a no brainer. Weekdays, it was better to keep some distance. There were seven days in a week, and a hundred divided by seven was fourteen-point-three. Except that in the modern world there wasn't really much of a difference between Sundays and weekdays. But Charlie was an old man. And old habits die hard. Maybe he remembered London as a ghost town on Sundays, and the M25 as farms.

I said, "What day is it today?"

Nice said, "Friday."

Bennett had hedged his bets by planning for both routes, calling option two the straight shot through the center, and option one the circle to the north on the North Circular. Not that it really mattered. Because obviously the circle would meet the straight shot somewhere, in this case way in the west, about nine o'clock on a dial. Which was the obvious place to put the pick-off point for the chase car. Two birds with one stone. Which is what Bennett had done. There was an aerial photograph of the place where the two roads met, which had a surreal acreage of blacktop, like a regular four-way stop suddenly swollen up to immense size, but uniformly, like Joey's house.

Charlie White's home address was shown as a push-pin graphic on a map, and his destination was shown as another, stuck into an address in Ealing, which was his opposite number's house. A summit meeting. There was a photograph of the place, which was a big, hand-some, not-quite-suburban red-brick pile. Not a mil-lion miles from Chigwell, except it was. The street was about thirty years older than Joey's, maybe, but it was there for the same kind of reason. Successful people had to live somewhere.

Charlie's latest Rolls Royce had a file all its own. With photographs. It was big and ugly, with weird suicide doors on the back, but it was very imposing. No doubt about that. Ninety-three-point-two percent of the time Charlie sat behind his driver, with a guard next to him on the back seat, and another next to the driver up front. The other six-point-eight percent of the time this linear deployment was changed to a di-agonal deployment, with the back seat guard placed behind the driver. No pattern had been discerned. Which I guessed was likely, with computers. No com-mon sense. Obviously Charlie's regular driver was short. The steering wheel was on the right side of the car, and the car was on the left side of the road, and maybe Charlie didn't feel comfortable next to the sidewalk, stopped at lights or slow in traffic, so he rode next to the crown of the road instead, behind his driver, which was OK because the guy was short, ex-cept the guy needed time off now and then, so on oc-casion Charlie was forced out from behind a taller replacement, maybe twenty-five days in a twelve-

month period, which might have been a legal minimum, and which was six-point-eight percent of a year.

I said, "I need to go buy a very sharp knife."

Nice said, "OK."

We walked eleven blocks on Piccadilly, and the
whole length of Bond Street, and we saw plenty of
knives, but some of them were solid silver, for eating
fish, and others were neat pearl-handled pocket knives,
for rooting around in briar pipes, and none of them
was any good to me. Until we happened upon a very
upscale hardware store. It was full of rugged tools,
most of them with dark-stained wooden handles, including a linoleum knife with a wicked hooked blade.
I bought two, plus a roll of silver duct tape, and the
counterman put all three items in a brown paper bag
that he gave me for free.

Then Nice wanted clothes, so we made Oxford
Street the third side of our square, and she picked out
a store, where she picked out a new outfit. At the
dressing room door she gave me her jacket to hold,
and she said, "You don't need to check. I've still got
one pill left."

Five minutes later she came out in her new stuff,
and she put her jacket back on, and we headed for the
street, but first we passed the escalator to the mens-
wear department, so I followed her hint and headed
upstairs. I got all new, except for pants, because none
would fit. But the coat was better than the Arkansas
golf jacket. Bigger pockets, and less of a Glock-shaped
silhouette. An upgrade, but I felt bad about ditching

the old one. Like burying a friend. Khenkin's brains had been on it, and Nice's tears.

Then we headed down through Grosvenor Square, past our embassy, toward the back of the hotel, and I said, "My guess is Bennett will offer us a government car tonight. In which case we're going to take it, but we're going to ditch it as soon as we can."

"Why?"

"I don't want to be tracked."

"Would they?"

"Of course they would. They need to cover their ass. And they need to file a report tomorrow. Twenty-point-two percent of the time I was scratching my head."

"Why do you need two linoleum knives?"

"I don't. I need one, and you need one."

"For what?"

"Like I said before, we need to think for ourselves now, and there may be orders we need to ignore."

She said nothing.

I said, "Best of both worlds. We're doing our jobs, but we're doing them our way."

She said, "OK."

"Which also means, tonight we leave our phones at home."

Chapter 44

Bennett came back again just after four in the afternoon. He gave us the keys to his silver Vauxhall and told us he had programmed the chosen cross-roads into the navigation system. He suggested we stand by a little ways west of the spot, to be ready to pick up the Rolls Royce immediately after the chase car had been cut loose. He felt Charlie White would neither wait for it nor intervene nor try to help it in any way. Etiquette was too important. He couldn't be late in Ealing. That would be discourteous, and even disrespectful. Such things were important to London gangsters.

Charlie was expected at the Serbian leader's house at ten o'clock in the evening, which meant there was an eighty-four percent chance he would leave home exactly one hour before, which would give him a twenty-minute margin in case of traffic or other delays. If necessary he would park around the block and wait. Such was his usual habit for sensitive destinations. Etiquette meant everything. Ten o'clock meant ten o'clock. But probably his east-west loop around the North Circular would be uneventful, and therefore he would likely arrive at the pick-off point before nine-thirty. Bennett said his crew would be on the scene on full alert from the top of the hour onward, and he advised us to do the same.

I said, "How are you coming along with my information about the glass?"

He said, "You'll get it as soon as I do."

"I know that. But when will you get it?"

"Tonight, at the latest. Hopefully before the nine o'clock start time. If not, then I'll get it immediately afterward."

"Where is it coming from?"

"You know I'm not going to tell you that."

"Who else did you talk to, and what kind of notes did you write?"

"Nobody, and none at all. It's as low profile as you can get. Which is probably why it's taking so long."

"OK," I said. "Relax. Take a break. We're going to. We'll see you later tonight. You might not see us, but don't forget, we're out there somewhere, and we're depending on you."

Bennett looked at me, but said nothing.

Then he left.

We ate at five-thirty, because we wanted to be full of energy and good nutrition three and more hours later, and human digestion gets slower with stress, not faster. Then we put our phones side by side on her window ledge, twenty floors above Hyde Park, and she said, "I'm going to tell General O'Day we suspected penetration by British intelligence. It's the only possible defense. I'm breaking strict orders here."

I said, "Understood."

"And it will only work once. They'll make some new trade where the penetration becomes legitimate, in exchange for something else. So then we couldn't come up with some entirely random new excuse a second time around without looking obvious. So this is the only time we can do it. Is it worth it, for the Brits?"

"We only need to do it once. There wouldn't be a second time."

"But why now?"

"It's as good a time as any."

"What does that mean?"

"We leave here at seven-thirty," I said.

At seven-thirty we were standing next to the silver Vauxhall, in the Hilton's carriage circle, pooling and piecing together our impressions of the local geography, and coming to an unfortunate conclusion. Which was, to get where we were going, we had to either try a tricky slalom through the back streets, or drive around Hyde Park Corner in the direction of Buckingham Palace. Casey Nice felt the back streets raised the odds too high, of getting lost and thereby missing our deadline for the most mundane of reasons. I agreed. Then she said on the other hand Hyde Park Corner was a racetrack, and fender benders or traffic tickets were equally mundane. I agreed with that, too. But then she said she supposed back streets could be just as bad for fender benders and traffic tickets. Narrow spaces, parked vehicles, no-left-turn, no-right-turn, no rolling stops, or whatever the rules were. Probably the risk was far greater. So Hyde Park Corner it was. I volunteered to drive, but she insisted. Which was good. She was better at it.

It was like jumping into a rushing river, and going with the flow, and then jumping out again at exactly the right spot, which was basically two bold maneuvers separated by a lot of held breath. But Nice got it right both times, and we made it out to Grosvenor Place, safe and sound, tight against Buckingham Palace's side wall, which looked a lot like Wallace Court's side wall. Maybe the same contractor had built them both. Maybe at the time he had a long list of prospective customers, all of them worried about the same kind of thing.

We dumped the car in a no-parking zone a hundred yards from the St. James's Park subway station. We felt a hundred yards was enough to keep our destination ambiguous. We could have been headed elsewhere. There was plenty of other stuff in the area. And the station itself served two separate lines, including the Circle Line, which like its name suggested ran in a subterranean circle, not as wide as the above-ground orbitals, but more like the downtown Loop in Chicago. The other line was the District Line, our old friend, the one we wanted, which ran all the way across London from the east to the west.

We stopped in at a bright white branch of Boots

the Chemist and bought two burner cell phones, with cash. Then we walked onward to the subway, and we used our cash-bought travel cards, and we went down to the platforms, where we waited for a train running east, away from Ealing, away from the giant four-way, and away from Bennett.

Chapter 45

We got out of the Tube at Barking, and we walked up to the Barking Minicabs office, where Nice fired up her new cell and called for a car from the sidewalk outside. There was the usual ragtag selection of sedans on the curb, old Fords and Volkswagens and Seats and Skodas, unfamiliar models to us, but clearly ideal for their line of work, like Crown Victorias in America or Mercedes Benzes in Germany. Within a minute a guy came out of the office. He was digging in his pocket for a key. He was middle aged, and he looked local, and a little sleepy. He saw us and didn't react in any way. Maybe he was part-time only, and unaware of late-breaking gangland APBs. He said, "Where to, folks?"

I said, "Purfleet," because I liked the sound of the name. I had seen it on a road sign. I figured it was east and a little south of Barking. The guy indicated a scraped-up Ford Mondeo the color of sewage, and he said, "Climb aboard."

Which we did, side by side on the rear seat. The guy slid in behind the wheel and took off, smooth and competent, left and right through the back streets, working the gearshift, keeping the diesel purr going. I figured he was aiming to join the main Purfleet road as late as possible, to beat the traffic, which worked for me. I waited until I saw a bleak stretch up ahead, with weedy sidewalks, and boarded windows, and a forlorn line of shuttered small-business workshops, and I pulled out my gun and waved it in the mirror, long enough for the guy to see it for what it was, and then I touched it to the back of his neck, and I said, "Pull over, right here."

Which he did, instantly sweating and panicking, and he said, "I don't have any money on me."

I said, "Have you been robbed before?"

He said, "Many times."

"This is different. We're not going to rob you. We're going to pay you for your time. Every minute. We'll even give you a tip. But we're going to drive now, and you're going to ride in the back. OK?"

The guy didn't answer.

I said, "Put your hands behind the seat."

Which he did, and I wrapped his wrists with about a yard of duct tape, and then his elbows with a yard more. Uncomfortable, but necessary, to keep him out of action. I asked him, "Do you breathe well through your nose?"

He said, "What?"

"No nasal congestion, no deviated septum, no adenoidal conditions, no current flu-like symptoms?"

He said, "No."

So I wrapped another couple yards around his head, over his mouth, again and again, and then I slid out of the car and opened his door. I found his seat recline lever, and I laid him on his back, and I taped his knees, and his ankles. Then I hoisted his feet up in the air and I shoveled him backward and upside down over his seat into the rear compartment. Casey Nice took his shoulders, and we got him laid out on the floor, a little compressed, but livable. I found a cell phone in his pants pocket, and I left it on the side-walk. I put two of the Romford Boys' fifty-pound notes in his shirt pocket. We figured that was a decent tip. Then Nice got in the front passenger seat, and I got in behind the wheel, and we drove off again, eight twenty-five in the evening, about three miles from where we wanted to be, which was Romford.

We navigated by a shifting mix of dead reckoning and memories, of our previous trips, and of the maps we had seen on Bennett's second computer, and we got to Romford OK, with about twenty minutes to spare, but then we agreed we needed more detail and precision, so I pulled over and Nice ducked out to a newspaper store and came back with an A-Z street atlas. We sat together with the taped-up guy grunting on the floor behind us, and we found Charlie White's address, which gave us a drive from one page to the next. Five minutes, maybe. Rush hour was over, and traffic was moving right along. But slower than it looked, clearly, because it took us seven minutes, not five, to get to the end of Charlie White's street.

Which was a hard-boiled, somewhat leaner-and-meaner version of Little Joey's street. The houses were a generation older, their chimneys a little taller, and their bricks a little shinier, but fundamentally the deal was the same. Lots of walls, lots of fences and gates, and lots of late-model automobiles.

Including a black Rolls Royce and a black Jaguar, parked nose to tail two houses down on the left, behind a fence just like Joey's. Part red brick, with a knee wall and tall spaced pillars, and part wrought iron, painted black and twisted into shapes like licorice, with two electric gates made of the same stuff, one for in and one for out. The Rolls Royce was parked ahead of the chase car, which made logical sense, at least linguistically. Both gates were closed.

There was an eighty-four percent chance he would leave home exactly one hour before.

Five minutes.

I looked at the map and said, "They're heading for the North Circular Road. They'll turn left out of the house. They'll drive away from us. We need to be at the other end of the street."

Nice said, "Do you want to risk a drive-by, or should we go around the block?"

"We took a minicab for a reason. We can get away with a slow cruise, like a guy looking for an address, and then turning around and pulling over and waiting for his customer."

"These people have drivers of their own."

"Not all of them. Only the working class heroes." I backed up a little and made the turn, and drove exactly like a guy looking for an address, slow and obvious, peering out the side window all the time. Charlie's place was a solid old pile, fairly ornate, built back when bricklayers were cheaper than bricks. The front garden was long gone, replaced by a shallow curving driveway, in one gate and out the other, over flagstone slabs and gravel shapes, between concrete urns and concrete angels, some of them with pans of water held high above their heads, for the birds to drink.

I turned around two houses later, and I pulled into the curb, and I waited.

Etiquette meant everything. And ten o'clock meant ten o'clock. Therefore exactly one hour before meant nine o'clock. And at eight fifty-nine on the nose Charlie's front door opened, and he stepped out. He looked just like his photograph. Seventy-seven years old, bulky, round-shouldered, with thin gray hair, and a plain face, and a nose the size of a potato. He was wearing a black suit with a black tie under a black raincoat. Behind him came a shorter old guy, who I assumed was the driver. Behind the short guy came a stream of six younger men, all plainly dressed, all with shaved heads, all a useful size. Four of them headed for the Jaguar, and the other two trailed along toward the Rolls Royce, now directly behind old Charlie himself, because by that point the driver had hustled on ahead to open his door.

Which was awkward, because it was a suicide door, with the handle at the front, one of a seamless pair with the driver's door handle, which was on a regular door, and Charlie was approaching from the rear, all of which meant Charlie had to pass by his driver, and then stand and wait until the guy opened up, and then reverse direction, and get in. But between them they got the job done eventually. Charlie settled back, and the driver closed the door on him, and he opened his own regular door, and he slid in, and the two guards got in on the other side, one in the front and one in the rear.

At nine o'clock exactly the gate started to move.

Chapter 46

I was clinging to two crucial assumptions, the first of which was that the short old guy in the Rolls Royce thought of himself as a bit of an artist. Maybe he was a veteran wheelman from way back, an old pro, adaptable to any circumstance, whether the requirement was for a fast getaway from a bank job, or a silent chauffeur for the top boy, but one who secretly colluded in his boss's obsessions, such as for precision timekeeping, especially with sensitive destinations ahead. Therefore I expected the guy to touch the gas when the gate was open some exact accustomed distance, such that it would be still wider open when the car actually got there, thereby allowing the car to pass through, fast and neat and fluent, but with only inches to spare, as if the guy's mechanical precision was somehow a homage or a tribute to his boss's chronological precision. I figured that was how an artist would play it.

Which meant I had to guess the guy's hit-the-gas

signal, and hit mine about three seconds earlier, because I was still some ways down the street, and I had distance to make up. But I couldn't afford to arrive either early or late, so I set off at a slow roll, which I thought was acceptable, because a minicab driver might need to make a note or put his pen away, before looking up and engaging his brain and taking off for real. I saw the Rolls Royce move when the gate was about two-thirds open, slow and smooth, a modest, whispering acceleration, as if the driver intended to take the turn into the street without pausing, as one fluid move.

I watched the speed of the gate and the speed of the car, and the depth of the sidewalk, and the distance between where I was and where I would need to be, and I let the back part of my brain make a quick and dirty decision about when to go, and I hit the gas when it told me to. The grimy old Ford jumped forward, ten yards, twenty, and then I stamped on the brake and the car came to a dead stop, right where the Rolls Royce wanted to be, so the Rolls Royce driver stamped on his own brake in turn, and he came to a stop with his majestic grille two feet from Casey Nice's door, and behind him the chase car stopped two feet from his back bumper.

Then the next split second was all about Casey Nice sliding out through her narrow gap and heading left, her gun out exactly like the federal agent she was, with me skittering around the hood from the other flank, gun out too, and heading right, breathless, for the all-bodyguard side of the limousine, for the twin door handles, right there side by side in the middle of the car, such that both handles could be grabbed at once, and both doors thrown open at the same time.

The second crucial assumption I was clinging to was that modern automobiles had a device that locked the doors automatically, but only when a predetermined speed had been achieved. Which I was sure had not been achieved. Not in this case. Not yet.

I held the Glock finger and thumb and put my hands on the handles.

And pulled.

Both doors opened.

And both doors opened on Nice's side, too, which put us exactly where we wanted to be in relation to the chase car, which was each of us safely behind our very own hunk of armored steel and armored glass. *The back doors and the back glass,* Bennett had said, in his sing-song voice. And the back doors were hinged at the rear, and they opened wide, to a full ninety degrees, so they stuck straight out sideways, like Little Joey's ears, thereby keeping us protected as we went about our business. *Only against handguns,* Bennett had continued, but I figured that was OK, because I was sure the guys in the chase car had nothing bigger. Not that I expected them to shoot at all. Too much risk of hitting Charlie. They would know the rear windshield was armored, but Bennett hadn't mentioned anything else, so they wouldn't risk a wild deflection through a soft-skinned area like the trunk, or a rear wheel arch, because it could come through the upholstery and hit a back-seat passenger anywhere from the ass to the neck. So I expected them to freeze for a second, and then to react, and then to change their minds, and finally to do what they should have done first, which was come swarming out of the car and straight at us. But they would do it fourth, not first, which would give me three clear seconds to get my business done, *one thousand, two thousand, three thousand,* like the long lonely flight of John Kott's bullet, through the cold Parisian air.

My business was to aim the Glock at Charlie White's head in a threatening manner, while using the linoleum knife in my other hand to cut the guard's seat belt, in two places, *slash, slash,* and then to lean in and launch a kind of backhand elbow to the far side of the guy's head, so he ended up falling out, and then to shuffle sideways and do it all again, to the guard in the front, *slash, slash,* the elbow, the guy falling out, and then to turn and kick the back-seat guy, in the head, and the front-seat guy, the same, to keep them out of action on the ground, and then to hustle back to the Ford, and move it out of the way, and jump out again, and turn, by which time I was into the fourth second, and they were out of their car.

But I had to fire anyway. All part of the plan. But not at their tires. The angle was wrong. The bullet would have bounced off, literally. Tires can be freakishly strong. Best way to disable a modern automobile is to fire through the grille. Under the hood. All kinds of wires there, and computer chips, and sensors.

Which is what I did. Four rounds, spaced but fast, crouched wide around my armored door, *bang-bang-bang-bang,* which set the four guys back a step, which gave me time to lunge forward and slam my front door shut, and to hurdle the guys on the ground, and to shuffle and pivot and dump myself down next to Charlie, and to haul my rear door shut, while Nice in the front hit the gas, having used her own Glock and her own knife on the short guy, and the Rolls Royce surged forward like a tidal wave and howled down the street. The four guys ran after us for half a block, just like in the movies, and then they stopped, and watched us go.

Chapter 47

The Rolls Royce felt exactly like it should, given the things people like to say. It was very hushed, and it was very smooth. The rear bench was built like an armchair in an officers' club. It was deep, and wide, and soft. Next to me Charlie White was still belted in. His body was facing front, but his head was turned, and he was staring at me. A strand of his hair had fallen out of place. His nose was like most of an avocado pear. But overall he looked exactly like a gang boss. He was full of power and strength and confidence.

I said, "Are you armed, Charlie?"

He said, "Kid, you know you just signed your own death warrant, right? Please tell me you're clear about that. No one does what you just did."

"But?"

"But nothing."

I said, "There's always something, Charlie."

"Do you have any idea how much trouble you're in?"

"So much I should cut my losses and shoot you in the head and walk away while I still can?"

He said, "You could do that. Or you could get a stay of execution just long enough to get out of town. That's what I'm offering. But I only ask once, and I take your first answer, so you better put your thinking cap on, kid, about what comes next, about how hard it's going to be, and how hard it's going to be every day for the rest of your life."

"What do you want us to do in exchange for that?"

"Get out of my car."

"Wrong answer, Charlie. My question was, are you armed?"

"I'm on my way to a memorial service. Of course I'm not armed."

"Is that an elaborate courtesy?"

"What?"

"Do you have a portable phone in your pocket?"

"Do I look like the kind of man who makes his own telephone calls?"

I said, "Strictly speaking, you *were* on your way to a memorial service. Now you're on your way someplace else. I'm going to have to tape your wrists. No way around that. And it would be better for me if I taped your mouth, too. But to be frank with you, Charlie, I'm concerned how well you breathe through that nose."

"You're concerned what?"

"You could suffocate if I taped your mouth."

"There's nothing wrong with my nose."

"Good to know. That's settled, then."

He said, "Exactly what is it you're trying to do here?"

I said, "Don't worry about it. You're just collateral damage."

"From what? I have a right to know."

From the front seat Casey Nice said, "No, Mr. White, you do not. As a matter of fact you have no rights at all. Legislation is not on your side. Your associate Joseph Green is harboring men who would be called terrorists by any court in the world."

"I don't know anything about Joey harboring anybody."

"He has guests."

"Friends of his, I expect."

"You're responsible for what he does."

"He hasn't done anything."

I said, "But he will," and Nice slowed the car, and took the turn for Chigwell.

We passed the pub, which we both remembered, and we did our best to follow the turns we had taken on foot, the huge car more at home there than in Romford, until we came to the board fence, with the yard-wide gap before the next fence began. Nice pulled over and stopped, and I made Charlie White take his seat belt off, and I made him squirm around with his back to me, and I taped his wrists, and his elbows, and his mouth, around and around, and then I leaned over and opened his door, and pushed him out, and followed after him, and hauled him into the mouth of the alley.

Nice drove on a hundred yards and parked equidistant from five opulent houses, compared to any one of which a gap in a fence a hundred yards away was invisible. She jogged back, fast, a little up on her toes, not relaxed at all, and she bundled into the alley after us, and then squeezed past us and led the way. I kept old Charlie moving behind her, with the old guy huffing and puffing, whether from indignation or lack of condition I couldn't tell, but either way he was proving himself an honest man when he said there was nothing wrong with his nose.

We made it into the grit clearing, Nice first, glancing left and right, then Charlie, stumbling, his best pants flapping, and then me, checking our backs, checking left, checking right, checking the wooden hut ahead, with *Bowling Club* over the door. Nice ducked down and moved the stone and stood up again and said, "There's no key."

Charlie White stood there, breathing hard.

I said nothing.

She said, "Yes, I'm sure it's the right stone."

I said, "Did they change the lock back?"

"Why would they?"

I didn't answer. A shed made of wood, built way back before I was born. *Take it up with whichever carpenter died fifty years ago,* Bennett had said. A good craftsman, probably, but working with poor postwar materials, plus sixty or so summers and sixty or so winters, which meant the shed would be strong, but not very strong. I took three long strides and smashed my heel through the lock and caught the door on the bounce.

The binoculars were gone.

The kitchen stools were gone, and the tripod stands

were gone. The clear lane in front of the windows was completely empty.

Casey Nice said, "Is this one of the weird things you told me would happen?"

I said, "No, I think it's even weirder than that. But like the man said, we get what we get."

I pushed Charlie White all the way in, and I made him sit in a corner, leaning on a bag of bowling club stuff. I switched on my phone, and I entered Bennett's number, which I remembered from the afternoon, and I sent him a message.

It said: *We have Charlie White.*

Then I pictured computers whirring in the county of Gloucestershire, and I switched my phone off again, immediately.

Nice said, "Will it work?"

I said, "I have no idea. But I'm sure something will happen."

Charlie White was watching us. His eyes would always take second place to his nose, in terms of distinguishing features, but they were handsome enough, and mobile, sliding back and forth between us, or perhaps between two different interpretations of his predicament. The first might be represented by me, some kind of a big American thug far from home and punching above his weight, stupid enough to go for a big score, which meant I was guaranteed to be dead, and he was guaranteed to be alive. It was just a matter of time. There would be a little discomfort along the way, but the final outcome was not in doubt. He was far too valuable a chip to be wasted. And a little discomfort was nothing to a Romford Boy. They had come up from worse.

But a second possible interpretation was represented by Casey Nice, with her youth, and her bustling energy, and her accent, downstate Illinois via Yale and Langley, all shot through with the kind of ringing clarity that must have come from growing up in a farmhouse with more than one dog. She was a type, a product of the modern world, perhaps recognizable even in London. She was federal, no question. In which case the taunts about collateral damage might have been true, which was another way of saying pawns in the game, and no way was Charlie White ever going to call himself a pawn in a game, but even bishops and knights got sacrificed sometimes. Because the world's governments were king, with all their three-letter agencies and their shadowy units, which had to be where the girl was from. What else could she be? She was part of some huge international operation, which for once wasn't all about London and Charlie, which removed his guarantee of survival. A pawn was not a valuable chip.

Charlie White didn't know what to think.

"Check," Nice said. "Bennett should have replied by now."

I switched my phone on again, and watched it hunt for its signal, and find it, and present me with everything I had missed in the interim, which was a single text message from Bennett. It said: WHERE ARE YOU MOST URGENT NEW INFORMATION RE-PEAT EXTREMELY URGENT NEW INFORMA-TION MUST DISCUSS IMMEDIATELY

No punctuation, no nothing.

Chapter 48

We had taken careful steps to avoid electronic surveillance, and now we were being asked to come right out and tell the British where we were. Casey Nice said, "I think we have to."

I said nothing.

She said, "You've been bugging him for data. About the glass. And now he has it. You have to hear what he has to say. It could be important. In fact it must be important. Look at his language."

"Unless he's faking. Maybe he's pissed we fell off the map. He's in charge. He's supposed to know where we are. Maybe he's taking it like a challenge."

"He's a brother soldier. Look at what he wrote. Would he lie to you that bad?"

"They didn't rule the world by being nice."

"Your call," she said.

I put my finger on my phone's off button, and I held it there, touching but not pressing, and then I changed my mind and handed the phone to Nice. Her thumbs were quicker. And smaller. I said, "Tell him to come alone."

I wasn't sure how long Bennett would have stuck around the giant four-way in the west of London, but probably he had twigged pretty early that things were not going to plan, so he might have already folded his tent and started for home. In which case he could be in Chigwell as fast as twenty minutes. Or as slow as forty, if in fact he had hung around until the bitter end. There was no way of knowing.

There was only one practical way to the bowling club, for a pedestrian, which was the yard-wide footpath. No doubt there were ancient easements and rights of way across neighboring lots, for lawnmowers and heavy rollers and whatever else it took to keep grass that smooth, and if SWAT teams came they would use helicopters and land on the green itself, but if Bennett came alone he would walk.

Charlie White was still watching us. Still unsure. I spent most of the time looking out the windows, but without the night vision and the magnification there wasn't much to see. Just dark space, vague trees, and the distant glow of Little Joey's street, a quarter of a mile away. No detail. I could barely make out his house, big as it was. Nice sat on a lumpy canvas bag, with both hands in her jacket pockets, one of them no doubt curled around the butt of her Glock, and the other maybe curled around her pill bottle. I wanted to say *I guess this ain't the night to quit Zoloft,* but I didn't, because I figured she would prefer me to take it seriously. And maybe she wasn't thinking about pills at all. In which case I certainly didn't want to remind her. Maybe she was just keeping her hands warm. The air had gone cold. It had been a pleasant day, but the temperature had dropped after sunset.

After fifteen minutes I went out, and closed the smashed door behind me, and hiked across the grit to the clearing's furthest corner, which gave me a sideways view of the line between the mouth of the alley and the bowling club HQ. Which was the best I could do. I didn't want to be in the alley itself. I didn't want to be on the street. I wanted an escape route, if necessary, and our best bet was through the gardens and over the lawns that surrounded us, not along the public highways and byways, which were full of dangers and perils.

And I wanted to be at least a little proactive, too. If Nice had to start shooting, she'd be firing out the front of the hut, so it made sense for me to be firing at ninety degrees. Basic triangulation. Lots of good reasons. Not that I could see very well. Clearly the bowling club had voted down any kind of exterior illumination. Some of the houses backing onto the space had lit-up rooms, and there was the usual kind of urban glow in the sky, the city itself reflected back off low nighttime clouds, all averaged out to smoky yellow, but apart from those two faint sources I was looking at nothing but pitch dark. The back part of my brain told me Bennett was a man of average size,

and his center mass would be thirty-seven inches behind his muzzle flash.

I waited.

I **was out** in the cold seven more minutes, which
when added to the original fifteen made twenty-two,
which told me Bennett had indeed quit early and
holed up somewhere central to wait on events. I heard
his footsteps all the way at the far end of the path, a
soft, whispering sound, amplified but also modified
by the parallel board fences. Then as he got closer I
heard the muted crunch of his soles on the thin scattering of grit, and at one point I heard a brief *rat-a-tat*
scuffle, as if he had swayed on the uneven ground and
something in his hand had brushed against the boards.
Something leather, I thought, given the sound.

He stepped into the clearing, and stopped. I could
see his face, just vaguely, a pale gleam, but I couldn't
see anything else. I couldn't see his hands.

I waited.

Then he spoke, in his normal sing-song voice, as if
we were in a room together and I was six feet away.
He said, "Reacher? I'm guessing you're ninety degrees to my left or my right. I have a flashlight with
me. I'm not going to shine it on you. I'm going to
shine it on myself, and then I'm going to shine it back
down the footpath so you can see I came alone."

I said nothing.

I saw a flashlight beam click on, dancing on the
ground, and then it reversed itself in his hand and he
played it all over himself, fast, like it was foam and

he was on fire. He was in his regular clothes. The thing in his hand was a briefcase. He ended up with the beam high over his head, shining straight down, like a shower head.

I said, "OK, I believe you."

He glanced my way, inside his cone of light, and then he swung the beam down and picked out his way to the door. I followed him in, and he balanced the flashlight upright on the floor, so the bounce off the ceiling lit us all up. He took a long hard look at Charlie White, and then he turned back to me.

I asked him, "What happened to the binoculars?"

He said, "I had them removed."

"Why?"

"They weren't just binoculars. Remember? They were video feeds. Think back through history. Who gets in the least trouble? The guy on the tape, or the guy not on the tape, because there was no tape in the first place?"

"You were looking out for us?"

"We're here to help each other."

"Thank you."

"I was expecting some action tonight."

"You got my information?"

He paused a second, and said, "I've got information."

"But not mine?"

"I think it's yours in a way. I think you should own it. A lot of the ideas were yours."

"What ideas?"

"The wrong ideas," he said.

He squatted down and popped his briefcase lid,

and I saw a photograph inside, black and white, which he picked up and lifted into the light. He offered it to me and Nice equally, like a ceremony, so she took its left edge and I took its right edge, and we held it between us. It was not a regular printed photograph. It had come out of a computer. The paper was thin, and the surface was dull. An e-mailed attachment, maybe, printed out on an office machine.

The picture showed a dead man in what looked like a hospital bed. In what looked like a foreign hospital. The finish on the wall looked different. Somewhere hot, maybe. The kind of place where a hospital could have yellow clay tiles on the floor. The bed was narrow, and made of iron pipe painted white. The sheet was tight and straight, and the blanket was pale and unmarked. High standards from the nursing staff, maybe. Or mugging for the camera. Because the picture was clearly part of an official documentary record. Someone had stood at the foot of the bed and taken a picture for a file. The angle and the framing said so. Like a crime scene photograph. There was a date and a time stamped in. Depending on exactly where in the world it was, it was either very recent, or extremely recent.

The man in the bed had not died easy. That was clear. He had what looked like a bullet wound in his forehead. The skin was all torn up. Not an entry wound. Not an exit wound, either. It was a furrow. Like a glancing blow, that shreds flesh but only cracks bone, instead of piercing it. Maybe an unlucky ricochet.

It was not a new wound. Far from it. I could practically smell it through the paper. I had seen wounds like that before. It was between twelve and twenty days old. That was my guess. And it hadn't healed. Hadn't even begun. It looked like it had gone septic early, and gotten messy, and no doubt the infection had caused a raging fever, and it looked like the guy had fallen for it hard, racked and sweating, tossing and shivering, losing weight, getting pale, becoming nothing more than glittering skin wrapped tight over jutting cheekbones, and then finally getting his picture taken by a bored government clerk. Rest in peace, wherever. It was impossible to say what the guy had looked like three weeks before, other than he was probably white, and his skull was a normal size.

I said, "So?"

Bennett said, "That's one of the retired snipers we keep an eye on."

"And?"

"He got hired all the way to Venezuela. But things went wrong over there. You know how it is. Everyone betrays everyone else. Our boy got in a gunfight with the police, and he got away, but not before getting hit in the head. Which he didn't get treated, because now he was on the run. He holed up in a chicken house somewhere, and tried to gut it out. He ate raw eggs and drank from a hosepipe at night. But the infection was bad. A woman found him delirious, and took him to the hospital in the back of her pick-up truck. By that point his blood work looked like toxic waste. He died a day later. He had no name and no ID. But he looked foreign to them, so they put his fingerprints on the Interpol system."

"And?"

"That's William Carson."

Chapter 49

Bennett said, "Kott is the only one not accounted for now. Which raises two possibilities. Which throws them into a panic, obviously. Because now they have to choose. Either you're wrong, and the same guy could make both shots, or they're wrong, and there are more snipers in the world than they know about."

I said, "Which way are they leaning?"

"I'm sure they'd like to blame you, but they're supposed to be rational. The truth is they just don't know."

"Not even the psychological subcommittee?"

"Not even."

"It's option one," I said. "Kott is on his own."

"What tells you that?"

"A toothless hillbilly in Arkansas."

"Are you admitting you were wrong?"

"I'm admitting I was misled."

"By what?"

"Doesn't matter yet. Doesn't change what we have to do next."

"Which is what?"

"We have to get Little Joey out of his house."

"How?"

"We're going to negotiate with him. Face to face, because of the size of the deal."

"Which is what?"

"We're going to sell Charlie to him."

"Like a ransom?"

I shook my head. "Like a purchase price. All anyone knows so far is that Charlie was snatched up by persons unknown, so now we can sell him on, under the table, and Joey can beat whatever kind of information he wants right out of him, and no one will ever be the wiser. Done deal, right there. Because now Joey's got the account numbers and the passwords and he knows where the bodies are buried. He's the new boss, automatically."

"Will he go for that?"

"Are you kidding?"

"I mean, will he understand the logic?"

"It's a DNA thing. Like rats. He'll come running. Which is what we want."

"Why were you not more surprised by Carson?"

"Just a feeling."

"About what?"

"Joey doubled his guard. He didn't triple it. Yet he likes to put on a show. There were only two people in the house. Joey and Kott."

"Why not Joey and Carson?"

"It was Kott's bullet in Paris. Chemistry says so. Trust me. This is all about John Kott."

"No, this is all about the G8."

"The G8 is safe. Trust me on that, too."

"It can't be safe until we get him. He's the last one."

"The G8 was never the target," I said.

"So what is?"

"I need my information about the glass."

"You'll get it. What's the target?"

"Something that doesn't change what we have to do next."

"We're not doing anything next. They're still talking."

"Who's talking?"

"The committees."

"John Kott is in Little Joey's house. That's all they need to know. Tell them that from me."

"They'll say your credibility is damaged."

"Then I'll do what my mother told me, whenever I got mad. I'll count to three."

"What does that mean?"

"Can you count to three?"

"Of course I can."

"Show me."

"One, two, three."

I said, "Do it like time ticking away."

He said, "One second, two second, three second."

"Is that how they say it in Wales?"

"That's how they say it everywhere."

"No, it isn't. We say one thousand, two thousand."

"It's supposed to sound like a ticking clock. Which

it does. Second, second, second. Like something with a pendulum, in your grandma's front parlor."

"That's pretty good."

"What was your point?"

I said, "John Kott is in Little Joey's house."

Bennett paused a beat, and then he looked over toward the corner of the hut, and he said, "We should confirm these wild rumors with Mr. White."

Old Charlie backed away a little when he heard those words. No doubt the Romford Boys asked questions from time to time, of reluctant sources, and no doubt they used methods that ran the whole gamut from brutal to fatal. And apparently he didn't expect a government agent to be lenient in comparison.

Bennett stepped over and considered the guy for a long moment. Then he took a switchblade from his pocket. A flick knife, in Britain. He thumbed the button and the blade popped out, with a solid *thunk*. An antique, probably. They had been illegal for so long it had gotten hard to find a good one. He balanced the handle on his thumb, with his four fingers spread along the upper edge, and he moved the blade close to Charlie's cheek, like he was a barber about to start a shave with a straight razor.

Charlie eased backward, until his head was jammed hard against the wood of the wall.

Casey Nice said, "Are we on the record here?"

Bennett said, "Don't worry."

He used the blade to pick at the edge of the duct tape I had wrapped around Charlie's mouth. He got some of it lifted and used a fingernail to pouch it out. He made a quarter-inch cut, and then started over, lifting, picking, cutting, a quarter-inch at a time, until the whole two-inch width was severed. He used the blade again, to lift a tab, which he grasped finger-and-thumb with his left hand, and then he peeled the tape away from Charlie's lips, neither fast nor slow, like a nurse changing a dressing. Charlie coughed and ducked his mouth to his shoulder, to wipe it.

Bennett asked him, "Who is staying with Joey?"

Charlie said, "I don't know."

Bennett still had the switchblade open. Charlie's hands were still taped behind his back. He was wedged as tight in the corner as he could get. No further movement was feasible.

Bennett said, "You sell guns to hoodlums everywhere in this country. You peddle heroin and cocaine. You lend a man with mouths to feed fifty pounds, but he pays you back a hundred, or you break his legs. You bring teenage girls from Latvia and Estonia and you turn them out, and when they're all used up, they go to Joey's. So on a scale of one to ten, how likely is it that anyone in the whole wide world will give a shit about what I do to you next?"

Charlie didn't speak.

Bennett said, "I need an answer, Mr. White. Just so we understand each other. On a scale of one to ten. Where ten is very likely and one is not very likely. Pick a number."

Charlie didn't speak.

"I get it," Bennett said. "You can't find the right answer. Because it's a trick question. The numbers don't go low enough. No one in the whole wide world is going to give a shit. Not one single person. And they won't even know anyway. Tomorrow you'll be in Syria or Egypt or Guantanamo Bay, even. We do things differently now. Your organization is harboring a rifleman planning to shoot the British prime minister and the American president. You're the new Osama Bin Laden. Or Khalid Sheik Mohammad, at the very least."

Charlie White said, "That's bullshit."

"Which part?"

"All of it. I wouldn't have the prime minister shot."

"Why not?"

"I voted for him."

"Who is staying with Joey?"

"I don't know who it is."

"But you know someone is there?"

"I never met the man."

Bennett said, "He killed Karel Libor for you, and he gave you a lot of money, and he induced you to shake hands with the Serbians, and you're providing twenty-four-seven shelter and security for him, and for a deal of that magnitude you never talked to him face to face?"

Charlie said nothing.

Bennett said, "I think you talked extensively. I think you know every detail. Including the target."

Charlie said, "I want my lawyer."

Bennett said, "Which part of Guantanamo Bay don't you understand?"

Charlie said nothing.

Bennett said, "Hypothetically, then. For now. If a hypothetical man in your hypothetical situation was involved in a deal of that type, would he not want to approve certain details?"

"Of course he would. Hypothetically."

"Including the target?"

"Of course the target."

"Why?"

"It would have to be acceptable."

"Who would be off limits?"

"Women and children, obviously. And the Royal Family."

"And the prime minister?"

"That would be a big step. Hypothetically, I mean. I believe such people haven't dabbled in that kind of politics before."

"Just the folding kind?"

"Hypothetically."

"So you know what the target is. Because you approved it."

No answer.

Bennett said, "This is like one of those philosophy questions that people debate in the newspapers. Suppose you had until the sun comes up to find the ticking bomb? How far could you go, legally and ethically?"

No answer.

"What's the target, Mr. White?"

Charlie said nothing. He was looking at Bennett, looking at me, looking at Bennett, back and forth, with some kind of a plea in his eyes, as if he wanted permission to give each of us a different answer.

I said, "Leave it for now, Bennett. It doesn't change what we have to do next."

Bennett looked at me, and at Charlie, and at Nice, and then he shrugged and stepped back to where he had been before, by the window, and as he got there the busted door crashed open and a man with a gun stepped in, followed immediately by another, the hut suddenly hot and cramped, six of us in there, and then it got worse. A leg the size of a tree trunk appeared, bent at the knee, and a massive shoulder, and a bent back, and a lowered head, way down under the lintel, where it said *Bowling Club* outside, and then Little Joey was right there in front of us, in the hut, upright, nearly seven feet tall, the pent of the roof exactly framing his massive head and shoulders.

Chapter 50

Joey's huge bulk pushed his two guys forward, and we didn't have room to retreat, so we ended up all packed together like a subway car, which meant contact between us and them was made early, with one of Joey's guys pressing up against Casey Nice, and seizing her elbow, and moving her in front of him, presumably with his gun in her back, and the other guy did same thing to Bennett, so I had no snap shot. The Glock stayed in my pocket. There was nothing I could do at all, except get a crick in my neck.

Up close and personal Joey was worse than I had feared. He was nothing like the athletes I had seen, years before, from visiting colleges on the West Point campus, the football players and the basketball teams. Those guys had been immense, but quiet and focused and above all contained, as if their frontal lobes were fully in command. Joey didn't look that way. He was the furthest thing possible from a small nervous guy, but he was twitching and throbbing with the same kind of spasms. He looked deranged. His eyes were buried deep and his lower lip was hanging down over his absent chin. His teeth were wet. His right foot was tapping on the floor. His left hand was bunched in a fist, and his right hand was arched open, completely rigid.

He looked at Charlie White first, and then he looked away. He looked at Casey Nice, up, down, and then at me, the same, up, down, and then at Bennett, right into his eyes, and he said, "You think I didn't notice the fence blew down? And the tree? You think I'm stupid? You think you're the only one who can afford night-vision binoculars? We thought you'd gone. But we checked anyway. And look what we found."

No reply from Bennett. I recognized both of Joey's guys. They had been in the little supermarket's parking lot. The security cordon, from the black Jaguar. Two of the four. The pick of the litter. Next to their boss they looked like miniature humans. I assumed the other two were out in the lot. In the cold and the dark. I assumed the driver was still with the Bentley, at the far end of the yard-wide footpath. I put my hands in my pockets. On the right I had the Glock, and on the left I had the linoleum knife. I glanced out the window at the shadowy contours of the street four hundred yards away, and I hoped Kott didn't have a night-vision scope on his rifle. He could have chosen which eye to plug me through.

Behind me Charlie White said, "Joey, get me out of here, will you?"

But Joey didn't answer right away, which gave me a

glimmer of hope. Maybe he was setting foot on a road that might lead somewhere useful. *It's a DNA thing. Like rats.*

Behind me Charlie said, "They're armed, Joey. They have guns and knives."

Joey nodded, an inch down, an inch up, which looked millimetric, given his bulk. The guy with Bennett let go of his elbow and started patting his pockets. He came out with the switchblade, now closed up again, and a Sig Sauer automatic, a P226, I thought, favored by Special Forces everywhere. Then the guy with Casey Nice did the same thing, and out came her Glock, and her linoleum knife, and finally her pill bottle, its lone occupant rattling quietly. Joey held out his hand, the size of a trash can lid, and the guy put the bottle in it, and Joey held it between a huge finger and a huge thumb, and he brought it up close to his face, and he said, "Who is Antonio Luna?"

Casey Nice started once, and started again, and said, "A friend of mine."

"Are you addicted?"

Nice paused a beat and said, "I'm trying not to be."

Joey used a thumbnail the size of a golf ball and popped the lid, which fell away to the floor, and he upended the bottle into his palm, where the lone pill looked tiny.

He said, "Do you want it?"

Casey Nice didn't answer.

"Do you?"

No answer.

"You do, don't you?"

No answer.

Joey slammed his palm to his mouth, and he swallowed the pill.

He dropped the bottle on the floor.

Charlie White said, "Joey, come on."

Joey reached out an arm the size of a tree limb and nudged his guys aside, one way and the other, making them haul Nice tight against the wall and Bennett tight against the window, elbows around their necks, guns visible now, aimed at me, Browning High Powers from Belgium.

I took my hands out of my pockets.

Joey turned sideways and came through the gap between his guys, one freakish stride, and then he stopped and stood face to face in front of me.

Or face to collar bone. He was six inches taller. And six inches wider. He was all bone and muscle. Not a bodybuilder. Like a regular guy, but a strong one, and all swollen up uniformly, like his house. He smelled of sweat, sharp and acid, and there was a pulse jumping in his neck. All of which hit the ancient parts in the back of my brain, especially the most ancient part of all, which had kept us safe for seven million years, and counting. The flight reflex, and mine was screaming at me to get the hell out of there. But I didn't. I had no place to go. Wall behind me, wall to the left of me, wall to the right of me, and Joey ahead of me. I looked up into his eyes, and in the recessed shadows I saw one pupil blown the size of a dime, and the other like a pinprick.

I said, "What else are you taking, Joey?"

He said, "Shut up."

He lifted his hands. His fingers were long and thick.

Not like sausages. Wrong description. They were wider than that, and harder. More like soda cans, jointed at the knuckles, with fingertips twice as wide as mine, and nails twice the size.

He hooked those fingertips into my coat pockets, and wormed them deep, four inches maybe, coming close, breathing on me, and then he jerked back and tore the pockets right off my coat. My gun and my knife spilled out and clattered to the floor. He scraped at them with his feet, and kicked them behind him. Then he turned and stepped back to the door, the same giant stride in reverse.

Charlie White said, "Joey, don't walk away from me."

Joey shifted his weight, one foot to the other, and the floor creaked, and the balanced flashlight fell over, and shone a rolling beam across our ankles. Charlie White started moving, getting impatient, testing the tape on his wrists. I figured Joey had about a second and a half to make up his mind. Any longer than that, and there was no going back. Bonds of trust would have been destroyed. Suspicions would permanently linger. Charlie would always know it had passed through his subordinate's mind to do exactly what I had outlined to Bennett.

A second and a half.

Joey chose wrong.

He turned his giant head and called out the door, "Get in here and take Mr. White home."

Which was impossible, as long as he was blocking the doorway. So he bent his head again, and hunched his shoulders, and bent his back, and bent his knees, and he squirmed his way out of the hut, sideways, right leg, duck, left leg, and then he was gone again.

The guys holding Nice and Bennett stayed on the ball, their elbows tight on their necks, their guns up diagonally, ready for instant action, aimed halfway between them and me. I looked at Bennett and said, "What do they call these new teams they've got you in?"

The guy holding him said, "Shut up."

I said, "Make me."

Which he didn't. He was not authorized to intervene, I guessed, except in dire emergencies. Other than that, our fate and our treatment was to be decided at a higher level, at a later time. Bennett said, "We don't really have a name. Not yet. It's all pretty fluid at the moment."

"Is your air force working with you?"

He nodded. "It's a completely integrated approach."

"Can you get us a flight out of here?"

"Home?"

"Fort Bragg."

"When?"

"Now would be great. But let's say a couple hours from now."

"You're optimistic."

"I try to stay cheerful, no matter what."

"Won't O'Day send a plane?"

"I want the Royal Air Force," I said. "I'll trade that for not meeting the Queen."

Then the guys from outside came in, and they hustled through the tight quarters and helped Charlie White to his feet. They cut the tape off his wrists and his elbows with knives of their own, and he rubbed his arms and rolled his shoulders to get some circulation back, and then he straightened up, no longer a hostage, but a gang boss again, full of power, and strength, and confidence. He looked at me and said, "You lose, kid. Pity about that. Because now comes the death warrant."

I glanced out across the bowling lawn, at the dark street nearly a quarter of a mile away. Was Kott watching? I pictured a hallway window, fifty percent taller and fifty percent wider than anyone else's hallway window, with a tripod behind it, and a pair of night-vision binoculars, bought off the Internet maybe, or stolen and smuggled out of a military depot anywhere in Britain or Europe, with Kott crouched behind them, eyes to the rubber rings, staring past where the fence had been, and the fallen tree, taking in all the precise silvery details. But the line of sight was narrow. We could see the house, and he could see the hut, but none of us could see much of anything else.

Which was good.

What would he hear, from a quarter mile away? The Browning High Power was a nine-millimeter weapon, and like all Fabrique Nationale products it was built tight and true, so it would be no noisier than it needed to be. But he would hear it. Gunfire would be audible, at four hundred yards, late in the evening in the suburbs.

Surely.

Probably.

Did he have a night-vision scope on his rifle?

I said, "Charlie, wait."

Charlie stopped and turned back, and I hit him in the face, a colossal right, all the way up from my planted feet, as hard as I could, partly because I didn't like the guy, and partly because I had to drive on through to the guy holding Nice, with no delay at all. Which was pretty much what happened. I caught Charlie dead on the nose, which admittedly was a big target, and I felt my fist drive through it, and beyond it, and then his falling body weight whipped his head out from under my moving hand, and my momentum carried me onward, shoulder-first into Nice, and then the guy behind her.

There were eight of us in there at that point, and the advantage of fighting in a small tight-packed hut with a flashlight rolling around on the floor was all the dark close-quarters pushing and shoving and stumbling, which made an accurate aim impossible, especially with the top boy in the mix somewhere, collateral damage just waiting to happen, especially because Bennett was messing with one of the guys, and I was messing with the other. Casey Nice knew exactly what was happening, and she peeled away like a wraith, but not before taking advantage of her relative geometry by kneeing her guy in the nuts as she spun. Which helped me considerably, because it meant the guy's head was jerking downward just as my elbow was jerking upward, which doubled the power of the blow, like money for nothing, which left me instantly free to turn on Charlie's escorts, who at that point were still empty-handed, and already moving away, thinking that Charlie was right behind them, which indeed he had been, right until he hit the deck.

One guy brought his hands up like a boxer, pretty high, so I hit him in the gut, which was a better close-quarters blow anyway, a tight body shot, no extension required. The other guy crowded in like he was going for a bear hug, which would have been a reasonable move, but he didn't get all the way there, because however crowded the quarters, there was always room for a head butt, which cracked in right on target, an inch of backswing, and a lot of fast-twitch muscle. He went down and I turned back to the guy I had hit in the gut and I popped a knee under his chin, and he went down, by which time we were about three seconds into it, and certainly noisy, but I wasn't worried about Joey rushing in, partly because Joey couldn't rush in, not through any kind of a normal doorway, and partly because even if he did, I wouldn't worry about him immediately.

Because I knew something about Joey.

Bennett was doing OK. He had a thumb in his guy's eye, and his other hand was crushing the guy's throat. In the active sense of the word. His fingertips were right in behind the guy's larynx, squeezing and tearing. They didn't rule the world by being nice. That was for damn sure. I picked up the flashlight and waited until Bennett's guy hit the deck, and then I searched the floor and under coats and came back with our original three handguns, plus four identical Browning High Power Model 1935s, from Joey's guys. The Brownings were all recent, with the ambidextrous safeties. Up for safe, down for fire. They were all fully loaded. But their chambers were empty. We had been safer than I thought. We shared them around, one each, and I took the magazine out of the fourth and gave it to Nice to put in her pocket.

I said, "Let's go find Joey."

I turned and headed for the door, but Bennett caught my arm and said, "We can't just walk out there. Especially not with a flashlight. We'd be sitting ducks."

I said, "Let's not over think this whole thing."

Bennett glanced at Nice, in mute appeal, like he thought I was crazy.

She said, "I'm sure we'll be fine."

I smiled. She had seen it, too. Probably from the thing with the pill bottle.

I said, "Joey is not armed. That's one thing we can be sure of."

Bennett said, "How can we?"

"Because we know in his whole adult life Joey has never fired a handgun, or a long gun, or a shotgun, or a BB gun, or any other kind of a gun."

"How do we know that?"

"Because no trigger guard on earth is big enough for his finger. He couldn't get it in there. No way, no how. He hasn't touched a trigger since he was maybe seven years old. And I bet even then it was a tight squeeze. He's out there, right now, in the lot, un-armed, and we've got a hundred and four rounds of live ammunition and a flashlight."

Chapter 51

Casey Nice had the flashlight. I had a gun in each hand, mainly because by that point I was short on pockets. Bennett was behind us, ranging left and right, watching our rear, watching our flanks. Nice flicked the flashlight beam from side to side, very fast, painting the night air, lighting things up like a stroboscope, letting our persistence of vision fill in the gaps.

No sign of Joey. Not at first. The beam reached a good long way down the yard-wide footpath, and he wasn't there. And he would have been, still, if he was making a run for it. Because it wouldn't have been much of a run. He would have had to take the path sideways, at a shuffle, which would have been slow. We checked the far corner, where I had waited for Bennett, and he wasn't there. We checked the opposite corner. Not there.

We stood still and listened. No sound. The yellow glow was still there in the sky, but the houses all around us were darker. Lights were going out. People were going to bed. Their children were already in bed. Pretty soon we would be completely boxed in by sleeping people. Here and there I saw the blue flicker of some night owl's television, a movie, perhaps, or soccer, or a documentary feature, which I hoped was illuminating in the educational sense, because it certainly wasn't in the physical sense. We were hunting a giant in the dark.

And getting nowhere, until I did fourth what I should have done first, which was to put myself in his shoes, to think like him, to be him, just for a moment. What would I have done? No gun, bodyguards down, driver too far away to summon, a sideways skip down the alley too slow. Not that I needed to run, and not that I needed support. I could do fine by myself. I was Little Joey Green, and I had been all my life.

But I liked an audience.

Of which there was a shortage, at that very moment. The lawn bowling World Series was not currently underway. All around us people were closing their drapes and closing their eyes. There was only one place Joey might find an audience. Possibly. An audience of one, admittedly, but committed. An ally, maybe even a friend already, and a fellow professional, Joey might like to think.

John Kott might be watching, through the night-vision binoculars.

Or through a night-vision scope.

I made a sign and Casey Nice killed the light, and we inched around to the far back corner of the hut, which put us level with the windows, which meant we were within a degree or two of the same view we had gotten before, through the binoculars, from where we had seen the whole fine square of lawn, which we saw again, but this time with Little Joey in the middle of it, the giant all alone under the yellow nighttime sky, dancing, swinging his hips, shuffling his feet, waving his arms, and jerking his head from side to side.

I knew immediately what he was doing, and how, and why. Some kind of animal cunning. Some kind of rodent intelligence. *It's a DNA thing. Like rats.* He had no gun in his hand. How could he take the guns out of our hands? *Boxed in by sleeping people. Their children were already in bed.* He was dancing to make us miss. Which we couldn't afford to do. Not there. Not that we would have missed. Not ninety-nine times in a hundred. Or better. *This is like one of those philosophy questions that people debate in the newspapers.* What odds would a responsible person need? But even a good clean hit could be a through-and-through. The soft tissue of the neck, maybe. Which wouldn't slow a bullet. Next stop, a bedroom painted blue or pink. Or the bullet might nick bone and skip away at an unpredictable angle, low and wide. It might hit a night owl, before the game had ended. Tied score, maybe, and into overtime. He would never know what happened.

Could I make the shot? Hell, yes. Little Joey was big enough. Should I take the shot? With sleeping children behind him, to the left and the right, behind thin panes of glass?

We pulled back into the shadows, and we leaned on the wall of the hut. We could afford to let him dance a minute more, I thought. It might tire him out. Which might help. I hoped.

Nice and Bennett slipped around the edge of the green, to the far side, on what looked like a well-worn gravel track. Maybe referees ran up and down. Or umpires. I had no idea of the rules of the game. Bennett went further than Nice, until they were about twenty feet apart, triangulated, so they both had the hut dead in line behind Joey, so if they had to shoot, with no alternative, then at least their misses might get stopped by the sixty-year-old wood. Or worst case, delayed.

I had no front pockets, so I put my guns in my back pants pockets. Then I stepped onto the grass. I tracked to my left, to keep Joey's bulk between me and his distant house, with its numerous firing positions behind its numerous oversize windows. Four hundred yards. Less than a second. Flash *one thoussa* game over.

I walked on, slowly. Toward Joey. He saw me coming, looming up out of the yellow gloom, and I saw a flash of teeth as he smiled, and he backed away, toward the far corner of the lawn, matching me step for step, leading me, keeping me lined up with his distant house. He wasn't dumb. After three backward paces he had moved out of Nice's safe zone, and after four he had moved out of Bennett's. I sensed their shoulders slump, and in the silence I heard Bennett's phone ding with a message. My information about the glass, I hoped. Which could be interesting. If I survived to read it.

Joey checked over his shoulder and adjusted his alignment and came to a stop. He started dancing again, hopping from side to side, bending one way, bending the other. His huge feet were stamping divots in the perfect grass. I guessed the bowling club was going to be seriously pissed. I hoped they had insurance. Or a big bag of seed.

I said, "Listen up, Joey. Here's the thing. I need to get in your house. Without you being there. Option one is agree right now."

He said, "What's option two?"

"I advise you to choose option one."

"An Englishman's home is his castle."

"I understand that, Joey. I really do. But you need to think of me like a Viking. Or a rebel marauder. Or some kind of an invader. I'm going to storm your castle. Better for you if you don't get hurt in the process."

"What if it's you that gets hurt?"

"You could help me there, Joey. You could tell me where Kott's hanging out, and his guards, and you could point out other dangers. You got any loose rugs? Any low furniture? I don't want to slip and fall."

"You're a dead man."

"How's that, Joey? You got a gun?"

He didn't answer.

I said, "I didn't think so. You got guys with you, apart from the four in the hut unconscious on the floor with broken bones?"

He didn't answer.

I said, "I didn't think so."

He was still dancing, just a little. He was moving left, and moving right, and I was moving with him, keeping him between me and the house. I was a couple of steps from him, which meant he was a single step from me. Close enough to worry about, given how fast I had seen him move, in the little supermarket's parking lot.

He put his hand in his pocket. Right side of his suit coat. A big hand. A big pocket. He came out with a cell phone. He held it up in front of his mouth and said, "Call Gary." Then he held it up by his ear, like a regular person. His fingers were too big to dial. His phone obeyed voice commands. Which worked, apparently, because the call was picked up.

Joey said, "Gary, it's Joey. Call me back in ten minutes, OK? If I don't answer, abandon ship. Every man for himself. Understood?"

And it was, evidently, because Joey clicked off the call and put the phone back in his pocket. And then he just stood there.

My mother had rules about fights. She was raising two sons on Marine bases, so she couldn't ban them altogether. But she hedged them around with restrictions. The first rule was strictly practical. *Don't fight when you're wearing new clothes.* Which I was, ironically. The second rule could be viewed as ethical or moral, but to my mother it was simply *correct,* which was a whole other word in French. The second rule was never start a fight. But the third rule was never lose one, either.

Which I argued about, as a little kid. Sometimes

you had to throw the first punch, or you weren't going to win, ever. I felt the two rules were incompatible. Based on experience. It turned into a big family thing. We had all kinds of discussions. It was the 1960s, and she was French. Eventually it was agreed the rules were indeed incompatible. So maybe they were a Rorschach test instead. Were you a rule two guy or a rule three guy? My brother Joe was a rule two guy. I was a rule three guy. For the first time my parents looked at us a little differently. We didn't know which was right or wrong. Their signals were mixed. They were decent people, but they were Marines.

I was a rule three guy. *Never lose one.* Served me well. Even if it meant stepping on rule two occasionally. Sometimes you had to start a fight. As in, for example, right then. Rule of thumb: I had to hit Joey before he hit me.

But then he spoke again. He said, "I'm a Romford Boy."

I said, "I guess someone has to be."

"We keep our word. To get near Mr. Kott, you'll have to come through me."

"Like going to the dentist. I will if I have to."

"You think you can fight me?"

"Probably."

He said, "I don't like Mr. Kott very much."

I said, "Me either."

"But I'm a Romford Boy. I keep my word."

"So?"

"So let's make it interesting." Then he paused, pensively, as if he had struck on a way to cut through a lengthy explanation. He pointed to his pocket. He said, "Did you hear my phone call?"

I said, "Yes."

"Gary is tonight's team leader, on Mr. Kott's security detail. You heard what I told him. If I answer the phone, it means you're out of the picture and we can go about our business as normal. I'm a Romford Boy, and I've kept my word. But I don't want my people dealing with this shit if I'm not here to supervise it. So if I don't answer the phone, they'll clear out immediately and Mr. Kott is all yours."

Chapter 52

Some kind of a Socratic method in a classroom might have teased out deep meanings in what Joey had said, involving high stakes, and imagined concepts of loyalty and honor and sacrifice, or maybe he just liked to fight, and couldn't get opponents without bribing them. In either case I paid no further attention, because he backed off a step and went into a crouch, like he was waiting for the bell to ring. Which he must have heard before I did, because he came out of the dark at me like a wrecking ball, twice as fast as the supermarket lot, crashing a right elbow at me, like lightning, clubbing down, a chill vision of exactly how I had hit the guy from the van. He wanted me gone, right at the beginning. *The only way to deal with a sudden incoming elbow was to twist and drive forward and take it on the meat of the upper arm.* Which I did. *Which is always painful and sometimes numbing.* Which it was. *But generally you stay on your feet.* Which I did.

But only just. Three hundred eight pounds, in the local weights and measures, coming on strong. To which the only response was to slide past him and turn him around. Which put my back to his house, so as agreed Casey Nice lit me up with the flashlight, just briefly, two seconds, which we figured would blind a night scope, and which had the added advantage of distracting Joey, just minutely, so I crashed a left hook into his throat, and a short right to his kidney, as hard as I ever hit anything, total focus, and then I backed off through the same wide circle, so that if Kott fired blind he would hit Joey and not me, and so I could see what damage I had done.

Which wasn't much. Which wasn't encouraging. Size was no big deal. Not in itself. The real guys to watch for were the ones who got so pumped up they became oblivious to pain. Some chemical thing. Their bodies couldn't tell them to quit. Then size became a big deal. Which was the case with Joey. I had hit him twice, no small deal, but he was still upright and cheerful, still six inches taller than me, and still sixty pounds heavier.

"Ten minutes," he said. "That's what you've got. A bit less now, I suppose."

He said it with some kind of bliss on his face, like an old bare-knuckle prizefighter, a nineteenth-century man loose in the twenty-first, a Londoner, like something out of a Charles Dickens movie. A young man, but old news, out of date long ago, a leg breaker, nothing more. Meanwhile the back part of my brain was telling me to keep with the kidney shots, on the right, in the hopes of accidentally busting the phone in his pocket, so that Gary wouldn't get an answer either way, which might make it easier for Nice and Bennett later on.

Joey shuffled in. A prizefighter, but not a great one. He launched a roundhouse right I saw coming a mile away, and I ducked, down and up like squats in a gym, and his fist buzzed over my head, and its momentum carried him onward in a curve, which meant his right kidney was coming toward me all the time, so I hit it again, another short right, a colossal blow, a blow that would have cracked a young tree or killed a mule stone dead. An all-time top three for me, which was saying something. He suffered all the appropriate mechanical effects. He bent violently backward from the force of the blow, and the breath *oofed* out of him as the shock hit the back of his lungs, and he tottered, and his leg went stiff.

But he didn't fall on the floor yelping with pain, which he should have. A normal person would be in a coma. Every internal organ on fire, a million knives in the back, too breathless to scream. But Joey just huffed once, and wriggled like some kind of amateur chiropractics, and took up his stance again. Maybe the Zoloft helped. I made a mental note to ask Nice about physical benefits.

And then I changed the plan, to a war of movement. If I couldn't knock him down, then maybe I could make him fall down all by himself. Because the end game had to be flat on the grass. No other way. I knew where the children weren't. I danced in, and then away, and around, and then back, by any other standards ludicrously clumsy, but by comparison with Joey for once in my life I was the neat little guy, bobbing and weaving and stinging.

The grass was soft, and he was very heavy, and three times he nearly tripped. I kept it going fast, mostly because of Kott, but partly because of a vague theory that in any contest the big guy would tire faster. We went around and around, and at one point his feet lagged his body by half a second, and I got a shot with my elbow, but he parried it the same way I had, and we bounced apart and started again.

I changed the plan for the second time. He wasn't going to fall down by himself. He was going to require assistance. Which I was happy to supply. And getting happier by the minute. *You think you can fight me?* Maybe Scarangello was right. *Couldn't bear to be challenged.* But not exactly right. It was never about the challenge. It was always about the other guy. I didn't like Joey Green. Partly for the right reasons, like the teenagers from Latvia and Estonia, and the man with the mouths to feed, but also for ancient, savage reasons, because for every year humans had been modern, they had been primitive for seven hundred more, which left a residue, and by that point the back part of my brain was firmly in charge. *My tribe needs you gone, pal. And you're ugly, too. And you're a pussy.*

I danced right, and danced left, and gambled on a leg getting left behind, and I smashed my heel into his kneecap, same angle and extension as breaking down a door, but harder than all the doors I have ever busted put together. Maybe his pain responses were all screwed up, but bone is a physical thing, and if it breaks it breaks, which his did. I felt the crack through my boot. But the kneecap is not a structural bone. He didn't fall down. Instead he stepped forward on his good leg and hit me in the chest, another roundhouse right but snappier, too fast to see coming, and I fell backward and twisted and went down, gasping and whooping and trying to breathe, and trying to roll away, and trying to get on all fours, which I did, and then I scuffled away before he could kick me to death, busted kneecap or not.

He was all pumped up by that point, seeing me down, and he came lumbering in, with some defect in his stride, maybe, but still fast enough to make me scurry and hustle. I got on my feet and dodged away and started again. I was fresh out of new plans, and I had about six minutes left. I kept on moving, always mindful of the distant house, always maneuvering, and at one point I got him all twisted up and I kicked him again on his busted knee, hard, a real moving violation, but at a cost, because he lashed out backhand, maybe just a furious reaction, maybe a sober calculation about where I would be, but either way he won the bet. The back of his massive hand swatted me on the forehead, which was like running full speed into a clothes rope.

I went flat on my back, but my earlier work saved my life. He couldn't turn around. He couldn't work out how. His knee was locked up solid. Painless, maybe, but engineering is engineering. I scrambled away on my back and hauled myself upright again. I stood for a second, hands on knees, breathing hard, and blinking, adrift in a real does-not-compute moment. I had hit the guy five times, a left and two rights, and two shots with my feet, and the guy was still upright. And the second right should have put any human down. Or horse, or gorilla, or elephant.

I had a problem.

Then I thought about the soccer the night owls might be watching, and I looked at the lawn, smooth and flat and even, slick with night mist. Joey was facing away from me. I backed off a step and ran in and went down and slid, like a ski turn, my hip kissing the grass just as my angled shins hit his calves from behind, a blatant foul in soccer, a yellow card offense, or even red, if there was malicious intent, of which there was plenty in my case. I plowed right through him, calves and ankles and heels, and he went up in the air and came down on his back as theatrically as any pampered European superstar.

Then it was about surfing back upright, and turning, and taking a short choppy stride, and snatching the Glock from my back pants pocket, and then leaping, like a kid aiming to go joyously knees-first into a snowdrift, except there was no joy involved, and the snowdrift was Joey's belly, and I was whipping the Glock around and down, so that all three points would land at the same time, in a perfect triangle, my left knee, my right knee, the muzzle of the Glock, which hit his solar plexus with all my weight behind it, two hundred and fifty moving pounds, punching it way down, and then I pulled the trigger.

I was a rule three guy.

In pathology class they would have called it a starburst entry wound. The muzzle had been hard against him, and naturally the first thing out was the bullet, which punched a neat nine-millimeter hole through his flesh, which didn't stay neat for long, because the next thing out was a blast of exploding gas, which had nowhere to go but straight down the bullet hole, deep inside Joey's body itself, which was not as hard as the steel of a gun barrel, so the gas swelled instantly to a hot bubble the size of a basketball, which burst the skin at the entry point, so that when it settled back down after the gas was gone, it looked like a five-pointed star.

The first advantage was it killed him instantly. At that kind of range, more or less dead center, there was a whole lot of stuff in there. Spine, heart, lungs, all kinds of arteries. The second advantage was the through-and-through, which it must have been, could have killed only earthworms. Maybe the larvae of parasitic grubs. In which case the bowling club should have thanked me.

The third advantage was the inside of Joey's whole chest cavity acted like a silencer. Like I had mounted a suppressor the size of an oil drum. He worked pretty well. The sound of the gunshot was very muted. But even so Bennett played it safe. He came over and said, "I heard that."

I said, "Of course you heard it. You were only fifty feet away."

"If I heard it the neighbors heard it."

He took out his phone and texted a word.

I said, "What's that?"

"It means it was one of ours. If someone phones it in to the local cop shop they'll be told it was a car backfiring, and not to worry."

"You can do that now?"

"I just did."

"Since when?"

"Some inconveniences were eliminated very early in the process."

I said nothing.

Little Joey's phone rang in his pocket.

And rang.

We let it ring until it stopped.

I said, "We need to get going. We need to be sure Kott doesn't run with his guards. We need to see the front of the house. But much closer than this."

Casey Nice said, "The shortest distance between two points is a straight line," and she set off the way the gale had blown, and we followed her, over the fresh-cut stump of some guy's tree, and through the gap in some other guy's fence.

Chapter 53

We trespassed through five separate yards, I figured, and we stayed in the last of them, behind a low ornamental wall, directly across the street from Joey's place. A close-up view. Better than any binoculars. There was a single black Jaguar on the driveway. The gates were closed. The giant door was closed. It had a brass letter slot, and a handle, and in the plate below the handle was a single keyhole. Some kind of a fancy multi-lever mortise lock, no doubt, recommended by insurance companies everywhere, not that Joey Green had needed insurance, other than his name.

Then right on cue the gates rolled back and the giant door opened and four guys spilled out, like parachutes streaming from a plane. The mood looked confused. The guys looked uncertain. They were stumbling, looking left, looking right, one guy hitching his coat on, another combing his hair with his fingers. They got in the Jaguar and drove through the out gate, to the street, and then they took off, fast, into the far distance, until they were lost to sight.

They left the gates open.

John Kott didn't come out.

Not in the first minute, or the fifth, or the tenth.

He was staying inside, to fight it out.

I looked at Bennett and said, "You got my information about the glass?"

"It's in French," he said.

He set it up for me on his phone. It was a scan of a Xerox or a fax of a classified document. It was very long. I had to swipe the screen to scroll. It was marked top secret in several different places. I said, "Does it set on fire in five minutes?"

Bennett said, "No, but I might."

I said, "Thank you for getting it."

He said, "Think nothing of it. But I hope it turns out useful."

It was in French because glass was a big deal in France. A manufacturing success story, all over the world. All kinds of stemware, and hotel ware, with an emphasis on industrial efficiency, and strength. You could throw a French restaurant tumbler like a baseball, and it would probably survive. Who better to move onward and upward into modern bulletproof technology? A research and development laboratory in Paris had taken up the challenge. As always, the mission was to combine optimum clarity with optimum strength. No point in putting a president behind something safe but murky. Visuals were important.

Security agencies in all the major NATO countries had contributed funding. The guys in Paris had taken the money and gotten to work.

First surprise was, it wasn't called bulletproof glass. It was called transparent armor. Second surprise was, it wasn't glass. Not even a trace. Previous bulletproof panels had been layered, with glass panes separated by and skinned by soft polycarbonate or thermoplastic materials. Some of the glass sheets were hard, and some were less so, to allow flexing. Results were usually good, but there were two problems. Edge on, the finished assembly could look like plywood. And the index of refraction was different for every layer, which at certain angles made it like looking into about six different swimming pools at once. Imperfect visuals. Bad for television.

So the scientists turned their backs on glass, and went for aluminum instead. Which sounded weird to me, but as always with chemistry, things were not exactly what they seemed. The substance in question was aluminum oxynitride, which they claimed was a transparent polycrystalline ceramic with a cubic spinel crystal structure composed of aluminum, oxygen, and nitrogen. A chemical formula was quoted, full of large letters and small numbers and graceful parentheses. The molecule was sketched, which looked like the chandelier in my great aunt's dining room, in New Hampshire.

The aluminum oxynitride started out as a powder, which was carefully mixed, like flour for a cake, and then it was compacted in something called a dry isostatic press, and then it was baked at an extremely high temperature, and then it was ground and polished, until it looked more like glass than glass itself. It was optically perfect. It was heavy, but not crippling.

And it was strong. The design brief was to survive a fifty-caliber armor-piercing round, and the test procedure was meticulous and detailed. I read it very carefully. I could understand most of the language used, although some of it was highly technical and therefore unfamiliar. But numbers were the same the world over, and I could recognize a hundred when I saw it. The test panels had scored a hundred percent against nine-millimeter handguns, and against .357 Magnums, and .44 Magnums, at ranges from fifty feet all the way down to contact shots, like Joey.

So then they flew the panels down to a place called Draguignan, in the south of France, near where my grandfather had stabbed the snake, where there was a huge military facility, with rifle ranges galore. They set up at three hundred feet, and the panels scored a hundred percent against .223 Remingtons and 7.62-millimeter NATO rounds. At which point the scientists doubled down. They must have been feeling good. They shortened the range to two hundred feet, which was unrealistically short for the larger calibers, and then they skipped right over worthy contenders like the .308 Winchester and the British .303, and went straight to the .44 Remington Magnum. From two hundred feet. Which was less than seventy yards. Like a battleship firing at the harbor wall.

The panels scored a hundred percent.

Then came the moment of truth. They loaded up

the fifty-cal and laid it on the bench. Armor-piercing ammunition. For which seventy yards was more than unrealistically short. But I understood the point they were hoping to make.

The panels scored a hundred percent.

And at a hundred feet, and at fifty, and even at twenty-five. Although the scientists were open enough to point out that the visible pitting at the shorter ranges would require replacement of the panels after every such incident. Even the scientists were political enough to understand a candidate couldn't show up behind gear already riddled with bullet holes from previous failed attempts. Like he had gotten out of Dodge just in time. Not good for the image. People might get a clue.

There was a lot of foreign money in the project, and a lot of valuable foreign lives depending on the outcome, so the test procedure was supervised every step of the way by representatives from all the interested parties. They checked the numbers, they asked the questions, they looked behind the curtain. They were all intelligence specialists, but scientifically literate. The old guard, with nothing better to do, all extremely experienced. The guys from Paris didn't mind. It was like any other peer review. Just compressed in time. I swiped the screen and scrolled down, through the list of participants, just a little ways, to *E,* for Etats-Unis d'Amérique.

The United States of America.

The Pentagon had sent Tom O'Day.

Chapter 54

I looked over the low wall at Joey's house. The gates were still open and lights were still burning. But nothing else was happening. I gave the phone back to Bennett, and I said, "Why don't you go take a short stroll?"

He said, "Why would I want to?"

"I need to talk to Ms. Nice alone."

"What are you going to say to her?"

"Something inaudible, from where you're going to be."

He paused a beat, and then he got up and disappeared in the dark, there one minute, gone the next, like on the apartment balcony in Paris. Nice and I squatted side by side, with our backs against the wall.

I said, "This is the scene where I try to get rid of you."

She didn't answer.

I said, "Not for the reasons you think. I could use your help a dozen different ways, and you'd be good at all of them. But this is between Kott and me. He wants me gone, therefore I want him gone. Not fair to involve other people, in a private quarrel. I'm going to tell Bennett the same thing."

"Bennett will stay away anyway. He has to. There are rules. But I'm free to do what I want."

"This is me and Kott. Which has rules, too. It's one on one."

"You're just saying that."

"Because I mean it."

"I think you're being kind."

"That's an accusation I don't hear often."

She said, "Why did he take my pill?"

"Take as in deprive, or take as in swallow?"

"Swallow."

"I'm guessing he took all kinds of pills. A guy that big gets aches and pains. In his back, and his joints. So he already likes the opiates and the painkillers, and then he starts to dabble in the bad stuff passing through his hands. Pretty soon, he sees a pill, he takes it. Occupational hazard."

"I don't want to take them anymore. Did you see his mouth? He was disgusting."

"Right now you can't take them anymore. Even if you wanted to."

"Is that the reason? You think I'm going to freak out?"

"Are you?"

"Not from anxiety, anyway. I can't even see anxiety in the rearview mirror."

"We'll be OK."

"We?"

"You out here, me in there."

"I should help."

"This is me and Kott," I said again. "I'm not going to gang up on him. Wouldn't feel right, afterward."

The gates were still open, but I didn't want to go in the front. It was the obvious point of entry. It was the main place Kott would watch. Probably MI5 would come up with a number. *Kott spent sixty-one percent of his time watching the front.* In second place would be the backyard. Third and fourth place would be the end walls. But which was third and which was fourth? I guessed third place went to the end facing the bowling club. That was where the action had been thus far. So I headed the other way, to the other end of the house, fourth place, away from the night vision, creeping through the shadows, then climbing the fence. Which was not easy, but it was feasible, because the ironwork had sculpted features that acted like rungs on a ladder. I stepped down into a flowerbed. The side of the house was right there, across a narrow path. There were eight ground-floor windows. They would all have been drawn small by the kid with the crayon, but I could have gotten through any one of them standing up.

I checked the nearest window. The sill was chest-high to me. A small room. Relatively speaking. A nook or a niche or a parlor. Or a library or an office or a sitting room. I moved on to the next window. Through which was a hallway. Which was much better. There was the foot of a staircase visible, about thirty-five feet away. I guessed the hallway turned ninety degrees to the right at some point, to reach the front door.

I stood still and took a breath. In, and out. Then again. Then I used the butt of the captured Browning, and I broke the window, *smash, smash, smash,* all the glass I could reach, until the hole was big enough to climb through. I figured Kott would instantly see it as a bluff. No more than a diversion. As in, he was supposed to investigate, and meanwhile I would come in the front door, behind him. He would predict that. So he would go guard the front door instead. Except he was professionally paranoid, so just as instantly he would call it a double bluff, and he would head for the window as planned, to meet me head-on. So I triple-bluffed him. I sprinted for the front. I knew the door was open. That kind of a lock, you have to stop and use the key, both ways, out as well as in. And the departing guards hadn't. They had gotten straight in the Jaguar, and hit the gas, no delay at all, putting on their coats, and slicking down their hair.

The door handle was a grand affair, a neat Georgian style swelled up to about thirty inches tall. The lever I turned was the size of most people's forearms. Inside I saw a lobby with black and white marble on the floor, and a chandelier the size of an apple tree.

No sign of Kott.

Which was good. It let me open the door all the way, for an unrestricted field of fire. Behind the lobby was a long section of hallway, with the staircase at the far end, which meant the part of the hallway with the busted window was on the left, at ninety degrees.

I stepped inside.

No sign of Kott.

Which meant if he had only doubled where I had tripled, he was right then staring at the broken glass, or searching room to room in the immediate vicinity, through all the pesky nooks and niches and parlors and libraries and offices and sitting rooms.

He was on my left, at ninety degrees.

I walked through the lobby to the hallway. Like any other hallway it was rectangular, much longer than it was wide, with hallway-style furniture, with doors left and right, to the kind of rooms that big houses always seemed to have. But I had been in big houses before, and Joey's place didn't feel like any of them. I remembered doors that looked way further apart than normal, implying huge rooms beyond, which turned out to look even bigger than expected, mostly because the walls went on and on, as if the room was saying, *you know I'm big, because my walls go on forever.* Proportion, in other words. Joey's place really was a regular house all swollen up in perfect lock step. The rooms were huge, but they didn't look it, because the doors were the regular distance apart, except the doors were more than nine feet tall, more than ten with the architrave frames, so the regular distance was an optical illusion.

The marble squares on the floor would have been two feet on a side in any designer magazine, but in Joey's house they were three. A full yard. The baseboards would have been twelve inches high in a fancy Victorian place. In Joey's house they were a full foot and a half. A regular door knob would hit me in the thigh. Joey's door knobs would hit me in the ribs. And so on. The net effect was I felt very small. Like I had been shrunk, by a mad scientist. Maybe the aluminum glass people would take it up next.

And I felt slow. Obviously. It took fifty percent longer to get anywhere. Three steps from A to B was really four and a half. It was like walking through molasses. Or walking backward. Always hustling, and getting nowhere. Like going up the down escalator. Disorienting, like a whole different dimension.

I stopped what I thought was six feet from where the hallway turned. But it could have been nine. Either way I held my breath and listened. And heard nothing. No crunching of broken glass underfoot, and no opening and closing of doors. So I inched toward the corner, or three-quarter-inched, or an inch and a half, or whatever it really was. I had the Browning in my left hand, and the Glock in my right, with one in the chamber and twelve in the magazine. Five rounds expended so far, four under the Jaguar's hood at Charlie's house, and one into the bowling club's subsoil, via Joey.

I figured if Kott was expecting a head to come around the corner, he would be expecting it at normal height, purely as a matter of default instinct. But what was normal? Eye level about five feet six inches from the ground, probably, which was fifty-five percent of a normal room's height. Which would translate to about eight feet three inches in Joey's funhouse world. Which would mean Kott would be staring way over my head. But even so I played it safe. I made sure he would be staring over my head. I knelt down low and took a look at baseboard level, which because of the millwork's exaggerated height, was perfectly comfortable.

I pictured my brow and my eyes, suddenly visible, but tiny next to the extravagant molding.

No sign of Kott.

I saw shards of glass on the marble. From the window. I saw closed doors. For parlors, and libraries, and sitting rooms. I didn't see Kott. Was he behind a closed door? Temporarily, maybe. Or perhaps he had never moved. Perhaps he was still upstairs, in the guest accommodations, patient like snipers were, with his fifty-caliber Barrett on a table, aimed directly at the door to the suite.

I thought back to the architect's blueprint we had seen. The guest suite was in the rear left quadrant of the house. Above the kitchen wing, basically. Up the stairs, and turn right. I stood up again, and checked all four ways, and breathed in, and breathed out.

Then I started up the stairs.

Chapter 55

The stairs went half the way up on the left, and then turned a 180 on a half-landing, and went the rest of the way up on the right. And like everything else in the house they were regular items, but expanded in size, so I had to labor up them, stepping fifty percent higher than normal each time, lurching forward half as far again as my muscle memory expected, to reach the next stair, and then repeating it all. Plus I was aware the back of my head was about to be visible in the upstairs hallway, through whatever kind of railings or spindles the carpenter had used. Kott could be up there, prone, with his muzzle right in line with the banister. He would get me in the back, just before I stepped up to the half-landing. At a range of about twelve feet. Which was four yards. And I wasn't made of aluminum oxynitride.

So I hugged the wall, and went up backward, until I could see the second floor hallway for myself. It was empty. No sign of Kott. I hustled the rest of the way and found myself in what looked like a repeat of the downstairs hallway, except the floor was carpet, not marble. Carpet as wide as a new-mown prairie. I saw a bunch of doors, all of them nine feet tall. A corridor, with more doors. All closed. Two on the left, two on the right, and one dead ahead, in the end wall. Which was the guest suite, I figured. I would be walking straight toward it.

But the advantage of walking straight toward it through a giant's house was I had plenty of wiggle room. Normally an upstairs hallway would be a narrow field of fire. But fifty percent extra gave me the chance to stay well off the center line. Because maybe Kott had something rigged. His gun, pre-aimed, locked down, ready to fire through the wood. Maybe there was an infra-red beam. Or maybe he had X-ray glasses.

But I made it to the end wall, safe, and I pressed myself alongside his door, and I flipped the Browning barrel-first in my hand, and I used it to knock.

I said, "Kott? Are you in there?"

No answer.

I knocked again, louder.

I said, "Kott? Open the door."

Which I figured he might. Ballistically it was already open. Either one of us could have fired straight through it. In his case he could have fired straight through anything. If he wanted to aim based purely on sound alone, he could. The walls and the floors didn't exist for him. He was living in a transparent house.

But he would want to watch. Surely. A guy who put a picture on his wall, last thing he saw at night, first thing he saw in the morning, he would want to watch me take the bullet. He would want to see me fall down. He had probably pictured it every day in yoga class. *Visualize your success.* He had waited fifteen years. He might open the door.

I said, "Kott, we should talk first."

No answer.

I said, "No harm, no foul. You forget about me, I'll forget about you. We can go our separate ways. You should get over yourself. No need to make a whole big thing out of it. I sent plenty of guys to prison and no one else got so mad about it."

I heard a creak, and for a second I thought it was the door, but it was in the other direction, at the top of the stairs. In the corner of my eye I saw a child flit by. Real fast. Up the stairs and across the hallway and out of sight. A small boy, I thought. How could Bennett not have told me? Where was the mother? What the hell was going on?

I eased my finger off the Glock's trigger.

Then the back of my brain said, not a child. Not chubby or bony or elastic. But stiff, and worn, and tense like an adult. A small man, maybe five-seven, running past a balustrade five feet high, in front of baseboards a foot and a half tall, under fifteen-foot ceilings.

Not a small boy.

John Kott.

I tried to call up the architect's blueprint in my mind. I wanted to see the details. The upstairs hallway ran front to back, from the top of the stairs to a feature window above the front door, and also side to side, toward the guest suite in one direction, where I was, and the other way, too, toward a huge master bedroom. Kott hadn't come my way, and I figured he wouldn't hang out by the feature window. Why would he? Therefore he was in Joey's bedroom.

Below me I heard a voice. Bennett, in the downstairs hallway. He called out, "Reacher? You OK up there?"

I called back, "Get out of here, Bennett. No reason for you to be involved."

I listened for a reply, but I heard nothing more.

I tried the guest suite's door. It was unlocked. I stepped inside. I looked around. I had seen similar places in hotels, but smaller. Living accommodations, all self-contained. A short private hallway, a powder room, a kitchenette, a living room, with two bedrooms, one to the left and one to the right, both with their own separate bathrooms. The left-hand bedroom was unoccupied. The right-hand bedroom had Kott's stuff in it. Of which there wasn't much. A bedroll and a backpack, Nice had guessed, back in Arkansas, and she had been more or less correct. The bedroll was a sleeping bag, and the backpack was a duffel bag, made of scuffed black leather, full of T-shirts and underwear and ammunition.

The ammunition was all either nine-millimeter Parabellum, or fifty-caliber match grade. Big visual difference. The handgun rounds looked small and dainty. Like jewelry. The rifle rounds looked like cannon shells from a combat airplane. The cartridge cases alone were four inches long.

I checked everywhere I could think of, and I didn't find a handgun.

But I found the rifle.

It was under Kott's bed, in a custom case. A Barrett Light Fifty, the real deal, more than five feet long, close to thirty pounds scoped and loaded. From Tennessee. The price of a used sedan, right there. I kicked the scope out of alignment, which is all I had time to do, and then I hustled back to the hallway.

The blueprint said I had to walk thirty feet, and turn right, and walk twenty feet, and turn left, into some kind of a three-sided anteroom ahead of the bedroom itself. On the plan it would be called a niche or a nook, no doubt. The bedroom door was in the wall facing the hallway. I kept the Browning in my left hand and the Glock in my right, like an old-time gunfighter in a black-and-white movie. Not that I believed those old stories. I never met a guy who could aim left and right simultaneously. Not well, anyway. Better to focus on the Glock, like it was the only gun I had, and if the Browning happened to blaze away at the same time, unaimed and unsynchronized, then so much the better. Couldn't hurt.

I made the first turn. Ahead of me was the feature window. But still a long ways away. I was getting better at decoding the funhouse dimensions. I had the Glock aimed hard on the near corner of the anteroom, the equivalent of three baseboards up, which would be four feet six, which would be high on Kott's chest. At that point I was fifteen feet away, and the nine-millimeter Parabellum was a speedy little bullet. If Kott stepped out, he would be dead about an eightieth of a second later. Plus my reaction time. Which would be very rapid. That was for damn sure.

Kott didn't step out. I arrived at the anteroom. The bedroom door was closed. Nine feet tall, ten with the frame, rib-high knob.

I heard a woman's voice behind it.

No words. Inarticulate. Not a scream or a moan, but a kind of frustrated gasp. She wanted to do something, or get something, or reach something, but she couldn't. But *want* was the wrong word. She wasn't annoyed. She was desperate. She *needed* to do something, or get something, or reach something.

But she couldn't.

I stepped back and called over my shoulder, "Bennett? You still down there?"

No answer.

Sudden silence in the bedroom.

I stepped to one side, in case he fired through the wood.

He didn't.

How do you make them come out of there voluntarily? No one knows. No one ever has. Normally I would have stood with my back against the wall and eased the door open, arm's length and out of sight, but Joey's doors were too wide for that. So like the neat little guy I was in that new environment, I dodged forward, twisted the knob, kicked the door, dodged back, and aimed.

And fired. And hit John Kott in the center of the forehead. Except I didn't. It was a mirror on the side wall. The gunshot roared and silvered glass sheeted down, and then the world went quiet again, and from inside the room Kott said, "What happened to forgetting about me and going our separate ways?"

I hadn't heard his voice for sixteen years, but it was him. The slow Ozark accent, the querulous pitch, the aggrieved tone.

I said, "You didn't answer me."

"Not worth answering."

"Who is in there with you?"

"Step inside and take a look."

I called up the blueprint in my head again. I said, "You're on the second floor of a very tall house. I'm at the only door out. I just fired a gun in London. Five minutes from now you'll have five thousand cops outside. You'll survive about three weeks without food. And then what will you do?"

He said, "The cops won't come."

I said, "You think?"

"Bennett will tell them it was one of his."

"What do you know about Bennett?"

"I know plenty about Bennett."

"Who is in there with you?"

"I could have showed you in the mirror, except you busted it. You're going to have to come on in."

I backed away a step and called over my shoulder. "Bennett? You down there still?"

No answer.

"Nice? Are you there?"

No answer.

I stepped back to the bedroom door and said, "I guess you know Joey is no longer with us. And you know his guys ran away. So I can stay here as long as I need to. You'll still starve to death, even if the cops don't come."

"And then you'll have more innocent blood on your hands. Because I ain't in here alone. But I guess you know that, right?"

And then he muttered something, not to me, maybe *tell him, kid,* and I heard the woman's voice again, still inarticulate, this time not a frustrated gasp, but a muffled scream. She was gagged. And if she was gagged, she was tied up, too.

The woman screamed again.

I said, "Is that supposed to impress me?"

Kott said, "I would hope."

"What am I, a social worker?"

The scream came again, a third time, long and loud, but muffled by the gag. It tailed off into a bubbling sob, full of pain and hurt and misery and indignity.

Kott said, "I got to say, it's impressing the hell out of me, at least."

The blueprint said the room was about thirty feet by thirty, with a bathroom to the left and a dressing room to the right. I stood exactly where I had stood before, and looked into the mirror, which showed me nothing, just rough-stained wood not meant to be seen, but when it was still glass it had shown me Kott. My angle was pretty tight, therefore his angle was pretty tight. They had to be equal. High school physics. Basic optics. Probably the head of the bed was right next to me, on the other side of the wall, and a bed was a logical place to put a woman, bound and gagged. In which case Kott was sitting on the end of the bed, probably. Which all made sense until I re-checked the angles, and figured the end of the bed would put him too close to me. Unequal. Not possible. Then I remembered Joey's bed was probably nine feet long, maybe ten, and it all made sense again.

I took a step. I knew nothing about domestic hardware or any kind of construction, but I had cyes and a memory, and I figured every door hinge I had ever seen had a barrel about half an inch across, which made Joey's barrels three-quarters of an inch, and a hinge was shaped to suit its task, which was to jack the door out of its frame, and swing it open. Simple math said the crack between the door and the jamb on the hinge side would maximize when the door was open exactly ninety degrees. Which would be a little over an inch, in Joey's case. But the door wasn't open ninety degrees. It was open about thirty degrees. Maybe a couple more. Which meant the crack was a hair over a third of an inch. Which in foreign weights and measures was about ten millimeters wide.

And a nine-millimeter Parabellum was nine millimeters wide.

Chapter 56

I kept my eye back from the crack, like a sniper keeps his eye back from the scope, because I didn't want Kott to sense a sudden subliminal darkening, or hear the huff of breath through a narrow channel. He was sitting on the end of the bed, half turned to face the door. He was easily sixteen years older. He had lines around his eyes, and lines around his mouth. He was all ground down, and all wised up. He was wearing brown pants and a brown shirt, cheap items, like I might have chosen. His hands were resting easy in his lap. He had a gun. A Browning High Power. The local favorite.

Next to him on the bed was a naked woman. I didn't know her. Her skin was white and her hair was yellow. She could have been anywhere between eighteen and forty. Her arms were twisted behind her and bound at the wrists. Her ankles were tied. She had a rag in her mouth.

Her arms were twisted with the insides of her elbows facing outward, and they were not a pretty sight. Green and yellow bruises, and scars, and clots of old blood.

Kott picked up a syringe and showed it to her, and then moved it near her elbow. She twisted her neck and watched, eyes wide. Kott touched the needle to her skin. She watched, and watched, and hoped, and hoped.

Kott moved the needle away again.

The woman slumped and gasped the same frustrated gasp I had heard before. Anguish, disappointment, and pain. *She needed to get something. But she couldn't.*

I stepped back one long pace, staying exactly in line, and I put my own Browning in my back pocket, and I stood feet apart, and I raised the Glock two-handed, an easy, natural motion I had made a thousand times before, and I fired through the crack, at the real John Kott, not his reflection. But I hit him just the same, in the center of his forehead. Fifteen feet. An eightieth of a second. I saw a neat black entry hole, instantly there, and then equally instantly the back of his skull blew off, which was anything but neat, and the roar of the shot rolled up my arms to my ears, and Kott just sat there, still as a statue, and sat, and sat, and then finally he toppled sideways and fell off the bed.

I didn't check Kott's condition. He had fallen on his face and I could see the inside of his brain. Which told me enough. Instead I went straight for his pockets and found a phone just like mine. Then I untied the woman's ankles, and her wrists, and I pulled the rag out of her mouth, and I half turned to look for a robe or a sheet or a towel to cover her with, whereupon she shoved me out of the way and grabbed the needle and stuck it in her arm.

She closed her eyes and pressed the plunger, slowly, slowly, all the way there.

She waited.

Then she made sounds I hadn't heard from her before, a hum of contentment, a sleepy giggle, a yawn of pure happiness.

She stood up, slow and dazed, a little wobbly.

She said, "I want to leave here."

She sounded foreign. Eastern European. From Latvia or Estonia, probably. Her accent shortened certain syllables. At first I thought she had said, *I want to live here.*

Maybe she had.

I said, "Take the needle out of your arm."

She did, and she dropped it on the floor.

I said, "Where are your clothes?"

She said, "I don't have any."

So I hiked across to the bathroom, and I found a towel the size of a twin-bed mattress. Probably just a hand towel, in Joey's world. I carried it back to the woman and draped it around her shoulders. She got the message and pulled it tight in all the right places.

I said, "What's your name?"

She said, "First you have to give me money."

She staggered a step, and I put the Glock in my

pocket, and took her elbows, and steadied her. I said, "Can you walk?"

She took a breath, and I knew from the shape of her lips she was about to say yes, but then her eyes rolled up in her head, and she passed out, with another murmured hum of sheer contentment, and I caught her as she fell and hoisted her in my arms. I figured I could carry her downstairs and leave her somewhere, until I found Bennett. He could call for an ambulance after Nice and I were gone. The woman could survive a short delay. She didn't need urgent care, and she wouldn't, not until she started coming down again.

I got her comfortable, for me and for her, and I carried her out to the weird little anteroom, and I turned into the hallway. Where I came face to face with Charlie White. He had a gun in his hand, yet another Browning High Power, and he was pointing it straight at my head.

Chapter 57

Charlie's funeral suit was soaked with blood all down the front, from when I had hit him in the face. His nose might have been crushed or broken, but it was hard to tell. His hair was all over the place. But he was vertical. Not bad, for a seventy-seven-year-old.

I said, "You lied to me. You told me you weren't carrying."

"I wasn't," he said. "This is Joey's. I know where he keeps them."

"Kept them," I said. "He isn't keeping anything anymore."

"I know. I found him."

"Hard to miss."

"Put the whore down."

Which I was happy enough to do, because it would free my hands. I laid the woman gently on the hallway carpet, and her head lolled toward Charlie, as if she was looking at him.

He said, "She's a good one. Hours of fun. I mean it. She'll do anything for a fix. Literally anything. You dream it up, she'll do it. You have to see it to believe it."

Then he lowered his aiming point, to the center of my chest. He was about eight feet away. Less than a hundredth of a second. He said, "Hold your arms out wide. Like you were trying to fly."

Which was the moment of truth. Hands up, or hands on your head, or wrists together out in front, any of those commands would have been conventional, ahead of restraint with handcuffs or rope, or to keep me unthreatening while he decided what to do next. But hands out wide was an execution. It would put me one, two, three, four, five sweeping moves from salvation. Hands down, reach back, grab the guns, hands up, and aim. However slow and befuddled the old guy was, he would nail me before I was halfway through. Eight feet. *Flash game over,* with nothing in between. Technically I would see the flash. Light travels faster than bullets. The flash would bloom when the bullet was about eight inches gone, and the light waves would instantly overtake it and hit my eyes well before it hit my chest. Whether I would have time to think *wow, that looks like a muzzle flash* was a different matter.

Probably not.

Charlie said, "Hold your arms out."

Something moved behind him. A shadow, on the stairs.

I said, "Think again, Charlie. You need to retire."

The shadow moved again. There was someone on

the staircase, moving slowly, pausing, moving slowly, very quiet. In front of a table light on a piece of furniture in the downstairs hallway, which was casting a long shadow. I realized I would have been visible from the upstairs long before my head crept into view.

I said, "This is not an old man's game, Charlie. And you just lost the next generation. Things are changing. You need to get out while you can."

He said, "Things are always changing. Usually for the worse." He nodded forward, at the gun in his hand. "Hasn't been the same since these things replaced a good old-fashioned beating."

The shadow moved again. Someone was coming up the stairs, silently, one big step at a time, fourteen inches a pop, like climbing boulders on a mountainside.

I said, "So it's time to quit."

"Not necessarily," Charlie said. "Joey is no big loss. We're moving out of that side of things anyway. We're looking at computers now. We can make more with credit card numbers."

The shadow resolved itself to a head and a pair of shoulders. Inching up. Or fourteen-inching up. I kept my eyes tight on Charlie's. I relied on peripheral vision alone. I didn't want to tip him off.

He said, "Hold your arms out wide."

I said, "Who was Joey's next of kin?"

"Why do you want to know?"

"Just thinking about how hard it's going to be to market this house. The buyer pool is going to be pretty small. Or big, depending on how you look at it."

The shadow grew longer still. A head, shoulders,

an upper body, on a riser, across a tread, on the next riser, on the next tread. Like a cartoon animal, run over, pressed into the shape of the stairs.

I said, "You should sell out to the Serbians. Before they take it all for nothing."

In the corner of my eye I saw hair, and a forehead. Blonde hair. Green eyes and a heart-shaped face. She was coming up backward, like I had.

Smart kid.

Charlie said, "The Serbians ain't taking nothing. They're going to stay out west, like always."

I said, "You plan to split Libor's business equally?"

He didn't answer.

In the corner of my eye I saw her from the waist up. She had her Glock in her hand, raised high, near her shoulder.

I said, "So you're not planning to split Libor's business equally. You think the Serbians are going to stand still for that?"

"We were here first."

"But who was here before you? You took it away from them, right? Whoever they were. I can imagine. Back when you were a young man, full of piss and vinegar. You remember that, right? That's the Serbians now. You should take some cash while you still can."

She made it to the half-landing. Ready for the 180 turn. Ready for the second half.

Charlie said, "I'm not here to discuss business."

She took the first stair. Fourteen inches.

I said, "So what are you here for?"

Another stair. Another fourteen inches.

Charlie said, "There are rules. You're way out of order."

Another stair.

I said, "I was helping you out. Culling the herd. Darwinism in action. You've got a weak crew, Charlie. I don't see the talent. And I don't see the brains for credit card numbers."

"We do OK. Don't worry about us."

She stepped up to the upstairs hallway. She was twenty feet behind him. He was a bulky, round-shouldered man. A broad back. Twenty feet in front of her.

I'm an average shot with no aptitude for hand-to-hand combat.

I said, "They know all about the pay-offs you make. Soon as you stop making them, they're going to take you apart."

She crept closer. Silent on the carpet. Seventeen feet, maybe.

I thought, *Keep coming. Then aim for center mass. Nothing fancy. No head shots.*

Charlie said, "I'm never going to stop making the payments. Why would I?"

One more silent step. Fifteen feet.

She stood still.

Too far.

She raised the Glock.

I said, "You ever fired a gun before, Charlie?"

She held her breath.

He said, "What's it to you?"

"The FBI released some figures. Research and analysis. Back home. The average distance for a successful handgun engagement is eleven feet."

She lowered the Glock.

She took a step forward.

Charlie said, "I'm already closer than eleven feet."

She took another step.

I nodded. "Just saying. It's trickier than it looks. But it needn't be. People overcomplicate it. Better just to relax. Make it natural. Like pointing a finger. That way you can't miss."

She took another step. ·

Charlie said, "I'm not going to miss. Although maybe I should. Deliberately. Maybe I should wound you first. That might learn you a lesson."

She took another step. She was nine feet away.

I said, "I don't need no education."

"You need to learn some manners."

Another step.

She was seven feet away.

I said, "Don't worry about me, Charlie. I do OK."

He said, "Maybe you did OK in the past. But you ain't doing so great now."

She straightened her arm. Her gun was four feet from his back. At which point I started to worry. About a whole bunch of different things. He would smell her. He would smell the gun. He would sense some kind of a disturbance in the air around him. Some primitive instinct. Seven hundred years of ancient evolution for every year of modernity. And if she fired from four feet the through-and-through would nail me, dead on, just the same as if he had fired.

I looked him right in the eye and I said, "One second from now I'm going to fall down on the floor."

He said, "What?"

And I did. I let go and fell like a coat coming off a hook and she fired into his back from four feet, and I saw a spit of flesh and blood splash out from the front of his chest, and the feature window behind me shattered, and I landed next to the woman in the towel, who stirred in her sleep and hooked a loose arm around my neck and kissed my ear and said, "Oh, baby."

Chapter 58

Less than two minutes later we were in the back of a mint-green Vauxhall. Up front was the couple who had delivered the computers. The man and the woman, both still quiet and contained, both still happy with their short-straw assignments. Good team players. We had left Bennett at Joey's house, and I didn't expect to see him again.

We had gotten on the East Anglia highway right out of Chigwell. The M11 motorway, as it was called on the local signs. We were heading for a Royal Air Force station in a place called Honington. Which was near a place called Thetford. Ninety minutes, Bennett had promised, but I figured it would be less. The woman was driving extremely fast. The land all around us was flat. Strategically Britain was an aircraft carrier permanently moored off the coast of Europe, and there was plenty of space for flight decks.

* * *

RAF Honington turned out to be a big place, mostly shrouded in darkness. The woman drove through gates and straight out to the tarmac. Just like the SEAL at McChord, which all seemed a long time ago. She drove the same kind of well-judged part-circle and came to a stop at the airplane stairs. We got out, and closed our doors, and the mint-green Vauxhall drove away.

The airplane was the same kind of thing as O'Day's Gulfstream, short and pointed and urgent, but it was painted dark blue, very shiny, with a pale blue belly under a gold coach line, and the words *Royal Air Force* above the windows. A man appeared above us, in the oval mouth of the cabin. He was wearing an RAF uniform. He said, "Sir, madam, please come up."

Inside there was no butterscotch leather or walnut veneer. Instead the leather was black, and the veneer looked like carbon fiber. It was severe but sporty. A whole different flavor. Like a modern Bentley, maybe. Like Joey's. The man in the uniform told us his last passenger had been royal. The duchess of somewhere. Cambridge, maybe. Which started me thinking about MI6 again, and MI5, and everything in between. Nice and I sat across the aisle from each other, but facing, head to toe. The man in the uniform disappeared, and a minute later we were in the air, climbing hard, heading west to America.

We were given a meal, and then the guy in uniform retired to some discreet compartment, and left us alone. I looked at Nice, across the aisle, close enough to touch, and I said, "Thank you."

She said, "You're very welcome."

"You OK?"

"About Charlie White? Yes and no."

I said, "Concentrate on the yes part."

"I am," she said. "Believe me. The way he talked about that girl. I heard him, from downstairs. They took pleasure in tormenting her."

"Plus the firearms and the narcotics and the payday loans."

"But we shouldn't be judge and jury and executioner all in one."

"Why not?"

"We're supposed to be civilized people."

"We are," I said. "We're very civilized. We're riding in a duchess's airplane. They didn't rule the world by being nice. And neither did we, when our turn came."

She didn't answer.

I said, "You proved one thing, at least. You can operate in the field."

"Without pills, you mean? Are you going to tell me to quit again?"

"I'm not going to tell you anything, except thank you. You saved my life. Take all the pills you want. But be clear about why, at least. It's a simple chain of logic. You're anxious, about your professional performance and your mother, but only one of those is a legitimate worry, therefore you're taking the pills because your mother is sick. Which is OK. Take them as long as you need. But don't doubt your skills. They're separate.

You're good at your job. National security is safe. It's your mom who isn't."

She said, "I'm not going to join the army. I'm going to stay where I am."

"You should. It's different now. You know what really happened. You just moved up a step. You're harder to betray."

We flew on, chasing the clock, but losing, and we landed at Pope Field at two in the morning. We turned and taxied, all the way to the small administrative building with *47th Logistics, Tactical Support Command* on it. The engines shut down and the guy in the uniform opened the door and lowered the stairs.

He said, "Sir, madam, you need the red door, I believe."

"Thank you," I said. I pulled out the fat rolls of British money, from Romford and Ealing, and I gave them to the guy. I said, "Have a party in the mess. Invite the duchess."

Then I followed Nice down the steps, and through the dark, to the red door.

The red door opened when we were still six feet from it, and Joan Scarangello stepped out. She had a briefcase in her hand. She had waited up for us, but she wasn't about to admit it. She was trying to look like she was just heading home after a long day at the office.

She stopped and looked at me and said, "I take it back."

I said, "Take what back?"

"You did very well. The British government is officially grateful."

"For what?"

"Your input helped their operative achieve a very satisfactory conclusion."

"Bennett?"

"He states in his report he couldn't have done it without you."

"How long were we in the air?"

"Six hours and fifty minutes."

"And he's already written a report?"

"He's British."

"What couldn't he have done without me?"

"He took Kott off the board inside a local gangster's house. Where he went solely at your suggestion. Hence the gratitude. Along the way he was forced to neutralize a number of gang members, including two really big names, and so Scotland Yard is grateful, too, and because of what he wrote some of that will rub off on us, so all in all I would say we're heading for a period of glorious cooperation. Our London operations will be better than ever."

I said, "He claims they're reading your signals."

She said, "We know."

"Are they?"

"They think so."

"What does that mean?"

"We built a new system, in secret. It's hidden in routine data from weather satellites. That's where we talk. But we kept the old system going. That's what they're reading. We fill it with all kinds of junk."

I said nothing.

She said, "We don't rule the world by being dumb."

And she walked away, in her good shoes and her dark nylons, and her black skirt suit, with her briefcase swinging, and I watched her for thirty yards, which was no kind of a hardship, because it all worked well together, especially the nylons and the skirt, and then she stepped out of the last pool of light and the darkness swallowed her up. I heard her heels a minute more, and then Casey Nice pushed the red door open and stepped inside.

The buffet room was empty. No pastries, no coffee. All cleared away, at the end of the day, pending new deliveries in the morning. We walked upstairs, fast and easy on the standard dimensions. Shoemaker's office was empty. The conference room was empty. But O'Day had his light on.

He was at his desk, in his blazer, with the sweater under it. He was leaning forward, on his elbows, reading. His head was down, and he looked up at us without moving it.

He said, "We'll do the debrief in the morning."

We waited.

He said, "I have one preliminary question, however. Why did you fly back with the RAF? Our own plane was standing by."

I sat down, on the Navy-issue chair. Casey Nice sat down next to me. I said, "Do we get to ask a preliminary question?"

"I suppose a fair exchange is no robbery."

"We flew back with the RAF just for the fun of it. We wanted to see how the other half lives."

"Is that all?"

"We wanted to make Bennett work for what he was getting."

I saw him relax.

I said, "Our question is, why can't either the NSA or GCHQ see the money?"

I saw him unrelax.

He didn't answer.

I said, "It was a year of Kott's rent, and his living expenses, and his fee, and the rifle itself, and all that practice ammunition, and the neighbor, and the private jet to Paris, and whatever the Vietnamese cost, and the two gangs in London, and presumably some kind of homeward transportation. That's not tens of millions of dollars, but it's more than 9-11 cost. Therefore I'm sure their computers wouldn't ignore it. And they're smart people. And motivated, because whatever happens, they'll get blamed, too. Because everything starts with money. So why can't they see it?"

"I don't know."

"Because it was never there."

"It had to be there. No money, no operation."

"Exactly. There was no operation."

"Did you get hit in the head? You were just in the operation. You just found Kott three miles from the scene."

I said, "The first bullet was supposed to break the glass. The second bullet was supposed to kill the guy. But there was no second bullet."

"Because the glass didn't break."

"But that didn't matter. You're not thinking like the second bullet. The glass breaking or not breaking was a future event. You saw the video from Paris. How long was it between the bullet hitting the screen and the security guys getting to the president?"

O'Day said, "A couple of seconds. They were very good."

"Now think about the range. Three-quarters of a mile. The bullet is in the air three whole seconds. Which means you can't wait. Because what happens if you do? You pull the trigger, you wait three whole seconds, and wow, the glass breaks, so you pull the trigger again, and you wait three more seconds, and the new bullet arrives. But by then the president is buried under secret service agents. You missed your chance. The only way to get the guy is to make the second bullet chase the first bullet through the air. It has to follow on, about half a second later. So both bullets are flying together, one after the other. In fact they travel together for more than two whole seconds before the first bullet even arrives at the glass. Whereupon the second bullet passes through the newly airborne debris and hits the president before anyone has time to react, including the president himself, who is after all closest."

O'Day said nothing.

"Or alternatively if the glass doesn't break, then the second bullet hits it too, half a second later, and the scientists get two little chips to look at, not one."

O'Day said nothing.

"There never was a second bullet. There was never going to be a second bullet. Someone sent Kott to Paris to fire one single round. At a bulletproof shield. Which was pointless. The glass either breaks or it doesn't, but if it does, then the bullet that breaks it will always shatter or deflect and be of no further use. You fire either two bullets or zero bullets. The only way you fire one bullet is if you know for sure the shield will work."

O'Day said, "The manufacturer? Like an advertisement?"

I said, "Like a type of advertisement, I guess. But not for the manufacturer, necessarily. Who else benefitted? You need to look back through your notes and check who came up with the audition idea."

"Does it matter who?"

"Suppose you're running an agency somewhere. You need a way to raise your profile. You happen to know for sure the new glass works. Right there you've got a cost-free method of putting yourself front and center. Kott fires his single round, the glass holds, you start the audition stampede, and suddenly you're the alpha dog in the world's biggest manhunt, with world leaders kissing your ass. How many agency heads would go that far?"

"Seriously? They'd all want to. But not many would trust themselves. A handful, perhaps, around the world."

"So let's narrow it down. Who can move slush fund money for unacknowledged assets like Kott, without the NSA or GCHQ seeing it?"

"That doesn't narrow it down. Everyone can do that."

"Whose profile was most in need of a raise?"

"By what objective measure? Wouldn't that be a personal perception?"

"Who knew the glass would work?"

"Anyone who witnessed the tests."

I said, "We're not narrowing it down much, are we?"

He said, "Not much."

"Who knew John Kott?"

He paused a beat, and said, "He might have been on a number of radars."

"Sixteen years ago."

He didn't answer.

I asked, "How many agency heads are still in place sixteen years later?"

He didn't answer.

I said, "Maybe we should add that in, as a dispositive factor. As another box to check. Which agency head still in place sixteen years later had a need to raise his profile and knew the glass would work and had a slush fund and knew John Kott?"

O'Day said nothing.

"We could discuss it point by point, if you like. Your profile was so low they were sending you to watch glass get tested. The great O'Day, humiliated. It was a hint, obviously. They wanted you to retire. Everyone knew. Even Khenkin, in Moscow. The SVR had you down as an old warhorse, put out to pasture. But you saw a way back. You knew Kott was about to get out. You'd been watching him. Maybe he worked for you, sixteen years ago. Maybe you were just as pissed at me as he was. So you made him an offer. If he goes to Paris and fires a single pointless round, then you'll promise him that sooner or later you'll serve me up on a platter, somewhere in the open air, within range."

O'Day said nothing.

I said, "I was the only target. Me personally. Not the G8 or the EU or the G20. That was all window dressing."

O'Day said, "Bullshit."

I said, "To keep him horny you feed him the bad parts of my file. He gets in quite a state. Good for the local economy. Whoever had the Xerox franchise had a pretty good year. Then finally you fly him out. He does the deed. You ramp up the audition talk. You're the big dog now. You tell Kott to hang tight. You tell him the ad is in the paper. And you find me fast. Kott is very pleased about that. You send me to Paris. You know for sure I'll be on that balcony, and you know approximately when. You called ahead. You set up the visit. You agreed to the itinerary. So Kott gets his shot, but he misses."

"Bullshit."

"So the circus rolls on to London. My phone has GPS in it. You know where I am. You're going to lead Kott to me. You're talking to him all the time. He has a phone just like mine. You know we'll check Wallace Court. But Ms. Nice doesn't tell you beforehand. Suddenly you see my GPS right there, but you can't move Kott in time. Insufficient warning. But never mind. Tomorrow is another day. And meanwhile you're king of the world. The politicians are panicking. They'll do anything for you. You have IOUs everywhere. All kinds of inconveniences are disappearing, all around the world. Even the London cops love you. Now they won't let you retire. Because you win both ways. If Kott gets me, you instantly sell him out to Bennett, and you've saved the world from behind the scenes. If I get Kott, you've saved the world by audacious use of unacknowledged assets. Either way you're a star again. You're back in the textbooks."

O'Day said nothing.

I said, "You gave the money to the neighbor. How else would you know he's missing a tooth?"

No response.

"Someone else knows," I said. "The three most dangerous words in the secrecy business. But there it is. I know, and Ms. Nice knows. Which is why we came back with the RAF. Because where would your plane have landed? Guantanamo, maybe. But it didn't, and we're back in America, free and clear. And we know. I'm sure you could crush Ms. Nice's career, but you'll never find me. I'll always be out there. And you know me, General. You've known me a long time. I don't forgive, and I don't forget. And I won't have to do much. Talking might be enough. Suppose the SVR found out it was you who got Khenkin killed? Some of those IOUs might get canceled. And they might retaliate. Rumors might start, about poor old Tom O'Day, who got so desperate he came up with a cockamamie scheme. Think of all those rookies laughing up their sleeves. All around the world. The whole community. That could be your legacy. It's a possibility, anyway. You'll have to live with it, I'm afraid. Or not. But don't think about ignoring it. It's you and me now, General. This thing won't have a happy ending."

I got up and put the Browning that Charlie White was going to kill me with on O'Day's desk, and then I followed Casey Nice out of the room, and down the stairs, and through the red door, and out into the night.

She drove me in the hideous Bronco, three miles to a crossroads, where I could get a night bus. We didn't talk. She stopped but couldn't get out, because she had to keep her foot on the brake, so we repeated the same chaste hug we had in London. I asked her to say goodbye for me, to Shoemaker, and I got out and walked to the concrete bench, and watched her wave and drive away, and then I lay down and watched the stars, until I heard the bus come close.

I went places I don't remember, but I know a month later I was in Texas, on a bus passing close to Fort Hood, where a man in uniform left an *Army Times* behind. O'Day's face was on the front. His obituary was inside. It contained corrections to earlier reports. The discharge had been accidental. He had been examining an unfamiliar weapon captured in Europe. Possibly the late hour explained the mistake. There was no truth in the rumor that a Royal Air Force plane had landed minutes earlier. O'Day was to be awarded three more medals posthumously, and a bridge was to be named after him, on a North Carolina state route, over a narrow stream that most of the year was dry.

No one knows suspense like
#1 *New York Times* bestselling author

Lee Child.

And there's no bigger name in suspense
than Jack Reacher.

If you enjoyed *Personal,*
please keep reading for the
Jack Reacher short story

Not a Drill

and then for an exciting preview of

Make Me

A JACK REACHER NOVEL

Coming in hardcover and eBook from
Delacorte Press
Fall 2015

Not a Drill

One thing leads to another, and in Jack Reacher's case, one warm and aimless August day, a hitched ride in an empty lumber truck led to East Millinocket in Maine, which led in turn to a decent mid-morning meal in a roadside restaurant near the highway, which led to a halting two-wary-guys conversation with the man at the next table, which led to an offered ride further north, to a place called Island Falls. The unspoken but clearly implied cost of the ride was the price of the guy's coffee and pie, but the establishment was cheap, and Reacher had money in his pocket, and as always he had no particular place to be, so he accepted.

One thing leads to another.

The guy's car turned out to be a softly-sprung old Chevrolet, lacy with rust, and Island Falls turned out to be a pleasant little place on a lake, way in the north, where Maine sticks out like a thumb up Canada's ass, with Quebec to the left and New Brunswick to the right. But most of all Island Falls was pretty close to the north end of I-95. Which was tempting. Reacher had a collector's instinct when it came to places. He knew the south end of I-95 pretty well. More than nineteen hundred miles away, just past downtown

Miami. He had been there many times. But he had never seen the north end.

He had no particular place to be.

One thing leads to another.

Getting out of Island Falls was easy enough. He had a cup of coffee in a hut next to a kayak rental slip, and stood in the buggy warmth of the lake shore and took in the view, and then he turned his back on it all and walked out of town the same way the old Chevy had driven in, back to the highway cloverleaf. He set up on the on-ramp heading north, and waited. Not long, he figured. It was August, it was warm, it was vacation country. The mood was amiable. It was daylight. He was clean. His clothes were only two days old, and his shave was only three. Ideal conditions, overall.

And sure enough, less than ten minutes later an old-model Jeep SUV with New Brunswick plates slowed and stopped. There was a woman at the wheel, and a man next to her, in the passenger seat. They looked to be somewhere in their mid-thirties, clearly outdoor types, ruffled by the wind and tanned by the sun. Heading home, no doubt, after an active vacation. Maybe they had been kayaking. Or camping. Or both. The load space in the rear of the truck was piled up with stuff.

The guy in the passenger seat let his window down, and the woman craned over for a look, too. The guy said, "We're only going to Fredericton, which isn't far, I'm afraid. Any good to you?"

Reacher said, "Is that in Canada?"

"Sure is."

Reacher said, "Then that's perfect. All I want is to get to the border, and then back again."

"Got something against Canada?"

"My passport expired."

The guy nodded. Gone were the days when a person could just stroll in and out of neighboring countries. Then the guy said, "But there's nothing much to see between here and there. Nothing much to see through the fence, either. You'd be better off staying where you are, surely."

Reacher said, "I want to see the end of the road."

The guy said, "That sounds heavy."

The woman said, "We think of it as the beginning of the road."

"Good point," Reacher said.

The guy said, "Hop in the back." He craned around in his seat and batted stray items aside. Reacher opened the door and slid in and used his hip to finish the job. He closed the door and the woman hit the gas and they took off, cruising easy through the last thirty-some miles of America.

* * *

The last exit was for a town called Houlton. Or the first exit, Reacher supposed, from the Canadian point of view. Then came a mile or so of hinterland, and a little queuing traffic, and barriers and booths and official signs. Reacher stayed in the Jeep until the last car's length, and then he said his thanks and his goodbyes and he slipped out, and he stepped ahead and put his foot on the last inch of blacktop, directly under the barrier pole.

The end of the road.

One thing leads to another.

He looped back and crossed to the southbound lanes and set up again thirty yards from the barriers. He wanted to give incoming drivers plenty of time to see him, but not enough time to be already going too fast to stop. Once again he anticipated no kind of a lengthy delay. August, daylight, sunshine, vacation country, warmhearted and relaxed Canadian drivers full of generosity and goodwill. Ten minutes max, he thought, maybe closer to five, and it wasn't outside the bounds of possibility that the first car through would be the one.

It wasn't. But the second car was. Which was more of a minivan, really. But not the kind of thing a soccer mom would be proud of. It was old and grimy, and somewhat battered. Light blue, maybe, when it left the factory, but now colorless, almost, faded by sun and salt. There was a young man at the wheel, and a young woman beside him in the front, and another young woman in the back. The van had New Brunswick plates, and it was trailing a puff of oil smoke, after pulling away from the customs post.

But Reacher had ridden in worse vehicles.

It slowed and stopped alongside him. The passenger window was already down. The woman in the front said, "We're headed for Naismith."

Which was a place Reacher had never heard of. He said, "I'm not sure where that is."

The guy at the wheel leaned across and said, "The Allagash, man. About an hour west of Route 11. After going north for a bit. It's a little town. Where you get on the wilderness trail through the forest. It's a really cool place."

Reacher said, "North of here?"

The guy said, "Beautiful country, man. You should see those woods. Really primeval. Step off the path, and you could be the first human ever to set foot. I mean, literally. Ten thousand years of undisturbed nature. Since the last Ice Age."

Reacher said nothing.

The guy said, "Get it while you can, my friend. It won't be there forever. Climate change is going to take it all down."

No particular place to be.

Reacher said, "OK, sure, thanks."

One thing leads to another.

He looped around the rear of the van and the girl in the back slid the door on a rusty track and he climbed in. Behind him in the load space were two big backpacks and one hard-shell suitcase. The seat was some kind of nylon cloth gone greasy with age. He got settled and slid the door closed and the van moved off, puffing smoke again, from the effort.

"Thanks," Reacher said, for the second time.

The trio introduced themselves. The girl in the back was Helen, and the girl in the front was Suzanne, and the driver was Henry. Henry and Suzanne were a couple. They ran a bicycle store in a place called Moncton. Helen was their friend. The plan was Henry and Suzanne would walk the wilderness trail north from Naismith, to a place called Cripps, which would take four days. Helen would be waiting there with the van to meet them, having spent the same four days doing something else, maybe antiquing in Presque Isle and Caribou.

"I don't like the woods," she said, as if she felt an explanation was required.

"Why not?" Reacher asked, because he felt a response was expected.

"Too creepy," she said. "Too dark. Too full of bugs."

They puttered onward past Houlton, and then Henry turned off on 212, which soon joined Route 11 going north, which was a pretty road. Saddleback Mountain was ahead on the right, and on the left was an endless expanse of woods and lakes. The trees were green, and the water glittered, and the sky was blue. Beautiful country, just like Henry had promised.

"I don't like the woods," Helen said again.

She was in her late twenties, Reacher guessed. Maybe thirty, tops. She was paler than her friends, and sleeker, and more cared for. Indoor, more than outdoor. Urban, rather than rural. Like her luggage. She was a hard-shell suitcase, not a backpack. Henry and Suzanne were stockier, and tousled, and wind-burned. But not older. Maybe they had all been college friends together, still a threesome more than five but less than ten years after graduation.

Henry said, "The woods are actually awesome, Helen."

He said it kindly, full of enthusiasm. No hint of confrontation or scolding. Just a guy who loved the woods, unable to understand why his friend didn't. He seemed genuinely intrigued by the possibility that he could walk where no other human had ever trod, in all of history. Reacher asked where they were all from originally, and it turned out that Henry and Suzanne were from the suburbs, of Toronto and Vancouver respectively, and it was Helen who was the real country girl, from what she called the trackless wastes of northern Ontario province. In which case he figured she was entitled to her opinion. She had earned it, presumably.

Then they asked where he was from, and his bio filled the next few miles. The Marine family, always moving, the dozen elementary schools, the dozen high schools, then West Point, then the U.S. Army, the military police, always moving all over again, some of the same countries, some new, never in one place long enough to notice. Then the drawdown, and the discharge, and the wandering. The hitched rides, the walking, the motels. The aimlessness. No particular place to be. Henry thought it was all very cool, Suzanne less so, Reacher thought, and he figured Helen didn't think it was cool at all.

They slowed and turned left onto a narrow rural two-lane that speared straight west through the trees. There was a rusted enamel sign that said *Naismith 40 miles*. It was possible the road had once had shoulders, but they were long overgrown with underbrush and broadleaf trees that reached forty feet tall. In places their branches met overhead, so that for hundreds of yards at a time it was like driving through a green tunnel. Reacher watched out the windows, left and right. Either side he could see not more than five or six feet into the vegetation. He wondered how much more primeval woods could get. Brambles and brush were tangled thigh high, and the air looked dank and still. The ground looked soft and springy, densely matted with leaf litter, damp and fecund. The blacktop ribbon ahead had turned gray with age, and the heat it was holding made the air above it thick with tiny insects. After five miles the windshield was soupy with slime, from a million separate impacts.

Reacher asked, "Have you been here before?"

"Once," Henry said. "We walked south to Center Mountain. Which was boring, man. I like to stay below the tree line. I guess I'm a forest dweller."

"Are there animals in there?"

"Bears for sure. Plenty of small stuff, obviously. But the underbrush never gets eaten, so there's no deer. Which is interesting as to why. Predation, most likely. But by what? Mountain lions, maybe. Or wolves, but no one ever sees them or hears them. But there's something in there, that's for sure."

"You sleep in a tent?"

"Pup tent," he said. "No biggie. Double-bag your food, wash around your mouth in a stream, and there's nothing for the critters to smell. Bears like to eat, but if you don't lay out a picnic for them they'll leave you alone. But you know all this, right? I mean, doesn't the army train everywhere? I thought you got sent out in every kind of terrain."

"Not in a forest like this," Reacher said. "Can't move through it, certainly can't move vehicles through it, can't shoot through it. Clearing it with napalm and explosives would take forever. So we'd have to maneuver around it. Best kind of natural barrier there is."

They drove on, over a surface that got progressively worse. The encroaching brush had nibbled out fist-sized bites of blacktop on both sides, and then tree roots had punched out deeper holes, and the winter freezes had elongated the cracks, and the state's fixes had been infrequent and hasty. The old van's suspension creaked and pattered. Overhead the green tunnels became more or less continuous. In places leafy vines hung down and whipped the roof.

Then exactly an hour after leaving Route 11 there was a cleared length of shoulder with a board sign on it, which had words burned into it with a hot poker: *Welcome to Naismith, the Gateway to the Wilderness.* Which Reacher felt was about an hour too late. He felt that particular threshold had been passed long ago.

Henry slowed the van and the road curved to the left and came out in a clearing about the size of a football stadium. Dead ahead was a lake shaped like a crooked finger, first pointing north and then curling east. The road became a kind of Main Street leading straight to the shore. At the far end was a kayak pier, and left and right were low wooden buildings, with vacation cabins near the water, and a general store and a diner and small residences further from it. There were side streets made of the same battered gray blacktop. Naismith, Maine. A miniature town, in the middle of nowhere.

Suzanne said, "I'm hungry."

"I'll buy lunch," Reacher said. "That's the least I can do."

Henry parked the van in front of the diner and shut down the motor. The world went silent. They all climbed out, and they all stood and stretched. The air was somewhere halfway between fresh and heavy, the tang of the lake water mixed with the smell of the trees, and there was no sound beyond a subliminal drone from a billion tiny insect wings. There was no wind, no rustling leaves, no lapping waves. Just hot stillness.

The diner was all wood, inside and out, rough stained boards worn shiny in places by hands and elbows and shoulders. There were pies in glass cases and eight square tables draped in red checkered tablecloths. The waitress was a flinty woman of about sixty, wearing a pair of men's eyeglasses and carpet slippers. Two tables were occupied, both by people who looked more like Henry and Suzanne than Helen. The waitress pointed to an empty table and went to get menus and glasses of water.

The food was the same as Reacher had eaten in a thousand other diners, but it was adequate, and the coffee was fresh and strong, so he was happy. As were the others, not that they were paying much attention to what they were eating and drinking. They were talking amongst themselves, running through their plans. Which sounded straightforward enough. They were all going to spend the night in pre-booked cabins, and at first light Henry and Suzanne were going to set out walking, and Helen was going to drive back to Route 11 and look for whatever she could find.

Four days later they were all going to meet again at the far end of the trail. Simple as that.

Reacher paid the check, said his goodbyes, and left them there. He didn't expect to see them again.

* * *

From the diner he strolled down to the kayak pier and walked out to the end of it, and stood with his toes above open water. The lake was a bright-blue spear pointing north and then turning east into the distance, more than ten miles long, probably, but not more than a couple hundred yards across at its widest bulge. Overhead was a vast high bowl of summer sky, completely cloudless, unmarked except for wispy contrails eight miles up, from transatlantic jet planes heading to and from Europe, in and out of Boston and New York and Washington, D.C. Great Circle routes, way up over Canada and Greenland, and then dropping down again to London and Paris and Rome. Straight lines on a spherical planet, but not on a flat paper map.

At ground level the forest crowded in on both sides of the lake, unbroken, a continuous green canopy covering everything that wasn't liquid. There were hundreds and hundreds of square miles of it. Ten thousand years of undisturbed nature, Henry had said, which was exactly what it looked like. The earth had warmed, the glaciers had retreated, seeds had blown in, rain had fallen, and a hundred generations of trees had grown and died and grown again. Elsewhere on the giant continent people had cut them down to clear fields for farming, or for lumber to build houses, or to burn in stoves and steam locomotives, but some parts had been left alone, and maybe always would be. You could be the first human ever to set foot, Henry had said, and Reacher had no doubt he was right.

He walked back past the vacation cabins, which were all quiet. People were out and about in other places, clearly, doing whatever it was they were there to do. He found a turn to the left, which was basically north, where there was a hundred-yard side street, which he followed, and at the end of it he found a wooden arch, lashed together from bark-stripped trunks stained dark brown, like a ceremonial thing. A literal gateway to the wilderness. Beyond it the trail started. It ran straight for twenty yards, all beaten flat by booted feet, and then it turned a corner and disappeared. Next stop, the town called Cripps, four days away.

He stepped under the arch and stood still on the first yard of the trail. Then he moved forward, twenty paces, to the first turn. He took it and walked onward, another twenty paces, another twenty yards, and stopped again. The trail was about four feet wide. Either side the forest crowded in. The trunks were spiked with dead branches all the way to the canopy far overhead. The trees had grown tall and straight, racing for the light. They were two or three feet apart in some places, and more or less touching in others. Some were ancient and mature, all gnarled and burled and a yard across, and some were younger and slimmer and paler, exploiting the gaps, like opportunistic weeds. Below chest height the undergrowth was dense and tangled, a mess of dark-leaved thorny runners snaking among dry and brittle twigs. The air was still and completely silent. The light was green and dim. He turned a full circle. He was forty yards from the ceremonial arch, but he felt like he was a million miles from anywhere.

He walked on, another twenty paces. Nothing changed. The path wandered left and right a little. He guessed some kind of parks authority kept the under-brush trimmed back, and left it to passing feet to crush new seedlings. He guessed without that kind of human intervention the trail would close up in a year or two. Three, tops. It would become impassable. Re-claimed by nature. He guessed wider bulges had been hacked out here and there, for campsites. For the pup tents. Near streams, maybe. There was nowhere else to sleep the night.

He stood for a minute more, in the green filtered light and the eerie silence. Then he turned around and walked back to Naismith's token Main Street, and he followed it out the way they had driven in, to the board sign on the shoulder, with the welcome. But there was no traffic leaving town, and after a moment's reflection he realized there wouldn't be, not until the next morn-ing. Presumably the check-out time for the vacation cabins was eleven or noon, which meant that day's exo-dus was already over. The diner and the general store would need occasional deliveries, but the odds were long that a returning truck would be passing by any-time soon. He stood in the heavy silence a minute lon-ger, for no real reason other than he was enjoying it, and then he retraced his steps, through the town toward the lake.

* * *

The vacation cabins were laid out haphazardly, like a handful of dice thrown down. Reacher figured the location furthest from the water would be the least desirable, and sure enough found it was being used as some kind of a resident manager's accommodations, with a front room done up as an office, with one of its window panes converted to an opening hutch, which had a shelf behind it with a little brass bell and a ballpoint pen on a chain. He rang the bell and a long moment later an old guy stepped up, slowly, like he had arthritis. Yes, he had vacancies. The overnight charge was a modest sum. Reacher paid cash and signed his name with the pen on the chain, and got a key in return, to what turned out to be a tiny wooden house that smelled hot and moldy. Not a prime position, but it had a partial sideways view of the lake. The rest of the view was all trees, inevitably. There was a bed and two chairs, and a bathroom and kitchen facilities, and a short shelf with creased and battered paperback books on it. Outside in back there was a small deck with two folding chairs slung with faded and sun-rotted fabric. Reacher spent the rest of the afternoon in one of them, with his feet up on the other, reading a book from the shelf, warm, alone, relaxed, as happy as he could remember being.

* * *

He woke at seven in the morning but lay in bed a whole extra hour, stretched out like a starfish, to let the walkers and the boaters get through the diner ahead of him. He figured they would be looking for an early start. He wasn't. He figured about ten o'clock would be optimum, to catch the first wave of departures. A ride back to Route 11 was all he needed. To I-95 would be a bonus, and Bangor or Portland or anyplace further south would be the icing on the cake. He figured he would head to New York next. Yankees tickets would be easy to get. The dog days of summer, folks out of town, plenty of space in the high seats in the sun.

He showered and dressed and packed, which consisted of folding his toothbrush and putting it in his pocket. He saw the maid on her way between two other cabins, and told her his was vacant and ready for her. She looked like she could have been the waitress's sister, from the diner, and probably was. He walked on, thinking about coffee, and pancakes, and a corner table in a quiet empty room, and maybe someone's abandoned newspaper to read.

He didn't get the quiet empty room.

Henry and Suzanne were in there, with about nine other people, all milling about, all talking in a tense and agitated fashion, like a scene in a movie where folks find out the mining company has poisoned their water. They all turned to look at him as he stepped inside. He said, "What's up?"

Henry said, "They closed the trail."

"Who did?"

"The cops. State, I think. They strung tape across the entrance."

"When?"

"In the night."

"Why?"

"No one knows."

"They won't tell us," Suzanne said. "We've been calling all morning. All they'll say is the trail is closed until further notice."

Another guy said, "It's closed at Cripps, too. We started that end last year. I still have the motel number. Same situation. Tape between the trees."

Reacher said, "It's a four-day walk, right? There must be a bunch of people still in there. Maybe something happened."

"Then why won't they tell us?"

Reacher said nothing. Not his problem. All he wanted was pancakes. And coffee, more urgently. He looked for the waitress, and caught her eye, and found an empty table.

Henry followed him straight to it. "Can they do that?"

Reacher said, "Do what?"

"Close the trail like that."

"They just did."

"Is it legal?"

"How would I know?"

"You were a cop."

"I was a military cop. I wasn't a park ranger."

"It's a public resource."

"I'm sure there's a good reason. Maybe someone got eaten by a bear."

One by one the whole disgruntled group came over and gathered around. Eleven people standing up, Reacher sitting down. The guy who still had the number for the Cripps motel asked, "How do you know that?"

Reacher said, "Know what?"

"That someone got attacked by a bear."

"I said maybe. Like a joke."

"Bear attacks aren't very funny."

A guy said, "Maybe it's just a drill."

"What kind of drill?"

"Like a rehearsal. For a medical emergency, maybe. For the first responders."

"Then why would they say until further notice? Why wouldn't they say until lunchtime today, or some such?"

Another guy asked, "Who should we call?"

Suzanne said, "They're not telling us anything."

"We could try the governor's office."

Another woman said, "Like he's going to tell us anything, if the others aren't."

"It can't be bears."

"Then what is it?"

"I don't know."

Suzanne looked at Reacher and said, "What should we do?"

Reacher said, "Go for a walk someplace else."

"We can't. We're stuck here. Helen's got the van."

"She left already?"

"She didn't want to eat breakfast here."

"Can't you call her?"

"No bars."

"Bars aren't open yet."

"I mean no cell phone coverage here. We can't call

her. We tried, from the payphone in the store. She's off the network somewhere."

"So go kayaking instead. That's probably just as much fun."

Henry said, "I don't want to go kayaking. I want to walk the trail."

* * *

Eventually the small crowd wandered away again, out through the door to the parking lot, still mumbling and grumbling, and the waitress came by to take Reacher's order. He ate and drank in silence, and he got the check, and he paid in cash. He asked the waitress, "Does the trail get closed a lot?"

She said, "It never happened before."

"Did you see who did it?"

She shook her head. "I was asleep."

"Where's the nearest state police barracks?"

"The kayak owner says it was soldiers."

"Does he?"

She nodded. "He says he saw them."

"In the middle of the night?"

She nodded again. "He lives nearest the arch. They woke him up."

Reacher put an extra dollar on her tip and walked out to the street. He turned right and took a step in the direction of out of town, but then he stopped and went back and found the hundred-yard side street that led to the trail.

Henry and Suzanne were right there at the arch. Just the two of them. They had their backpacks on. The arch had tape tied across it, three lengths, one knee high, one waist high, and one chest high, all two-inch plastic ribbon, blue and white, twisted on itself in places, saying *Police Line Do Not Cross.*

Henry said, "See?"

Reacher said, "I believed you the first time."

"So what do you think?"

"I think the trail is closed."

Henry turned away and stared at the tape, like he could make it dematerialize by willpower alone. Reacher walked back to Main Street, and onward out of town, to the welcome board on the shoulder. Ten minutes, he thought. Maybe less. He figured that morning's exodus would be brisker than normal.

* * *

But the first vehicle he saw was coming, not going. Into town, not out. And it was a military vehicle. A Humvee, to be precise, painted up in black and green camouflage. It roared past, all thrashing gears and whining tires. It took the curve and disappeared.

Four guys in it, hard men, all in the new Army Combat Uniform.

Reacher waited. A minute later a car came driving out of town, but it was full. Two in the front, two in the back. No room for a hitchhiker, especially one as large as Reacher. He recognized people he had seen in the diner, disconsolate and complaining, boots on and ready, backpacks piled in the corner, no place to go.

He waited.

Next up was another Humvee, heading in, not out. Roaring engine, thrashing drive train, howling tires, four guys wearing ACUs. Reacher watched it around the corner and even at a distance he heard it slow, and change gear, and speed up again. A right hand turn, he thought, and he would have bet the few bucks in his pocket it was heading for the wooden arch.

He stared after it, thinking.

Then another car came driving out of town. A sedan. Two people. An empty back seat. The driver was the guy who still had the number for the motel in Cripps. He slowed and stopped and the woman next to him buzzed her window down. She asked, "Where are you headed?"

Reacher said nothing.

She said, "We're going back to Boston."

Which would have been great. Three hours from New York. Multiple routes. Lots of traffic. But Reacher said, "I'm sorry, but I changed my mind. I'm going to stay here."

The woman shrugged and the car took off without him.

* * *

He walked back to the cabin rental office and rang the bell. His cabin was still available. He paid for another night, and got the same key in return. Then he headed for the arch, a hundred yards along the side street, and when he got there he found the two Humvees and their eight occupants. The Humvees were parked side by side, noses out, blocking the whole width of the road. Their occupants already had their boots on the ground. They were all armed with M16s. They were setting up an exclusion zone. Reacher knew the signs. Two squads, four hours on, four hours off.

Military police, for sure. Reacher knew those signs, too. Not the National Guard, either. Regular U.S. Army. Not a drill. No one was going to get past them.

There was no sign of Henry or Suzanne.

Reacher said, "Sergeant?"

One of the grunts turned around. Chevrons on the tab in the center of his chest. Twenty years younger than Reacher, at least. A whole different generation. The military police has no secret handshake. No magic word. And no real inclination to shoot the breeze with some ancient geezer, no matter who he might claim to have been, one day long ago, way back when.

The sergeant said, "Sir, you need to step back ten yards."

Reacher said, "That would be a hell of a long step, wouldn't it?"

Two PFCs were hauling sawhorses out of a Humvee. A-shaped ends, and planks to fit between, marked *No Entry*.

Reacher said, "I'm guessing your orders are to keep people out of the woods. Which is fine with me. Knock yourselves out. But close observation of the terrain will reveal the woods start where the woods start, not a Humvee's length plus ten yards down the street."

The sergeant said, "Who are you?"

"I'm a guy who once read the Constitution."

"This whole place is woods."

"So I noticed."

"So back off now."

"Unit?"

"345th MP."

"Name?"

"Cain. Spelled *C, A, I, N,* with no *E.*"

"You got a brother?"

"Like I haven't heard that one before."

Reacher nodded. He said, "Carry on the good work, sergeant," and he turned and walked away.

* * *

He went back to the cabin rental office, and rang the bell again. The old guy stepped up, creakily, and Reacher asked him, "Are my friends still here? The people I came in with? Henry something and Suzanne something?"

"They checked out early this morning."

"They didn't come back again?"

"They're gone, mister."

Reacher nodded, and headed for his hut, where he spent the next four hours on the back deck, sitting in one lawn chair, his feet up on the other, watching the sky. It was another beautiful day, and he saw nothing except bright blue emptiness, and wispy contrails arching way overhead, eight miles up.

* * *

In the early afternoon he headed to the diner for a late lunch. He was the only customer. The town felt deserted. No trail, no business. The waitress didn't look happy. Not just about the lack of revenue. She was on the wall phone, listening to someone, concern on her face. A tale of woe, clearly. She hung up after a long minute and walked over to Reacher's table.

She said, "They're sending search parties south

from Cripps. For the walkers. They're grabbing them and hustling them out. Real fast."

Reacher said, "Soldiers?"

She nodded. "Lots of them."

"Weird."

"That's not the worst of it. They're holding them for questioning afterward. They want to know if they saw anything."

"Soldiers are doing that, too?"

"Men in suits. My friend thinks they're the FBI."

"Who's your friend?"

"She works at the motel in Cripps."

"What are people supposed to have seen?"

"All we have is rumors. A bear gone rogue, maybe. A man-eater. Packs of wild coyotes, mountain lions, bigfoot monsters. Or some vicious murderer escaped from the penitentiary. Or wolves. Or vampires."

"You believe in vampires?"

"I watch the television, same as anyone else."

"It's not vampires," Reacher said.

"There's something in those woods, mister."

* * *

Reacher ate a tuna melt and drank coffee and water, and then he headed back to the arch for a second look. The sawhorses were in place, ten yards upstream of the parked Humvees. Four grunts were standing easy, weapons shouldered. A show of force. *No entry.* Not a drill. Pleasant duty, overall, given the season. Winter would have been much worse.

Reacher walked back to town. Just as he hit Main Street the colorless minivan came around the corner.

Helen was at the wheel. She pulled over next to him and buzzed her window down.

She said, "Have you seen Henry and Suzanne?"

He said, "Not since breakfast time."

"People say the trail is closed."

"It is."

"So I came to pick them up."

"Good luck with that."

"Where are they?"

"I think Henry is a hard man to dissuade."

"They went anyway?"

"That's my guess."

"After it was closed?"

"There was a brief window of opportunity. After the tape went up, before the soldiers arrived."

"I heard about the soldiers."

"What else have you heard?"

"There's something bad in the woods."

"Vampires, maybe," Reacher said.

"This isn't funny. I heard it might be escaped prisoners or rogue military units. Something very dangerous. Everyone is talking. It's on the local AM station. There are anchors in Cripps already."

"You want a cup of coffee?"

* * *

Helen parked in front of the diner, and they went in together, to the same table Reacher had used before. The waitress brought coffee, and then hustled away and got on the wall phone again. To her friend in Cripps, presumably. For updates, and gossip, and rumor.

Helen said, "Henry is an idiot."

"He likes the woods," Reacher said. "Can't blame him for that."

"But there's something in there now, obviously."

"I guess there is."

"Which he must have known. It's not brain surgery. He's an idiot, but he's not an *idiot*. But he went in anyway. And dragged Suzanne in with him. He is an idiot. Both sorts."

"Suzanne could have said no."

"Actually, she's just as bad. No impulse control. I heard they have search parties moving south from Cripps."

Reacher nodded. "I heard that, too. Straight from the horse's mouth. Or slightly secondhand, I suppose. Our waitress has a friend up there."

"What are they searching for?"

"People like Henry and Suzanne. They're getting them out and asking questions about what they saw."

"But they'll miss Henry and Suzanne. Won't they? It's inevitable. They're expecting a three-day pipeline. They'll stop when they get all the people who started out yesterday morning. Henry and Suzanne will be twenty-four hours behind them. They'll leave them in there. With whatever else is in there. This is not good."

"It's a big woods."

"The thing could be roaming and hunting. Or if it's escaped prisoners they'll stick close to the trail anyway. They would have to. Henry and Suzanne will be in there alone with them."

Reacher said, "It's not escaped prisoners."

"How do you know?"

"I went to see the soldiers at the arch. They're military police, like I was. But technically what they're doing isn't entirely kosher. The military can't perform civilian law enforcement duties. There are all kinds of rules about that. But their sergeant told me his unit number with no hesitation at all. And then he told me his name, just as fast. He even spelled it out for me. *Cain,* with no *e.*"

"What does all that mean?"

"It means he's not afraid of anything. So he can get right in my face. Which means he has a solid gold get-out-of-jail-free card. Which must be urgent orders from somewhere very high up. From an unimpeachable source. As in, if some citizen like me makes a fuss, I'm going to get crushed by the machine. He's going to get a medal. Which makes this a national security issue. It's showing all the signs. And people escaped from the penitentiary isn't national security. That's a state affair."

Helen was quiet for a second.

Then she said, "A national security issue could be a rogue military unit. Or a band of terrorists. Or escaped prisoners from Homeland Security. Or some kind of mutant has gotten free. Like a genetic experiment. Or someone else's genetic experiment, *set* free. On purpose. Maybe this is an attack. And they're right there in it."

"It's none of the above," Reacher said.

"How do you know?"

"Because I sat in a chair all morning and watched the sky."

"Which told you what?"

"No circling spotter planes, no drones, no helicopters. If they were hunting a warm-blooded creature or creatures, they'd have been up there all day with heat-seeking cameras. And air-to-ground radar, and whatever other fancy things they have now."

"So what do you think they're looking for?"

"They aren't looking. I told you that. No aerial surveillance."

"Then what aren't they looking for?"

"Something with no heat signature, and too small to show up on radar."

"Which would be what?"

"I have no idea."

"But something they don't want us to see, obviously. Something we can't know about."

"Evidently."

"It could be a cold-blooded creature. Like a snake."

"Or a vampire. Are they cold-blooded?"

"This isn't funny. But OK, maybe it's not a creature at all. Maybe it's a piece of secret equipment. Inert, somehow."

"Possibly."

"How did it get in there?"

"That's a great question," Reacher said. "I think it must have fallen off an airplane."

* * *

They got refills of coffee, and Helen worried away at the problem in her mind, and eventually she said, "This is very bad indeed."

Reacher said, "Not really. Henry and Suzanne don't

have much to fear from a piece of inert equipment. It's not going to jump up and bite them in the ass."

"But it is. That's exactly what it's going to do. Figuratively speaking. They're in the woods illegally, twenty-four hours behind anyone else. That looks secretive. Like their job is to find the thing and smuggle it out. Suppose it's a bomb or a missile? That happens, right? Bombs and missiles fall off airplanes. Accidentally. Sometimes, right? I read it in a book. But more likely deliberately. Like it's one big conspiracy. What do we do if Henry and Suzanne are taken to be the designated retrieval party? It wouldn't take much imagination. They sneak in through the tape, they're all alone in a deserted twenty-four-hour time window, their job is to grab the missile ahead of your government, and pass it on down the chain, until one day an airliner comes down at JFK and it's 9/11 all over again."

"Henry and Suzanne are hikers. Wilderness enthusiasts. It's the summer vacation. They're Canadians, for God's sake."

"What does that mean?"

"Nicest people in the world. Almost as good as being Swiss."

"But whatever, they'll check them out."

"Names and numbers, in a couple of databases. Nearest thing to doing nothing at all."

"Suzanne has a history."

Reacher said, "What kind?"

"She's a lovely person. You have to understand that. She has sympathy for everybody."

"Is that a problem?"

Helen said, "Of course it is. Because *everybody*

means everybody. Plain English. Which means if you focus the spotlight one particular way, you can see sympathies going where your country doesn't want them to go. Out of context and more than balanced by other things elsewhere and not at all fair, but facts are facts."

Reacher said nothing.

Helen said, "And she's very passionate politically. And very active."

"How active is very active?"

"It's what she does. Like a job. Henry runs the bike shop on his own most of the time."

"So she's in more than a couple of databases. A couple hundred, at least."

"Red-flagged in most of them, probably. I mean, she's not Che Guevara or Chairman Mao, but computer memory is very cheap these days, and they have to fill it up with something. She's in the top million, I'm sure. And I'm equally sure they have preprogrammed responses ready. The screens will light up like a Christmas tree and she'll be hauled off to Egypt or Syria. She'll be in the system. They might let her come home in a year or so, all weird and slightly off. If she lives through it."

Reacher said, "It might not be a missile. It might be some boring black box full of coded data. Maybe it fell off a satellite, not an airplane. No possible use to anyone else. Which makes the idea of a retrieval party insane to them. They're not going to be chasing shadows. If they see Henry and Suzanne coming around the corner, dressed like hikers, walking like hikers, and sounding like hikers, then they're going to call them hikers. They're going to give them a drink of water and send them on their way."

"You can't be sure of that."

"It's one of a number of possibilities."

"What are all the others?"

"I guess some of them could come uncomfortably close to the kind of thing you're worried about."

"How many of them?"

"Practically all of them, really. Bottom line is she's a foreign national with a history in the middle of a national-security lockdown."

Helen said, "We have to go get them out."

* * *

Resistance was futile. Reacher knew that right away. He was a realistic man. A Stoic, in the original meaning of the name. A guy who accepted circumstances for what they were, and didn't seek to change them. He asked, "How fast do they walk?"

Helen said, "Not very. They're communing, not commuting. They're stepping off the path and making footprints in the virgin earth. They're looking at everything. They're listening to the birds and the wind in the trees. We should be able to catch up to them."

"Better to get ahead of them."

"How?"

* * *

They started in the diner's kitchen, where the bewildered day guy gave up two machete-like weapons. Cleavers, possibly, for cutting meat. Then they hustled down to the kayak dock and rented a slim two-place vessel. It was bright orange in color. It had waterproof fabric around the seat holes. To tie around the rower's waist, Reacher figured. Like wearing the boat like a pair of pants. To stop water getting in. Which he thought was overkill, on a fine day in August, on an inland body of water about as placid as a millpond.

Reacher took the back seat. It was a tight fit. Helen looked better, in the front. The rental guy let go of a rope and they paddled away, chaotic at first, then getting better. Much better. All about building up a rhythm. Long, steady, propulsive strokes. Like swimming. But faster than swimming. Faster than walking, too. Certainly faster than communing, and putting prints in the virgin earth, and listening to birds. Maybe twice as fast. Maybe more. Which was good. The lake turned like a crooked come-on finger, which gave them a natural outflanking maneuver, at first running parallel to the trail, and then cutting up and in, all the way to the far end of the finger, right to where the nail would be, which would be as near the trail as they could hope to get. Because after the turn the lake dug into the woods, just like Maine itself dug into Canada. Like a blade. Like a knife wound. The far tip might dump them just a couple hundred yards from the path itself. A quarter mile, maximum. The primeval part of the forest was not wide at that location. Because of the water. Like a bay. Like a river estuary.

They paddled on. Not a sprint. A middle-distance race. The mile, maybe. Black-and-white film of skinny gentlemen pounding around cinder tracks. Baggy white shirts. Grimaces. Digging in. Enduring. The machetes were between Reacher's feet. They slid backward and forward, backward and forward, with the pulse of every stroke.

* * *

The far tip of the finger was a rocky V tight up against tree trunks. Which made it easy to steady the ship prior to getting out. There were handholds everywhere. But it made it hard to move more than a foot ashore. It was all about squeezing through, leading with one shoulder, leading with the other, being careful with the trailing foot, like crossing a crowded room at a party, except with statues instead of people, all of them as solid as iron. And not in candlelight, but in a strange green glow, from the bright sun behind a billion still and silent leaves.

And any wider clearing was no real bonus, either, because they were all tangled with vines and brambles, which to some extent could be blundered through, but nine times out of ten the machetes were needed in the last yard or two, to release ankles all snarled up and fresh out of momentum.

Reacher asked, "You OK?"

Helen answered, "In what way?"

"You don't like the woods."

"You want to take three wild-ass guesses as to why? As in, right now this minute?"

They pressed on, Reacher leading, making a big hole in the vegetation, Helen coming through it close behind, both of them making prints where maybe no human had ever walked before. And then they sensed rather than saw the trail up ahead, a slit, a discontinuity, an absence. A hole in the woodland sounds. A change in the sky. A seam in the canopy. And then they came upon it, stepping over gnarled trunks bent like knees, turning, squeezing, and finally falling out on what was literally the beaten track. The air above it was damp and still, and noticeably cool.

Helen said, "So are we ahead of them?"

"I think so," Reacher said. "For sure, if they're sightseeing. Maybe not, if something spooked them and they hustled. But I'm pretty sure we made it. And when it comes to speculation, I'm a very cautious man."

"So we wait here?"

"The most efficient use of our time would be to move and meet them head-on. By definition we'd turn them around closer to Naismith than here."

"We might be walking away from them."

"Life's a gamble, I guess."

"It was a spooky situation from the start. Maybe they were hustling all the way. Just to be able to say they'd done the miles. They could have passed here thirty minutes ago."

"I'm guessing they didn't hustle. They seemed really into this stuff. I think they're strolling slow, stopping all the time, looking at this and that. All on their own. It's just them and the forest. I say they're thirty minutes in front of us."

"You've done this kind of thing before, right?"

"From time to time."

"Did you get them right?"

"Some of them."

She took a breath and said, "OK, we'll hope to

meet them head-on. And if we don't, I'm going to call you some very un-Canadian names. Some with several syllables."

"Sticks and stones," Reacher said.

"I'll go first," she said.

* * *

The trail was much easier underfoot, and it was a straight shot, with no twisting or dodging, which meant they could pay a little attention to things more than a foot and a half away. Of which there were many. And which in the end slowed them down more than the tripwire brambles. Because there was a lot to look at. *Primeval* was the right word. Not necessarily Reacher's thing, but he couldn't deny some sense of primitive connection. It could have been that a hundred generations of his ancestors had lived in the woods. They had to live somewhere. The trees were spotty with lichen and smooth with light green moss, and they bent and twisted and jostled for light and space, and the gloomy shapes they made seemed to talk, just faintly, like a distant hum. *Perfect ambush location ahead and left, so take care. Two defensive positions ahead and right, so plan to use the first, with the second to fall back on if necessary.* A hundred generations, and by definition all of them survived.

They walked on, through cool air, like cellar air, still and damp and undisturbed. The trail itself was soft and springy, a dark, leaf-rich loam. Like carpet.

No hikers up ahead.

Not in the first five minutes, or the first ten. Which

made each new minute more and more likely. Two couples on exactly opposite vectors, one moving fast, one moving slow, fifteen minutes already gone. The window in which the encounter would have to take place was getting smaller and smaller. If it was going to happen, it was going to happen soon.

It didn't.

Not in the next five minutes, or the next ten. Which was getting arithmetically difficult. It was hard to imagine Henry and Suzanne could be slow enough to make the big numbers work. Unless they had chickened out and turned around, straight back to Naismith. Second thoughts, maybe, and an honorable retreat. They might have stepped out behind Sergeant Cain at the exact same moment Reacher and Helen had paddled away from the kayak dock.

No way of knowing.

No hikers up ahead.

Helen said, "Reacher, you blew it."

He said, "Start with the polysyllabic examples. I'm always interested."

She said, "Maybe something already happened to them."

"But what? There are no search parties coming north out of Naismith. No other hikers. The missing equipment is not jumping up and biting them in the ass. Not actually. You can say so later, figuratively, but so far nothing much can have happened to them."

"Then where are they?"

"They must be static. Maybe they pitched their tent already. Maybe they found the perfect spot."

"I think they hustled and we missed them. I think we came in behind them. You blew the call."

"Life's a gamble," Reacher said again.

* * *

They moved on, speeding up a little, ignoring the sylvan glades to their left and right, every one of them a separate curiosity, like a room in a museum. There was a new breeze high above them, and the canopy was rustling, and tree limbs were clicking and groaning. Small furtive animals made darting sounds in the underbrush. Insects hung in tight clouds, to be avoided if possible, or batted through if not.

Then the trail jinked right and left around a huge mossy bole four feet wide, and up ahead in the gloom they saw two bright objects stacked side by side on the forest floor. Red and orange and yellow, nylon, straps and buckles.

Backpacks.

"Theirs," Helen said.

Reacher nodded at her side. He had seen the backpacks before, most recently at the wilderness arch that morning, hoisted into place and ready to go. They walked on and stopped next to the luggage. It was not abandoned. Both packs were set upright, leaning one on the other. They had been carefully placed.

"They stepped off the trail," Reacher said. "A little side excursion. No point hauling bags through the brush."

"When?" Helen said.

"Recently, I hope. Which would mean they're close by."

Behind the click and the hum of the living woods there was nothing but silence all around. No gasps, no calls, no feet ripping through the tangled undergrowth.

Nothing.

Helen said, "Should we shout?"

Reacher said, "Not too loud."

"Henry? Suzanne?" She said their names like a fierce stage whisper, louder than talking, but far from yelling, with an anxious questioning cadence rising on the ends.

No response.

"Suzanne? Henry?"

No response.

She said, "They can't be far away, surely."

Reacher studied the brush to the left and the right. Logic said if they had stepped off the trail, they would have done so near their bags. No sense in stacking the packs and then choosing an exit point a hundred yards away. So Reacher knew where to start looking. But he was no kind of an expert tracker. Not out in the wilds. Not like the movies, where the guy squats down on his haunches and ponders a moment and says, *They passed this way three hours ago, and the woman has a blister on her ankle.*

But there were broken shoots and torn leaves in one location. Easy enough to imagine a planted foot, and the sweep of a short, cautious stride, and the next foot, and a second person following behind, leading with one shoulder, then leading with the other, squeezing through the gaps.

Helen said, "Should we try it?"

Reacher said, "Call their names again."

"Henry? Suzanne? Where are you?"

No response. No echo off the trees.

Reacher pushed his way into the brush, scanning ahead, looking for disturbances, for kicked twigs, for sap oozing from crushed stalks. It was an inexact process. In most places there was no obvious new direction to follow. He was forced to stop every few yards, and examine a whole arc ahead of him, and choose the least-worst possibility from among a number of equally plausible angles. He figured rabbits and other small animals could sweep blades of grass aside just as easily as a brushing foot, but only human weight could break anything thicker than a pencil, so he based his guesses on the presence or absence of bright new wood on the inside faces of busted twigs. On and on, like an algorithm, yes and no and no and yes.

Deeper into the woods.

Every ten yards they stopped and listened, the backs of their brains filtering out the normal sounds and scanning for the abnormal. But hearing nothing, not on the first stop, or the second, or the third, but the fourth time around Reacher felt he could sense held breath nearby, a tense human vibe, which the ancient part of his mind interpreted as either predator or prey, and therefore of interest either way. A hundred generations, and they all survived. Then he heard a tiny sound halfway between a wheezing click and a whirring crunch, all spiky with tiny squeaks and whistles and mechanical resonances, and bathed in faint but cavernous echo. Like a Nikon camera, but not really. An electronic imitation, reedy and insubstantial.

A cell phone, taking a picture.

And another.

Reacher pushed on, stepping high to keep clear of vines, squeezing through gaps, and then suddenly seeing Henry and Suzanne, standing shoulder to shoulder not ten feet from him, looking down, taking cell phone snaps of the thing on the ground in front of them. *No heat signature, and too small to show up on radar.* That was for damn sure.

* * *

It was a dead human, a man, small, dark-skinned, lean and ascetic, in old orange prison garb. He was on his back, and the angle of his neck and his limbs made no kind of anatomical sense. He looked soft inside, almost liquid, as if his bones were smashed and his organs crushed.

Reacher said, "He fell out of an airplane. Not off an airplane, exactly. Out through the door. Way high up. So he blacks out because he has no oxygen, or maybe the sudden cold gives him a heart attack right then and there, but either way he falls like a rag doll, and he smashes through the canopy, and he hits the forest floor, where he's DOA for sure. The canopy bounces back, so there's nothing to see from above, and he's cooling fast, down to ambient temperature, so the infrared can't find him, and as far as radar is concerned, he looks exactly like a tree root or a little pile of broken branches."

Suzanne said, "I hope he had the heart attack from the cold."

Reacher said, "The question is, did he jump or was he pushed?"

"He jumped."

"Who is he?"

"He's a Canadian citizen. He was supposed to come down in Toronto. But he missed."

"And who are you?"

"Just another Canadian citizen."

"Who are the pictures for?"

"His family."

"Who is he?" Reacher asked again.

"I see both sides," Suzanne said. "I would do anything to stop another attack. But it's getting insane now. They fly these guys from Guantanamo to Egypt and Syria, where they get a good working over, and after a while the ones who survive have to come back, because the Egyptians and the Syrians can't have them hanging about forever, but you don't want them back, because what are you going to do with them? Guantanamo is always full, and you can't just say never mind and let them go, because they've all got stories to tell."

"So what do they do with them? And tell me how you know."

"There's a network, for people of conscience. Way down in the dark web. Certain facts are established. Your ground crews bypassed a couple of failsafes, and made it possible to open the airplane door during flight. At very low speeds, and very low altitudes, mostly over the far north Atlantic, in the radar shadows, where they would come down low and slow, and open the hatch. That's what they do with them. Problem solved."

"So?"

"So word gets around, and this guy knows he's either going to die under torture or get thrown out of the plane on the way home. There's no happy ending here. So he decides to jump out the door on the outward flight. To take them by surprise. Somewhere over Toronto. To make a statement. A sympathetic foreign press, a chance to apply some external pressure."

Reacher nodded. *Like a thumb up Canada's ass.* Toronto wasn't very far away. He said, "What went wrong?"

"Not very much. They have access to information and experts of every kind. They knew the route, which never changes, and they knew the timing. It's just a question of counting the minutes in your head, and then going for it. Which I guess can't ever be totally accurate. Although he trained for months. And a gust of headwind counts for a lot, I suppose. Small errors multiply."

"Who are the pictures for?" Reacher asked again.

"His family. There's nothing else to be done. None of this exists on paper. The denials would be instant and convincing. They'd say the photos were faked. Low green light, a little grainy. Foreign radicals with a bike shop. The whole thing wouldn't last a day."

"Would it have lasted longer in Toronto?"

"They thought so. Cities and suburbs are different. There are lots of witnesses, and cops, and TV. Things don't go away so easily. They thought it could be a watershed moment."

"You seem to know a lot about how they think."

"I try to learn how everyone thinks. It's the key to understanding. Not that this was some innocent sweetheart. He was a thug straight from the Middle Ages. He was a vicious killer. I was glad he was jumping out of the plane. But he had already told them what he knew. And they were sending him anyway. Just out of habit. It's insane now."

"How did you know where to look?"

"Postgame analysis from the experts."

"Why you?"

"We were closest."

"Out of how many choices?"

"Many."

"Including Helen?"

Helen said, "Of course."

Henry said, "It was her idea to pick you up and bring you along. At least that way we get an American witness. You've seen it now. You can't un-see it."

Reacher said, "We need to get back to Naismith."

* * *

But they didn't make it far. Not as a group. They retraced their steps. It was easy to follow Reacher's blundering trail in reverse. Then thirty yards short of the path he heard noises ahead, and he saw a blink of movement through the trunks. He held out his hand in warning, and Suzanne and Helen and Henry froze behind him. He crept on without them, leaning rather than moving, straining forward, peering ahead.

Four guys in ACUs. One of which was Sergeant Cain. They were all staring at the backpacks. Carefully placed. One leaning on the other.

Reacher eased back, and they all four ducked their heads together, and he whispered, "Stay in the woods another hundred yards. Loop around. Hit the trail south of them, and then leg it. Jump in the van and head straight for home. Best of luck all the way. Don't come back again."

They all shook hands, and the three of them moved off, and Reacher waited. He gave them three minutes, and then he moved toward the four soldiers, as noisily as possible, brushing things and snapping things at every opportunity. They heard him ten yards out, and they turned as one, and their M16s came up, and Reacher heard four quiet snicks as four fire selectors were turned up a notch. Clean precise sounds, hard and real, not like the phony photo shutter.

He said, "Long guns are a poor choice in the woods, Sergeant Cain. You can aim all you want, but there's always going to be a tree in the way. That's your first mistake. Let's hope it's also your last."

Cain called back, "Are those people with you?"

"Which people?"

"The infiltrators."

"They were hikers, from Canada. I haven't seen them since this morning."

"I don't believe you."

"Let it go, sergeant. Play it smart. There are no medals in this one. By tomorrow morning it won't have happened at all."

"They might have seen evidence of a covert operation."

"They saw what they were supposed to see."

Cain said, "What does that mean?"

"Like a magician on stage," Reacher said. "A big showy flourish with the left hand, attracting all the attention, while the right hand does the real work. There are activists in the world, Sergeant Cain. We can't wish them away. They're always looking for something to piss and moan about. So we give them something. A big showy flourish with the left hand. Something to get all agitated about. But not too agitated, because after all who really gives a shit about vicious killers straight out of the Middle Ages? Meanwhile, the right hand does the important stuff undisturbed. Classic misdirection."

"Who are you?"

"I was an MP once. I was your boss's boss's boss. And my brother did a spell in Military Intelligence. I met some of his people. Some sly minds there, sergeant. There was an old guy called O'Day. A buck gets ten this scheme is one of his. Think about it. Hundreds of people, a secret website, all kinds of planning and scheming. It's an energy sink. Like a sponge. It keeps them where we can see them."

No answer.

"Let it go, sergeant," Reacher said again. "Play your part, which is to look sinister next to your Humvees. No one's going to thank you if you screw up your lines. These things are very carefully orchestrated."

Then Reacher stepped back and shut up, and let Cain's career caution do his work for him. After a minute Cain gave the word and all four of them formed up and jogged back the way they had come. Reacher followed five minutes behind them, but he took the precaution of looping the last hundred yards through the brush, and coming out on a parallel street. Two minutes later he was back at the welcome board, waiting for a ride out of town.

Make Me

Chapter 1

Moving a guy as big as Keever wasn't easy. It was like trying to wrestle a king-size mattress off a waterbed. So they buried him close to the house. Which made sense anyway. The harvest was still a month away, and a disturbance in a field would show up from the air. And they would use the air, for a guy like Keever. They would use search planes, and helicopters, and maybe even drones.

They started at midnight, which they figured was safe enough. They were in the middle of ten thousand acres of nothingness, and the only man-made structure on their side of any horizon was the railroad track to the east, but midnight was five hours after the evening train and seven hours before the morning train. Therefore, no prying eyes. Their backhoe had four spotlights on a bar above the cab, like kids had on their pick-up trucks, and together they made an aimed pool of halogen brightness. So visibility was not a problem either. They started the hole in the hog pen, which was a permanent disturbance all by itself. Each hog weighed two hundred pounds, and each hog had four feet. The dirt was always chewed up. Nothing to see from the air, not even with a thermal camera. The picture would whiteout instantly, from the steaming animals themselves, and their steaming piles and pools of waste.

Safe enough.

Hogs were rooting animals, so they made sure the hole was deep. Which was not a problem either. Their backhoe's arm was long, and it bit rhythmically, in fluent seven-foot scoops, the hydraulic rams glinting in the electric light, the engine straining and roaring and pausing, the cab falling and rising, as each bucket-load was dumped aside. When the hole was done they backed the machine up and turned it around and used the dozer blade to push Keever into his grave, scraping him, rolling him, covering his body in dirt, until finally it fell over the lip and thumped down into the electric shadows.

Only one thing went wrong, and it happened right then.

The evening train came through five hours late. The next morning they heard on the AM station that a broken locomotive had caused a jam a hundred miles south. But they didn't know that at the time. All they heard was the mournful whistle at the distant crossing, and then all they could do was turn and stare, at the long lit cars rumbling past in the middle distance, one after the other, like a vision in a dream, seemingly forever. But eventually the train was gone, and the rails sang for a minute more, and then the taillight was swallowed up by the midnight darkness, and they turned back to their task.

Twenty miles north the train slowed, and slowed, and then eased to a hissing stop, and the doors sucked open, and Jack Reacher stepped down to a concrete ramp in front of a grain elevator as big as an apartment house. To his left were four more elevators, all of them bigger than the first, and to his right was an enormous metal shed the size of an airplane hangar. There were vapor lights on poles, set at regular intervals, and they cut cones of yellow in the darkness. There was mist in the nighttime air, like a note on a calendar. The end of summer was coming. Fall was on its way.

Reacher stood still and behind him the train moved away without him, straining, grinding, settling to a slow rat-a-tat rhythm, and then accelerating, its building slipstream pulling at his clothes. He was the only passenger who had gotten out. Which was not surprising. The place was no kind of a commuter hub. It was all agricultural. What token passenger facilities it had were wedged between the last elevator and the huge shed, and were limited to a compact building, which seemed to have both a ticket window and benches for waiting. It was built in a traditional railroad style, and it looked like a child's toy, temporarily set down between two shiny oil drums.

But on a signboard running its whole length was written the reason Reacher was there: MOTHER'S REST. Which he had seen on a map, and which he thought was a great name for a railroad stop. He figured the line must cross an ancient wagon-train trail, right there, where something had happened long ago. Maybe a young pregnant woman went into labor. The jostling could not have helped. So maybe the wagon train stopped for a couple of weeks. Or a month. Maybe someone remembered the place years later. A descendant, perhaps. A family legend. Maybe there was a one-room museum.

Or perhaps there was a sadder interpretation. Maybe they had buried a woman there. Too old to make it. In which case there would be a commemorative stone.

Either way Reacher figured he might as well find out. He had no place to go, and all the time in the world to get there, so detours cost him nothing. Which is why he got out of the train. To a sense of disappointment, initially. His expectations had been way off base. He had pictured a couple of dusty houses, and a lonely one-horse corral. And the one-room museum, maybe run part-time and volunteer by an old guy from one of the houses, or the headstone, maybe marble, behind a square wrought-iron fence.

He had not expected the immense agricultural infrastructure. He should have, he supposed. Grain, meet the railroad. It had to be loaded somewhere. Billions of bushels and millions of tons each year. He stepped left and looked through a gap between structures. The view was dark, but he could sense a rough semicircle of habitation. Houses, obviously, for the depot workers. He could see some lights, which he hoped were a motel, or a diner, or both.

He walked to the exit, skirting the pools of vapor light purely out of habit, but he saw that the last lamp was going to be unavoidable, because it was set directly above the exit gate. So he saved himself a further perimeter diversion by walking through the next-to-last pool too.

At which point a woman stepped out of the shadows.

She came toward him with a distinctive little burst of energy, two fast paces, eager, like she was pleased to see him. Her body language was all about relief.

Then it wasn't. Then it was all about disappointment. She stopped dead, and she said, "Oh."

She was about forty, Reacher guessed, with dark hair worn long, and she was wearing jeans and a T-shirt under a short coat. She had lace-up shoes on her feet. Five-nine, maybe, and a hundred and fifty pounds. She was no kind of a waif.

He said, "Good evening, ma'am."

She was looking past his shoulder.

He said, "I'm the only passenger."

She looked him in the eye.

He said, "No one else got out of the train. So I guess your friend isn't coming."

"My friend?" she said. A neutral kind of accent. The kind he heard everywhere.

He said, "Why else would a person be here, except to meet the train? No point in coming otherwise. I guess normally there would be nothing to see at midnight."

She didn't answer.

He said, "Don't tell me you've been waiting here since seven o'clock."

"I didn't know the train was late," she said. "There's no cell signal here. And no one from the railroad to tell you anything. And I guess the Pony Express is out sick today."

"He wasn't in my car. Or the next two, either."

"Who wasn't?"

"Your friend."

"You don't know what he looks like."

"He's a big guy," Reacher said. "That's why you jumped out when you saw me. You thought I was him. For a second, at least. And there were no big guys in my car. Or the next two."

"When is the next train?"

"Seven in the morning."

She said, "Who are you and why have you come here?"

"I'm just a guy passing through."

"The train passed through. Not you. You got out."

"You know anything about this place?"

"Not a thing."

"Have you seen a museum or a gravestone?"

"Why are you here?"

"Who's asking?"

She paused a beat, and said, "Nobody."

Reacher said, "Is there a motel in town?"

"I'm staying there."

"How is it?"

"It's a motel."

"Works for me," Reacher said. "Does it have vacancies?"

"I'd be amazed if it didn't."

"OK, you can show me the way. Don't wait here all night. I'll be up by first light. I'll knock on your door as I leave. Hopefully your friend will be here in the morning."

The woman said nothing. She just glanced at the silent rails one more time, and then turned around and led the way through the exit gate.

Chapter 2

The motel was bigger than Reacher expected.
It was a two-story horseshoe, a total of thirty rooms,
with plenty of parking. But not many slots were occupied. The place was more than half empty. It was
plainly built out of stuccoed blocks, painted beige,
with iron stairs and railings, painted brown. Nothing
special. But it looked clean and well kept. All the light-
bulbs worked. Not the worst place Reacher had ever
seen.

The office was the first door on the left, on the
ground floor. There was a night clerk behind the desk.
He was a short old guy with a big belly and what
looked like a glass eye. He gave the woman the key for
room 214, and she walked out without another word.
Reacher asked him for a rate, and the guy said, "Sixty
bucks."

Reacher said, "A week?"

"A night."

"I've been around."

"What's that supposed to mean?"

"I've been in plenty of motels."

"So?"

"I don't see anything here worth sixty bucks a night. Twenty, maybe."

"Can't do twenty. Those rooms are expensive."

"Which rooms?"

"Upstairs."

"I'm happy with downstairs."

"Don't you need to be near her?"

"Near who?"

"Your lady friend."

"No," Reacher said. "I don't need to be near her."

"Forty dollars downstairs."

"Twenty. You're more than half empty. Practically out of business. Better to make twenty bucks than nothing at all."

"Thirty."

"Twenty."

"Twenty-five."

"Deal," Reacher said. He took his roll of cash out of his pocket and separated a ten, and two fives, and five singles. He laid them on the counter and the one-eyed guy swapped them for a key on a wooden fob marked 106, taken from a drawer, with a triumphant flourish.

"In the back corner," the guy said. "Near the stairs."

Which were metal, and which would make a clanging noise when people went up and down. Not the best room in the place. Petty revenge. But Reacher didn't care. He figured his would be the last head to hit the pillow that night. He didn't foresee any other late arrivals. He expected to be undisturbed, all the way through the silent plains night.

He said, "Thank you," and walked out, carrying his key.

The one-eyed guy waited thirty seconds, and then dialed his desk phone, and when it was answered he said, "She met a guy off the train. It was late. She waited five hours. She brought him here and he took a room."

There was the plastic crackle of a question, and the one-eyed clerk said, "Another big guy. A mean son of a bitch. He busted my balls on the room rate. I gave him 106, in the far corner."

Another crackling question, and another answer: "Not from here. I'm in the office."

Another crackle, but a different tone and a different cadence. An instruction, not a question.

The one-eyed guy said, "OK."

And he put the phone down and struggled to his feet, and stepped out of the office, and took the lawn chair from outside 102, which was empty, and dragged it to a spot on the blacktop where he could see his own door and 106's equally. *Can you see his room from there?* had been the question, and *Move your ass somewhere you can watch him all night* had been the instruction, and the one-eyed guy always obeyed instructions, if sometimes a little reluctantly, as at that point, as he adjusted his angle and dumped his bulk down on the uncomfortable plastic. Outside, in the nighttime air. Not his preferred way of passing his shift.

From inside his room Reacher heard the lawn chair scrape across the blacktop, but he paid no attention. Just a random nighttime sound, nothing dangerous, not a shotgun jacking a round, not the hiss of a blade on a sheath, nothing for his lizard brain to worry about. And the only non-lizard possibilities were a lace-up footstep on the walkway outside, and a knock on the door, because the woman from the railroad stop seemed like a person with a lot of questions, and also some kind of expectation they should be answered. *Who are you and why have you come here?*

But it was a scrape, not a footstep or a knock, so Reacher paid no attention. He folded his pants and laid them flat under his mattress, and then he showered away the grime of the day, and climbed under the bedcovers. He set the alarm in his head for six o'clock in the morning, stretched once, yawned once, and fell asleep.

The dawn came up entirely gold, with no hint of pink or purple. The sky was a rinsed blue, like an old shirt washed a thousand times. Reacher showered again and dressed, and stepped out to the new day. He saw the lawn chair, empty, oddly placed in the traffic lane, but he thought nothing of it. He went up the metal stairs as quietly as he could, reducing the likely clang to a duller pulsing boom, by placing his feet very carefully. He found 214 and knocked on its door, firmly but discreetly, like he imagined a bell-boy would, in a fine hotel. *Your wake-up call, ma'am.* She had about forty minutes. Ten to get going, ten to shower, ten to stroll up to the railroad again. She would be there well ahead of the morning train.

Reacher crept back down the stairs and headed out to the street, which was wide enough at that point to qualify as a plaza. For farm trucks, he guessed, slow and clumsy, turning and maneuvering, lining up ahead of the weighbridges and the receiving offices and the grain elevators themselves. There were train tracks embedded in the blacktop. It was a whole big operation. Some kind of a hub facility, probably, serving the locality, which in that part of America could have meant a two-hundred-mile radius. Which explained the large motel. Farmers would come in from far and wide, and spend the night before or after a train ride to some distant city. Maybe they would all come at once, at certain times of the year. When futures were for sale, maybe, up in Chicago. Hence the thirty bedrooms.

The wide street or the plaza or whatever it was ran basically south to north, with the railroad track and the shiny infrastructure defining the eastern limit, on the right, and what amounted to a de facto Main Street defining the western limit, on the left. The motel was there, and a diner, and a general store. Behind those establishments the town spread out in a loose westward semicircle. Low density. Sprawl, country style. A thousand people, maybe less.

Reacher headed north on the wide street, looking

for the wagon-train trail. He figured it would come in across his path, from east to west, which had been the whole point of wagon trains. *Go west, young man.* Exciting times. He saw a crossing fifty yards ahead, after the last of the elevators. A road, perpendicular, exactly east to west. On the right it was bright with the morning sun, and on the left it was long with shadows.

The crossing had no barriers. Just red lights. Reacher stood on the tracks and gazed back south, the way he had come. There were no other crossings for at least a mile, which was about as far as he could see, in the pale light. There were no other crossings for at least a mile to the north, either. Which meant that if Mother's Rest laid claim to its own east-west thoroughfare, he was standing on it.

It was reasonably wide, and slightly humped, built up with dirt taken from shallow ditches dug either side. It was covered with thick blacktop, grayed with age, split here and there by weather, and random like frozen lava on the edges. It was dead straight, from one horizon to the other.

A possibility. Wagon trains went dead straight when they could. Why wouldn't they? No one put in extra miles just for the fun of it. The lead driver would steer by a distant landmark, and the others would follow, and a year later some new party would find the ruts, and a year after that someone would make a mark on a map. And a hundred years later some state highway department would come by with trucks full of asphalt.

There was nothing to see in the east. No one-room

museum, no marble headstone. Just the road, between infinite fields of nearly ripe wheat. But in the other direction, west of the tracks, the road ran through the town, more or less dead center, built up on both sides for about six low-rise blocks. The corner lot on the right had expanded northward about a hundred yards. Like a football field. It was a farm equipment dealership. Weird tractors and huge machines, all brand new and shiny. On the left was a veterinary supply business, in a small building that must have started out as an ordinary residential house.

Reacher made the turn and walked on the old trail, due west, the morning sun faintly warm on his back.

In the motel office the one-eyed clerk dialed the phone, and when it was answered he said, "She went back to the railroad again. Now she's meeting the morning train too. How many guys are these people sending?"

He was answered by a long plastic crackle, not a question, but not an instruction either. Softer in tone. Encouragement, maybe. Or reassurance. The one-eyed guy said, "OK, sure," and hung up.

Reacher walked six blocks down and six blocks back, and he saw plenty of stuff. He saw houses still lived in, and houses converted to offices, for seed merchants and fertilizer dealers and a large-animal veterinarian. He saw a one-room law office. He saw a gas station one block north, and a pool hall, and a store selling beer and ice, and another selling nothing but rubber boots and rubber aprons. He saw a laundromat, and a tire bay, and a place for stick-on boot soles.

He didn't see a museum, or a monument.

Which might be OK. They wouldn't have put either thing right on the shoulder. Back a block or two, probably, for a sense of reverence, and to stay out of harm's way.

He stepped off the wagon-train trail into a side street. The town was laid out on a grid, even though it had grown up semicircular. Some lots were more desirable than others. As if the giant elevators had a gravitational system all their own. The furthest reaches were undeveloped. Closer to the apex, buildings were shoulder to shoulder. The block behind the trail had one-room apartments that might have started out as barns or garages, and what looked like pop-up market stalls, for folks who had given over an acre or two to fruits and vegetables. There was a store that did Western Union and MoneyGram and faxing and photocopying and FedEx and UPS and DHL. There was a CPA's office, but it looked abandoned.

No museum, and no monument.

He quartered the blocks, one after another, past low shacks, past diesel engine repair, past vacant lots full of weeds as fine as hair. He came out at the far end of the wide street. He had covered half the town. No museum, and no monument.

He saw the morning train pull in. It looked hot and bothered and impatient about stopping. It was impossible to say whether anyone got out. Too much infrastructure in the way.

He was hungry.

He walked straight ahead through the plaza, almost all the way back to where he had started, past the general store, and into the diner.

At which point the motel keeper's twelve-year-old grandson ducked into the general store, to the pay phone on the wall just inside the door. He dumped his coins and dialed a number, and when it was answered he said, "He's searching the town. I followed him everywhere. He's looking all over. He's doing it block by block."